INHERITORS OF
THE NEW KINGDOM

V K McGivney

Printed and bound in Great Britain by Clays Ltd, St Ives plc

Authors Reach
www.authorsreach.co.uk

ISBN: 978-0-9957883-6-7

With thanks to Todd, Maggie, Rashmi, Corinna and Jill for their encouragement and helpful comments and to Gina for her patience.

Part 1
The Blitzgreen

Chapter 1

Was it a change in the direction of the wind? A shifting of the Earth's tectonic plates? A sudden and unusual noise? Whatever it was that occurred on that night in April, it was sufficiently disturbing to rouse the residents of Coronation Close from their slumbers.

Mrs. Brennan, the Irish widow at number one, sat up in her bed and crossed herself, murmuring, 'Jesus, Mary and Joseph.'

Marjorie Phelps at number three, opened her eyes, peered anxiously over the duvet but seeing nothing untoward, hissed, 'Stop it, Stanley!'

Accustomed to taking the blame for everything, her husband rolled over and grunted, 'Sorry, dear', but on hearing no further complaint, sighed and settled back on his pillow.

At number five, Pugwash, the Perkins' bull terrier, sprang from his basket, uttered a fusillade of barks and sniffed the air for interlopers. There being none, he returned to lie on his blanket, uttering occasional warning growls and keeping open one wary eye.

His owners in the bedroom above stirred uneasily. 'Bloody dog!' grumbled Reg Perkins, plucked unwillingly from a pleasant dream in which he was engaged in a close encounter with the lissom young lady who was his current secretary.

At number seven, a solitary light burned in an upstairs window. Behind it, a young man sat bent over his laptop. Richard Jarman, his face furrowed with concentration, was struggling to complete the final chapters of his thesis on the regeneration of local communities in the aftermath of a catastrophic natural disaster. *The evidence from these two parts of the developing world,* he wrote, *leads to the conclusion...* At this point something prompted him to abandon the sentence and walk over to the window.

In the daytime, the back windows of houses on the lower side of the Close commanded a view of a descending line of uniformly-shaped, tiled rooftops, ending at the point where the steep slope of Bridlington

Hill came to an abrupt halt at the T-junction with Browning Rd. At night, this scene metamorphosed into an undifferentiated dark mass, relieved only by the dim pinpricks of light marking the existence of the small shopping parade at the bottom of the hill. Now, however, this nondescript view had been transformed. The nearest rooftops were clearly silhouetted against a sky that, to Richard's surprise, looked extraordinarily bright; almost translucent. Stepping back to his desk, he turned off the lamp then returned to the window.

He could see now that, without the neutralising effect of background light, the sky wasn't so much translucent as coloured – striped, in fact, with vivid streaks of orange and yellow. As his vision adjusted, he noticed a shower of sparks descending in ever diminishing arcs, like fading fireworks. He opened the window, leaned out and peered upwards to locate their source then uttered a gasp. High above the rooftops, a huge and dazzling stationary object hung suspended in space like a balloon. Only it wasn't a balloon. He gaped at it for a few seconds then squeezed his eyes shut and opened them again. The object was still there. Cylindrical in shape but narrower in the middle than at the ends, it blazed with an effulgence that suggested it was lit from within by an extraordinarily powerful light.

He uttered another gasp, for the object had started to revolve. It turned slowly at first, then faster and faster and ultimately with such velocity that it lost its straight lines and became a brilliant spinning orb that reminded him of the glitter ball that used to dangle from the ceiling at school discos. Then suddenly, and with unimaginable speed, it shot upwards at a sharp angle and disappeared from view. Within seconds, the coloured streaks and sparks faded and the sky resumed its normal night-time obscurity.

Dazed, Richard continued to peer into the darkness but there was nothing more to be seen. Ducking back into the room, he shut the window and stood wonderingly in front of it. What had he just seen? A satellite or surveillance plane? He thought it unlikely. The object had moved at a speed far in excess of anything he thought a man-made machine was capable of. The remains of a spent rocket? Debris from a meteorite or asteroid? Those might explain the sparks but not the shape and abrupt upward trajectory of the object. A weather balloon? No. The object was far too big. Whatever it was, he decided, there was probably a perfectly rational explanation. Other people would surely have witnessed the same phenomenon.

He returned to his desk, switched on the lamp and stared at his unfinished sentence: *leads to the conclusion*... What conclusion? His mind was a blank; his earlier train of thought had completely evaporated. Sighing, he saved the chapter, closed the laptop and went to bed.

Chapter 2

Waking from a troubled sleep, Richard gazed blearily round his bedroom, the one he had occupied throughout his childhood and which had been preserved in a time warp by his mother. Here, in precisely the same position as when he was a boy, were his desk with its anglepoise lamp, his bookshelves bowed with the weight of old comics; his chest of drawers topped with a framed photograph of himself holding a football.

As he dragged himself into full consciousness, he realised that his mobile was ringing. He swung his legs over the side of the bed, stumbled over to the desk and picked it up.

'Ric, you old tart!'

Richard winced on recognising the voice of Phil Banks, a former colleague at *Global Geographic*, or GG as the journal was affectionately known by its staff.

'Welcome back! How about comin' for a few jars tonight?'

'Sorry, Phil, got a deadline. I'm finishing my thesis.'

'Bollocks! We've all got deadlines.' The voice became wheedling. 'I'll tell you all the goss about GG and Wanker-in-Chief.'

Glancing at his watch, Richard saw that it was after ten. He had no desire to spend time with Phil Banks but he did need to discuss some matters with his academic supervisor. 'I suppose I could go to the university this afternoon and meet you afterwards,' he muttered unenthusiastically.

'You're on! See you in *The Green Man* around six.'

Richard put down his mobile, stumbled drowsily into the bathroom and splashed his face with cold water. More alert now, he suddenly recalled the vivid colours in the sky and the spinning object that had accelerated away at unimaginable speed. Returning to his room, he opened the window and looked out, half expecting to see some traces of his night-time vision. But the morning view over the rooftops was exactly the same as it always had been. He crossed the landing and peered out of his parents' bedroom window. Coronation Close also looked the same: an unchanging stage set with the same, unchanging group of characters - Mrs. Perkins pulling her ugly dog on a lead; Stan Phelps clipping his front hedge; little Mrs. Brennan coming out of her gate, carrying an enormous shopping bag. Everything in the Close appeared normal; horribly, boringly normal.

Richard disliked the suburban backwater where he had spent his childhood, but finding himself homeless after conducting the field research for his thesis, he had readily accepted his parents' invitation to house-sit while they celebrated their thirtieth wedding anniversary on a world cruise.

As soon as he had finished breakfast he rang his academic supervisor and arranged to see him that afternoon. After the call, he checked the news on his laptop but there was no mention of any strange aerial phenomena during the early morning hours. Nor, in the other websites he opened, was there any reference to a passing satellite, asteroid or meteorite. For want of a better explanation, he was obliged to conclude that what he had seen was a UFO - a term broad enough to cover any unusual appearance in the sky. He consulted *Wikepedia*. 'Unidentified flying object,' the online encyclopedia informed him, 'is the popular term for any apparent aerial phenomenon whose cause cannot be easily or immediately identified by the observer.' This fitted the case exactly. He exited from the internet and made a second call on his mobile.

A pleasant male voice answered. 'Daniel Morrison.'

'Hi, Dan. It's Ric.'

'Ric! How's the thesis going?'

'Fine, nearly finished.'

'Great! Hang on, I'll just shut the door.' There was a faint click then Dan's voice again. 'You OK?'

'Fine. Just wanted to ask you something.'

'Ask away.'

'Do you happen to know if there was any unusual aeronautical activity last night... over north London - surveillance planes, satellites ... that kind of thing?'

'Eh? That's not really my bag, Ric. I may work for an airline but I see more computer screens than sky. Why do you want to know?'

Richard strove to keep his voice casual. 'Last night I was working late on my thesis and I saw something really weird.'

'Oh? What was it?'

'I looked out of the window and there were these amazing lights. The sky had kind of ... streaks in it, incredible colours, and there was, like, this thing, just hanging there.'

'What kind of thing?'

'It was a sort of cylinder; absolutely dazzling, unbelievably bright. It started spinning then shot away faster than anything I've ever seen.'

'Oh yeah?' Dan chuckled. 'Were you out on the piss last night?'

Richard felt slightly affronted. 'No. I was working on my thesis till about one.'

'Well you must have been staring at the screen too long. It was probably an optical illusion.'

'No, I saw it, Dan, as clear as anything, but ...' he forced a laugh '... there's probably a perfectly rational explanation.'

'There usually is for these things, Ric. It could have been an international space station. They occasionally flash across the sky, or a weather balloon, or even a Chinese lantern. They're often mistaken for UFOs.'

'You're probably right.' Richard began to feel a little foolish. 'I just wondered if you could check it out.'

'OK. I know someone in Air Traffic Control at Swanwick. I'll give him a bell if you like.'

'Cool.'

Richard returned to his laptop and brought up his unfinished sentence, *leads to the conclusion that* ... He reflected for a moment then typed, *the main conditions necessary for* ... Bollocks! This was a crucial chapter, the conclusion of over two years' research. But he couldn't concentrate. He decided to abandon his work and go into town earlier than he had intended.

A few minutes later, walking towards the corner of the Close, he stepped into the road to avoid his neighbour Stan Phelps who was sweeping up hedge clippings. 'Hi, Mr. Phelps.

Stan straightened up. 'Hello, Ricky!'

Richard winced. Being called Ricky made him feel about ten years old. 'You've made a good job of that hedge,' he said politely.

'I'm supposed to be on leave,' Stan muttered grumpily, glancing up towards the house.

Following his gaze, Richard spotted Stan's wife, Marjorie, watching beadily from an open window. He smiled sympathetically. 'No rest for the wicked, eh?'

'You can say that again! Have you heard from your mum and dad?

Are they enjoying the cruise?'

'They're having a great time, thanks.'

Stan shook his head. 'Wouldn't suit me, being cooped up in a cabin all that time.' He glanced up at the house again. 'Depends who you're travelling with, I suppose.'

Richard swallowed. 'Mr. Phelps, you didn't see anything odd last night, did you? About one o'clock?'

Stan laughed. 'One o'clock? We're always in bed at that time. We don't stay up late like you youngsters. Why?'

'Oh, it's nothing really. Something disturbed me while I was working on the computer last night. I'm not sure what it was.'

Stan thought for a moment. 'Come to think of it, I did wake up. It must have been pretty late. Dratted dog next door was barking. I don't remember hearing anything else. Maybe there was a prowler. Marjorie thinks we ought to start a Neighbourhood Watch. She --'

As if to order, a sharp voice came like a pistol shot from the open window. 'Stanley! Haven't you finished that hedge yet?'

Stan smiled apologetically. 'Better get on. What was that you were saying, Ricky?'

'It's not important. See you, Mr. Phelps.' Richard turned out of the Close, descended the hill and walked across Browning Road to the shopping parade.

Physically unchanged since his schooldays, the parade contained a minimarket, a newsagent-cum-post office, an Indian takeaway, a discount hardware store, a women's hairdressers and a chemists - all, as Marjorie Phelps periodically complained, owned by "foreigners". There was still a petrol station at the end of the parade, but a charity shop had taken over the premises of what had previously been an off-licence chain. The only other innovation Richard had noticed since his return to the area, was a hole-in-the-wall cash dispenser outside Mr. Patel's mini-market. As he walked past this on his way to the bus stop, he nearly tripped over an elderly bearded man squatting on the pavement, surrounded by plastic bags. A huge mongrel dog with a piece of red cloth tied around its neck, sprawled by his side. The man stared at Richard and mumbled something unintelligible.

Ignoring him, Richard hurried past. Waiting for the bus that would carry him to Rayners Lane tube station, he gazed at the poster that covered one side of the bus shelter. It depicted a well-endowed young man, clad only in underpants, his feet obscured by a caption warning against the dangers of sexually-transmitted diseases. Chance would be a fine thing, Richard thought glumly. There had been no-one since Emma, his former girl friend, although several exquisite girls in Kashmir and Bangladesh had been obligingly offered to him as potential brides. No-one in either society could comprehend how a man could still be single at the advanced age of twenty six. He had declined the offers.

Chapter 3

After leaving the university at six o'clock, Richard walked to Euston Station. He wished he hadn't agreed to meet Phil Banks who, he remembered, could down six pints in an evening without any visible effect. The early phone call had caught him off guard.

He bought an *Evening News* and scanned the headlines while waiting on the crowded platform for a Victoria Line tube: *Terrorist Attack in Iraq; Dozens Killed at Wedding Feast in Afghanistan; Celebrity Sues Surgeon for Botched Boob Job* - the usual juxtaposition of the terrible and the trivial. He opened the paper and just as a loud rumble and rush of malodorous air announced the arrival of a train, caught sight of a headline on the second page, *Mystery Fire at North London Recreation Ground.* He pushed his way on to the train and, squashed among the crush of passengers by the doors, held the page up to his eyes.

Residents in the Northolt area were shocked this morning to find that a large part of their local recreation ground, Fonthill Park, has been destroyed, apparently by fire. Most of the vegetation in the seventy-acre park has been obliterated. Local resident, Graham Maddox, 49, told reporters, 'When I looked out of the window this morning, I couldn't believe my eyes. The park's gone. It's just a heap of grey dust.'

Police are investigating the possibility of arson. According to a spokeswoman, 'the damage is so extensive that it is unlikely to be the action of a single person.'

Richard reread the item as the tube clattered its way south. He knew the park well having played there often as a boy. It was about a mile from Coronation Close, a pleasant green oasis that created a welcome contrast to the grey uniformity of the surrounding residential streets. Why would anyone want to destroy it? He was still pondering the question as he left the tube at Oxford Circus.

Seconds before he arrived at *The Green Man*, his mobile vibrated and he found a text message from Dan: *ATC say zero on radar last night.*

His spirits fell as he entered the pub. The dingy interior hadn't changed since the days when he used to frequent the establishment with his colleagues at *Global Geographic*: the same threadbare carpet; the same faded upholstery on the chairs and bar stools.

The pub was full of its habitual early evening clientele, mostly suited men delaying the moment of returning to their domestic lives. Some were busily tapping into laptops and smartphones. It didn't take him long to spot Phil Banks. He was standing at the bar, chatting to the barman. Richard hailed him with a heartiness he didn't feel. 'Hi, Phil. How's it going?'

Phil turned and waved his glass in greeting. 'Ric! Welcome back to civilisation! What you 'avin'?'

Richard didn't consider *The Green Man* "civilisation" but let this pass. 'Pint of lager, please. How's life at *GG*?'

'Bloody awful!' Phil gave the order to the barman then turned back to Richard. 'Wanker-in-Chief called me in yesterday. Bastard said I wasn't pulling my weight!'

Having once shared an office with Phil, Richard was inclined to agree with this assessment, but he forced his features into a sympathetic expression. 'That's too bad.'

They took their drinks to a table next to a window offering an uninspiring view of continuous passing traffic.

'You did the right thing leaving when you did,' grumbled Phil as they sat down. 'Place is goin' to pot.' He peered gloomily into his glass then looked up with an air of false cheerfulness. 'So, Professor, 'ow's the *magnum opus*? Get lots of gen on the natives?'

Richard recoiled at the language. 'Nearly finished. I'm writing the last section.' Knowing that Phil would have little interest in his research, he didn't bother to elaborate. This gave his companion an opportunity to launch into a tirade against his editor.

'Wasn't my fault the spring issue was be'ind schedule. Stupid tossers in Graphics sent the wrong bloody cover design.'

Subjected to a lengthy account of Phil's multiple grievances, Richard began to find his grumbles and the cockney accent he affected (someone having once unwisely told him that he resembled a famous cockney actor), were getting on his nerves. Seeking to change the subject, he found himself relating the details of his previous night's experience.

Phil stared at him incredulously. 'Pull the other one!' he chortled. 'You were off your 'ead, 'allucinatin'.'

'No, Phil, I was wide awake and I don't do drugs. I've never seen anything like it.'

'Take a look around you, old son!'

Richard was puzzled. 'What do you mean?'

'Can't you see all those little guys?'

'What little guys?'

'This is *The Green Man*! Little *Green Men*! Geddit?' Phil laughed up-roariously.

Richard realised there was no point in continuing the conversation. To hide his irritation, he went to the bar and ordered two more pints. Returning to the table, he diverted Phil's attention by asking him for news of other former colleagues, a topic on which his companion was only too pleased to enlarge.

After another fifteen minutes, Richard got up to leave, citing the urgency of his deadline.

'You can't go yet,' Phil protested. He grinned lasciviously. 'I thought we could make a night of it; go on to *Hot Totty*.'

Richard had no desire to visit a lap-dancing club. 'Sorry, I need to get back.' He shook off Phil's restraining hand and hurriedly left the pub.

By the time he arrived in Browning Road, the shops were shuttered and the parade deserted. He walked briskly up Bridlington Hill which was now almost devoid of traffic. Back in his parents' house, he returned to his laptop and reviewed the previous night's work. Consulting his notes, he started to write, resuming the train of thought that had been so abruptly interrupted the night before.

It was nearly midnight when he stopped working. Yawning, he stood up to stretch his limbs then, on an impulse, went over to the window. He opened it and peered up into the sky, but this time there was nothing unusual to see. Convinced that there must be some explanation for what he had witnessed the previous night, he returned to his desk and began to search the internet for information on UFOs. He was stunned by the number of listed websites, far too many for him to investigate. He opened some, dismissing those that seemed overly absurd and fanciful, and scanning only those that seemed more sensible. A number of the latter expressed scepticism about UFOs, claiming that the majority were either conventional objects such as aircraft or balloons, or astronomical phenomena such as meteors or bright planets.

He read part of a report that had been reluctantly released by the

Ministry of Defence under the Freedom of Information Act. The report declared that "unidentified aerial phenomena" posed no threat to British airspace since they were "natural, atmospheric and other not yet fully understood phenomena." Nevertheless the report quoted Russian research findings that humans who had approached UFOs or UFO landing zones had suffered (unspecified) "effects" and some aircraft that had pursued UFOs had been destroyed.

In a separate document, an employee who had led UFO investigations for the Ministry during the 1990s, claimed that although eighty per cent of the sightings reported during that time were due to meteors, satellites or weather patterns, the evidence relating to fifteen per cent was "inconclusive" while that relating to the remaining five per cent "could be something more intriguing".

Richard opened other websites at random. The number of reported UFO incidents in or near the UK made his head reel. Some particularly caught his attention. During the 1960s and 70s, there were over a thousand reported sightings of UFOs in Wiltshire, mainly in Warminster where residents had witnessed lights, glowing cigar-shaped objects and other unidentifiable forms in the sky. These unexplained incidents became known by the collective title of "The Warminster Thing".

He was particularly intrigued by an incident reported in Wales. In 1977, a woman was woken by strange noises and very bright lights. Looking out of her window, she claimed she saw an object like an "upside-down saucer" in the field below, and beside it, two silver and faceless "humanoid creatures". This was only the start of a series of strange occurrences in what became known as "the Broad Haven Triangle".

Richard perused the details of countless similar accounts with growing excitement. He had always been profoundly sceptical about the existence of UFOs. Now he found himself gripped. He noted that the people who claimed to have seen unexplained aerial objects weren't necessarily cranks or fantasists. Some of the phenomena reported in the area near the Pennines during the 1970s were witnessed by formerly sceptical police officers. Mysterious lights that appeared in the sky above Rendlesham Forest in Suffolk in 1980 were observed by credible witnesses from nearby US air bases. UFOs had also been reported by experienced airline pilots.

In 1991, an Alitalia passenger jet bound for Heathrow Airport had a near miss with an unidentified flying object over Lydd in Kent. The pilot was appalled to see a large cigar-shaped craft moving at speed within only three hundred metres of his plane. Investigations by the Civil Aviation Authority ruled out the possibility that the object was a missile, weather balloon or space rocket. No explanation for the incident was ever found.

In 2007, pilots in a plane flying over the Channel Islands saw two stationary, cylindrical objects of immense size in the sky near Guernsey. This was also investigated by the Civil Aviation Authority and a secret copy of their air incident report was apparently sent to the US Air Force Space Agency. If this was true, Richard mused, it contradicted a claim in the Ministry of Defence report that there was no collaboration between the UK and other countries on the subject of UFOs.

He was struck by the fact that many of the objects described had features in common: a cylindrical or cigar shape, extreme brilliance and incredible acceleration. Another common factor was that many witnesses said they had been pressurised (by whom it wasn't clear) to keep quiet about what they had seen.

He realised how easy it was to become obsessed by the subject but felt exhausted after so many hours staring at the computer screen. He closed his laptop and went to bed.

Chapter 4

When he got up the next morning, Richard felt a strong compulsion to visit the ruined recreation ground, Fontwell Park. He wasn't sure what this would achieve or even what he wanted to achieve. He knew that he should be getting on with his thesis, but for some reason witnessing the damage for himself seemed more important.

As he made his way along the shopping parade, he spotted the homeless man he had seen the day before, squatting with his dog near the cash dispenser.

The man looked up as Richard approached and mumbled something inaudible.

This time Richard stopped. 'Yes? Did you say something?'

The man gazed up at him. His scanty grey beard was unkempt and his eyes almost hidden in a cross-hatching of wrinkles. His words came out in a hoarse whisper. 'The light shineth in darkness but the darkness don't compre'end it ... John, One, Five.'

'What?' Richard stumbled backwards as the dog jumped up and sniffed at his trousers.

The man stared at him impassively without enlarging on his gnomic statement.

Richard fumbled in his pocket and handed him a coin, then proceeded to the newsagents where he bought a local paper. He stood outside the shop and quickly scanned the contents. An inner page was dedicated to the Fonthill Park incident. The details were identical to those he had read in *The Evening News* but they were augmented by a blurred photograph of the ravaged area and the quoted reactions of several local residents. He noted with surprise that none of those interviewed had heard or seen anything untoward that night. Nor had they smelled smoke or burning, which, given the size of the area affected, seemed odd. He was struck, however, by the comments of a Mrs. Norman who lived close to the recreation ground. She claimed that she had woken during the night and was amazed to find her bedroom bathed in brilliant light. '*It was so bright I thought it must be lightnin' but I didn't hear no thunder. I went to the window but it suddenly went dark again. It all happened so quick.*'

Richard pondered the woman's remarks as he made his way to the park. Could there be a connection between its destruction and what he had seen in the sky?

There were several police cars parked along Fonthill Road and he could see two uniformed officers calling at the doors of the houses nearest to the recreation ground. The north entrance to the park was cordoned off and a large notice had been erected in front of it. On it was written in large red letters, *DANGER. NO ENTRY.* Underneath, in smaller letters, was a warning that the dust left after the fire could cause skin problems or damage to the eyes. Smaller, handwritten notices had been placed at intervals along the side of the road: *Incident in Fonthill Park. Information wanted.* The words were followed by a telephone number. After a moment's hesitation, he entered it on his mobile.

A policewoman was questioning people who had gathered on the pavement. 'Excuse me, Sir, do you live in this area?' she asked as Richard approached.

'No. I live about a mile away.'

'Were you in this area on the night of April the seventh?'

'No, I read about what happened in the paper. Do you have any idea what could have caused it?'

'Not yet. Excuse me, Madam …' the policewoman moved on to the next person.

Richard climbed on to a bench and craned his neck to peer over the fence that surrounded the park. He was dumbstruck. What confronted him was a scene of total devastation. The area that had once been an expanse of grass was covered in a dark grey substance and all that remained of the shrubs and trees that had lined the paths were blackened stumps.

Investigators wearing masks and white protective clothing were making their way across the ruined green, examining the ground and placing samples of dust in plastic bags.

A breeze sent the dust swirling in the air. Some of it stung Richard's face and judging from the squeals around him, he gathered that others were also affected. He jumped off the bench and walked round to the main park entrance.

A number of police cars and vans were parked in front of the tall gates which were open and guarded by two uniformed officers. Pushing his way through a group of people peering through the gates, Richard caught a glimpse of the café and public toilets at the end of the car park. The buildings were intact. He moved rapidly out of the way as two men came through the gates, carrying bags of the samples they had collected from the ravaged ground. One raised his mask as he passed. 'Be careful,' he warned. 'The dust is toxic. If you live near here, keep your windows shut.'

The men climbed into one of the vans and the policemen closed the gates.

Richard set off for home, his mind in turmoil. If it was arson, it must have taken a considerable effort to blast such an extensive area. Yet, according to the accounts he had read, none of the people living near the park appeared to have noticed flames or the smell of smoke or burning. What if the damage had been caused not by fire, but by something else? Maybe, just maybe, there could be a connection with what he had seen in the sky.

He came to a decision. He would do his civic duty and tell the police what he had witnessed on the night the recreation ground was destroyed. He rubbed his face, surprised to find that it was sore. When he got home and looked in the bathroom mirror, he found that several angry-looking spots had erupted on the cheek where the dust had struck him. He splashed cold water on them then took out his mobile and rang the number he had copied into his contacts.

Eventually a female voice responded. 'Metropolitan Police.'

'I have some information that may be connected to the incident at Fonthill Park --'

'What is your name, please?'

'Richard Jarman.'

'Address?'

He gave her his parents' address and phone number.

'What is the nature of your information, Mr. Jarman?'

'I saw something that might be connected with the fire at Fonthill Park. But it might not. I thought I'd report it, just in case.' Richard briefly described what he had seen.

'I'll pass on the information. Someone will contact you shortly. Thank you for calling.'

* * *

It was unfortunate that the police car drew up in Coronation Close at exactly the same moment that Marjorie Phelps and Doris Perkins stopped to chat on the pavement. As Richard opened the door, he glimpsed them staring curiously at the man who was standing on the front step. He wasn't in uniform and was aged about forty, with a long, mournful face that reminded Richard irresistibly of a basset hound.

'Richard Jarman?'

'Yes.'

'I am Detective Sergeant Johnson.' The man presented his ID card and Richard quickly ushered him into the living room.

DS Johnson sat down on one of the two armchairs that faced each other on either side of the fireplace. 'You are Richard Jarman?' he asked, extracting a notebook from his jacket pocket.

'Yes.' Richard said, surprised. He hadn't changed his name in the time it had taken to walk from the front door to the living room. He sat down in the other armchair.

'Date of birth?'

'Tenth of February, 1986.'

'What is your occupation, Mr. Jarman?'

Richard wondered how this could be relevant. 'I'm a PhD student. I'm writing a thesis on--'

The police officer cut him short. 'Stu…dent', he repeated with a hint of a sneer, and laboriously wrote the word in his notebook before asking his next question.

'I am investigating what happened at Fonthill Park during the night of the seventh of April. I believe you have some information relating to the incident?'

Richard felt slightly embarrassed. 'Well I'm not sure that it's relevant, but I did see something strange that night.'

'Were you in or near the park that night?'

'No, I was here.'

'Here?'

'Yes, here, in the house.'

DS Johnson raised his eyebrows. 'But this is nowhere near Fonthill Park.'

'I know it isn't, but the night the park was destroyed, I saw something out of my bedroom window which might have been connected with what happened.'

'What time was this, Mr. Jarman?'

'About one o'clock.'

The officer wrote the detail in his notebook. 'And what was it you saw?'

Richard took a deep breath. 'Well, first I noticed a strange light.'

'A light?'

'It was incredibly bright, almost like daylight, and there were amazing streaks of colour in the sky. Then I saw this extraordinary thing just hanging there.'

'Thing? What kind of thing?'

'It was huge and incredibly bright; cylindrical but a bit narrower in the middle, like one of those old-fashioned French cafetières, only laid on its side.'

'An old-fashioned French what?'

'Cafetière. You know, one of those aluminium coffee pots they have in France, that you put on the stove. There was one in a gîte my parents rented once when we went to France on holiday. But you don't see them so much these days.'

The officer stared at him incredulously. 'You saw something that looked like a … coffee pot?'

'Yes, only without the handle …'

'Without … the … handle,' DS Johnson repeated slowly. He snapped his book shut. 'If this is a joke, Mr. Jarman, I must inform you that wasting police time is an offence.'

Richard flushed with indignation. 'It's not a joke. I only called the police because I thought it might help your enquiries.'

'Well if it isn't a joke, may I suggest that you were either dreaming… or were on something you shouldn't have been.'

'I'm not in the habit of taking drugs,' Richard retorted angrily. 'Anyway, I can't have been the only person who saw it.'

There was a short silence during which DS Johnson gazed thoughtfully at Richard, his face more mournful than ever. 'Nobody else has reported a … flying coffee pot.'

Richard felt himself flushing again. 'I can't help that. I can only tell you what I saw.'

So why, Mr. Jarman, do you think this … thing that looked like a coffee pot might be relevant to the Fonthill Park incident?'

'Because it was over in the west, where the park is. There were, like, sparks coming from it. It started spinning then it shot off at an angle, unbelievably fast. I've never seen anything move so quickly in my life.'

'Could you show me exactly where you saw this … object?'

Richard escorted the officer to his bedroom, opened the window and pointed.

DS Johnson put his head through the window and peered into the empty sky. After a few moments, he ducked back into the room, his face expressionless. 'Thank you for the … information, Mr. Jarman. If we need any more details, we'll be in touch.'

Richard shut the window and they descended the stairs in silence. When he accompanied the inspector to the front door, he noticed his two female neighbours still hovering on the pavement nearby. As soon as the police car had disappeared, he shut the door and started to count. He had barely reached twenty when, as expected, the bell chimed.

Re-opening the door, he feigned surprise. 'Mrs. Phelps! What can I do for you?'

His neighbour's face was a mask of solicitude. 'Has there been an accident, Ricky? I saw the police officer and as your parents are away, I was a bit concerned.'

'No, there hasn't been an accident.'

'Then is something wrong?'

Richard racked his brains to find a plausible reason for the police visit. 'My bike. It's been stolen.'

'Stolen?' She looked at him sharply. 'I haven't seen you on a bicycle. Have you, Doris?' She turned, revealing Mrs. Perkins who was standing a few paces behind her.

The other woman shook her head. 'I don't think so, Marj.'

Richard was uncomfortably aware that one lie usually begets a succession of others. 'I don't use it much. I … I left it outside the … post office. Stupidly forgot to put the security chain on.'

Marjorie Phelps gave him a searching look. 'Are you telling me a police officer came to the house just because of a stolen bicycle?'

'It was a pretty decent bike,' Richard replied lamely.

'Well I'm delighted to know that the police are taking thefts of private property seriously. And kindly keep the volume down when you're playing music! ' She waddled back down the path muttering to Doris Perkins.

Richard shut the door with a bang. *Nosy old bat!* And that po-faced policeman obviously thought he was a nutcase. He wished now he had mentioned that some of the strangest UFO incidents he had read about on the internet had been witnessed by *police* officers. One still maintained, after nearly thirty years, that what he had seen looked like a double-decker bus! Was that more credible than something shaped like a coffee pot?

Chapter 5

Too agitated to resume work on his thesis, Richard thought a walk might help him regain his composure. With no clear idea of where he was heading, he strode down Bridlington Hill and across Browning Road. He was passing along the shopping parade when he was startled to hear a gravelly voice somewhere around the level of his knees. 'Because you 'ave seen, you 'ave believed!' it intoned expressionlessly. 'Blessed are them that 'aven't seen but 'ave believed: John, Twenny, Twenny nine.'

The vagrant sitting outside the mini-market leered up at him revealing stained and broken teeth between the matted grey strands of his shaggy beard.

This time Richard was in no mood to stop. Silly old fool was off his rocker. But the man's curiously appropriate words continued to reverberate inside his head as he hurried past. *Mario's*, the nearest decent coffee shop, was about ten minutes' walk away. He decided he would go there and have an espresso.

A young woman was strolling along the road ahead of him. Her dark, shoulder-length hair swung as she walked and he could see that she was listening to something on headphones. He glanced at the girl as he overtook her and thought she looked vaguely familiar.

A musical voice called after him. 'Ric? It is Ric isn't it? Ric Jarman?'

He turned round and stared at the girl. She removed the headphones and grinned. 'It's Fiona, Curtis that was. We were in the same year at Bridlington High, remember?'

As soon as Richard saw the slight gap between her top teeth, his mind travelled back in time. Fiona Curtis! She had been one of the brightest students of his year but had dropped out of school without finishing her GCSEs. There was gossip. Pregnant, they said. Paul Harris was the major suspect. Afterwards it was rumoured that they had got married.

'Of course!' he said. 'I thought you looked familiar? How are you?'

'I'm fine,' she said. 'How about you?'

'I'm fine too.'

They smiled uncertainly at each other.

'Oh dear,' she said after a moment, 'have you hurt your face?'

Self-consciously, Richard fingered the small blisters that had come up on his left cheek. 'It's nothing, just a couple of spots. What are you up to these days?'

'I'm a phlebotomist at the hospital. What about you? What have you been doing for the last … how long is it? Twelve … thirteen years?'

'I went to uni … Warwick, then worked for a journal for three years. Now I'm doing a doctorate at London University.'

She looked impressed. 'Wow! You must be dead brainy! Are you still living round here?'

'Only temporarily. I'm house-sitting while my parents are on a cruise.'

She grinned. 'I'm back at my parents' house too. Yo-yo kids, that's what they call us. They think they've got rid of us then we move in again.'

'But didn't I hear you were married?'

'I was, to Paul Harris. Remember him? It didn't work out. We were much too young. I couldn't afford to rent somewhere on my own so I moved back into Mum and Dad's place with my daughter, Polly. And you? You married?'

'No. I lived with someone for a while but it didn't work out either. She met someone else'.

'Oh, I'm sorry.'

'Don't be. It was the best thing that could have happened.'

'Oh?' She sounded puzzled.

'Look,' he said impulsively. 'I'm going to *Mario's* for a coffee. Like to join me? Do you have the time?'

'Sure, I was only going to the supermarket.'

Mario's was quiet at that time in the afternoon. They sat opposite each other at a scrubbed wooden table and filled each other in on the years since they had left school.

He told her how, after graduating, he had worked for several years on a journal specialising in climate research. 'I know some people are sceptical about global warming,' he said earnestly, 'but glaciers and ice caps are shrinking at a terrifying rate. If sea levels rise one or more metres, it could have a terrible impact on low-lying land masses…' He paused, embarrassed. 'Sorry, didn't mean to give you a lecture. But I can't understand why so many people won't believe what's happening when the effects are clear to see.'

She smiled at him reassuringly. 'I think you're absolutely right. We need to take climate change more seriously.'

Richard decided to drop the subject in case she thought he was boring. 'Tell me about your life since Bridlington High.'

She described the period she had spent with Paul Harris. 'We should never have got married but it seemed the right thing to do at the time. And I've got Polly, so it was worth it.'

Richard told her about his relationship with Emma who worked for a women's magazine. 'After we moved in together we found we actually had very little in common. I was preoccupied with climate change and natural disasters. She was obsessed with clothes and cosmetics. I thought she was frivolous. She thought I was boring.' He grinned ruefully. 'We were probably both right! Then I discovered that she was having a relationship with someone called Rodney. After a while, I moved out and he moved in.'

'That must have been hard,' Fiona murmured sympathetically.

'Actually it galvanised me. I needed a new direction. I left *Global Geographic* and enrolled on a doctorate in the Department of Geography, Environment and Development Studies at London University. It meant living on a shoestring, but it's been worth it.'

'Cool,' she exclaimed. 'What are you working on?'

Richard hesitated. People's eyes tended to glaze over whenever he gave details of his research. 'It's about the rebuilding of communities after a huge disaster like a hurricane or a tsunami,' he said timidly. 'I was lucky enough to get a grant from an international foundation, so I did my field research in an area in Bangladesh that had been destroyed by floods, then in a part of Kashmir where there'd been an earthquake.'

Instead of glazing over, Fiona's eyes widened with interest. 'Wow! That must have been amazing. What was it like?'

Richard was flattered. 'Both of them were real eye-openers. You don't know how terrible conditions are for survivors until you're actually on the spot. But I learned a lot. I realised that it's not just the practical things like providing shelter that help to rebuild communities. It's all about attitudes; mental resilience. People stuck in refugee camps waiting for assistance often become depressed and listless. You have to encourage self-help. I met one old woman who'd lost her home and entire family. She was looking after eight orphaned kids on her own. She had them organised, getting food from the distribution centre and collecting firewood.'

Fiona was listening raptly, her elbows on the table, her face cupped in her hands. Flecks of froth from her Cappuccino had stuck, charmingly he thought, to her lips. Her eyes were a colour he couldn't pin down. A moment ago he could have sworn they were grey, but now they looked green.

'It must have been an extraordinary experience.' she commented admiringly.

'It was, even though it was difficult seeing the plight so many people were in. When I've finished my thesis, I'm going to try to get a job with an overseas aid agency.'

'Cool.' She glanced at her watch. 'Sorry, better go. I promised Mum I'd get the shopping.' She stood up.

He rose reluctantly to his feet. 'I should be getting back too. I hope I haven't bored you. Not many people are interested in my research.'

She smiled. 'No, it sounds fascinating. It's good to speak to someone who's been doing something useful. Most of us only think of ourselves.'

As they moved towards the door, Richard glanced at the pile of newspapers provided on a shelf for the benefit of customers. One of the local papers had a front page headline, *Mystery Fire Destroys Park*.

'You heard about Fonthill?' he asked as they walked out into the street.

Fiona nodded. 'Yes, isn't it terrible?'

'I went there yesterday. It looked as though it had been blasted by a bomb.'

'They say it was arson, but why would anyone have done it?'

'It may not have been any "one",' Richard muttered grimly.

She looked at him curiously. 'What do you mean?'

Despite his earlier decision not to mention the incident again, Richard found himself describing what he had witnessed a few nights before.

'Gosh!' she exclaimed. 'You're dead lucky seeing something like that.'

'Lucky?' He gave a derisive laugh. 'No-one believes me. I rang the police and the miserable guy who came round accused me of wasting police time.'

'Well I believe you. What do you think it could have been?'

'I've been through all the possibilities but nothing seems to fit. It must have been a UFO.'

'That's really cool. I'd love to see a UFO.' She stopped outside the doors of a supermarket. 'It's been great seeing you again, Ric.'

'Wait,' he said hurriedly. 'You wouldn't like to come out for a drink or something one evening, would you?'

She looked pleased. 'Sure. How about Saturday?'

'Saturday would be good.'

Her face fell. 'No, sorry, I forgot. I've got a ticket to see Morgana Delph at the theatre.'

'Who's Morgana Delph?'

'She's that famous medium, the one on TV, in the paranormal slot, *Voices from the Other Side*.'

Richard shuddered. 'A medium? One of those people who say they receive messages from the dead?'

'Yes. She's absolutely fantastic. She comes out with stuff she couldn't possibly have known about. Why don't you come along? I could try to get another ticket though we might not be able to sit together. We could go for a drink afterwards.'

'OK, why not?' Richard could think of better ways of spending an evening than listening to a load of psychic claptrap, but it might be a laugh, and after the visit from the lugubrious detective, a laugh was exactly what he needed.

They exchanged mobile numbers and went their separate ways.

He returned to Coronation Close in a decidedly better frame of mind than when he had left it.

Chapter 6

On Saturday evening, Richard left his father's car in a public car park then walked the few hundred yards to the Princess Royal Theatre - an ornate white and gold nineteenth-century edifice towering incongruously over the neighbouring modern shops. Posters in front of the entrance advertised a special appearance of "Britain's Greatest Medium".

He pushed his way through the crowd in the foyer and found Fiona waiting by the box office. She was wearing a navy raincoat and had tied her hair in a pony tail. She looked absurdly young, like the teenager he remembered from school.

She brandished two tickets at him. 'They had some returns so I exchanged my ticket and managed to get two together in the dress circle. Clever or what?'

Richard was relieved. He hadn't relished the prospect of sitting on his own at an event he imagined would be grotesque.

When they took their seats, he was surprised to see cameras being set up around the stage. 'You didn't tell me it was being televised.'

'Didn't I? It's going to be shown next week on *Voices from the Other Side*. We could watch it again.'

Richard thought one live viewing would probably be quite enough.

The stage was bare except for a microphone, a chair and a table on which stood a vase of flowers, a bottle of water and a glass. The backdrop was a huge, blank screen. Low music was playing in the background. It was of a New Age type that Richard detested: metallic notes accompanied by whooshing and tinkling sounds and a high-pitched noise he suspected was a whale song.

After the final warning bell, the last ticket holders trickled in and noisily took their seats. The lights dimmed and there was an expectant hush in the auditorium.

A bearded man came to the microphone at the front of the stage and addressed the audience. 'Ladies and Gentleman, welcome to what I'm sure will be an exciting evening with Madame Morgana Delph, the UK's leading medium.'

There was a ripple of applause.

'When Madame Delph appears, there will be many spirits clamouring for her attention and I would ask you to kindly remain as quiet as possible so as not to disturb her concentration . She will respond to the most persistent voices and call out a name and perhaps other information. If you have that name and recognise some of the details, please stand up and someone will bring a microphone to you. It will soon become clear to Madame Delph if you are the right person. You may feel embarrassed or self-conscious, but I promise you those feelings will rapidly evaporate as Madame Delph channels messages to you from the spirit world.'

The man exited through the wings amidst an expectant murmur from the audience. The house lights dimmed and there was tumultuous applause as the medium made her entry.

Richard, who had been expecting someone of exotic appearance, was slightly disappointed to see that she was small, plump and grey-haired.

She walked slowly to the front of the stage and welcomed the audience in a broad Yorkshire accent. She then spent several minutes describing how she had recognised and developed her psychic gift and what her work involved. 'Like all mediums, I am assisted by spirit guides,' she declared at the end of her exposition. 'I have two principal guides, Dr Hu, a Chinese healer and Soaring Eagle, an Indian, or what they call now native American, chief. And occasionally Tante Sabine, a French lady who lived in the eighteenth century, steps in to assist when a spirit has trouble making contact. Because spirits reside on another plane, it can sometimes be difficult for them to tune in.'

Richard suppressed a yawn. He glanced at Fiona who was listening attentively to the medium. He wished he was sitting next to her somewhere else, in a pleasant pub, or in a restaurant or at a gig.

Morgana Delph surveyed the audience. 'None of you should be afraid or intimidated,' she said reassuringly. 'The spirits who communicate through me bring only messages of love and advice.' She moved to the microphone beside the table, took a sip of water and closed her eyes.

The audience waited expectantly.

'I 'ave a gentleman with me,' she announced suddenly, 'an elderly gentleman ... Michael ... Mike ... yes, I've got it, dear ...A dog? Woolwich? Olive? You want to speak to Olive, or is it Olivia? Yes, dear, I'll try and make the connection.'

She opened her eyes and addressed the audience. 'Is there an Olive or Olivia among you who has a relative or friend called Michael in the spirit world, someone who may have lived in Woolwich?'

There was a silence.

'Come on, don't be shy!' urged the medium.

A seat banged in the stalls and the camera focused on a slight, middle-aged woman. Her face, hugely magnified on the screen at the back of the stage, was a picture of alarm. Someone brought her a microphone.

'Are you Olive, love?' asked Madame Delph.

'My name's Olivia,' the woman mumbled self-consciously.

'Does the name Michael mean anything to you?'

'My grandfather was from Woolwich, his name was Mick.'

'I heard barking. Did your granddad have a dog?'

'No, but his surname was Barker.'

The audience tittered.

'Then it's you he wants to speak to, love. There's no need to be frightened.' Madame Delph shut her eyes and listened for a moment. 'What's that, dear?' she asked the unseen presence. 'Ah yes, I understand'. She addressed the woman. 'Has there been a feud in the family, my love? Over your grandmother's rings?'

The woman looked mortified. 'Yes ... There have been some arguments,' she admitted tremulously.

'Between you and your sisters?'

'Yes.'

'Well your granddad says the family shouldn't fall out over material things. You must sort the problem out now; compromise ... He says it's important.'

The woman's eyes filled with tears. 'Yes,' she whispered. 'I will.'

'Your granddad sends his love to you.'

Richard squirmed uneasily in his uncomfortable seat. He found the scene excruciatingly embarrassing. Fiona obviously did not. She turned to him, her eyes shining with excitement. 'Isn't she fantastic?'

He forced a smile but didn't reply.

Several other members of the audience received messages allegedly emanating from the spirit world. One man was instructed by his late uncle to take greater care of his vegetable plot; another was commanded by his mother to overcome his fears and go to the dentist. A blonde woman wearing lots of gold jewellery was sternly advised by a relative who had died long before she was born, to be more discriminating in her choice of gentleman friends.

Given the astounding banality of these messages, Richard was surprised by the emotional reactions of the recipients. Many of them burst into tears.

Finally Madame Delph sank, exhausted, on to the chair. The lights came back on. It was the interval.

Fiona was bubbling with excitement as they joined the crowds drifting towards the bar. 'She's amazing, isn't she? She couldn't possibly have known about those rings or that that man had a painful abscess.'

Richard was surprised that someone so intelligent could be taken in by such rubbish. 'It could all be a fix, couldn't it?'

She looked shocked. 'No, I'm sure it's not. I think she's absolutely genuine.'

'Did you know her real name is Margaret Entwhistle?'

'You're kidding!'

'No, I looked her up on the internet!'

She giggled. 'No wonder she changed it. Morgana Delph is more ...'

'Exotic?'

'Yes.'

Richard wondered whether he could endure sitting through the second half. All too soon, however, he found himself back in his cramped seat in the dress circle.

Morgana Delph returned to the stage. As before, she stood by the table, took a sip of water and shut her eyes. A few seconds passed. Then she opened her eyes and addressed the audience. 'Eeeh, it's a funny one is this! I can't make it out. I don't know whether it's a man or a woman but it's very insistent.'

She listened intently, gasped and her eyes rolled upwards so that only the whites were visible. Then, to Richard's horror, a deep, guttural male voice issued from her mouth. 'Fire! Destruction!' it shouted.

There were startled cries from the audience.

'Someone has witnessed the sign,' called the unnerving voice. 'The sign of The Coming! Ri...Ri...Richard!'

Richard shrank back in his seat

'Burning!' Madame Delph staggered and clutched the back of the chair to steady herself.

There was a murmur of alarm around the auditorium. The bearded man emerged from the wings and walked quickly to the front microphone. 'Ladies and gentlemen, please don't be alarmed. Madame Delph is occasionally taken over by spirit and when this happens, she is in an altered state of consciousness. Is there someone named Richard in the audience for whom her words are significant? If so, please stand up.'

No-one moved.

Fiona nudged Richard with her elbow. 'Go on,' she whispered, 'it must be you. Stand up.'

'No way!' he hissed. He had broken out in a cold sweat.

'Burning! Destruction!' The strange voice continued to reverberate through the theatre. The words it uttered were all on the same note, stilted, almost staccato, reminding Richard of a Dalek in the *Dr Who* series he had watched as a child.

Morgana Delph had started to shake uncontrollably and the bearded man appealed again to the audience. 'If there is anyone here tonight who finds this message meaningful, please stand up. As you can see, Madame Delph is in some distress.'

Fiona nudged Richard again. 'Stand up, Ric. It must be you.'

Reluctantly he got to his feet. His seat made a loud clacking sound as it folded back behind him. The audience buzzed with excitement and people twisted round to stare at him. The cameras swung towards him and he was horrified to see his face on the screen magnified to such an extent that every pore was exposed.

Madame Delph's eyes snapped open and she peered intently up at the dress circle. 'Richard!' she called in the same sepulchral voice, 'watcher at the window! You have seen the sign. Find the poet, philosopher and healer ... but take *great care*.'

Richard froze.

There was a brief silence, then, '*Evil*' she shrieked, and the audience collectively jumped.

The medium uttered a groan and collapsed on to the chair. Two men rushed from the wings. Each taking an arm, they pulled her gently to her feet and half carried her off the stage.

There was a renewed murmur around the theatre and Richard realised that he had become the object of intense curiosity. As he sank back in his seat, Fiona pressed his hand reassuringly.

'Ladies and gentlemen, please be patient,' announced the bearded man who had remained at the front of the stage. 'After Madame Delph has been taken over by spirit, she needs time to recover. The perfor mance will be resumed shortly.'

The house lights came on and the irritating New Age music started up again.

Richard was dripping with perspiration. 'I'm sorry,' he muttered to Fiona, 'I've got to get out of here.' Without waiting for her to answer, he stood up, clambered over the feet of the people sitting next to him, and hastened towards the exit.

Grabbing her bag and raincoat, Fiona scrambled after him.

Outside the theatre, he leant against a lamppost and took deep gulps of air. It was raining but he didn't care, as long as he was away from that awful voice.

Fiona stood uncertainly in front of him, pulling on her raincoat. 'Are you OK, Ric? What's the matter?'

'That voice … it freaked me out. '

'I'm not surprised. It was really weird. Who do you think it came from?'

'I don't know. I don't care. Let's go for a drink. I need one.'

Hunched against the rain, they made their way to a nearby wine bar. It was noisy with the chatter and laughter of young people enjoying an evening out. Richard felt reassured by the normality of the environ-ment. It was a place where he was unlikely to be exposed to spirit voices and whale songs. He ordered white wine for Fiona and a brandy for himself. He didn't usually drink spirits (from now on he would even avoid the word), but felt he needed something strong.

'I'm sorry I dragged you out before the end,' he said as they sat down.

'It doesn't matter.' She draped her raincoat over the back of her chair. 'I know it was a bit scary, but don't you think she was impressive?'

'No,' he snapped. 'I thought she was horrific. All that rubbish about evil and finding a poet and healer.'

'But how could she have known that you saw something in the sky that night? And that stuff she said about burning and destruction was spot on, wasn't it, after what's happened in Fonthill and Hertfordshire?'

'Hertfordshire?'

'You know, the incident in Hertfordshire yesterday.'

'What incident?'

'Didn't you hear? It was in the papers.'

'I haven't seen any papers. I've been trying to finish my thesis. What happened?'

Fiona pushed a wet strand of hair off her forehead and took a sip of wine. 'Another green area has been destroyed, razed to the ground. They think it must be arson but it happened overnight and no-one saw anything.'

He stared at her, astonished. 'You mean like what happened at Fonthill?'

'Exactly the same, apparently. The police believe there may be a connection.'

'Christ!' Richard gave an involuntary shiver and put down his glass. He felt suddenly very frightened. 'I'm sorry, Fiona. I know we were going to make a night of it, but do you mind if we go now? I'll drive you home.'

'Now?' She looked crestfallen. 'I suppose so, if that's what you want.' She swallowed the rest of her wine then put her raincoat back on.

'Sorry to cut the evening short,' he mumbled as the car drew up outside her parents' house. 'Perhaps we could go out another evening?'

'Perhaps.' She slammed the passenger door and ran up the front path without a backward glance.

Chapter 7

As soon as Richard arrived home, he went upstairs, opened his laptop and searched the internet. It didn't take him long to find what he was looking for: *Mystery Conflagration in Hertfordshire. Police are investigating the mysterious destruction by fire of Mayfield Common.* The brief details confirmed what Fiona had told him: the common had suffered a fate identical to the damage inflicted on Fontwell Park.

He lay awake most of the night, puzzling over what had happened during the Morgana Delph show and the significance of the second arson attack in Hertfordshire.

When he got up in the morning, he decided to go and buy a newspaper before working on his thesis. As he passed along the Close, he came face to face with Stan and Marjorie Phelps and was struck anew by what an ill-assorted pair they were: she, huge-chested and triple-chinned; he, short and slight, his face scaly with psoriasis. What could have brought them together forty odd years ago? He tried and failed to imagine Mrs. Phelps as an attractive young woman.

'Well, Ricky. Did they find it?'

'Find what, Mrs. Phelps?'

'Your bicycle! The one you said was stolen.'

'No, not yet. Sorry, in a hurry.' Richard strode rapidly round the corner before she could comment and made his way down the hill to the shopping parade.

As he passed along it, a rasping voice made him start. 'I seen it!'

'What?'

'I seen what you seen.' The elderly vagrant was standing in front of him, so close that Richard could smell his unpleasant odour of alcohol and unwashed flesh.

'What do you mean?'

The man loomed over him. Though stooped, he was surprisingly tall. 'That night.'

'What night?'

'That night when there was lights in the sky and that shiny thing that went off like, wheeeeeee!' The man waved an arm in the air and laughed, revealing his stained and broken teeth. 'I aint never seen nothin' move so fast. I seen you watchin' it too, from the winder.' He stopped laughing, his eyes blazed and to Richard's alarm, his voice became a high-pitched wail. 'The sun an' the air was darkened by the smoke o' the bottomless pit and the locusts was told that they shouldn't 'urt the grass of the earth nor any green thing, but only them what didn't 'ave the sign o' God on their 'eads. John, Apoc'lypse, Nine.'

Stunned, Richard hastily stepped past the man and, pursued by the wailing voice, hurried to the newsagents and bought a paper. He didn't know whether to laugh or cry. He had finally found someone else who had witnessed the UFO, but it was a crazy, Bible-spouting vagrant.

He hurried home and spread the newspaper on the kitchen table. The Hertfordshire incident was covered on the inside pages. Trees and shrubs and a large expanse of grass on the common had been totally destroyed and the ground was covered in a residue of toxic dust. The damage appeared to have been inflicted during the small hours and there were no witnesses. No-one had smelt burning or seen smoke or flames.

The article was accompanied by a smudgy photo of the ravaged green and the obligatory range of comments from perplexed local residents. One snippet caught his attention. Sister Francis, a nun at the nearby Benedictine Convent, had reported seeing bright lights and a dazzling object in the sky during the night of the conflagration. *Police believe this was an overflying aircraft and have discounted any connection with the incident.*

Richard, however, did not discount it. This was surely too much of a coincidence. Could the nun have witnessed the same object that he had seen? He felt compelled to find out. But how could he contact her? He thought he could probably find the convent's telephone number, but would a nun be allowed to receive a call from a stranger? And if he did ring the convent, what would he say to whoever answered the phone? 'Hello. I saw something in the sky the other night and was wondering whether it was the same thing Sister Francis saw.' That would probably put an end to the conversation!

He concluded that it would probably be easier to go to the convent and speak to the nun in person. If she wasn't available, he could at least visit Mayfield Common and witness the damage for himself.

He looked up the convent's address on the internet and set off in his father's car, estimating that it would take him about an hour and a half to get there.

Because of heavy traffic, the journey was agonisingly slow and he finally arrived at the common just before twelve. As had been described, the area was a scene of blackened devastation, now roped off, with stern notices restricting entry to all but emergency services. Lines of forensic investigators, wearing facemasks and protective clothing, were slowly crossing an expanse of blackened ground, their heads lowered as they searched for clues to the source of the destruction.

Police officers were stationed at intervals around the perimeter of the common, keeping crowds of curious onlookers at bay. Large signs on the pavement advised people to keep away from the area and avoid contact with the poisonous dust.

Richard checked the map. Our Lady of Lourdes Convent was in Chestnuts Crescent, about a mile away from the common. It only took him a few minutes to drive there. The crescent was instantly recognisable by its double line of majestic chestnut trees, already resplendent with pink blossoms. The convent was set back from the road and surrounded by a high stone wall.

He left the car by the roadside and walked up to the wrought iron gates which were locked. Through them he glimpsed a stately gravel drive leading to the entrance of an imposing mock Gothic building. In sharp contrast to the scene he had just witnessed, the lawn on either side of the drive was a sparkling green and the borders were radiant with spring flowers.

He pressed the buzzer on the right gatepost and after a few moments, a sharp disembodied female voice answered through the intercom. 'Yes?'

He took a deep breath. 'Good morning. Could I speak to Sister Francis?'

'Sister Francis? What is the nature of your business with her?'

He had intended to say that it was a private matter, but decided he needed a more plausible reason for his visit. Fortunately the voice supplied him with one. 'Are you from the shelter? Sister Francis usually gets the food boxes ready in the afternoon.'

'Erm … yes,' he mumbled, 'it's about the boxes.'

The intercom went dead and through the decorative scrollwork of the gates, he saw an elderly nun wearing a dark blue habit and a white headdress emerge from the main doors and walk stiffly down the drive. When she arrived at the gates she peered at him suspiciously. 'Mr.

Carter usually collects the boxes.'

'Erm … not today,' he stammered, feeling uneasy about telling a lie to a nun. 'I just wanted a quick word … about the boxes. It won't take a moment. I'm sorry I didn't give any prior notice.' He smiled at her appealingly.

Her expression softened. 'Very well. Sister Francis is in the kitchen garden. I'll take you to her.' She pressed a button on her side of the gates and they noisily swung open.

Richard breathed a sigh of relief and stepped on to the drive. 'What a lovely garden,' he said, gazing round at the flower beds.

The nun looked pleased. 'Thank you. It takes a lot of looking after. Sister Francis does most of it. There are only eight of us left at the convent now.'

'Only eight?'

The nun sighed. 'There were more than twenty of us when I came here as a novice, but very few young women have the vocation these days. We may have to move out. The convent's far too big and expensive to maintain.'

She led him round the side of the building and along a narrow brick path that ran between several dilapidated greenhouses. At the end of the path there was a large vegetable patch striped with rows of neatly planted furrows. Green shoots and leaves were sprouting under cloches and emerging at the base of bamboo canes. At the end of one of the rows, a small plump nun wearing a plastic apron was kneeling on a gardening stool, digging vigorously.

'Sister Francis, you have a visitor,' called the elderly nun.

The other nun looked round in surprise.

'This young man is from the shelter. He wants to talk to you about the food boxes.'

Sister Francis peered at Richard through a triangle of pea-stick supports. 'Thank you, Sister Benedict.' She put down her trowel and hauled herself to her feet.

The other nun shuffled away.

Sister Francis wiped her hands on a cloth she produced from her apron pocket. She was tiny, barely five feet high, with a round red face and bright blue eyes behind small rimless glasses. She beamed at Richard. 'Well this is a pleasure, so it is. I don't get many male callers these days, especially good-looking young ones!' She held out a plump hand. 'And one with red hair; a Celt like me!'

Richard grasped her hand, blushing furiously. He wasn't used to being flirted with by elderly nuns. 'Hello, I'm Richard Jarman.'

'Are you a volunteer at the homeless shelter?' she asked, then before he could answer, 'Was there something wrong with the last box? We're a bit limited at this time of year. Once the sprouts and leeks are finished, we have to wait for the spinach and caulis. But I've got some broad beans and there are things coming on in the greenhouses. I might have some purple and white broccoli in a few weeks. And there are always the food donations that people bring us.'

'I'm sorry,' Richard stuttered, 'but I haven't come from the shelter. I've come from London.'

'London?' She looked astonished. 'Sister Benedict said you'd come about the boxes.'

'She thought I had and I'm afraid I didn't contradict her. I just needed an excuse to see you.'

The nun stared at him. 'Me? Why?'

'I'm really sorry to turn up out of the blue, Sister. But it's about what happened at Mayfield Common.'

Her face fell. 'Oh, you're not a reporter are you? Mother Ignatius has asked me not to talk to journalists.'

'No, I'm not a journalist. I'm a mature student.'

She looked even more bewildered. 'A student? So why do you want to see *me*?'

He swallowed. 'It's because I read in the paper that you saw something strange on the night that Mayfield Common was destroyed. Something very similar happened to me. I *saw* something strange in the sky the night Fonthill Park was burnt. I wanted to compare notes.'

'What did you see?' she asked sharply.

'The sky was all lit up with incredibly bright colours, and I saw an amazingly bright object ... something absolutely dazzling. It had kind of sparks coming off it. It started spinning incredibly fast, then it suddenly shot upwards and disappeared.'

Sister Francis looked agitated. 'What did it look like? What shape was it?'

'It was huge and sort of cylindrical, with an indentation in the middle.'

'Yes, yes,' she repeated excitedly. 'That's exactly what I saw. I couldn't sleep so I got up to say the rosary. I was standing near the window and the sky suddenly lit up with such bright colours, I thought the angels had come, so I did. And when I looked out, there was this dazzling thing in the sky, just the shape you described. It was spinning at such a speed, then it shot away and disappeared so fast I thought I'd been dreaming and--'

Richard interrupted her. 'Who did you tell about it? '

She clasped her hands together. 'I told Mother Ignatius the next morning, and after we heard about Mayfield Common, she rang the police. They said it was probably an aeroplane or a weather balloon, but I knew it wasn't. Mother Ignatius didn't want me to talk about what I saw to anyone else in case we had visitors who believe in ... what's the word now?' She lowered her voice. 'You know ... flying saucers, that kind of thing. But I stupidly mentioned it to someone who comes to Mass at the convent, and the next thing we knew, a journalist came calling.'

Although there was no-one else around, Richard also lowered his voice. 'Don't you think it's significant, Sister, that on the nights when we both saw something strange in the sky, two green spaces were completely destroyed, and no-one saw anything burning or smelled any smoke? Don't you think there could be a connection?'

She gazed at him in alarm. 'May the Lord bless and save us! It was so beautiful I thought it must have been a sign from God. But if it had something to do with that terrible incident at Mayfield Common, perhaps it was the work of the Devil.' She crossed herself.

'I don't know about that,' Richard said gravely, 'but I think it's quite possible that the object we saw could have been responsible for both of the fires.'

Sister Francis looked distressed. 'If what we saw is evil, then we need our Saviour's assistance. We must pray to Him to deliver us. Will you come and pray with me, Robert? We must pray that what we saw wasn't an instrument of the Devil.'

'Oh ... I ...' He coughed. 'My name's actually Richard.'

'Will you come and pray with me, Richard?' she repeated.

He felt it would be churlish to refuse. 'Yes ... OK.' Reluctantly he followed the little nun through a door at the back of the convent.

She took off her gardening apron and led him down an echoing corridor and into a small chapel that smelled of incense and candle wax.

Fascinated, he gazed around him. There were about twelve rows of pews facing an altar over which hung a huge wooden crucifix. An alcove on the right side of the altar contained a life-size plaster statue of the Virgin Mary, holding her arms wide and her palms open. Her robes were painted blue and white and there were shiny pink Mother of Pearl teardrops in the corner of her eyes. Beneath the statue, the stubs of several candles were burning in holders on a metal stand. Two nuns were kneeling in front of them, murmuring over rosary beads.

Sister Francis motioned Richard into a pew then knelt down beside him and bent her head. Richard lowered himself self-consciously onto his knees and assumed what he hoped was an expression of piety. His mind, however, wasn't on prayer. He was wondering if the object he, the old vagrant and the nun had seen, had indeed destroyed the two large green areas, and if so, why?

After about ten minutes, he followed Sister Francis out of the chapel and she accompanied him back to the gates. Before opening them, she handed him a rosary. 'Keep this with you now, Richard, and the Blessed Virgin will protect you against evil.'

'Thank you.' He looked dubiously at the rosary and thrust it into his jacket pocket. Then on an impulse, he wrote his mobile and home telephone numbers on a scrap of paper and handed it to her. 'Just in case,' he muttered, 'in case you see that thing again.'

She stowed the paper in the folds of her habit and smiled sweetly at him. 'We're not supposed to make personal calls, but I'll keep your number as you're such a nice young gentleman. It'll be our wee secret.'

She opened the gates and waved him off.

Back at the car, Richard checked his mobile and found a text from Fiona: *don't forget morgana delph prog on tv tonite.*

He shuddered. He had no intention of watching the programme and re-experiencing the embarrassment and humiliation of being singled out by the mad medium. Fortunately the programme was on one of the minor Freeview channels, so hopefully no-one he knew would watch it either.

He pocketed his mobile and drove home.

Chapter 8

That night he dreamed that flames were devouring great swathes of land while a raucous voice exhorted him repeatedly to seek the "Poet, Philosopher and Healer". Eventually the voice changed into another sound: a shrill, insistent noise that forced him into consciousness. The landline phone was ringing in the hall.

He rose stiffly from his bed and stumbled downstairs to answer it.

'Did I wake you up?' asked his sister Saskia.

'Yes. What's up?'

'Just wanted to know if you're OK?'

'Yes, why shouldn't I be?'

'I've had an email from Mum. She said she hasn't heard from you for a week.'

Richard felt a rush of guilt. He had been too preoccupied with recent events to respond to his mother's emails. 'I've been working on my thesis. Didn't have much to say.'

'Well send her a message, will you? She wanted to know if you're having any problems in the house.'

'Of course I'm not having any problems,' he said irritably. 'Was that all you rang about?'

His sister chuckled. 'Just checking on my little brother.'

Richard yawned. 'I'll email Mum today. How are the boys?' He was fond of his twin nephews, although he saw them infrequently as they didn't live near his parents.

'They're fine. Come and visit us soon.'

'I will,' he promised, 'after I've finished my thesis.' He replaced the receiver, then went to the kitchen and put the kettle on only to discover, when it had boiled, that he had forgotten to buy any milk. It meant a trip to the shop. Cursing, he returned to his bedroom and got dressed.

He left the house at the same moment that Doris Perkins, his neighbour at number five, emerged from hers. After exchanging greetings, he quickened his pace but she fell into step beside him.

'Well Ricky, you're quite the celebrity!' she commented inexplicably as they set off together down Bridlington Hill.

'Me? What do you mean, Mrs. Perkins.'

'I saw you on *Voices from the Other Side* last night.'

His heart sank.

'I said to Reg, "That's Ricky from next door, isn't it?" I didn't think a young man like you would be into paranormal stuff.'

'I'm not *into* paranormal stuff,' Richard protested. 'I only went because a friend invited me.'

'But wasn't it exciting to get a message from Spirit? You looked quite shocked. What did she say to you again? It sounded very odd. Something about evil and finding a poet?'

'I don't remember exactly.'

'But Morgana Delph is usually very accurate, Ricky. Didn't it make sense to you?'

'No, it didn't. To be honest, I thought it was a load of rubbish.' He skilfully changed the subject to one he knew was dear to her heart. 'Mrs. Perkins, your back garden is a real picture. I can see it from my bedroom window.'

She beamed. 'Thank you, Ricky. It's at its best now the spring flowers are out and the cherry tree's in blossom. I put a load of bulbs in last autumn …'

As she chattered on about her garden, Richard made polite noises while attempting to mask his agitation. Had any other acquaintances seen him on the Morgana Delph show? It was a horrifying thought.

After they separated at the shopping parade, he made his way to the minimarket, noticing, as he entered, that the homeless man wasn't in his usual place by the cash dispenser.

'Where's the old guy with the dog this morning?' he asked Mr. Patel while paying for his carton of milk and sliced loaf.

'Paddy? They took him away,' replied the shopkeeper, closing the till.

'Who took him away?'

'When I was serving a customer yesterday morning, I heard a commotion outside, men shouting and a dog barking. I went to the door and saw two men pulling the old man into a car. He was struggling, kicking…' The shopkeeper grinned. He appeared to have enjoyed the scene.

Richard stared at him. 'Who were the men? The police?'

Mr. Patel shrugged. 'I don't know. They weren't in uniform.'

'But why would they take the old guy away? Didn't anyone try to stop them?'

The shopkeeper shrugged again. 'No. People just watched.'

'What about the dog?'

Mr. Patel chuckled. 'It bit one of the men on the leg. He got in the car quick, then they drove away. The dog ran after the car and I haven't seen it since ... Good morning, Madam!' Another customer had put her wire basket on the counter.

Richard felt uneasy as he left the shop. Maybe the old man had fallen victim to the Vagrancy Act if it was still in force. But even if it was, his violent removal from the shopping parade seemed disproportionately harsh.

He was half-way up the hill when he heard a dog whining. It was the kind of piteous noise that issued from next door whenever Pugwash was left in the house on his own. Looking in the direction of the noise, he spotted the old man's dog on the other side of the road. It was running up and down in front of a disused and vandalised bus shelter. He crossed the road and approached the dog cautiously, mindful that it had bitten someone. As it backed away, he saw that it was a bitch of no recognisable breed. She was pitifully thin and her matted grey fur was in a poor condition, with some bare patches.

The shelter showed signs of recent habitation: sandwich wrappers and empty lager cans were strewn across the broken bench, and the floor was littered with old newspapers and plastic bags. A filthy sleeping bag protruded from under the bench.

Watching Richard intently, the dog stood protectively in front of the mess that probably comprised the totality of her owner's belongings. She was quivering. He wondered whether she had had anything to eat since her owner had been taken away. 'Here, girl,' he said, gently holding out his hand.

The dog whined and looked at him with filmy eyes.

'Come on, I won't hurt you.' He remained very still, with his hand outstretched.

After a few moments, she moved forward and sniffed his fingers.

Richard stroked her gently. 'Are you hungry? I'll get you something.'

Mr. Patel looked surprised when he re-entered the supermarket. 'You forget something?'

'Yes.' Richard took some cans of dog food and a bag of dog biscuits from the shelves and carried them to the till.

The shopkeeper placed the items in a plastic bag. 'You got a dog, then?'

'No. These are for someone else's dog.'

She was still whining when he arrived back at the bus shelter. He scattered the biscuits on the ground and she wolfed them down in seconds. Returning home, he opened one of the cans of dog food and tipped its contents into a breakfast bowl. He filled another bowl with water, then carried both back to the bus shelter.

After noisily gulping the food and slurping some of the water, the dog snuffled hopefully round his legs.

'That's all for now.' Richard picked up the empty food bowl and carried it home. He wondered whether he should ring the RSPCA but decided not to. Hopefully the old man would soon return and reclaim the animal.

After eating his own delayed breakfast, he returned to his desk and switched on his laptop. He reread some of the last sentences he had drafted. *It is a question of regeneration, not just of the natural and manmade environments, but also of the spirit of stricken populations. The rebuilding of communities depends on survivors' collective resilience, fortitude and self-belief ...*

His mind began to wander. For the last two years he had been preoccupied with the consequences of natural disasters. What was worse, he now wondered: destruction wrought by catastrophes such as earthquakes or floods, or destruction caused by preventable disasters such as wars, terrorism or ... arson?

His thoughts were interrupted by the doorbell. He ran downstairs.

Two men were standing on the path. They were tall and smartly dressed in dark suits. They smiled at him, wide insincere smiles that revealed implausibly white and even teeth.

'Yes?' Richard muttered.

'Good morning, Sir,' said one in what sounded like an American accent. 'Could you spare us a few minutes?'

'What for?'

The second man leaned forward, smiling so broadly that Richard thought he could almost see his face reflected in the gleaming teeth. He held out a pamphlet. 'Sir, we have a special message just for you.'

Richard felt a rush of anger. He had received quite enough "special messages" lately. 'And I have a special message just for *you*.' he snapped. 'Piss off!'

He slammed the door then stood in the hall for a moment, wondering if he had been unnecessarily rude. He peered cautiously through the small window next to the front door. The two men were conferring on the path. He ducked out of sight as one of them walked back to the door. He heard the click of something being pushed through the letterbox. After waiting a few seconds, he picked it up. It was a leaflet on which was written in large red type: *Repent your sins and prepare for the Second Coming! Only the righteous will enter into the New Kingdom.*

He tossed the leaflet into the kitchen bin. When he looked out of the hall window again, the men had disappeared.

He returned to his desk but was unable to recover his previous train of thought. Sighing, he abandoned the attempt, opened the internet and scrolled through the latest news bulletins. After a few minutes, he uttered a gasp. He had spotted a heading: *Essex Common Ravaged by Mysterious Fire.* His stomach lurched.

Local police, he read, *in partnership with those in north London and Hertfordshire, are investigating the possibility that a gang of arsonists is working its way around green areas on the outskirts of London, using an inflammable substance that creates rapid devastation but doesn't give off smoke or flames.*

There were no other details.

Richard opened some Essex newspaper websites. They had brief and identically-worded accounts of the latest incident which bore exactly the same features as those at Fonthill and Mayfield Common.

Shaken by this new development, he felt an urgent need to express his growing sense of unease to someone else. Fiona was the only person who hadn't dismissed his story about the UFO. He sent her a text: *Can we meet later tday?*

Taking Poll to swimming pool at 4pm, she texted back.

C u there, he replied.

* * *

He arrived at the leisure centre, which was within walking distance, at half past four. The glass walls of its indoor swimming pool imparted light and a sense of airiness but did not absorb the noise – the deafening, echoing sound of children shrieking and splashing. There was a strong and unpleasant smell of chlorine.

At the shallow end, a young woman was demonstrating swimming strokes to a group of children. A number of adults watched from the raked rows of seats overlooking the pool. Richard spotted Fiona among them and made his way towards her. Catching sight of him, she waved and smiled. Her dark hair hung loosely round her face and it struck him how attractive she was - not glamorous like Emma, who would never leave the flat they had shared without putting on thick layers of make-up, but naturally attractive in a way that didn't rely on cosmetics.

He sat down next to her. 'This is a trip down memory lane. I haven't been here since I was about seventeen.'

She laughed. 'It hasn't changed much, has it?'

He noticed that her upper lip was fuller and more prominent than the lower one and found this oddly endearing. 'Which one's Polly?' he asked, glancing down at the line of children queuing to enter the water.

He didn't have to wait for an answer. A girl of about ten with long, coltish legs and dark hair, was about to take her turn at the edge of the pool. She waved to Fiona and gave a gap-toothed grin before disappearing with a huge splash under the water.

He laughed. 'Spitting image!'

'Everyone says that.' Fiona watched Polly performing an exaggerated breast stroke then turned back to him. 'Did you watch *Voices from the Other Side*?'

'No, couldn't face it. Did you?'

'Yes. The message she gave you seemed even weirder on TV.'

He shuddered. 'Don't tell me. I don't want to know.'

'Chicken!' She made a gesture of applause as Polly scrambled out of the pool and looked proudly up for her approval.

'Fiona,' he said when her attention switched back to him. 'Something really weird is going on.'

She looked at him enquiringly. 'What do you mean?'

'Did you hear that a common in Essex was destroyed last night? It was burnt, exactly like the other two.'

Her eyes widened. 'You're kidding. Another one?'

'Yes, and I think what's happening may be connected to that thing I saw in the sky.'

She looked dubious. 'What makes you think that?'

He frowned. 'It's too noisy to talk in here. Can we go somewhere quieter?'

She looked at her watch. 'The swimming lesson should be finished soon. We can go to the café while Polly gets changed.'

He hoped he could compress all he wanted to tell her in the short time it would take the girl to get dressed.

While they drank tea in the café, he related what the homeless man and Sister Francis had told him. 'When I read about the third incident in Essex, I felt I needed to talk about it to someone.'

She looked puzzled. 'You're right. There does seem to be something weird going on. Why would three areas of greenbelt have been destroyed in quick succession?

This is getting scary, Ric.'

'I know. A lot of strange things do seem to be happening. The local shopkeeper told me that he saw the old homeless man being manhandled into a car yesterday and driven away.'

She frowned. 'Why? Who would want to kidnap an old man?'

'I don't know. The shopkeeper said it wasn't the police. I found the old man's dog this morning. It was waiting for him in an old bus shelter. Poor thing was very hungry.'

'What a shame. Do you know his name?'

'Whose? The man's or the dog's?'

'The man's of course.'

'The shopkeeper called him Paddy. Why?'

'A nurse at the hospital where I work told me an old man was brought in yesterday afternoon. He'd been badly beaten up.'

Before Richard could respond, Polly arrived at their table. With her grey-green eyes and straight dark hair, she could have been Fiona's younger sister. 'Mum, did you see me?' she asked excitedly. 'I swam six strokes underwater and I didn't swallow any.' She stared curiously at Richard.

'Great stuff, Poll Doll! This is Ric. He went to the same school as me.'

The girl continued to stare at him unblinkingly. 'Was that in the olden days?'

He laughed. 'Yes, in the Dark Ages when your mum and I were as young as you.'

After Fiona had bought Polly some crisps, he accompanied them to their bus stop.

'Let me know if you hear anything else about what happened in Essex?' Fiona said as the bus came into view, 'and I'll try and find out more about the guy in the hospital.'

'Yeah, let's keep in touch.' He regarded her hesitantly. 'Would you like to come out again one evening?'

She seemed pleased. 'Cool. Wednesday's best for me.'

'Wednesday it is. I'll ring you'. He was relieved that she didn't appear to hold the abrupt curtailment of their previous outing against him.

He waved to them as the bus left, then made his own way home on foot.

He had completely forgotten about the dog until he saw her prowling forlornly up and down in front of the bus shelter on the hill. He hurried back to the house, opened another can of dog food and took a bowl of it back to her. She swallowed it in seconds and looked hopefully up at him for more.

'Later!' He retrieved the empty bowl and returned home.

Back at his desk, he searched for information on the third incident in Essex but could find nothing new. Eventually he abandoned the attempt and sent an email to his parents assuring them that the house hadn't burned down (an unfortunate choice of words, he later realised), and claiming that he was leading a quiet and uneventful life writing his thesis.

After closing the laptop he went to the window. Nothing stirred outside. He yawned and put his hands in his pockets. His right hand closed over something lumpy: the nun's rosary beads. He hung them over the window catch.

Chapter 9

'How's the write-up coming along?' It was Monday morning and Professor Salter, his academic supervisor, was on the phone. 'Don't forget the deadline's nearly due.'

'It's nearly finished.' Richard stalled, mentioning a few details that might suggest this statement was true. In truth he was getting anxious about the progress of his thesis. The recent series of events had undermined his concentration. He resumed work immediately after breakfast, continuing without a break for several hours.

At about midday his mobile rang and his heart sank on hearing the nasal tones of Phil Banks.

'Hi, Phil. What's up?'

'I've bloody well been made redundant, that's what's up.'

Richard made sympathetic noises. 'Bad luck. You did say it might be on the cards.'

'That doesn't make it any easier. I've only been there six years, so the package is fuck-all.'

'Have you consulted the union? You could argue for better terms.'

Phil snorted. 'Went to see the NUJ rep last week.'

'Was he helpful?'

'It was a *she*. No! Snooty bitch made me feel about as welcome as a fart in a lift. She said what they're offerin' is quite legal. There's no chance of gettin' anythin' better.'

'Oh.' Richard wished he could bring the conversation to an end but Phil's voice with its contrived cockney accent continued to grate into his ear. 'The reason I'm ringin' you, old mate, is because I'm 'avin' a farewell bash on Friday at *Loonies*. All the usual suspects. Wanna join us? '

The prospect of an evening at *Loonies*, a club inexplicably popular with his former colleagues, filled Richard with horror. He had reluctantly accompanied them there on several stag nights in the past. The dress code - *as outrageous as possible* - was taken seriously by many clients and there was a small platform on which they were at liberty to display any talents they felt they possessed. He recalled a man in sequinned shorts who stood on his head for about half an hour while people pelted him with peanuts and beer mats.

'I'd like to come, Phil, but --'

'Come on, Ric, it's the end of an era. For me at any rate.'

'I'll think about it. Not much time at the moment.'

Phil sniggered. 'Too busy with little green men? Scary Mary in Reception saw your ugly mug on the telly the other night. She said some crazy old tart was sendin' you spooky messages. What's with this weirdo crap you're into these days?'

'Sorry, gotta go. I'll let you know about *Loonies*.' Richard abruptly ended the call and uttered an expletive. Why hadn't he kept his head down during the Morgana Delph show?

As soon as he had pocketed his mobile, it rang again. This time it was a more welcome caller.

Fiona's voice was slightly breathless. 'Ric, I've found out about the old man who was brought in the other day, the one who was beaten up. His name's Paddy McAllister. He had a slight heart attack after he was admitted. Apparently he never stops ranting religious stuff, bits of the Bible. Sounds like the guy you described.'

Richard gave a low whistle. 'Yep, that's him alright.' He thought for a second. 'Do you think I should go to see him, tell him I've been feeding his dog?'

'Why not? Might make him feel better. He's in Warburton Block, Ward Nine. Visiting hours are three to five.'

* * *

Ward Nine was full of elderly men, several of whom were mumbling to themselves. Some had visitors at their bedsides. Richard looked round for Paddy and eventually heard his unmistakable hoarse voice amid the general hubbub. He followed the sound and found the old man lying in a bed with the curtains drawn on both sides. There was a blood-stained bandage round his head and a drip connected to a cannula in his arm. A monitor on a stand behind the bed was recording his heartbeat. His face was bruised and swollen but his formerly long and matted beard had been trimmed. On seeing Richard, he fell silent for a second then resumed a stream of rambling biblical utterances.

As Richard dragged a chair closer to the bed, he inadvertently pulled aside the curtain that acted as a screen between Paddy and the patient in the neighbouring bed.

The man glared at him. 'Are you that bloke's son?'

'No, just an acquaintance.'

'Well, can you tell him to shut the fuck up? That religious stuff's getting on my nerves. I keep asking the nurses to move him to another ward.'

Richard nodded sympathetically, adjusted the curtain and sat down next to Paddy's bed.

The old man stared at him through bloodshot eyes, as though trying to remember who he was, then abruptly sat up and wailed, 'Maggie!'

Richard leaned towards him. 'Who's Maggie, Paddy? Is she a relative? A friend? Can I get in touch with her for you?'

'Maggie!' the old man moaned again.

Richard noticed that he was missing a front tooth. 'Tell me where Maggie is and I'll get in touch with her.'

'Left 'er at the shops. Bin wi' me since a pup ...'

Enlightenment dawned and Richard patted the old man's arm reassuringly. 'Don't worry about Maggie, Paddy. She's OK. I've been feeding her. She's fine.'

Paddy focused on his face but said nothing.

'Tell me what happened,' Richard urged. 'Who beat you up?'

The old man started babbling incoherently and it was several minutes before he spoke clearly enough for Richard to understand.

'Two of 'em ... took me away ...'

'Who did? Who took you away?'

'In'eritors.'

'Inheritors?' Richard repeated, puzzled. 'Who are they?'

'Said I 'ad betrayed the Truth ... Took me to a garage ... beat me up.' Paddy started to thrash about, almost dislodging the drip in his arm. 'The souls of the right'ous are in the 'ands o' God,' he yelled, 'an' no torment shall touch 'em!'

His heart monitor beeped alarmingly and the zigzag lines went into triangular peaks.

Richard was about to summon a nurse when the old man suddenly became calm and more coherent. 'I told 'em I seen the sign in the sky, the sign o' the Second Comin'.' His bruised mouth twisted into a semblance of a grin. 'That shook 'em! I sez I wasn't the only one 'oo seen it.

They asked 'oo else seen it. So I tell 'em, a young feller who lives in a road off the 'ill was lookin' out o' a winder an' 'e seen it too. They asked 'oo you was, but I didn't know your name ... didn't know the name o' the road neither, but they kep' thumpin' me just the same ... Maggie!'

Richard shivered with apprehension. Would the old man's assailants now come searching for him? He consoled himself with the thought that there were a number of roads off Bridlington Hill from which the UFO could have been spotted.

'Resist not evil!' bellowed Paddy, falling back on his pillow. "Oooso-ever shall smite thee on thy right cheek, turn the other side to him! Matthew, Five, Thirty ...'

'Belt up, will you?' shouted an exasperated voice from the neighbouring bed.

Richard beat a hasty retreat.

On his way home he purchased some dog biscuits and took them to the bus shelter where Maggie was still pacing up and down, waiting for her master. He wondered if any passers-by had rung the RSPCA.

* * *

That night he woke with a start. *What was that?* He thought he could hear a noise outside. Was it the rain? He sat up and listened. The illuminated face of his watch showed it to be ten past two. He yawned and lay down again. But there it was again: a soft, insistent scraping sound that seemed to be coming from the front of the house. He took a deep, calming breath. It was probably a cat or a fox trying to get into the rubbish bag he had left at the bottom of the front path. He yawned and lay down again.

For a while he heard nothing, then the noise started again. He stiffened. It was too close to the house to be the rubbish bag; it was somewhere near the front door. He listened intently. What if someone was trying to get in? Maybe the men who had beaten up poor old Paddy had managed to trace him. He rolled out of bed and stood uncertainly beside it for a moment, wondering what to do. Should he ring the police? He decided against it. If it wasn't someone trying to break in, he would only make a fool of himself again.

He padded across the landing to his parents' room. The noise was louder on this side of the house and it was definitely coming from outside the front door, but without opening the window and leaning out, he couldn't see who was there. With the blood pounding in his ears, he tiptoed downstairs, steeling himself for action. He knew his father kept his golf clubs in the cupboard under the stairs. Opening the cupboard door, he poked around in its dark interior until he located the golf bag. He extracted one of the clubs then stood in the hall listening. The scraping noise had stopped. He crept to the front door, unbolted it as quietly as he could and turned the handle. He pulled the door open and with a loud shout, lifted the golf club and brandished it in front of him. As he did so, something large and wet dived past his knees into the house, giving him such a fright that he yelled again.

The intruder whimpered and Richard almost sobbed with relief. The old man's dog! A light came on in the house opposite and he hastily shut the door. He dropped the club and switched on the hall light.

Maggie shook herself, sprinkling him with drops of rainwater, then whined. Her coat was bedraggled and the rag around her neck was sodden.

He sighed. 'Well, as you're here, I suppose you'd better stay the night.' He went into the kitchen and took a tea towel from a drawer.

Maggie padded behind him and didn't resist when he tried to dry her matted fur. She smelled terrible.

He opened one of the remaining tins of dog food and gave it to her in a bowl. While she was wolfing this down, he fetched an old blanket and put it on the floor, then switched off the light and shut the door. Poor thing was probably covered in fleas and he didn't want her spreading them through the house. Ashamed of his earlier timidity, he went back to bed.

* * *

Maggie was waiting patiently in the kitchen when he came downstairs the next morning. Wagging her tail, she attempted to jump up at him, but as she still exuded a strong and unpleasant doggy smell, he pushed her away. What on earth was he going to do with her? Now that he had become her principal feeder, she would probably hang around him until the old man returned from hospital. He had enough complications in his life without the responsibility of looking after a dog, although - the thought came suddenly to him - she might deter any intruders who had it in mind to attack him like they had her owner. On the other hand, if the old man's assailants recognised the dog, she might lead them directly to him! He gave her a handful of dog biscuits and watched her eat them, trying to come to a decision.

After devouring the biscuits, Maggie gave a short bark and went to the front door. When he opened it, she bounded down the path and on to the pavement. She was squatting next to the gatepost when Marjorie Phelps appeared at the corner of the Close, carrying a shopping bag. On seeing Maggie, she came to a halt, stared at her, then stomped to the bottom of Richard's front path. 'What,' she demanded, pointing at Maggie, 'is that?'

'It's a dog, Mrs. Phelps!'

She quivered indignantly. 'I can see it's a dog! But what's it doing here?'

Richard felt a strong desire to laugh. Ever since he was a boy, he had enjoyed winding Mrs. Phelps up. 'She's been paying me a social call, Mrs. Phelps.'

She glared at him. 'It belongs to that old tramp down at the shops, doesn't it? I recognise that filthy rag round its neck. I don't know what your mother would say if she knew that dirty mongrel was here, fouling the Close.'

'Have a nice day,' he said cheerily and went back inside. *Nosy old bag*!

A few minutes later he heard scratching at the door. He opened it and sighed as Maggie rushed through to the kitchen. It seemed he had no choice in the matter: he had acquired a house guest. He shut her in the kitchen with a bowl of dog food and returned to his desk.

Flicking swiftly through several news websites, he was unable to find any new information about the incident in Essex so tried instead to resume work on his final chapter, but his mind was elsewhere. He left his desk, went to the window and gazed down at the back garden. It was a beautiful morning and the remaining raindrops on the daffodils and forsythia were sparkling in the sun. But he was too preoccupied to appreciate the view. Musing on what had happened to Fonthill Park, Mayfield Common and the common in Essex, he concluded that whoever or whatever had caused their destruction seemed to be moving in an eastward arc around London. That suggested that similar incidents could also happen - indeed might already have happened - in Kent or

Surrey. He felt the need to confide in someone who would take him seriously; someone who might bring an informed perspective to bear on recent events. He reflected for a moment before a name came to him. Mark Davenport! Mark, one of his colleagues at *Global Geographic*, had a doctorate in Environmental Sciences and was a specialist in ecological issues. If anyone would have a theory about what was going on, it would be him. He took out his mobile.

Mark had a deep and warm baritone voice of a kind Richard associated with radio and television newsreaders. 'Good to hear from you, Ric. How's the doctorate going?'

'It's nearly finished, thank God.'

'Great stuff. Phil said he'd seen you.' Mark's voice dropped to a whisper. 'You heard he got the push? Things are fucking awful here at the moment.'

'Yes, he told me.' Richard wasn't in the mood to talk about Phil Banks. 'Mark, there's something I'd like to run past you. Are you free at all this week?'

'Not immediately, I'm afraid. Got a deadline for an article on global warming. But aren't you coming to *Loonies* for Phil's wake? We could meet there.'

'I haven't decided. It's not the ideal place for a chat, is it?'

'No, but I'll have an hour or so to kill after work, so we could meet beforehand if you like. I could meet you in the *Lion and Unicorn* around seven? '

'Cool. See you then.'

Richard put his mobile back in his pocket. A bark downstairs reminded him that he had a guest. First things first. He would buy Maggie a collar and lead then perhaps take her to a dog-grooming place for de-fleaing and a shampoo and set.

Chapter 10

The elaborately made-up young woman at the reception desk looked appalled when Richard entered Wagtails Grooming Parlour with Maggie. 'I don't think we can help you,' she told him curtly, her tone clearly indicating that the business did not cater for scruffy, flea-ridden mongrels. The message was reinforced by the framed photographs of pedigree dogs that lined the walls. The smart new collar Richard had bought for Maggie served only to accentuate her neglected condition.

He stood his ground. 'This is a *dog grooming* parlour isn't it? Well this is a dog and she needs grooming.'

The receptionist gave him a hostile look. 'Just a moment, please.' She turned her back on him and disappeared through a door. He heard her conferring with someone in another room and shortly afterwards she returned, followed by an older woman in a white coat who regarded Maggie with raised eyebrows.

Richard swiftly adopted another tack. 'Please, ladies,' he appealed, 'this is Maggie. She belongs to an old man who's very sick. He's in hospital and isn't able to look after her. I want to surprise him when he comes out.'

The older woman walked round Maggie and inspected her from every angle. 'Hmm. She's not the kind of dog I normally work with.' She bent down and smoothed back Maggie's ears, recoiling at her offensive smell. 'Poor old girl. You *have* been neglected, haven't you?' Straightening up, she addressed Richard. 'She's in very bad condition and it will be quite a challenge. But leave her here and I'll do what I can. Come back in a couple of hours.' She led Maggie through the door at the back of the premises.

Richard's eyes watered when the receptionist informed him what the fee would be. What was he doing spending so much money on a dog? Resignedly, he left a deposit.

While Maggie was being spruced up, he bought a paper and repaired to a local coffee shop to read it. He sat down at the nearest free table and scanned the items on the front page: The economic situation, the war on terrorism, the acrimonious divorce of an "A List" celebrity – all boring, predictable stuff. He turned the page and froze on seeing the headline, *Fire Menace Continues: Arsonists destroy parts of Kent and West London.*

Stunned, he read the article. By now, the details were familiar, but one of the places attacked was Richmond Park - one of the *royal* parks - a small area of which had been destroyed, albeit fortunately not the part where the resident three hundred red deer had been grazing. According to the report, the damage inflicted on this old and beloved piece of Crown land had sent shock waves round the country and police in the capital and neighbouring counties had been put on high alert. Small vigilante groups were being formed to watch over other cherished green-belt areas and a call had gone out for volunteers to join them. A strongly-worded editorial called on the Government to find out who was responsible for the wave of destruction and take immediate action to bring it to an end.

His mobile rang. It was Dan at Heathrow. 'I shouldn't be telling you this,' he said in a hushed voice, 'but I've heard from my mate at Swanwick Air Traffic Control. Apparently they've picked up unexplained objects on the radar this week. The Ministry of Defence is involved.'

'Do you think it's connected with the arson attacks?'

'Could be. I'll keep you posted.'

Richard gave an involuntary shiver of alarm. Had his instincts been correct?

* * *

The receptionist at the grooming parlour told him that Maggie hadn't taken kindly to having a bath and had struggled so ferociously that they were obliged to put a muzzle on her. When the older woman led her out, he almost didn't recognise her. Without the accumulated dirt of years, her coat had lightened to a soft silvery grey. Her previously sparse and matted fur was fluffy and combed in a way that hid the bare patches where she had been scratching herself to ease the irritation caused by fleas.

Richard fondled her head, surprised at the surge of affection he suddenly felt. She smelled clean and her fur was soft and pleasant to touch. He thanked the woman and paid the receptionist. He couldn't wait to see Paddy's face when he came out of hospital and witnessed his dog's transformation. He realised now that he had decided to keep her until the old man returned.

Maggie clearly wasn't accustomed to being on a lead. On their way home, she galloped ahead, dragging him behind her for a few yards and coming to an abrupt halt whenever she came across an interesting smell. She had just stopped to sniff a gatepost when Richard's neighbour, Reg Perkins passed by with his dog, Pugwash. The two dogs leapt at each other in a frenzy of barking while the two men hauled strenuously on their leads to keep them apart.

Reg looked puzzled. 'Didn't know you had a dog, Ricky.'

'She's not mine. She belongs to an old man who's in hospital. I'm only looking after her for a few days.'

'Good. Pugwash won't take kindly to a new kid on the block.'

Richard was relieved that Reg hadn't recognised Maggie as the dog belonging to the homeless man from the shopping parade, although he felt sure Marjorie Phelps would soon put him right on that score.

After returning home, he fed Maggie, spent the afternoon on his thesis, and in the evening set off to meet Mark Davenport.

He arrived at the *Lion and Unicorn*, a short distance from *Loonies*, a little after six and ordered a beer. The pub had resisted modernisation and still had its traditional brass fittings and worn leather chairs. Noisy groups of young people were standing drinking at the bar. Loud pop music was playing in the background.

Mark arrived a few minutes later. He looked stockier since the last time Richard had seen him, and his fair hair had started to thin.

The two shook hands and took their drinks to a table in the less populated part of the pub.

'What did you want to talk to me about?' asked Mark after they had exchanged initial pleasantries. 'You don't want your old job back, do you? Don't fancy your chances in the current climate.'

'No, it's not that.' Richard told him about the UFO he had seen and his theory that there could be a link between it and the trail of destruction around the outskirts of London.

After he had finished, Mark remained silent, staring thoughtfully into the distance.

'You probably think it's a load of old cobblers,' Richard ventured timidly, 'but there might be something in it.'

Mark took off his glasses and polished them slowly with a paper tissue. 'It's a wider problem than you're probably aware of.'

'What do you mean?'

'I told you I'm doing a piece on global warming? Well, I've been communicating with a journalist in the States who campaigns on the environment. He told me that what's been happening here, arson attacks on areas of vegetation, has also been happening over there.'

Richard gasped. 'You mean parkland and green spaces have been destroyed?'

'Yeah, and he said that there's a substance, a kind of dust, left on the ground after the attacks, that no-one's been able to identify. If any of it touches the skin it apparently produces a nasty blister.'

'Exactly the same as here!' Richard exclaimed. 'So why haven't we heard anything about it? Is there a restriction on sharing information?'

Mark's voice lowered to a whisper and he glanced around to make sure no-one was within earshot. 'There seems to have been some kind of news black-out. The American authorities don't want any panic. But now things are hotting up, people are getting jumpy. My friend in Washington says there's been some communication between the Pentagon, the Ministry of Defence and the EU because there have also been similar incidents in Europe, and in parts of Asia.'

Richard stared at him aghast. He vaguely remembered a news item about arson attacks in Europe some weeks before the Fonthill incident, but he had been so engrossed in his work that he hadn't paid much attention.

'How about another beer?' Mark suggested. 'Thinking about fires has made me thirsty.' He put his glasses back on, and made his way to the bar.

'So what do *you* think is going on?' Richard asked when he returned with two foaming pints.

Mark frowned. 'It's hard to say. But there have been leaked reports of people seeing bright and extremely fast-moving objects in the sky at the time of some of the attacks.'

'So there *could* be a connection between what's happening and what I saw!'

'Well, one has to wonder why the authorities are trying so hard to cover those reports up. The official line is that terrorists are responsible.'

'I know it's being fanciful,' Richard ventured hesitantly, 'but do you think the lights and objects might be from, like, somewhere else?'

'What do you mean?'

'Well, just for the sake of argument, isn't it possible that … something extraterrestrial could be responsible for the destruction?'

Mark gazed at him incredulously. 'You've got to be kidding!'

'But you said yourself that other people besides me have seen weird objects in the sky. And a friend of mine at Heathrow said something that moves with fantastic speed and manoeuvrability has been caught on radar.'

Mark laughed. 'That doesn't mean we've been invaded by aliens, Ric! You're letting your imagination run away with you, old son.'

'But it's not beyond the bounds of possibility,' Richard persisted. 'I've been investigating UFOs on the internet and there have been loads of unexplained sightings over the years.'

'You mean Roswell and stuff like that? That's been discredited, hasn't it?'

'Maybe, but there have been loads of other incidents over the years. Do you think the authorities play them down because they would cause panic, not least in the stock market?'

Mark laughed again. 'Don't get carried away! A lot of the most publicised UFO reports can be discounted. I've read that the Americans have manipulated reports of UFOs in order to cover up the advanced aerospace technology they've been developing for military operations. They've been secretly testing new prototypes in their airforce bases for years. They've created amazing machines that move so fast and look so weird that they're often taken for UFOs.'

'Well from what I've read, not all UFO sightings can be explained,' Richard said rather huffily. 'And you can't tell me that American military aircraft are responsible for what's happening. They wouldn't be destroying their own green spaces, would they? That would be absurd.'

'Yes, I suppose it would.' Mark took a long swig of his beer then assumed a tolerant expression. 'OK, boyo, let me indulge your wild imaginings for a moment. Let's say that there is a bunch of alien fuckwits, for want of a better word, up there, who are doing this. That begs a couple of questions: one, *how* would they have got here? And two, *why* would they have come here?'

'And three,' Richard added, 'why would they want to destroy our vegetation?'

Mark scratched his chin thoughtfully. 'OK, just to humour you, let's say … let's say some aliens *have* arrived and they want to destroy life on this planet, for whatever reason --'

'If that's the case,' Richard interjected, 'why not attack the world's population, infrastructure or buildings? What's the point of annihilating green spaces?'

Mark pondered again. 'Well, what better way to destroy life on this planet than to destroy the very thing that *sustains* life --?'

'You mean vegetation, plants?'

'Of course. Without vegetation and photosynthesis, the Earth would just consist of stony or sandy land masses stuck in the middle of the oceans.'

Richard reflected for a moment. 'But if destruction of Earth's vegetation *is* the intention, why wouldn't your bunch of alien fuckwits target much bigger areas, like rainforests and stuff?'

Mark frowned. 'Good point, though I suppose we're making a pretty good job of that ourselves. Think of creeping desertification. No-one's managed to persuade some communities in Africa to stop cutting down trees for fuel yet. And some big companies are falling over themselves to destroy rainforests for commercial gain, even though they're essential to our survival as they absorb so much Co2. I don't have to tell you this, Ric, you know this stuff better than I do.'

'Yeah, *I* know it, but how would a bunch of extraterrestrials know it?'

Mark grinned. 'Bear with me, Ric. I'm only trying to imagine a scenario that will fit your wild imaginings.'

Richard gazed pensively into his glass. 'But destroying parks and green spaces around urban areas doesn't make sense. Wouldn't they be far too small to attract alien attention?'

'There could be a perverse logic behind it.' Mark tapped the table with a finger nail. 'Think about it. What do all the incidents that have happened so far - at least those we know about - have in common?'

Richard stared at him blankly.

'As far as I know, they have mostly taken place around large conurbations: major cities. Our clever bunch of extraterrestrials might assume that targeting vegetation in or around places with the greatest volumes of population will have more of an immediate impact than targeting empty countryside.'

'Yes, that figures,' Richard conceded. 'But surely a plan like that wouldn't work in the long term because vegetation on scorched earth usually regenerates itself, doesn't it? They'd be shooting themselves in the foot... if they have a foot, that is!'

Mark removed his spectacles again and held them up to the light to inspect the lenses. 'Vegetation will recover after controlled or selective burning. It can even recover after wild fires, if they don't go too deep and destroy the subsoil. But whatever's causing this destruction is a very noxious substance. It may have been designed to prevent regeneration of vegetation and eco-systems, like Agent Orange, that deadly stuff the Americans used to defoliate forested and rural land in Vietnam.'

'OK.' Richard scratched his head as he collected his thoughts. 'But why would aliens *want* to destroy a planet that's no threat to them?'

'Maybe they want to get rid of us so that they can colonise it themselves.'

'In that case, wouldn't it be defeating the object to destroy the conditions necessary for life on Earth?'

'That's assuming that the conditions necessary to sustain *their* life are the same as those necessary to sustain ours.' Mark carefully replaced his glasses on his nose. 'Life can arise under many conditions, so if extraterrestrials do exist, they may have evolved in an entirely different way to us. They may have come from a much hotter or colder planet than ours. They may not need as much oxygen as we do. If they're used to hotter temperatures, they may actually want to create more CO_2 in the atmosphere.'

A shiver ran down Richard's spine. 'If anyone had suggested a scenario like this to me a few months ago, I would have laughed in their face, but now ...'

'Now?'

'I'm not so sure. Nothing's impossible, I suppose. After all, a hundred years ago, who would have believed that men could walk on the Moon or that we could send probes to Mars?'

'Or split the atom, discover DNA, clone a sheep? The boundaries of possibility are expanding all the time.'

Richard swallowed the rest of his beer. 'So, if we can't find a rational explanation for what's happening, aren't we forced to consider one that seems *ir*rational?'

'Maybe,' Mark replied. 'But, hey! What we're talking about is more than irrational, it's impossible, just a flight of fancy. There has to be a more plausible explanation for what's happening than an alien invasion.' He glanced at his watch. 'Better go. Time to meet the gang.'

Although he felt that a visit to *Loonies* was inappropriate after such a conversation, Richard rose to his feet and reluctantly accompanied Mark through the backstreets to the basement in which the club was located.

The noise hit him like a sledgehammer - a combination of deafening pop music, raucous laughter and shouted conversations. *Loonies* was already heaving and they were immediately surrounded by a circle of shrieking girls dressed in skimpy clothing and with flashing rabbit ears attached to their heads, who were gyrating suggestively to the music. They hooted lewdly at Richard and Mark as the two pushed their way into the room, passing en route a group of boisterous young men dressed as Elvis look-alikes.

Near the bar, people in lurid fancy dress were batting a huge phallus-shaped balloon above their heads. Bar staff wearing plastic aprons picturing a life-sized naked female torso were weaving their way through the crowd, collecting empty glasses. Coloured spotlights on the ceiling were turning people's faces successively a bilious yellow, a sickly green, then a livid red.

The percussion beat of the music sent uncomfortable vibrations through Richard's body as he and Mark fought their way through the throng. To his alarm he was encircled by four figures wearing V-shaped green masks with slits for eye-holes. One of them slapped him on the back. 'Glad you could make it,' Phil Banks yelled above the din. 'Like the get-up, Ric? I thought it would be right up your galaxy!'

Before he could protest, Richard found himself propelled through the seething mass of bodies to the bar.

Chapter 11

His head was throbbing painfully and there was a sour taste in his mouth. A dog was barking somewhere in the distance. It took him a few moments to realise that it was Maggie. Gingerly, he levered himself out of bed experiencing, as he did so, a wave of nausea and dizziness. The last thing he could remember of the night at *Loonies* was standing on the stage with Phil Banks and his other former colleagues, singing a coarse rugby song. He had a faint recollection of being bundled into a cab, but what happened after that was a complete blank. As he had woken up in his bed, he assumed he had managed to pay the driver and enter the house without mishap.

The clothes he had worn the previous night were strewn across the bedroom floor. He picked them up and checked his jacket pockets. He no longer had any of the money he had taken out with him. The evening out had obviously proved costly.

He dressed and stumbled downstairs, his head pounding at every step. When he entered the kitchen, Maggie leapt up at him, nearly knocking him over. He pushed her away. 'Careful! I'm a bit fragile to-day.'

Realising that she needed to go out, he opened the front door, flinching at the glare of the morning sun. When his eyes adjusted to the light, he was mortified to see a pool of vomit on the path. Maggie sniffed at it curiously. He hastily returned to the kitchen, hoping that none of his neighbours had spotted this testament to the previous night's excesses. But the moment he emerged with a kettle of water and a bottle of disinfectant, Marjorie Phelps came out of the house next door. She had evidently been calling on the Perkins.

Glaring at him across the low fence that divided the two front gardens, she pointed at the mess on the path. 'That is absolutely disgusting! You should be ashamed of yourself, Ricky Jarman. I assume it was *you* we heard singing at the top of your voice at three o' clock this morning?'

As his head was spinning painfully, Richard had neither the energy nor the inclination to reply. He poured the water and disinfectant over the vomit, swilling it to the side of the path.

Mrs. Phelps' eyes glittered with outrage. 'I don't know what your parents would say if they knew you were carrying on like this, coming home drunk at all hours ...' Spotting Maggie who was squatting in the gutter in front of the house opposite, her voice rose to a shriek. 'And that dog...It's fouling the Close. You should be fined! I shall bring this up at the next meeting of the Residents' Association.'

Richard hastily returned indoors to fetch a plastic bag. When he re-emerged, Mrs. Phelps had disappeared and Maggie was joyfully chasing Satan and Gabriel, Mrs. Brennan's two cats. They escaped rapidly up a tree and sat watching her balefully from the safety of a branch.

The day didn't get any better. Bending to clear up Maggie's mess gave him such an attack of vertigo that he was incapable of doing anything else for the rest of the morning. He put on some music and slumped inertly on the living-room sofa while Maggie lay patiently on the carpet in front of him. Thoughts chased each other haphazardly through his mind. One moment he was replaying his conversation with Mark; the next, he was fretting guiltily over his failure to complete the final section of his thesis.

A shrill noise drilled painfully into his skull. Pulling himself up into a sitting position, he removed his mobile from his trouser pocket.

Fiona's voice sounded sombre. 'Ric, I'm afraid I've got some bad news.'

'What?'

'The old guy, Paddy. He died yesterday. I thought you'd want to know.'

'What?' he heard himself repeating stupidly.

'He died, poor old chap.'

Richard's heart sank. 'From his injuries?'

'His heart gave out, but they probably contributed.'

'Oh dear,' Richard mumbled, then, conscious of the inadequacy of this reaction, added, 'did they find out any more about him? Did he have any relatives?'

'He told one of the nurses that he didn't have any family. He spent most of his life in some kind of religious commune. He ran away from it a few years ago and had been living rough ever since. I've got to go. Speak later.' She rang off.

Richard felt dazed. He was sorry that the old man had died, very sorry, but what was he going to do about Maggie? Should he take her to the RSPCA or the local dog pound? He didn't like the idea but a dog didn't fit into his plans for the future, and he knew his neighbours wouldn't welcome her continued presence in the Close. Moreover, how would his parents react if they returned to find a large mongrel installed in their neat home?

He looked down at Maggie. 'What am I going to do with you, old girl?'

She gazed up at him with moist adoring eyes.

He swallowed some water, sank back on the sofa and dozed for a while. About midday he woke with a start and a sense of deep uneasiness, as though he had experienced an unpleasant dream. As he opened his eyes, he became aware of something heavy pressing against his thigh. Sitting up, he found that Maggie had joined him on the sofa and was sleeping peacefully, coiled up in the space normally occupied by a seated human being. With a jolt he remembered what was disturbing him: the old man had died and he was now stuck with his dog.

Feeling too queasy to engage in purposeful activity, he sat up, reached for the TV remote and started flicking desultorily through the channels. He paused on one that provided continuous news updates and watched abstractedly, gently stroking Maggie's head with his left hand.

A scene on the screen caught his attention. He leaned forward to watch more closely. It was showing a recorded interview, conducted by a journalist earlier in the day, with a minister at the Home Office and a senior police officer. They were discussing what action should be taken about the conflagrations that had reduced formerly verdant areas to charred, grey landscapes.

The journalist was addressing the police officer. 'You are, of course, aware of the increasing concern being expressed in London and the Home Counties about these attacks? The damage caused to Richmond Park - Crown land - has caused particular outrage.' As he spoke, film footage of the devastated area appeared on the screen.

'What are the police doing to deal with the situation?'

The police chief cleared his throat. 'I can assure you that everything that can be done *is* being done. All the affected areas have been sealed off and officers from the respective forces are involved in full-time investigation--'

'But,' the journalist interrupted, 'this is extremely serious. Don't you have any idea who is behind it?'

'We don't yet know who's responsible,' admitted the police officer, 'but we are following several leads. I can promise you that we'll soon have some answers.'

The journalist looked sceptical and turned to the minister. 'Minister, what is the Government doing about this situation? We know that questions have been asked in the House, and we have heard reports that there has been communication with governments of other countries that have suffered similar incidents. Can you tell us something about the nature of those discussions?'

The minister stared, rather shiftily Richard thought, at the camera. 'Well, the Ministry of Defence is now involved and I can't reveal more about that at this moment in time. However, I *can* tell you that we are cooperating fully with governments elsewhere in trying to determine whether the incidents are part of a concerted attack by terrorists--'

Again the journalist cut in. 'So you believe this is the work of a terrorist group as some commentators have been suggesting?'

'It seems the likeliest explanation, although these actions don't conform to any known terrorist pattern. Terrorists usually target strategic areas, transport systems, administrative buildings, embassies and so on. These attacks are very different. It's very difficult to discern the motive behind them.'

'What is being done to protect the public?' the journalist demanded. 'So far as we know, no-one has yet been injured in these attacks but the dust left behind has apparently caused skin complaints.'

The minister produced a reassuring smile. 'Fortunately, any stinging that occurs as a result of contact with eyes or skin is only temporary. However, we have arranged for protective masks to be available at chemist shops and GP surgeries throughout the country.' A photograph of a white mask with dangling strings appeared on the screen.

'I would advise members of the public to keep away from the targeted areas,' the minister continued, 'but if you happen to live or work in the vicinity of one, you should wear a mask. Long sleeves and gloves are also advisable. And I would ask everyone to be vigilant. If you become aware of an incendiary attack in your locality, please ring this number ...' a telephone number appeared on the bottom of the screen. '... and if possible, remain indoors.'

The journalist fixed the minister with a penetrating gaze. 'There have been reports that unusual aerial phenomena have been witnessed on the nights the attacks occurred, and some have suggested that we may not be dealing with a ... human agency. '

The minister gave a forced laugh. 'That's nonsense; sheer fantasy. Some people have overactive imaginations. I can assure the British public they have absolutely nothing to fear on that account. Nothing--'

'That's right,' the police officer said emphatically. 'The public should dismiss such alarmist reports.'

The extract ended and another topic took its place.

Richard turned off the TV and gazed at the blank screen. It was interesting that people were now openly speculating about whether the damage could have been caused by non-humans. But before he could reflect on this further, the phone in the hall rang.

A faint female voice addressed him. 'Mr ... er ... Richard?'

'Yes?'

'It's Sister Francis, at the convent. You came to see me.'

'Sister Francis! ' He had almost forgotten the little nun. 'How are you?'

'I'm grand, thanks be to God.' Her northern Irish accent sounded much stronger on the phone. 'I'm sorry to bother you, so I am, but I only have a moment. It may mean nothing at all, but I thought I should mention--'

'Mention what?'

'You know I take care of the convent accounts? It's one of my tasks here.' Before he had time to reply, she continued. 'Well, yesterday afternoon I went to the bank, and when I came out, there were two men standing by the door. I didn't take much notice of them, but they followed me and before I knew it, they were walking on either side of me and talking to me.'

Richard was perplexed. 'Who were they? Reporters? You said one called at the convent.'

'No, I don't think they were reporters.'

'What did the two men look like?'

'They were quite young and very smartly dressed and they had very white teeth, so they had ... like in those toothpaste advertisements.'

Richard felt a pang of apprehension. 'What did they want?'

'Well, I said to them, very politely, "Good afternoon, gentlemen, can I help you?" and one of them, he had an accent, American I think , he asked me whether I was the nun who had seen something in the sky on the night that Mayfield Common was destroyed. I said I was, but it wasn't important because the police said it was probably a plane or a weather balloon. Then …' her voice tailed off.

'What then?' Richard prompted.

'Well, the other man, he became very … agitated, so he did. He caught me by the arm and started shouting … raving … about the Book of Revelations and … trumpets! He said I'd witnessed the preparation for the Second Coming. It was nonsense to be sure, but I was a wee bit alarmed.'

'I'm not surprised.' Richard was beginning to feel alarmed himself. 'They didn't hurt you, Sister, did they?'

'Oh no, not at all, thanks be to God. Father Doyle was passing on the other side of the road and when he came across, they ran off.'

'Did you tell Father Doyle what had happened?'

'I did indeed and he insisted on walking back to the convent with me. He said the men were probably a bit queer in the head, but maybe I shouldn't leave the convent for a while. He advised me not to mention what I saw in the sky to anyone else. But after that talk you and I had in the garden, I thought I'd better let you know what had happened.'

Richard thought it wise not to mention the attack on Paddy or his own visit from two smartly dressed young men with dazzling white teeth. 'I'm sure you don't need to worry, Sister,' he assured her. 'But I think Father Doyle's right. It would probably be wise not to leave the convent for a while in case they try to bother you again.'

'But you saw the same thing as me, Richard. What if those men come looking for you as well?'

'You mustn't be anxious on my account, Sister. If they do, I'll chase them off with the rosary you gave me.'

He heard her chuckle. 'You're a good young man, so you are! Take care of yourself now. I'll pray for you.'

After she rang off, Richard stood brooding by the phone. What would have happened if the priest hadn't come along at that moment? He looked down at the dog lying at his feet then took out his mobile and sent a text to Fiona: *Can u find name of religious cult old man belongd*

2.

After sending the message he returned unenthusiastically to his laptop and brought up the unfinished last section of his thesis. For over fifteen minutes he stared listlessly at the words on the screen but the fast moving events in his own life had displaced his interest in the impact of disasters in faraway lands. Unable to concentrate, he abandoned the chapter and wrote a grovelling email to Professor Salter requesting an extension to his deadline because of personal problems.

It was several hours before he received a reply reluctantly allowing him a month's extension and expressing the hope that his "personal difficulties" would soon be resolved. *Don't forget I'm going on a year's sabbatical in October*, the message continued, *so I'll need to rearrange your viva as soon as possible.*

Not long afterwards, Richard received a text from Fiona responding to his question: *Inheritors of the New Kingdom.*

His heart missed a beat. He remembered the old man telling him that it was "inheritors" who had beaten him up.

He opened the internet and began to search for information on the Inheritors of the New Kingdom. After scanning numerous websites ranging from the earnestly serious to the seriously mad, he managed to find only a few references to the sect. So far as he could make out from the sparse details available, it was a shadowy religious organisation that had broken away from the Mormon Church in the 1930s. Like similar fundamentalist groups, the Inheritors dismissed the theory of Evolution and took the Bible, especially the Book of Revelations, literally. Members were required to abide by a set of extremely strict rules and to donate their money and belongings to the sect. Men were allowed to practise polygamy and have up to three wives. According to several anonymous accounts, transgressions of the rules and desertion from the sect were severely punished.

Another report stated that the sect was proscribed in the United States and its leaders were being sought by the FBI for "fraud, abduction and sexual abuse of underage girls".

One of the websites Richard opened displayed a blurred photograph of the religion's founder, a hawk-featured man with a long beard and shoulder-length dark hair. He was wearing a turban and a profusion of chains and amulets dangled from his neck. Under the photo was written the name, *Abraham R* and under the name ... Richard gasped as he read the words ... *Poet, philosopher and healer.*

He gaped at the screen. Those were exactly the same words uttered by the medium, Morgana Delph, during the awful show he had attended with Fiona. Did she know Abraham R? If so, why had she instructed him in that awful voice to find him?

Insistent barking from downstairs disturbed his troubled thoughts. Maggie was demanding a walk. And after the shock he had just experienced, he decided he needed one himself.

He clipped on the dog's lead and left the house. He wandered round the corner and strode up Bridlington Hill with Maggie trotting contentedly by his side. At the top of the hill, a quiet residential area, he let her off the lead and sat down on a bench thoughtfully provided for weary pedestrians. It was a beautiful day and the sun bathed the distant buildings in a radiance that imparted a certain beauty to their habitual stark aspect. He remembered reading that April had become "the new summer", a consequence of the process of climate change. But his feeling of wellbeing was rapidly replaced by a sense of uneasiness. Was the fact that he had encountered the description of the Inheritors' leader a second time significant or merely a coincidence?

He took out his mobile and rang Fiona, realising, as he did so, that she had now become his principal confidante.

'Has something happened?' she asked.

'Yes. Is there any chance of meeting up this afternoon?'

'I'm taking Polly to the cycle track to try out her new roller blades after school. Do you want to join us? It'll be around four. '

'I'll meet you there.' As Richard pocketed his mobile, he was startled to hear a female voice screeching, 'Get away! Get out of it!'

Turning, he found an elderly woman standing at a gate behind him.

'Is that your dog?' she demanded, pointing into her garden.

He stood up and spotted Maggie's tail wagging vigorously as she inspected some flower beds. 'Yes,' he admitted with some embarrassment.

'She's just done her business in my garden!'

'Oh... Sorry. I'll clear it up.' Fortunately he had remembered to stuff a plastic bag in his pocket before leaving home. He followed the irate woman through the gate and after removing the offending deposits from the lawn, clipped Maggie's lead back on and pulled her out of the garden.

The woman banged the gate shut behind them. 'Dogs should be kept on a lead!' she snapped. 'And it's an offence to allow them to foul public places.' She indicated a notice to this effect attached to a nearby tele-graph pole, then stumped back up her path.

'A front garden isn't a public place,' Richard retorted to her retreating back. 'And you should keep your gate shut!'

Chapter 12

The cycle track encircled a small sports ground used for athletics practice and cricket matches in the summer. That afternoon there were few cyclists but a number of scantily-dressed joggers were pounding determinedly round the circuit. Dodging out of their way, Richard eventually caught sight of Polly. She was sitting on a bench while Fiona crouched in front of her, helping her on with her roller blades.

As he approached, Polly pointed excitedly at the shiny blue boots. 'Look! Grandma and Granddad gave them to me for my birthday.'

Richard admired the roller blades fulsomely before introducing Maggie. 'Fiona and Polly, I'd like you to meet my dog, Maggie.'

'Hello, Maggie' said Fiona, solemnly proffering her hand to the dog who sniffed it curiously.

'Hello, Maggie,' repeated Polly.

Fiona grinned at Richard. 'Now you're here, you can help me take Polly on her maiden run.'

They each held Polly by a hand and she wobbled between them on her blades, while Maggie trotted alongside, giving short barks of encouragement. After a few minutes' practice, the girl grew more confident and proceeded unsteadily ahead of them, holding cautiously onto the railings with her left hand.

'Watch out for the joggers, Poll,' Fiona warned as they followed slowly behind. She turned to Richard. 'So, what's happened?'

He told her about the two men who had accosted Sister Francis and his suspicion that they were members of the same sect that the old man had belonged to. 'I've been doing a search for the Inheritors on the internet.'

'What did you come up with? Hang on!' She broke into a run as Polly, who was a few yards in front of them, tumbled backwards, landing on her bottom.

Richard also rushed forward and, with Maggie weaving unhelpfully between their legs, the two of them hauled the girl to her feet.

Polly was laughing. 'I didn't hurt myself. I'm getting the hang of it now.' She steadied herself then set off again. While she glided ahead, Richard summarised the details he had discovered about the Inheritors of the New Kingdom.

Fiona gave a whoop of excitement when he came to the description of the sect's leader as "poet, philosopher and healer". 'There you are!' she cried, 'I told you Morgana Delph was amazing.'

'It certainly is a coincidence,' Richard conceded grudgingly, 'but she could be one of the Inheritors herself, couldn't she? She could be a member.'

'No way! She's a spiritualist. She wouldn't belong to a group like that.'

'If she isn't a member, why did she give me the same description of that man that I found on the internet?'

'It wasn't her, Ric. It was someone speaking *through* her. And whoever that was also said something about burning and destruction. So maybe that guy, the poet or whatever he is, has got something to do with the arson attacks.'

'Well even if he has, what's it got to do with me?'

'I don't know, Ric.' Fiona patted him on the arm. 'But Morgana said you had to find this poet guy and now you know who he is, you can.'

'But why do *I* have to find him?'

She shrugged. 'Who knows? But the message must be important. You must have been specially chosen to receive it.'

'I don't want to be specially chosen,' Richard muttered sulkily. 'And there's no way I'm going looking for the leader of some weird religious sect. Anyway, how would I know where to find him? He could be anywhere.'

'Ric, you're the researcher, not me! There has to be an Inheritor cell somewhere in the UK. That poor old guy, Paddy, used to belong to one, didn't he? My guess is if you can find out where it is, you'll be able to find Abraham whatever his name is.'

'But I don't want to find him. And what would I say if I did find him? "Hi, Abe! A mad medium told me to look you up, so here I am!".'

She laughed. 'I suppose you could say you're interested in Inheritor beliefs.'

'But I'm not!'

'I know that! You'd have to pretend that you are; tell him you're seeking religious enlightenment or something.'

Richard snorted. 'You've got to be joking. Anyway, he might not appreciate someone snooping around if the FBI's after him.'

'I suspect these sects are more concerned with getting people in than keeping them out.'

'No.' He quickened his step. 'This is crazy. I don't have time to go searching for the leader of a loony sect for no apparent reason.'

She hastened to catch him up and gave him a playful nudge with her elbow. 'Didn't you tell me you've been given a month's extension on your deadline?'

'That's irrelevant. Look, I don't care what that crazy woman said. There's no way I'm going in search of a scary-looking man in a turban. The Inheritors sound like a pretty nasty lot. Anyway I couldn't leave Maggie.'

She grinned. 'No problem. Me and Polly could look after her.'

'You? What about your parents?'

'They know Polly wants a dog. She's been talking about it for ages. They're intending to get her one for Christmas, though probably not one that looks like a cross between a sheep and an Irish wolfhound! If Polly says she wants Maggie to come on a visit, they'll agree. They can't deny her anything.'

'Mum, Ric, watch me!' Polly glided past them, steady now on her feet and grinning proudly.

'That's terrific, Poll!' called Fiona. 'So what do you say, Ric? There's no harm in trying to find out where the nearest Inheritor cell is, is there?'

Richard was beginning to feel boxed into a corner. 'I'll do another internet search,' he said morosely, 'but that's all.'

'Fine,' she said, bringing the discussion to an end. 'So where shall we go on Wednesday?'

'What would you like? A drink, meal, cinema?'

'I don't mind. Whatever.'

'OK, I'll think of something.' Richard experienced a moment of anxiety. The funds he had put aside while he was writing his thesis were dwindling. He might have to ask his sister for a loan.

* * *

Back in his room, he reluctantly resumed his search for information on the Inheritors of the New Kingdom. He found a few more references to the sect subsumed within general discussions of different Christian belief systems, but they contained no contact details. He was relieved. Why should he embark on a quest to find the leader of the Inheritors of the New Kingdom just because a crazy medium had picked him out during a trance and an old man he barely knew had been beaten up?

On the other hand, there was a disturbing detail that seemed to link him, as well as Paddy McAllister and Sister Francis, to the Inheritors. The two smartly-dressed men who called at the house had left him a leaflet about the Second Coming; Paddy's assailants had reacted strongly when he told them he had seen a sign of the Second Coming, and one of the men who accosted Sister Francis had apparently "raved" about the Second Coming. Could it have been the same two men on all three occasions?

This prompted a sudden and alarming thought. Maybe he didn't need to go in search of the Inheritors of the New Kingdom. If they were intent on finding people who had seen a UFO on the nights when the arson attacks had occurred, they might come looking for him again. Fearful though he was of such an eventuality, perhaps all he had to do was await *their* second coming.

Chapter 13

Richard was taken aback when Fiona opened the door early on Wednesday evening. She was wearing a short denim skirt, a strappy black top and gold loop earrings.

Noticing his admiring expression, she laughed. 'Do I scrub up well?'

'I'll say! You look great.'

He took her to a local wine bar having heard that it served good and reasonably priced food. They sat at a table by a window and by unspoken agreement, avoided the subject they had discussed at the cycle track. Over glasses of wine, they exchanged anecdotes from their past and reminisced about their former classmates and schoolteachers. They discussed films and TV programmes they had seen, books they had read and the kinds of music they liked.

After a waiter had brought their meals, Richard decided it was time to broach the subject that was preoccupying him; his suspicion that the two smartly-dressed men might come to the house again, looking for him.

Fiona looked worried. 'What if they attack you like they did poor old Paddy? You told me you slammed the door on them when they called on you before. They might not be so tolerant another time.'

'Well I've got Maggie to protect me now,' he said with a nonchalance he didn't feel. 'She may have acquired a taste for biting Inheritor legs. I imagine they beat Paddy up because he was a deserter. I've read that the Inheritors punish members of the sect who run away.'

'But you've never been a member of the Inheritors. Why would they be interested in you?'

'Because they may believe that I've also seen a sign of the Second Coming, like Paddy and Sister Francis.' He chewed a mouthful of burger. 'I suppose I could accelerate the process. Find them before they come looking for me.'

She blinked. 'How could you do that?'

'By sending them a message.'

'But you said you didn't want to find them.'

'That's true.' Richard was distracted by the way her hair was reflecting the rays of the late evening sun shafting through the window.

She looked puzzled. 'You also said you couldn't find any contact details for them.'

'I couldn't. I wish now I'd kept that leaflet they pushed through the door.' He speared a chip with his fork. 'I suppose I could try posting a message on an internet forum, one of the more extreme religious ones. You never know. They might pick it up.'

'They probably don't use computers. They may think the internet is an abomination, the work of the Devil!'

'That's possible I suppose. On the other hand, if they want to disseminate their beliefs and create new converts, they'll need to use modern communication channels. It's worth a try.'

She wrinkled her brow. 'Are you sure you want to contact them? Why have you changed your mind?'

'I don't know.' Richard realised he had no idea why he had suddenly decided to follow the medium's instruction to find the "poet, philosopher and healer".

Fiona was still looking dubious. 'I'm not sure it would be wise, Ric. All sorts of weirdoes might contact you if you contribute to one of those forums.'

'They might, but I wouldn't have to give my real name and address. I could make up a contact name and any responses would just be sent to the forum. A former colleague of mine, Phil Banks, was always writing to forums and social networking sites when he should have been working. He called himself "Windbreaker"! '

She chuckled. 'I hope you'll find a more dignified name than that. But even if you do post a message, how would the Inheritors know that it's you?'

'By a process of elimination. If I mention Fonthill Park and the UFO I saw, they could put two and two together from what Paddy said to them.'

'What exactly would you write?'

He smiled at her. 'I was hoping you would help me with that. I could claim that I've seen a sign of the Second Coming. That's what seems to excite them. How about coming back to my gaff when we've finished eating, and we could draft something together?'

She nodded. 'OK. Though I can't stay too late. But you must be careful, Ric. Those people sound dangerous to me.'

Her concern sent a surge of elation coursing through his veins. He reached across the table and took her hand. 'Don't worry about me, Fiona. But what's changed *your* mind? Not that long ago, you were urging me to find Abraham R.'

She looked embarrassed. 'I know. It was silly. I was so impressed that Morgana Delph got Abraham R's description right that I thought you should follow her instructions. But after what you've told me about the Inheritors, I think it would be better if you didn't.'

* * *

After they had finished their meal, Richard drove back to Coronation Close and parked his father's car in a residents' bay. As he and Fiona walked past number three, he caught a glimpse of Mrs. Phelps watching them through a front window. *Nosy old bat!*

Maggie greeted them ecstatically and he let her out in the back garden. She had now reached a state of peaceful coexistence with Pugwash next door and they often sniffed at each other in a friendly fashion through the adjoining fence. Richard had stopped worrying about his mother's reaction to the fouling of her lawn, although whenever he remembered, which wasn't often, he removed any visible deposits.

He made coffee then brought down his laptop and placed it on a low table in the living room. He switched it on and joined Fiona on the sofa. He was acutely aware of the pressure of her thigh against his and a tingle of excitement ran through his body. He took a deep breath. For the moment, there were other things to think about.

While they drank their coffee, they scanned the threads on some of the more extreme religious forums on the internet. Many of the messages, ostensibly from Christians, consisted of savage denunciations of homosexuals, divorcees, feminists, single parents and those who supported abortion. Some claimed that the devastation of green areas was divine vengeance for such "wickedness". Richard noticed that few of them denounced more obvious evils such as wars, genocide, torture and poverty.

'Bloody hell!' he exclaimed after a while, 'some of these people are off their trolley.'

Fiona looked worried. 'Are you sure you want to get mixed up in this kind of thing, Ric?'

'No, I'm not. But can you think of another way of smoking out the Inheritors?'

'No, but do you know what you're going to do *if* you manage to smoke them out?'

'No,' he said ruefully. 'I honestly don't have a clue.'

A bark reminded him that Maggie was still in the garden. He opened the patio doors to let her in, and she flopped down on the shaggy off-white carpet, looking comically like an extension of it herself. He took a pad and a pen from his parents' writing desk then resumed his seat beside Fiona on the sofa.

'Shall we toss some ideas around? First, what do I call myself?' He gazed thoughtfully up at the ceiling. 'Skywatcher?'

'Stargazer?' she suggested.

'Not serious enough. How about Receiver of the Message?'

'That's a bit OTT isn't it?'

'Maybe. Perhaps I should choose a name that suggests I'm a repentant sinner, a lamb returning to the fold, that type of thing.'

She chuckled. 'I never had you down as a sinner, Ric.'

'That's only because you don't know about my wicked past!' He wrinkled his brow in concentration. 'OK. What do you think of this one: Witnesser of the Light? It's a bit clumsy but it could convey a coded message like I've seen the lights in the sky and I've also seen the light in a religious sense.'

She laughed. 'Cool. That should do it. Though it might be a bit too subtle for them.'

Richard scribbled the words then chewed the end of the pen. 'Now I need a tag that will attract the Inheritors, if they actually look at these forums. I'll need to mention Fonthill Park so they'll know it's from me, something like: Divine lights over Fonthill - fulfilment of ancient prophesies?'

'No. Too long-winded.'

'What about this then: Fonthill destruction is divine retribution?'

'Yes, that's better. That should catch their attention.'

'OK.' He scribbled on the pad. 'Now I've got to think of a message, something really portentous to suggest that I could be converted to their beliefs.' He frowned at the paper then started writing again. After a few minutes he looked up.

'What do you think of this? The prophets got it right. I have seen the message in the sky. Fonthill Park was just the beginning. We are witnessing the beginning of the end of the world. Man must repent his evil ways.'

Fiona giggled. 'That's really good. It's the same nutty style as some of the others.'

He beamed with pleasure. 'But I think it needs something more, don't you?' He scribbled something else on the pad, then read it to her. 'Only the righteous will be spared. We who have witnessed the divine warnings must prepare ourselves for the Second Coming.'

She giggled again. 'Great. I think a biblical quote might come in handy after that, don't you?'

'Good idea. I think there's a Bible in the dining room.' He went into the adjoining room and emerged with a Bible which he handed to her. 'Why don't you find an appropriate quotation while I write this up? I'll do a draft in *Word* then paste it on some of the forums.'

She leafed through the Bible while he tapped busily on his keyboard. After a few minutes she gave a small whoop. 'Yes! Got one. *Watch therefore for ye know not what hour your lord doth come.*'

Richard laughed. 'Brilliant!' He finished typing the message, added the biblical citation, and pasted it on the forums that contained the most extreme comments.

'Gosh, it's nearly midnight.' Fiona got to her feet. 'I'd better be getting back.'

'I'll drive you.'

After the car drew up outside her parents' house, he shyly put a hand on her shoulder. 'Thanks for a lovely evening, Fiona, and thanks for your help.'

She grinned, then impulsively leaned across and kissed him on the lips.

He responded enthusiastically and they remained locked together for a few moments until she finally broke away from him and opened the passenger door.

'Let me know if you get any replies.' She swung her legs out of the car and tripped lightly up to the house, turning to wave after she had turned the key in the lock. 'See you soon, Witnesser of the Light!'

Smiling broadly, Richard drove home in a heightened state of sensual excitement that all but wiped out the anxiety of the previous few days.

* * *

When he checked the following morning, there were already a number of responses to the message he had posted. They ranged from the obscene and abusive (the mildest from "Old Nick" called him "a Bible-thumping wanker"), to the mind-numbingly tedious: incoherent sermons laced with lengthy extracts from The Book of Revelations. There was nothing to suggest that any of the responses were from Inheritor members, although he searched for possible hidden messages. All he could do was wait. In the meantime, he decided to call the convent to make sure that Sister Francis had recovered from the fright she had experienced when accosted by the two men.

He rang the number stored in his mobile and eventually a sharp female voice barked, 'Our Lady of Lourdes Convent…'

'May I speak to Sister Francis?'

There was a pause before she replied suspiciously. 'Who is this?'

'My name's Richard.'

'Are you a relative of Sister Francis?'

'No, just an acquaintance.'

'Why do you want to speak to Sister Francis?'

He struggled to find a suitable explanation. 'I called to see Sister Francis a few weeks ago. She was working in the kitchen garden and while we were talking, I confided … a … personal matter to her. She took me to the chapel and we prayed together, then she gave me a rosary.'

There was a short silence at the other end of the phone. 'Ah, yes,' the nun said at last, 'I remember. You're the young man who came about the food boxes for the homeless shelter.'

'She asked me to keep in touch, so may I speak to her?'

'I'm afraid that is not possible.'

'Then please would you tell her I called?'

The nun's voice trembled slightly. 'That isn't possible either. I suppose you may as well know … Sister Francis is missing.'

'Missing? You mean she's no longer at the convent?'

'She's disappeared. We've had to call the police. May the Good Lord keep her safe.'

Dumbstruck, Richard took a moment to take this in. 'But how? What happened?'

He heard her sigh. 'I suppose it can't harm to tell you. When Sister Francis didn't come in for lunch on Monday, one of the other sisters went to the kitchen garden to fetch her and we heard her shouting that something terrible had happened. We all ran out and, Holy Mother of God! It looked as though there had been a hurricane ... pots overturned, her lovely vegetable plots trampled. The side gate was open and the padlock had been smashed.' Her voice broke. 'But why? Why would anyone want to take our sweet Sister Francis? Such a good and holy soul. We're praying for her, day and night, and Father Doyle is saying a special Mass every morning until she's found.'

Richard was almost too shocked to speak. He took a deep breath. 'You think she's been kidnapped?'

'It looks as though there was a struggle. She's only a tiny wee thing as you know, but strong! She did all the heavy lifting in the garden. She would have put up a good fight. Father Doyle told us that two men accosted her in the street after she went to the bank the other day. Surely to goodness they didn't think she would be carrying money. He gave their description to the police. They've been here looking for clues but we haven't heard anything back from them yet.'

'This is terrible,' Richard said hoarsely. He cleared his throat. 'I can't believe it. Why would anyone want to kidnap Sister Francis?'

The nun resumed her former brisk tone. 'Now, young man, the police want me to inform them if anyone calls to enquire about Sister Francis. They'll need to know your name and phone number, and where you live.'

He supplied the details and expressed the hope that Sister Francis would soon be safely restored to the convent. He felt numb with shock. How could anyone have managed to get through the side gate of the convent without being seen? Thinking back, however, he remembered that Chestnuts Crescent, the road in front of the building, was wide, with rows of evenly spaced trees that were now in full foliage. It wouldn't have been be difficult for someone to park a car and break into the kitchen garden without being seen from the nearest houses.

Why, he agonised, hadn't he told the Reverend Mother, assuming it was she who had answered his call, the real reason for his visit to the convent? If the police contacted him he would have to tell the truth and they were bound to find it suspicious that he had visited the convent under false pretences.

He stood up and walked distractedly round the room. As he passed the window, he noticed Sister Francis's rosary hanging on the catch. He put it in his pocket. 'Come on, Maggie, walk!' he called as he descended the stairs.

Doris Perkins, who was putting out her recycle box, looked up as they left the house. 'You've still got that funny-looking dog, then?'

'Yes.' Richard felt resentful. Maggie looked far more presentable these days. With regular feeding, her body had filled out and he had started grooming her with a wire hairbrush of his mother's that he had found in the bathroom.

'What will you do with it when your parents get back?'

'I don't know.' He walked briskly down the Close and round the corner.

He allowed Maggie to dictate the direction of their walk. She trotted ahead and turned into a residential side street where a tall box hedge promised exciting smells. While she nosed enthusiastically around the roots, he fretted over what could have happened to poor Sister Francis. He had no doubt that her abductors were members of the Inheritors of the New Kingdom, but why would they have abducted her? He realised that he now had a concrete reason to search for the sect, but how could he discover where its headquarters were? He remembered that he hadn't yet got round to googling Abraham R. If the leader of the cult was, as grandiosely claimed, a poet and philosopher as well as a healer, then the chances were that he had published something.

He turned rapidly back into Bridlington Hill, hauling Maggie on her lead behind him. None too pleased at being so abruptly removed from the site of so many interesting odours, she resisted by sitting down on the pavement and it was only after an unseemly tussle that he managed to drag her home.

Back at his desk, he opened the internet and typed in the name, Abraham R. To his surprise, the search engine responded with hundreds of entries. He started to scroll through them, dismissing those whose surname was Abraham or whose surname did not begin with R. Many of the remainder were biblical or historical characters.

It was only after a lengthy search that he found two references to people described simply as "Abraham R". One was a drummer in a boy band and the other was an Israeli historian. He decided to refine his search. This time he typed in *Abraham R Philosophical Works*. This generated another shoal of entries, most of which were dedicated to the works of Jewish and other religious scholars, both living and dead.

After clicking on a number of other sites, he finally came across something that sounded promising - a pamphlet entitled *The End Time Debate* by one Abraham Rosenberg, "downloadable free of charge". According to the blurb, this described the fulfilment of prophecies foretold in the Book of Revelations. The pamphlet alleged that the end of the world and the Second Coming were imminent, as evidenced by the "trumpets of doom" - the spate of earthquakes, hurricanes and other natural disasters that had recently afflicted so many parts of the world.

He bookmarked the page, then googled *Abraham Rosenberg Poetry*.

Bingo! A direct reference immediately appeared on the screen. He gasped when he opened the website. It showed the front cover of a black volume on which the title, *Poetic Revelations*, was printed in glaring yellow. Beneath it was a startling image of the globe engulfed in bright orange flames.

He stared at it open-mouthed, then clicked on the contents page. The titles of the first two poems, *Catastrophes to Come* and *Prepare ye for the End Time*, told him all he needed to know. He had found his man! He clicked on the second title and read:

Prepare ye for the end time
And the beginning
Of the new beginning
When God cometh again
To give his judgement
The old world will die
Together with the evil ones
The end will be the beginning
The end of sinning
A new world will receive the just
Prepare ye for the end time.

He returned to the beginning of the volume and gave a whoop of triumph on finding the name of the publisher - *Kingdom Press (KP)*. With mounting excitement, he conducted another search. The website, a terse single page, revealed that it was a tiny, non-commercial outfit that produced religious pamphlets and poems, mostly written by one Abraham Rosenberg. The address given, 5 Holton Road, was in Potters Bar. There was no telephone number or email address.

Wasn't Potters Bar in Hertfordshire? He googled it. Yes! It *was* in Hertfordshire and, he realised with a swift intake of breath, not that far from Our Lady of Lourdes Convent.

He left a message on Fiona's mobile, telling her about the nun's disappearance and what he had found on the internet. A little while later, she sent him a text, *Check it out*.

Now that he had an address, he decided to drive to Potters Bar then play it by ear. He would take a look at the premises and if the office was open to the public, he would venture inside, express an interest in Inheritor beliefs and ask if he could look at some sample publications. With any luck, these might contain information about the sect's location. If he was treated with hostility or suspicion, he would beat a hasty retreat.

A problem, however, presented itself: Maggie. If he left her in the house or garden on her own for a lengthy period, she would probably start barking and disturb his neighbours. Remembering Fiona's earlier offer to look after the dog, he scribbled her a note.

Going to check out Kingdom Press and leaving Maggie at home. She's been out and fed. Will text on way home. If you haven't heard from me by 5pm, could you take over dog care? Enclose spare key. Dog food is under kitchen sink. Sorry to be a nuisance. Love, WoL.

He put the note in an envelope with a spare key, fed Maggie and let her have fifteen minutes in the garden, then drove to Fiona's parents' house and dropped the envelope through the letterbox. As he set off for Potters Bar, he switched on the car radio and listened to a half-hourly news bulletin. "The Blitzgreen", as it was now called, was still headline news. According to the newsreader, it had spread to some nature reserves and ancient woodlands. Police and volunteer groups were patrolling open spaces believed to be at risk. The Government was instituting emergency measures to prevent any further devastation of precious greenbelt land.

Richard turned north towards the M1, wondering what awaited him in Potters Bar.

Chapter 14

The road in which the office was located was lined with terraced properties, each of which had stone steps leading directly from the pavement to the front door. Brass plaques indicated that the premises were used for business rather than residential purposes. As Richard drove slowly along the road, he noticed an estate agent, several legal firms, a dental surgery and a letting agency. Number five had two plaques attached to its door. From the car, he could just about make out the names: *Bailey and Thring, Chartered Accountants* and *Kingdom Press*.

He drove to the nearest Pay and Display car park and put in enough change for two hours. Afterwards, he walked back to Holton Road and was about a hundred yards from number five when he saw two men in dark suits come out of the building and descend the steps. His heart missed a beat. They looked disturbingly similar in dress and build to those who had recently paid him a visit. One of them glanced briefly in his direction then turned away and the two walked briskly down to the far corner and turned right. Quickening his pace, Richard followed. On reaching the corner, he was just in time to see the two men turn into another road. He hastened after them.

The road had shops on each side, some of them boarded-up. A group of elderly women were chatting outside a launderette. A younger woman walked past him, pushing a whining toddler in a buggy. An elderly Asian man was standing in the doorway of a shop that smelt strongly of spices. A rack on the pavement outside displayed strange knobbly-shaped vegetables

The two men were about a hundred yards ahead of Richard and he saw them disappear round the side of a tall white building. To his surprise, he saw four other men in identical dark suits approaching from the opposite direction and turn into the side of the same building. With a nervous glance behind him, he walked nonchalantly up to the place where they had disappeared.

The building was a disused theatre or cinema with a crumbling white stucco frontage. Its name, *The Palace*, still discernible on a large and sloping neon sign, seemed to him sadly at odds with the building's advanced state of decrepitude. Tattered remnants of posters attached to weather-bowed boards indicated that at some time in its history, it had suffered the indignity of being downgraded to a Bingo hall.

On the far side of the theatre there was an alley. Looking quickly to left and right, Richard turned into it but could see no sign of any of the suited men. There were three doors on the side of the building, each with the peeling remnants of green paint. The first two were fastened shut with rusty padlocks. On one of them, the words *Upper Balcony* were still faintly visible. The third door had a new-looking padlock which was unlocked and dangling from the handle. Richard tentatively pushed the door open and stepped inside. He found himself in a dark corridor and had barely ventured a few yards along it when he heard footsteps and voices coming from the alley. He dived into the first room he passed and hid behind the door.

It was completely dark inside and smelled musty. A few seconds later, he heard several people come through the outer door and hurry along the corridor. When the sound of their footsteps had receded, he emerged cautiously from the room and, his heart pounding, stole down the corridor. Towards the end of it, a dim light emanated from an open doorway. There was a hum of male voices that grew louder as he approached. When he reached the door, he heard a resonant voice rise above the general hubbub. 'Brother Persuaders, is everyone here?'

There was a chorus of assent followed by a loud clattering suggesting that chairs were being moved.

'Then I'll begin,' declared the voice.

Richard moved stealthily forward and, holding his breath, peered cautiously through the open door. He was looking into a long, windowless room with a bare wooden floor - a rehearsal room perhaps. To the side of the door he could make out some tall fabric screens. At the far end of the room, there was a small platform illuminated by angle-poise lamps placed on the floor. It was furnished only with a table on which there was a large cardboard box. Behind the table, a tall man with grey hair was unfurling something shaped like a window blind and holding it up to show a group of other men who were sitting in an untidy semicircle in front of the platform.

The grey-haired man turned to hang what he was holding on the wall behind the platform. While his back was turned, Richard tiptoed quickly behind the nearest screen and squinted at the platform. He could see now that the man was hanging up a map of the world.

The man took some coloured counters from the box on the table and started to stick them on the map, then he turned and addressed the group seated in front of the platform. Richard could hear only some of his words which were greeted with enthusiastic murmurs from the seated audience: *Fulfilling the prophecy ... cleansing has begun... punishing the unjust...*

In order to see better, Richard pressed his head against the side of the screen and screwed up his eyes. He noticed that some of the counters had been placed on parts of Europe while others were scattered around a wider area. He stifled a gasp when he heard the man listing the places he had marked. They were all areas that had been mysteriously destroyed by fire.

The man turned away from the map and the group engaged in an animated discussion, much of which was inaudible to Richard. Eventually he heard someone ask in a loud voice, 'When will we know the time?'

There was a brief silence then the grey-haired man declared in ringing tones, 'The Healer will soon reveal the time.' He clapped his hands and the group in front of him stood up, raised their arms high above their heads and started to chant in unison. This time Richard could hear every word and his skin prickled.

Prepare ye for the end time
And the beginning
Of the new beginning
When God cometh again
To give his judgement
The old world will die
Together with the evil ones
The end will be the beginning
The end of sinning
A new world will receive the just
Prepare ye for the end time.

The men stopped chanting and bowed their heads in silence.
Richard's face had been pressed for some time against the side of the

dusty fabric screen and he suddenly felt the need to sneeze. Although he tried desperately to suppress it, the sneeze resisted his efforts and erupted explosively, echoing through the room.

There was a chorus of startled exclamations.

For a fraction of a second Richard remained paralysed with fear, then seeing a dozen heads turn towards him, he darted swiftly from behind the screen and through the door, hearing shouts and the clatter of falling chairs behind him. Without looking back, he sped down the corridor and out into the alley, momentarily blinded by the afternoon sunlight. He ran back up the road and practically fell into the shop displaying knobbly vegetables. The Asian man he had seen earlier was behind the counter. He looked up in surprise as Richard bounded through the shop and concealed himself behind the shelves at the back.

Moments later, Richard heard pounding footsteps outside.

The shopkeeper materialised by his side. 'Can I help you, Sir?'

Richard peered earnestly at the shelves. 'Erm ...' He grabbed a packet of turmeric. 'I'll take this,' he stuttered, 'and ... this.' It was a tin of coconut milk. Thinking it would be prudent to detain the shopkeeper at the back of the shop, he held them both up. 'What do you make with these?'

While the shopkeeper elaborated on the exotic dishes it was possible to create with the ingredients he had chosen, Richard kept an eye on the open shop door. It was only after he spotted his pursuers walking disconsolately back down the road that he deemed it safe to move. He paid for the two items and a packet of cumin seeds that the shopkeeper persuaded him was an essential ingredient for a curry, then set off at speed towards the car park. Panting for breath and with the blood singing in his ears, he flung himself into the driver's seat of his father's car. He had never been so frightened in his life.

When he had stopped trembling, he sent a text to Fiona telling her he was on his way home.

Driving through the afternoon traffic, he castigated himself for his cowardice. What had his journey achieved? Although he had come across some of the Inheritors, he had neither located Sister Francis nor discovered the whereabouts of Abraham R. It had been a waste of time.

After parking the car in the Close, he was dismayed to see Marjorie Phelps emerge from her front door and advance purposefully towards him.

'The police were looking for you again,' she announced without any kind of a greeting.

He feigned surprise. 'Were they?'

She glared at him. 'Don't tell me you've had *another* bicycle stolen?'

He didn't bother to reply.

'And that dog,' she hissed. 'It's been barking all afternoon. I don't know how Doris and Reg put up with it.'

'Well Pugwash does his fair share and I've never complained,' Richard retorted, fumbling with his keys. He turned away and strode up the path to the front door.

'You're lowering the tone, Ricky Jarman!' she shouted after him. 'This used to be a respectable neighbourhood.'

He unlocked the door and slammed it behind him.

He left a message for Fiona on her mobile: *Lots to tell you. I saw the Inheritors. Can we meet at the weekend? The police came to the house looking for me while I was away. By the way, do you know how to make curry?*

Chapter 15

The police returned the next morning. This time there were two of them – a stocky man with thick black eyebrows and an older woman whose greying fair hair was scraped severely back from her face.

Maggie, who had accompanied Richard to the door, barked furiously at the intruders.

'Mr. Jarman?' enquired the woman.

'Yes, that's me. Shut up, Maggie!'

'This is Detective Constable Evans and I'm Detective Inspector Mercer.' They held identity cards up for his inspection. 'May we have a word, Sir? We're investigating the disappearance of a nun, Sister Francis, real name Mary Donnelly.'

'Come in.' Richard was aware that lace curtains would be twitching round the Close and hoped the police car hadn't been parked where it could be seen from Marjorie Phelps' front windows. He pushed Maggie into the kitchen and led the officers into the sitting room.

The policewoman gazed at him steadily. She had very pale blue eyes, he noticed, so pale that the irises were almost indistinguishable from the whites. 'I believe you rang the convent yesterday and asked to speak to Sister Francis?'

'Yes, I did.'

'Could you tell us why you rang her?'

'I wanted to make sure she was OK.'

'And why did you think she might not be OK?'

'Because she called me a few days before and told me about an incident--'

She called *you*?' interrupted the policewoman, looking surprised. She and DC Evans exchanged a glance. '*When* did she ring you?'

He reflected for a second. 'Saturday I think. Yes, it was on Saturday.'

DI Mercer wrote this in her notebook. 'And what was the nature of her call.'

'She was frightened. She told me that two men had accosted her after she'd been to the bank.'

'Why should she tell *you* about that?'

Richard's mouth had gone dry. 'Because she was afraid they might accost me.'

'Accost *you?*' exclaimed the policewoman. 'Why would they want to accost you?'

'Because ... because ... it's a long story. ' They were both staring at him so intently that he was beginning to feel uncomfortable.

After a short pause the male officer took over the questioning. 'Perhaps you could tell us about your relationship with Sister Francis.'

Richard swallowed nervously. 'It isn't a relationship. I hardly know her.'

The officer's bushy brows formed an interrogative arch. 'But the Reverend Mother told us that you called at the convent to see her several weeks ago.'

'Yes I did go to see her, but only that once.'

'The Reverend Mother informed us that you were enquiring about the food boxes that the sisters supply to the homeless shelter.' He smirked. 'Are you a grocer, Mr. Jarman?'

Richard felt his face go hot. 'Of course I'm not, and I didn't go to see her about the food boxes.'

'You didn't?' DC Evans responded sharply. 'Then what exactly did you go to see her about?'

Richard took a deep breath. 'I read that Sister Francis had seen a strange object in the sky on the night that Mayfield Common was destroyed. It sounded exactly like something I saw on the night Fonthill Recreation Ground was damaged, so I wanted to ask her about it.'

'You're saying you went to see the nun to talk about what you both witnessed, but you claimed you were from the homeless shelter?'

Richard blushed again. 'I didn't say I was from the shelter. The nun who opened the gate just assumed it.'

DI Mercer regarded him severely. 'Why didn't you admit the real reason for your visit?'

'I thought they wouldn't let me in if I told them the real reason.'

'In other words, you entered the convent under false pretences?'

'I suppose so.'

'Did you tell Sister Francis you were from the homeless shelter?'

'No, I told her exactly why I'd gone to see her; I wanted to hear about what she'd witnessed in the sky because I'd seen something very similar. She said she'd been advised not to speak about it to anyone.'

'Yet she was willing to speak to *you*?'

'Yes, she wanted to talk about it. She was disturbed by what she saw, just like I was. She asked me to pray with her and even gave me a rosary.' Richard took the beads from his pocket and dangled them in front of the two police officers who regarded them impassively.

DC Evans took a notebook out of a pocket and glanced at it, before resuming the questioning. 'Mr. Jarman, are you a member of *Greenpeace*?'

Richard was startled. 'I was once. Not any more. Why?'

'And were you not involved in the action against *Esso* petrol stations in 2003?'

He was baffled. 'Yes, but that was years ago.'

'And the following year, didn't you chain yourself to a tree in Somerset to stop it being felled? I believe you were subsequently taken into custody?'

'Yes, but only overnight. I was a student then.'

'I gather you're a student *now*!'

'A postgraduate student.'

'And an activist?'

'Not now, but I was then. Most of us were in those days. We wanted to save the planet.'

DC Evans frowned and glanced down at the notebook. 'In 2006 you wrote an article supporting the Eco Activists Climate Camp that was trying to close down a nuclear power station in Hartlepool. And in 2007 you wrote another article, supporting activists who were trying to shut down Heathrow in protests against plans for expansion.'

'So what?' Richard snapped in exasperation. 'I'm entitled to my opinions, aren't I? And I don't see what any of this has to do with Sister Francis's disappearance.'

The officer changed tack. 'Can you tell us, Sir, where you were on Monday morning?'

'Monday morning? I don't remember. Why?'

The officer ignored the question. 'Please try to remember what you did on that day?'

A wave of hot indignation washed over Richard. 'Are you trying to implicate me in Sister Francis's disappearance? Do you think I have a nun hidden under the floorboards or something?'

DC Evans managed a faint smile. 'We need to know where you were on Monday morning, Sir, and if anyone saw you ... just for the record.'

Richard was beginning to feel distinctly uneasy. He made an effort to remember the morning in question. 'I think I was at home most of the time... though I did take the dog for a short walk.'

'Where did you go?' asked DI Mercer.

'Just to the top of Bridlington Hill.'

'Did anyone see you while you were out?'

'No ... I mean, yes. I sat on a bench for a few minutes and a woman came out of her gate. She was pissed off because my dog got into her front garden.'

'What time would that be?'

'Late morning. Between eleven and twelve, I think.'

'And can you tell us where that woman lives?'

'In a side street at the top of the hill. I think it's called Gladstone Walk or something like that. Hers was the house on the corner. I sat outside it for a while, on a bench.'

DI Mercer noted this in her book. 'Do you think the lady would remember you?'

'Probably not, but I expect she'd remember the dog.'

'We'll check.' She gazed unblinkingly at him. 'Let's go back to that phone call you say Sister Francis made to you on Saturday. She told you two men had accosted her on the previous day. Did she say anything else?'

'Yes, she told me the two guys made off when a priest crossed the road. He escorted her back to the convent and advised her not to go out again for a while.'

'Yes, we've spoken to Father Doyle. But I'm still not quite clear why she rang to tell you about it.' DI Mercer gazed at him searchingly, her pen poised.

'I've already told you,' Richard snapped impatiently. 'She wanted to warn me because the two guys seemed threatening. She thought that because I'd seen the same thing in the sky that she saw, they might come looking for *me* next.'

The two officers stared at him incredulously.

'She said they asked her about what she'd seen in the sky the night that Mayfield Common was destroyed, then one of them started shouting about the Second Coming.'

DI Mercer looked baffled. 'The Second Coming?'

'It's what some religious groups believe … that the Messiah will come to Earth again.'

She exchanged a glance with her colleague. 'Go on.'

'That's all there was to it,' Richard continued. 'I told her not to worry about me, but to do what the priest said and not leave the convent for a while.'

'So why did you ring the convent on Thursday?'

'Just to see if she was OK. I was shocked when I heard that she'd disappeared.'

DC Evans resumed the questioning. 'Do you have any idea what has happened to Sister Francis?'

Richard hesitated. 'Well, it's only a theory, but I think she may have been taken by the Inheritors of the New Kingdom.'

'The *who*?' the officers exclaimed in unison.

'It's an American religious sect that believes in the Second Coming. I think the two men who accosted her in the street belong to it.'

There was a short silence during which the two officers watched him carefully.

'Why do you think the two men who accosted her belonged to this sect?' asked DI Mercer.

'Because…' There was no going back now and Richard embarked on a stumbling account of recent events: the attack on Paddy McAllister, the visit he had received from two smartly-dressed men, his internet search for the Inheritors, and his trip to Potters Bar. He decided not to mention Morgana Delph's message to him during her appearance at the theatre.

After Richard had finished his narrative, DC Evans cleared his throat. 'If you believe this group, the … Kingdom Inheritors, was responsible for the nun's disappearance, why didn't you contact us?'

'Because I didn't think you would believe me,' Richard muttered sullenly.

There was another silence broken only by the scratching of the policewoman's pen and intermittent barks from the kitchen.

DC Evans frowned. 'Can you give us the address of the theatre where the meeting you say you witnessed took place?'

'I didn't notice the name of the road but it should be easy enough to find.' He described the theatre and its crumbling façade.

'And what do you think the man on the platform was marking on the map?'

'He listed some of the areas where green spaces have been destroyed. I remember him saying something about the fulfilment of a prophecy.'

The officers exchanged another glance then stood up.

'Thank you, Sir, you've been very helpful,' said DI Mercer. 'We'll make some enquiries and we may be in touch again.'

Richard accompanied them to the front door.

Before stepping outside, DC Evans smiled at him sardonically. 'By the way, Mr. Jarman, do you *still* want to "save the planet"?'

'Yes,' Richard snapped, 'but believe it or not, kidnapping a nun isn't on my agenda.'

He slammed the door behind them.

Chapter 16

'Why would the police think I've got something to do with Sister Francis's disappearance?' he grumbled to Fiona as they sat overlooking the swimming pool in which Polly and a friend were happily splashing and ducking each other.

'I don't know. You don't seem like a nun-napper to me?' She craned her neck to watch Polly.

Richard felt irritated. He desperately wanted to tell her about his experiences in Potters Bar, but the only opportunity to meet had turned out to be Saturday morning at the leisure centre. He found it difficult to talk against the cacophony of splashes and squeals from the pool, and Fiona was too preoccupied with ensuring that Polly and her friend didn't stray into the deep end to give him her full attention.

When the girls finally tired of swimming and went to the changing room, he and Fiona retired to the cafeteria. There, over coffee, he described in detail what he had witnessed in the disused theatre and his subsequent flight.

She was horrified. 'Ric, those men sound scary.'

'They were! They scared the pants off me.'

'Do you think the police are going to check them out?'

'Possibly, though the chances of their finding anything in that theatre are minimal. It didn't look like a permanent meeting place to me. They'll probably think I made the story up.'

'Why should they? And surely they can't think you're responsible for the nun's disappearance.'

'Can't they? You should have heard them! ' He imitated the male officer's flat tones. '"What were you doing on Monday morning, Mr. Jarman? Can anyone confirm your whereabouts?" My only alibi is a fucking dog turd! I just hope that woman remembers Maggie messing in her garden.' He gazed moodily into his coffee cup.

'What motive could you possibly have for abducting a nun?'

'God knows.' He laughed in spite of himself. 'That's true. God probably *does* know more about nuns than I do! But seriously, Fi, going to Potters Bar was a waste of time. I'm no nearer to finding her or Abraham R than I was before.'

Fiona pushed a strand of shining dark hair behind her ear. 'Have you checked the forums where you posted the message?'

'Not for a day or two. I'll have another look when I get home.'

'If the two men who came to your house were in that theatre, do you think they would have recognised you?'

He shook his head. 'It's unlikely. The most they would have seen of me was my back when I flew out of that room like a bat out of hell.'

'So there's nothing to connect the eavesdropper in the theatre with the "Witnesser of the Light".'

'Nothing.'

Polly and her friend Anna, damp hair clinging to their heads, joined them.

Still pink from her exertions in the pool, Polly threw her bag and jacket onto an empty chair. 'Can we get a drink, Mum?'

'I suppose so.' Fiona gave Polly some money and the two girls sped off. She smiled. 'They remind me of myself at that age.'

Looking at her generous mouth, Richard recalled the kiss they had shared on her doorstep on Wednesday evening and had a strong urge to repeat the experience.

'When are you free, Fi?' he asked. 'Let's have another evening out.'

She thought for a moment. 'How about Tuesday? Mum and Dad are staying in that night.'

'Great. What would you like to do?'

'Maybe we could go to the pictures? There's a new *Bond* film on.'

'Good idea.' He reached over and tentatively took her hand just as the girls returned to join them.

Polly looked searchingly at Richard as she sat down. 'Are you and Mum an item?' she asked solemnly, opening her can of Coca Cola with a loud snap.

Fiona blushed. 'Polly! You shouldn't ask questions like that.'

'Your mum and I are just old friends.' As soon as the words were out Richard realised how pompous they sounded.

Polly and Mia dissolved into fits of giggles.

Fiona smiled at him, but he felt slightly discomfited. 'I'd better be going,' he muttered, rapidly finishing his coffee. 'I don't like leaving Maggie alone in the house for too long. I'll check the forums as soon as I get back.'

'Let me know if you get any replies.'

'Will do. I'll be in touch about Tuesday.'

His mobile rang as he was leaving the leisure centre. It was Mark Davenport. Richard hadn't heard from him since the memorable night at *Loonies*.

'Ric, remember what we were talking about the other evening?'

'Yes?'

'I've heard again from my contact in Washington. This is serious stuff, Ric. Some incredibly bright flying objects were caught on US radar the other night. The Yanks have used their most sophisticated hardware to try and catch them.'

'Hardware?'

'They've sent up Reapers. You know, unmanned drones full of laser-guided missiles. They're piloted remotely by satellite link. But although they can travel at great speeds, Steve says they haven't managed to catch up with any of the targets. Those flying machines have astonishing powers of acceleration.'

Richard was stunned. 'Do the Americans know what they are?'

'Well if they do, they're not giving anything away. Apparently there have been top-level meetings at the Pentagon and secret meetings with foreign powers. The public aren't being told anything. I'll keep you posted if I hear any more.'

Richard made his way home in an uneasy daze.

Back at his desk, he found a dozen new replies on the forums where he had posted his message. As before, they included the abusive, the downright weird and the mind-blowingly tedious. He waded through them, searching for a clue that one of them might have emanated from the Inheritors. He had almost decided to give up when he spotted something on the third and final forum. The message was shorter than most and extremely cryptic: *Witnesser of the Light, those who are prepared for the End Time will be spared.*

He punched the air. 'Yeees!'

Come forward into the light, the message continued. *Redemption will be found where end follows harp in one high place 11 of 5 -15.*

Richard stared at the words for a long time. What was the point of leaving him a message that was totally incomprehensible? He wasn't a member of *MENSA*. Overcome with frustration, he took out his mobile and rang Fiona.

'I've had one reply that I'm pretty sure is from the Inheritors.'

'Wow! What does it say?'

He read the message out to her. 'Can you can make sense of this gobbledygook?'

He heard her laugh. 'No. Are you sure it's from them?'

'Yes. That bit about the End Time gives it away.'

'Well read it to me again and I'll write it down. I'll call you back if I have any inspiration.'

After dictating the message, Richard continued to try to decipher it but eventually abandoned the attempt. The rest of the day stretched ahead of him but he felt too restless to resume work on his thesis. He took Maggie for a walk, listened to some of his favourite music, and finally rang Dan whom he hadn't seen for some time.

'Will you be at home this evening? I'm at a loose end.'

'Yes, we're here,' his friend replied. 'Come and have dinner with us. Stop over if you like. We haven't seen you for ages.'

'Thanks, but I'll have to bring the dog.'

'What dog? I didn't know you had a dog.'

'I seem to have acquired one.'

'Hang on.' He heard Dan conferring with his wife. Seconds later he returned to the phone. 'The Lady of the Manor says the dog can come too, so long as you leave it in the conservatory at night and bring whatever food it eats with you.'

'You're on.' Richard was pleased. It would be good to see Dan and Kate again as well as potentially useful. He could ask Dan whether he had picked up any more information from Air Traffic Control.

* * *

'Blimey, Ric!' exclaimed Dan when he opened the door of his house in Ealing at six o'clock that evening. 'What kind of a dog is that?'

'A bit of this and a bit of that.' Richard smiled fondly at his friend. With his floppy fair hair and baggy t-shirt, Dan looked much younger than his twenty-eight years.

'What's his name?'

'It's a she and her name is Maggie!'

'Maggie?' Dan exploded with laughter. 'Good choice! *Shaggy*

Maggie!'

'Not *my* choice. I inherited her and her name from someone else. Hi, Kate!'

Richard kissed Dan's wife, a slender, attractive woman with curly auburn hair and bright hazel eyes, and dutifully admired Liam, the baby she was carrying on her hip.

Every surface in his friends' tiny living room seemed to be covered with baby clothes and equipment. "Shaggy Maggie" settled herself on the floor in the gap between a bundle of cuddly toys and a nappy-changing mat. She didn't seem to mind when Liam crawled up and tugged her fur with his podgy little hands.

Dan moved some crumpled baby clothes from an armchair so that Richard could sit down. 'We haven't had time to cook. Take-away suit you? Do you like crispy duck?'

'Love it.'

'Great, I'll phone the order. It'll probably take about an hour. That'll give Kate time to get his lordship settled.'

After Kate carried Liam upstairs for his bath, Dan disappeared into the kitchen. He returned several minutes later with a bottle of white wine and some glasses.

'How's the *magnum opus*?' he asked, pouring Richard a glass of wine and offering him a bowl of peanuts.

Richard took some peanuts and hesitated before answering. 'It's on hold for the moment.'

'Oh? I thought you had a deadline.'

'I managed to get an extension. Things have been a bit...difficult lately. I just couldn't concentrate on it.'

'Why, what's been happening?'

'It's a long story, Dan. Remember I told you about what I saw in the sky.'

'Your UFO?'

'Yes, I reported it to the police.'

'What did they say?'

'Nothing. They thought I was a nutcase! And now they think I've kidnapped a nun!'

Dan laughed so much he almost choked on a peanut. 'You *are* joking?'

'No,' Richard muttered, grumpily, 'I wish I was. He took a sip of wine then launched into an account of everything that had happened to him during the previous weeks. He realised how bizarre his story must sound, but Dan listened without laughing, interrupting only to ask for clarification.

After Richard had finished his narrative, Dan gazed at him thoughtfully.

Upstairs, Liam started to cry and Richard could hear Kate's voice soothing him.

Dan shook his head slowly. 'Now let me get this straight. You've been trying to track down the leader of a cult, what did you say they're called --?'

'Inheritors of the New Kingdom.'

'You're trying to track him down because a batty medium told you to?'

'Not just because of what she said,' Richard replied hastily. 'Because of the nun, Sister Francis.'

'You're not responsible for finding a missing person, Ric. That's the police's job.'

'But I'm sure the Inheritors had something to do with her disappearance, Dan. I don't have any proof, but if I manage to decode the message they left me, maybe I'll find out where they are and then perhaps I'll be able to find her. I wrote the message down. Take a look.'

He fished a scrap of paper out of his pocket, unfolded it and handed it to Dan who glanced at it briefly then tossed it back to him with a laugh.

'This is just cod's wallop, Ric! I wouldn't dignify it with a moment's thought.'

Feeling slightly aggrieved, Richard replaced the paper in his pocket. 'I'm certain it's a message from them, Dan. The reference to Abraham R's poem is quite clear.'

Dan looked doubtful. 'Well even if it is from them, why would they want to get in touch with you? And why would they have abducted the nun? I just don't get it.'

'I believe it's something to do with the UFO she and I both saw. I'm sure there's some connection. The Inheritors seem to have a real interest in the greenbelt areas that have been destroyed. The man in the theatre listed some of them when he was putting markers on the map.' He drained his glass and put it on the coffee table.

Dan refilled it. 'OK, so this group, Inheritors of Kingdom Come or whatever they're called, is interested in the Blitzgreen. That's not surprising, is it?'

Richard gazed reflectively into his glass. 'It's more than interest, Dan. When I was in that derelict theatre, I had the impression that they actually welcome what's been happening. They seem to believe the arson attacks are a sign that the end of the world is coming. It's creepy.'

Dan laughed. 'Well they're not the only people who think the end of the world is nigh. Religious crackpots have been predicting that for as long as I can remember. Didn't a whole bunch of them go up a mountain in the year 2000 to wait for it?' He thrust some peanuts into his mouth, chewed and swallowed them, then lowered his voice. 'I told you that the guys at Swanwick picked up some unexplained aerial objects on the radar?'

Richard nodded. 'Yes, and they've also appeared in the States. One of my ex colleagues told me that the American military sent Reapers after them but they couldn't get anywhere near. He said they have amazing powers of acceleration, far in excess anything a man-made machine can achieve.'

Dan looked worried. 'If they're not man-made, what do they think they are?'

At that moment Kate entered the room. 'He's asleep at last.' She placed a baby alarm on the sideboard. 'You're both very quiet. Where's my wine?'

Dan swept a bundle of clothes off an armchair, and handed her a glass with a flourish. 'At your service, Madame!'

'Cheers!' She took a gulp before sinking into the chair. 'What have you two been talking about?'

Dan tapped the side of his nose. 'Boys' talk, my petal.'

'We've been catching up.' Richard experienced a pang of envy for their easy companionship.

'How's the thesis going, Ric?' Kate enquired, taking some peanuts from the bowl.

He cleared his throat. 'Well, it's--'

'Ric's got other things on his mind at the moment,' interrupted Dan, giving him a warning glance.

Kate smiled knowingly. 'Aha! Are you seeing someone, Ric?'

He laughed. 'You sound just like my mother! Yes, as a matter of fact I am. An old school friend. But nothing serious. It's early days.'

'Good. We never thought Emma was right for you, did we Dan?'

'Now you sound even *more* like my mother!'

Dan topped up their glasses. 'Does your dog need to go out before the Chinese nosh arrives?'

Richard had almost forgotten about Maggie who was snoozing peacefully in the middle of the chaos on the floor. 'She's OK. I'll take her out after dinner.'

* * *

The rest of the evening passed pleasantly and neither Dan nor Richard made any further reference to their earlier conversation. They didn't resume it until after lunch the following afternoon.

'I didn't want to talk about it front of Kate,' Dan said as he accompanied Richard and Maggie back to the car, 'but something really serious must be happening if the Yanks are sending up fighter planes. Who or what the hell is up there?'

'God knows, but I don't buy the terrorist explanation they're trotting out.' Richard pushed Maggie into the back of the car then climbed into the driver's seat.

Dan leaned through the car window, his expression anxious. 'Take care, Ric. I wouldn't mess with those Kingdom nutcases if I were you. They're a pretty nasty bunch if they're into beating up old men and kidnapping nuns. Take your Uncle Dan's advice. Have nothing more to do with them and finish your thesis before the world *does* come to an end!'

Chapter 17

It was the middle of the afternoon by the time Richard arrived back in Coronation Close. As he walked up the path with Maggie, he saw his immediate neighbour, Doris Perkins, polishing a front windowpane with a vigour that failed to disturb the tight corrugations of her grey hair. Hearing his footsteps, she turned and called to him.

'Ricky, I hope you won't mind me mentioning this, but--'

'Yes, Mrs. Perkins?'

She smiled apologetically. 'It's that dog.' She glanced down at Maggie.

'What about her?' His mind ran rapidly through some retaliatory complaints he could make about *her* dog if necessary.

'It's none of my business of course, but Eileen, your mum, I know she's really fussy about her back garden and I couldn't help noticing from our bedroom window, that there's rather a lot of, erm, mess on it.'

'Is there?' he asked blankly. 'I hadn't noticed.' He stooped to remove Maggie's lead.

'Yes, and it's ... well, it's a bit of a health hazard, especially now that the weather's getting warmer. Reggie and I clear up Pugwash's mess as soon as he does it. It's automatic. But as you only recently got that dog, I suppose you haven't got into the habit yet. I just thought I'd mention it.'

Richard strove to hide his annoyance. He had been thinking about the end of the world and this woman was worrying about a few dog turds. 'Thank you, Mrs. Perkins. That's very thoughtful of you.'

'By the way, Ricky,' she called as he was unlocking the door, 'a policewoman called yesterday when you were out.'

'Oh?' He opened the door and disappeared rapidly inside. He assumed that the policewoman was the one who had called before. She was bound to return, arousing yet more curiosity and suspicion around the Close.

Grumpily, he took a plastic bag from the kitchen and after removing the offending mess from the back lawn, flushed it down the toilet. Then, as it was a warm and sunny afternoon, he brought down his laptop and took it on to the back patio. Perching on one of the metal garden chairs, he switched on the machine and read the latest email from his mother:

Darling, Alaska's wonderful! Such dramatic scenery. Fabulous glaciers and volcanoes. We've seen whales and taken loads of photos. I can't wait to show them to you. We're looking forward to Vancouver. It's hard to keep up with everything that's happening in the world when you're on a cruise, but we've been hearing about those arson attacks. Someone told us Richmond Park has been damaged. It's very worrying. Who would do such a thing?

Hope the thesis is going well. Dad sends his love, Mum xxx

Richard was composing a bland and uninformative reply when Maggie's barking alerted him to the fact that the front doorbell was ringing. His heart sank. Did the police make calls on Sunday afternoons? Reluctantly he went to the door, but to his relief, his visitor wasn't a police officer, it was Fiona.

She beamed at him. 'I've worked it out.' She staggered back as Maggie jumped up and put her paws on her shoulders.

'Worked what out?' Richard pulled Maggie off her and ushered her inside.

'The message of course! The one on the internet forum.'

'You mean you've managed to decipher it?'

'Yes,' she declared triumphantly. 'After I'd looked at it for a while, it became perfectly clear.' She reached up and kissed him lightly on the cheek. 'Aren't I the clever one?'

'We'll have to see.' He gave her a hug. 'Come into the garden and you can enlighten me.' He led her through the house and on to the patio. 'Would you like some tea?'

'After I've told you what the message means.' She sat down, smiling broadly. In the afternoon sunlight her eyes looked light green, reflecting the colour of her t-shirt.

He took the crumpled piece of paper from his pocket, smoothed it out and laid it on the garden table. 'OK, Clever Clogs, what does it mean?'

She leant over the table, pushed a strand of hair out of her eyes, and pointed at the words. 'Well, the first bit - *Redemption will be found where end follows harp* - I think this means that you'll find redemption in Harpenden.'

'Harpenden!' Richard exclaimed. 'I'm not sure I'd find anything in Harpenden, let alone redemption. I don't even know where it is.'

She grinned at him. 'You'll be interested to know that it's in Hertfordshire, north of St Albans, and not all that far from Potters Bar.'

'Hertfordshire again?' He stared at her. 'Wow! Whereabouts in Harpenden?'

'They give you the actual address. One High Place. There must be somewhere in Harpenden called High Place, and the meeting will be at number one.'

'But what about the rest? All those numbers?'

'Well they also give you a date and a time.' She pointed at the paper. '11 of 5 must mean the eleventh of May, and 15 probably means three o'clock. Looks like they're inviting you to a meeting, Ric!'

The eleventh of May? That's on Tuesday.' Richard's frisson of excitement was mingled with fear. 'Christ!' He gazed at the paper, then at Fiona, then at the paper again. 'Fiona Harris, you're a genius! I'm not sure I could have worked that out for myself. I showed the message to my mate Dan yesterday, and he thought it was a load of cobblers.'

She laughed. 'It wasn't all that difficult. What do you think? Will you go?'

He hesitated. 'I suppose I'll have to, if only for Sister Francis's sake. I'm not going to bottle out this time.'

Her expression changed to one of concern. 'It could be dangerous, Ric. Are you sure you want to do this?'

'Not really,' he said, 'but there's more at stake than my own safety.'

She leant across the table and took his hand. 'Well you're braver than I am! After what happened in Potters Bar, I don't think *I'd* want to meet those guys again. Why don't you take Maggie with you, for protection?'

'No. If the two guys who abducted Paddy are there, they might recognise her and smell a rat.'

'Well Polly and I can look after her. Mum and Dad won't mind.' She hesitated then grinned. 'Well *maybe* they won't mind if Polly asks them. You can drop her off before you go. I'll be at home for an hour at lunchtime. But aren't we going to the pictures on Tuesday?'

'I should be back in time for the film. It doesn't start till eight. Would you like some tea now?'

'No, I'd better go.' She stood up. 'I've got to pick Polly up from Mia's.'

'Can I give you a lift then?' he asked, reluctant to lose her company so soon.

'No thanks, it's so lovely out this afternoon, I'd rather walk.'

'Maggie needs a walk. We'll come with you.'

As they descended the hill, Richard took Fiona's hand and kept hold of it until they reached Polly's friend's house. When they stopped at the gate, he hesitated, then drew her to him and kissed her. She responded eagerly.

A second or so later, he heard peals of giggles, and lifting his head, spotted Polly and Mia standing at the open door.

'O-oh, we're under surveillance!' Fiona pulled away from him and ran up the path, turning to wave as she joined the girls at the door. 'You'll bring Maggie over at lunch-time on Tuesday then?'

'Yes,' he replied. 'I'll pick her up when I get back.'

His mobile beeped as he and Maggie made their way home. It was a text from Mark Davenport: *Prog on Chan 4 tonite abt life on other planets.*

* * *

The programme consisted of a discussion, interspersed with displays of charts and images of heavenly constellations, between a well-known British astronomer and an American astrophysicist.

The astronomer, whose bushy eyebrows, undisciplined mop of grey hair and excitable manner were familiar to British television audiences, was outlining at length the hypothesis that there could be thousands of alien civilisations with the potential to make contact with Earth.

'Planetary formations around stars are commonplace,' he declared with a theatrical flourish of his hand, 'so we can't assume that our planet is the only one that harbours life. Most astronomers now believe that there are countless planets capable of supporting life. There are a hundred billion stars in our Milky Way galaxy alone. Many of them may have planetary systems, some of which could be similar to Earth. NASA's Kepler spacecraft is expected to find thousands of rocky Earth-like planets some of which could be in the "Goldilocks Zone".

He turned to the camera and explained, 'The Goldilocks Zone is an area of space where it's neither too hot nor too cold and where there could be liquid water which is generally assumed to be a prerequisite for the formation of basic organisms.'

'I assume any estimates are premised on Drake's equation,' observed the American, a balding man with steel-rimmed glasses.

'Naturally,' responded the astronomer. 'Drake's formula has enabled us to estimate the combination of stars and planets needed to form life-supporting solar systems. More recently, scientists have used computer models to ascertain the likelihood of life on other planets.'

'Yeah.' The American said eagerly. 'Didn't they come up with three possibilities?'

'That's right. They applied certain hypotheses to the models...' a chart with diagrams and numbers appeared on the screen '...The first assumed that although it's very difficult to have the right conditions for life to form, once life is formed, it will eventually evolve into *intelligent* life. According to this hypothesis, there could be, at the very least, hundreds of intelligent civilisations in our galaxy alone.'

The astronomer paused as the first chart was replaced by a second. 'The next hypothesis assumed that, given the right conditions, life can easily be formed, though the chances of its evolving into *intelligent* life are relatively slight --'

'Meaning it would just be bacteria, single cell organisms,' interjected the American.

The astronomer peered earnestly at the unseen viewers. 'We define life as living organisms that have the possibility of growth, reproduction and metabolism.'

He paused until another chart appeared on the screen. 'The third option explored the possibility that life can pass from one celestial body to another through a collision, say with another planet or an asteroid. Many scientists believe it was just such a collision that kick-started life on Earth. This option suggests that there could be up to thirty eight thousand intelligent life forms in our galaxy! That's a staggering thought, eh?'

'That depends on what they mean by "intelligent".'

'They use Drake's definition - planetary civilisations capable of communicating with others. As you know, Drake himself estimated that the number of these in our galaxy alone would be about ten thousand.'

'But,' interjected the American, 'if intelligent life does exist on other planets, it won't necessarily resemble any of the life forms we are familiar with.'

'Correct. We tend to understand intelligent life in terms of human beings, but because of the different elements and conditions that may exist on another planet, there may be life forms that have evolved in totally different ways. It would be arrogant to believe that we are the most developed form of life in the universe. There may be far more evolved civilisations out there which look very different from us.'

'Granted there probably is life out there ...' the American took off his glasses and waved them upwards as if to indicate the universe. '... but if it is *intelligent* life as Drake defined it, we're obliged to ask the same question that Fermi posed in 1950, where *are* they? Why have we never received any signals? The SETI team--'

'The Search for Extra Terrestrial Intelligence,' the astronomer explained to the viewers.

'SETI have been scanning the skies for years, but they haven't yet picked up any radio signals.'

The astronomer smiled. 'SETI can only search a restricted number of radio frequencies at any one time. And of course we are talking about unbelievably immense distances.' He spread his arms wide. 'Our Milky Way galaxy is roughly a hundred thousand light years across. A message from the opposite side of the galaxy could take a hundred thousand years to reach us. And for all we know, other civilisations may have tried transmitting signals to Earth thousands of years before we had the ability to receive them.'

'Hmmm.' The other man looked unconvinced.

'But why ... ' the astronomer's head bobbed so vigorously that his hair looked as though it might fly off into the universe by itself '... why do we assume that the only way aliens might make contact is through radio waves? Radio signals may seem the logical way to send messages over colossal distances, but intelligent aliens could have developed other, more effective means of communication. We can't assume that our communication systems are necessarily compatible with those that might be used in a different planet. If an alien civilisation has a thousand years technological advantage over us, or even just a hundred, they could have developed technology beyond our wildest imaginings.'

The astrophysicist nodded. 'Yeah. Some believe that a more advanced way extraterrestrials might communicate through intergalactic space could be by smashing together muon particles to create an intense beam of neutrinos.'

This was completely over Richard's head. What on earth were "neutrinos" and "muon particles"? he wondered. With little understanding of its scientific content, he watched the rest of the programme in a daze.

The two men were now poring over charts and exchanging further impenetrable facts and comments. He picked up occasional words and phrases - *the NASA Terrestrial Planet Finder Mission, the Herschel Space Satellite, Darwin Space Mission, Hubble, Keck Observatory, the Kepel Satellite, the Kepler Mission, adaptive optics, gamma ray detectors* - none of which meant much to him, but his imagination was set on fire. There was, he was now convinced, life beyond Earth. He wondered if Dan was also watching the programme and revising his earlier scepticism.

When the discussion came to an end, he switched channels to catch the ten o'clock news bulletin. Back to life on Earth! After the urgent introductory music, the newsreader listed the items that were to be covered: job losses in British manufacturing industry; corruption charges against a well-known MP; a plane crash in South America, and, Richard caught his breath, '*Mystery arson attacks continue.*'

He waited impatiently for details of the final item. It was delivered by a male newsreader standing against a photographed backdrop of a blackened forest.

'The destruction of vegetation has spread further round the world,' he declared gravely. 'Green areas around Russian cities and several cities in the Far East have been incinerated in overnight arson attacks. Reports are just coming in about the extent of the damage. Members of the United Nations are holding top-level meetings on how to deal with the attacks which are believed to have been launched by an unknown terrorist group.'

There were no more details and the news bulletin ended.

'Bloody hell!' muttered Richard. 'Bloody fucking hell!'

Chapter 18

He awoke the next morning with a start. The doorbell was ringing, accompanied by a volley of barks from Maggie downstairs. His watch showed it to be nine fifteen. Who on earth would be calling on him at this time on a Monday morning? The bell rang again. 'Yes,' he shouted, 'I'm coming.' He quickly pulled on jeans and a t-shirt and stumbled downstairs.

'Good morning, Mr. Jarman.' DS Johnson, the mournful-looking officer who had visited him the first time, bared his teeth in the semblance of a smile.

'What do you want?' Richard asked warily.

'Just a few questions, Sir. May I come in?'

'I suppose so.' Richard reluctantly led him into the living room. He wondered whether he should offer the policeman a cup of tea, but immediately dismissed the thought. It might prolong the visit.

DS Johnson sat on the sofa and leant back against the cushions with an air of studied casualness. 'We've been following up your activities, Mr. Jarman, on the day that the nun, Sister Francis, disappeared.'

'I've already told your colleagues,' Richard said wearily, 'I walked the dog up the hill and a woman--'

'Yes, your story has already been investigated, Mr. Jarman. We found the woman and she told us that ...' He took a notebook from his pocket and with obvious relish read from it, 'a stupid young man allowed his ugly dog to foul my front garden.'

Richard bridled at the adjectives. 'Well if she confirmed that she saw me, what do you want now?'

'You told my colleagues that you went to Potters Bar in search of a group called the Inheritors of the New Kingdom who you believe may have abducted the nun?'

'That's right'

The officer smiled. 'That has been followed up too.'

'And?'

'We went to an office rented by this group and so far as we can tell, it is a perfectly legitimate enterprise --'

'I didn't say it wasn't,' Richard retorted. 'But I have read that the sect is proscribed in America.'

'That may be so, but it isn't proscribed in this country, and for the moment we are concerned only with finding a missing person. The gentleman in the office said he had no knowledge of any meeting held last Thursday and that he deals only with the distribution of religious pamphlets and other publications produced by the group. We then checked out the disused theatre where you claim you saw a group of men looking at a map.'

'And?'

'The theatre is owned by the council and is under a demolition order. They say it has been boarded up for years. We were given permission to search the premises, but there was nothing in the room you described except some screens, a platform and a stack of plastic chairs.'

'Well those guys definitely held a meeting there,' Richard protested. 'It was pretty dusty so there must have been footprints and stuff.'

DS Johnson read aloud from the notebook he was holding. 'There was evidence that someone may have broken into the premises. The padlock on one of the side doors was shiny whereas the others were rusty. There were a number of footprints in the corridor and in a former rehearsal room. Two eyewitnesses who were in a launderette on the afternoon in question, told us that at about four o'clock, a group of men ran up the road as though in pursuit of someone, then returned some minutes later.'

'There you are. That's exactly what I told your colleagues,' said Richard triumphantly.

'OK.' The policeman leaned forward and fixed him with a severe gaze. 'Let's say that you did go to that theatre and that you *did* meet some … gentlemen there. We have no evidence that those men were members of a proscribed American sect called Inheritors of the New Kingdom.'

'But I saw some of them came out of the publications office,' Richard muttered sulkily.

'That doesn't prove anything. And what we still don't understand is why you believe the sect called Inheritors of the New Kingdom is responsible for the nun's disappearance.'

Richard sighed. 'I've already explained this to your colleagues. I thought the men who accosted Sister Francis in the street could have been the same ones who called on me and beat up the old homeless guy. He used to be a member of the Inheritors but he ran away. That's probably why they attacked him. I've read that the Inheritors punish deserters.'

'McAllister's attackers haven't yet been identified. But why would the same men who attacked the vagrant then accost the nun? And why would they visit you? So far as I know, you and the nun aren't members of the sect.'

'Of course we're not. The only thing Sister Francis and I have in common is that we both saw something weird in the sky on the nights when two local recreation grounds were destroyed.'

'Ah yes,' sneered DS Johnson. 'Your UFO.'

Richard felt his face go red. 'I don't know what else to call it.'

'You believe those men may have taken the nun just because she saw a UFO?'

'Yes.'

'That seems rather far-fetched, Mr. Jarman, if I may say so.'

'You may say whatever you like,' Richard retorted, 'I'm only suggesting what might have happened to her. And the men I saw in that theatre were definitely talking about the arson attacks.'

'That is an entirely separate issue, Mr. Jarman. 'I'm concerned with a missing person and I believe you know more than you are admitting.'

'That's crazy,' Richard snapped. 'You have absolutely no reason to think I had something to do with Sister Francis's disappearance.'

'Oh but we have, Mr. Jarman! You claim that two other people besides yourself have been approached by members of a mysterious sect. One of them was viciously assaulted and has since died, and the other has disappeared in mysterious circumstances. But you, Mr. Jarman, you have not been accosted and you have not disappeared!' DS Johnson's brows formed arcs of mock surprise. 'Not only have you *not* been attacked or abducted by these people, but you claim to have gate-crashed one of their meetings, in the course of which there was some kind of an altercation from which you escaped totally unscathed. You must admit this looks a bit odd, Mr. Jarman.'

'It wasn't an altercation,' Richard countered indignantly. 'When they heard me sneeze, they ran after me and I escaped.' He realised with a sinking heart how feeble this must sound. He wondered whether to mention the Inheritors' message on the internet forum, but decided against it on the grounds that it would only reinforce the officer's suspicion that he was either lying or mad.

'I find it very odd,' the officer continued, 'that although you say you witnessed exactly the same phenomenon as the vagrant and the nun, you have neither been attacked nor abducted by the people you describe as extremely dangerous.'

'I've just been lucky,' Richard replied morosely. 'If they'd caught me when I ran away from that theatre, they probably *would* have attacked me.'

'Well when they do attack you, be so kind as to let me know!' The policeman passed Richard a card and rose from the sofa. 'Here's a direct number for you to ring. The fact remains, Mr. Jarman, that you were the last person outside the convent who contacted the nun before she disappeared. So when you decide you're ready to tell us the whole story, please give me a call.'

Part 2
The Inheritors

Chapter 19

On Tuesday morning, Richard put on his smartest trousers and a white shirt. As an afterthought, he slipped the rosary Sister Francis had given him into his jacket pocket. Although he had no particular religious beliefs, the humble object had become a kind of talisman against evil and it seemed appropriate to take it with him on his quest for the missing nun. He had no idea what awaited him in Harpenden or what he would do when he encountered the Inheritors of the New Kingdom. He wasn't even sure if he *would* encounter them. Although he assumed Fiona had deciphered their message correctly, he had failed to locate an area called High Place on the map he downloaded. Maybe it was too small to merit a mention.

Before leaving, he took Maggie round to Fiona's parents' house.

'You will be careful, won't you, Ric?' she asked anxiously.

'Don't worry about me,' he replied with a nonchalance he didn't feel. 'I should be back in time for the cinema, but take this…' he handed her DS Johnson's card…'in case the Inheritors decide to abduct *me* as well as Sister Francis!' Despite his forced laugh, he felt extremely nervous. What was he getting into?

He left Fiona some tins of dog food and set off in his father's car.

On arriving in Harpenden, he asked a taxi driver for directions. The man scratched his head, reflected for a moment and said he thought there was a housing estate called High Place a few miles north of the town. He gave Richard elaborate instructions how to get there.

He set off again and after several wrong turns and twice doubling back on his tracks, he eventually found himself on the edge of a small housing estate which he assumed was the right one although he couldn't see a street sign. He was puzzled. With its tiny terraced houses and minuscule front gardens, it didn't seem the kind of location where a religious sect might hold a meeting.

He stopped outside number one and was surprised that there were no other cars parked nearby. A dog in the neighbouring house barked furiously as he walked up to the door and rang the bell.

There was no answer. He rang again and waited. Out of the corner of his eye, he glimpsed a movement. The net curtain behind the nearest window was pulled aside, revealing the anxious face of an elderly woman. 'Who is it?' she quavered.

Richard stepped up to the window and gave what he hoped was a reassuring smile. 'Hello! I've come for the meeting.'

She looked confused. 'The what?'

'The New Kingdom meeting.'

Her face disappeared and after a few moments he heard a bolt being pulled back. The door opened slightly and the woman peered at him suspiciously through the small gap allowed by a security chain. 'Who did you say you're looking for?'

He smiled again. 'I'm looking for a group called the Inheritors of the New Kingdom. They're holding a meeting at this address.'

The woman looked bewildered. 'Meeting? There's no meeting here. This is my house. You've been given the wrong information.'

'But this is High Place?'

'No, this is Hyde Place.'

Richard cursed inwardly. The taxi-driver must have misheard him. 'I'm sorry to have bothered you,' he said politely. 'I don't suppose you know where *High* Place is?'

'No.' She shut the door then re-opened it a crack. 'I think there was somewhere called High Place a couple of miles away, near the old railway yard.'

Richard stepped eagerly back to the door. 'Can you tell me where that is?'

The old woman rattled off some garbled directions.

It took him about fifteen minutes to locate the old railway line, now covered in a profusion of weeds. He drove alongside it for about a mile, then turned left into a steep and narrow road which came to an abrupt end in a desolate open space littered with burnt-out cars and rusted pieces of machinery. Plastic bags, squashed drink cans and broken bottles were strewn across the ground. A scrawny grey cat prowled nervously among the piles of rubbish.

He got out of the car and gazed dubiously around him. Could this be the right place? After taking a few steps away from the car, he spotted a building a few hundred yards away, partially hidden behind some trees. As he picked his way towards it, he saw that it was abandoned: many of the windows were broken and the walls daubed with graffiti. He stepped cautiously over the flattened stakes of a collapsed wooden fence and came to a halt when he reached a crumbling gatepost. The name on the stone plaque was still faintly visible, *1 High Place*. His heart began to pound when, a little further on, he saw, neatly lined up under the trees, three gleaming black saloon cars.

He took a deep breath and ignoring the stern injunction to *fuck off* spray-painted on the wall next to the gatepost, marched with as much confidence as he could muster to the front door of the building. Before he could reach it, it swung open with a suddenness that made him start.

A man with close-cropped dark hair emerged. He smiled, revealing a set of unbelievably white teeth, and extended his hand. 'Witnesser of the Light?'

'Yes.' Richard cautiously took the man's hand and winced as his own was crushed and retained in a vice-like grip.

'Welcome! I am Brother Kevin. We hoped you would understand our message and find your way to us. You're very late!'

With difficulty, Richard prised his hand free. 'It took me a while to find the house.'

'Come in, Brother, the others are waiting.'

Brother Kevin led him along a passage and into a gloomy and dilapidated room. The wallpaper was peeling and it was devoid of furniture except for about ten plastic bucket chairs arranged in a circle. The men sitting on them fell silent as Richard and his escort entered. In their identical dark suits, he thought they looked sinister, like a coven of male witches.

Brother Kevin prodded him forward. 'Brothers, this is Witnesser of the Light. He received our message.'

Richard couldn't make out whether the collective murmur was a greeting, approval or surprise.

A grey-haired man stood up. With a start, Richard recognised him as the one who had unfurled the map on the platform in the disused theatre. Once again his hand was clasped in a bone-crunching grip.

'Welcome brother! I am Brother Isaac, leader of the British Chapter of the Inheritors of the New Kingdom. And you are…?'

'Richard--'

'That will suffice. The Inheritors use only Christian names. We are delighted to have you with us, Brother Richard.' The man's smile didn't quite reach his eyes. He did a rapid round of introductions that Richard barely heard as he attempted to calm his nerves. Each of the men stood up and shook his numbed hand, and he was uncomfortably aware of them encircling him in a manner that made flight impossible. The way they spoke struck him as odd. Although they had an accent he took to be American, their speech was formal and rather old-fashioned without the kind of colloquialisms he would have expected Americans to use.

'We understand that you have seen the light?' continued the man who had introduced himself as Brother Isaac. He leaned close to Richard so that their faces were almost touching.

Richard backed away. 'Yes.'

Brother Isaac fixed him with an unblinking gaze. 'Few people find their way directly to us. We usually have to find *them* and *persuade* them to come to us. That is why we - my companions here and I myself - are called the Persuaders. What exactly led you in our direction, Brother Richard?'

Richard tried to conceal his mounting panic. 'I… had a strange experience. I saw something recently that made me believe … that … something great and significant is about to happen.'

The men greeted this in silence.

'Please continue, Brother Richard,' murmured Brother Isaac silkily.

'Well, I … saw something that … erm … suggested that we might be approaching the end of the world. I tried to tell people about it but no-one would believe me. Then I went on the internet to try and find others who had come to the same conclusion. I found some references to the Inheritors of the New Kingdom, and when I looked you up and found a text about the End Time. I knew you were the group I was looking for.'

'*That* is how you found us?' Brother Isaac didn't sound convinced.

'I couldn't find an email or HQ address,' Richard continued, trying desperately to stop his voice coming out as a nervous squeak, 'so I left a message for you on some internet forums hoping you would pick it up.'

He gave a false laugh. 'You're not easy to find. I was expecting you to have a church or a permanent headquarters.'

Brother Isaac smiled grimly. 'Our communities are scattered and we are obliged to keep their location secret. There are people who find our beliefs and practices unacceptable and who would like to destroy us. For that reason we always hold our meetings in different and secret locations.'

'And this is one of them?'

Brother Isaac looked at him searchingly. 'We have been concentrating our mission near areas where certain events have recently taken place. You understand my meaning, Brother Richard?'

Richard nodded. 'You mean the destruction of green areas? Plant life?'

'Precisely. Events that are precursors to the End Time that will soon be upon us.'

There was a collective murmur from the group of men.

'Do you share our mission, Brother Richard?' continued Brother Isaac. 'Do you share our desire to save those who are worthy of being redeemed, in readiness for the Second Coming?'

'I do,' Richard answered nervously. For the first time it struck him that the two men who had come to his door may not have been searching specifically for him. They may simply have been going from house to house, proselytising after the destruction of Fonthill Recreation Ground.

'Have you been joined by others who have witnessed the sign?' he asked, hoping to be given a clue to Sister Francis's whereabouts.

Brother Isaac ignored the question. 'If you are joining us, Brother, you must undertake an initiation process.'

Richard gulped. 'What kind of initiation?'

'In preparation for the Last Judgment, all new members must be cleansed of their former wrongdoing and offer their allegiance to the Healer.'

'The Healer?'

'Our supreme leader, Abraham R.'

At the sound of the name, the men bowed their heads and murmured some words that Richard couldn't understand. It sounded like some kind of invocation or prayer.

'Brother Noah?' Brother Isaac beckoned to someone standing behind Richard, 'It is time to depart.'

Before Richard realised what was happening, a piece of cloth was wrapped round his eyes and secured tightly at the back of his head. 'Hey!' he cried, tugging at the material. 'What's going on?'

Hands seized his shoulders and he was forcibly turned and propelled back along the passage. He stumbled but the press of men around him kept him upright. Behind him he heard Brother Isaac's voice intoning, 'The day of His wrath is coming and who shall be able to stand?'

He was marched outside. He heard car doors open and slam. Someone pushed his head down and he was bundled roughly into a car and on to the back seat. Someone else with an overpowering smell of aftershave, climbed in beside him. 'Move up!' he ordered. Another man got in on his other side, pressing against him so that he was squashed uncomfortably between the two. The car shook as others climbed into the front seats.

'You can't do this!' Richard protested, trembling with panic. 'This is abduction. Where are you taking me?'

Brother Isaac's voice came from the front of the car. 'You are not yet one of us, Brother Richard. Until you are, we cannot reveal our destination.'

The car started and after a few minutes he felt it jolting back along the track he had recently driven along himself. Squashed between the two men, he experienced a gamut of emotions: terror, indignation and rage. 'Where are you taking me?' he repeated, striving to prevent his voice from shaking.

'To one of our communities,' replied Isaac.

'But *where* is that?'

As there was no reply to his repeated questions, Richard abandoned his attempts to elicit information but his ears remained alert to every sound. The men on either side of him were silent and he could hear the two in front conversing in low voices. Behind the buzz of their voices and the noise of the engine, there was a roar of passing traffic and he deduced that they were now travelling on a main road or motorway.

His stomach knotted in panic. What would happen to his father's car that he'd left in the disused railway yard? And what about Maggie? If he wasn't released, how long could Fiona continue looking after her? And how soon would she leave it before contacting DS Johnson?

An interminable period passed. He felt slightly nauseous and his mouth was dry. He realised that he hadn't had anything to eat or drink since breakfast. 'Could I have some water?' he asked eventually. 'And something to eat?'

There was a grunt from one of the men in the front and about twenty minutes later, the car stopped. The vehicle shook as some of the men, including the one sitting on his right, climbed out. Richard could hear voices and engines stopping and starting up outside. Perhaps they had arrived at a service station or a café. Some minutes elapsed then the car door on his right opened again.

'Take this, Brother. It's water. I've loosened the lid.' A small bottle was thrust into his hands. He pulled off the lid and gulped some of the water, then felt the car shake again as the man resumed his seat next to him. He addressed Richard again. 'Here's something to eat, Brother. Hold out your hand. I've removed the wrapping.'

Something soft and flabby was pressed into Richard's right hand. It felt like a sandwich. He took a bite. The filling was cheese, a piece of which fell onto his lap. From the sounds around him, he could tell that the other men in the car were also eating and drinking.

Eventually the car moved off again. Soon afterwards, he heard traffic passing at speed. Another motorway? The blindfold was tight and beginning to chafe. 'Look, guys,' he said, making an effort to sound calm, 'can't you take this thing off? I came to meet you of my own free will. There's no need to cover my eyes.'

Brother Isaac answered from the front. 'We cannot take any risks, Brother Richard, until we know that you are a true believer.'

'But it's too tight. It hurts.'

'It can be loosened.'

Richard felt hands fumble behind his head and the blindfold was slackened.

Snatches of speech and music were now coming from the front of the car. One of the men appeared to be trying different radio stations, finally settling on one that was broadcasting a news bulletin. Richard didn't pay much attention to it until one of the items claimed his immediate attention. 'There are reports,' announced a female voice, 'that parts of some tropical rainforests in South America have been damaged by fire.'

'Turn it up!' One of the men exclaimed excitedly.

'There are no reports of human casualties although people living in the forests are being encouraged to move away. The United Nations Emergency Council has called a meeting to discuss ways of counteracting these acts of eco-terrorism.'

The newsreader's voice was replaced by the grave tones of the UN Secretary General. 'These acts of aggression threaten to create a worldwide catastrophe that we must all unite to prevent. The World Health Organisation is circulating information on precautions ...'

His next words were drowned by sounds that sent shivers down Richard's spine. *Laughter!* The men in the car seemed to be exulting in what they had heard.

'Brothers!' Isaac's voice again. 'Rejoice! The Earth has started to die, just as the Healer prophesied. We are nearing the End Time.'

Richard gasped as the men gave a collective cheer.

The man on his left elbowed him in the ribs. 'Not long to wait now, Brother. The non-believers will die and meet their just deserts.'

Richard winced but made no comment.

'You do not rejoice, Brother Richard?' one of the men asked.

Richard hesitated before muttering, 'I can't welcome the death of innocent people.'

'In that case,' Brother Isaac responded, 'we must teach you to distinguish between the innocent and the guilty.'

Sensing an atmosphere of menace in the car, Richard made no further comment. Rigid with stress and anxiety, he wished he had never left Coronation Close. For all its dreariness and irritating residents, it was familiar and *normal.* He wished he could turn the clock back and return to the uneventful life he had been leading before he saw that UFO. He wished he could see Fiona, her quirky, gap-toothed grin and the endearing way in which she tossed back her shining curtain of hair. He wished he could be anywhere but stuck in this car with sinister men who thought the end of the world was a cause for celebration.

Someone switched off the radio and the four Inheritors lapsed into silence.

Richard's nervousness was replaced by exhaustion and after a while he dozed off. He woke to find someone tugging on his arm. It took him a moment to remember where he was and when he did, it was with a renewed sense of shock and panic. He felt a blast of cold air as the car doors were opened.

'We're getting out for a moment, Brother,' said the man who had roused him. 'You need to do the same.'

The man on Richard's other side gave him a push, causing him to stumble out of the car and nearly fall in the process. His legs were stiff and he had pins and needles in his hands. Wherever they were now, it was quiet and traffic-free. His arms were grasped again and he was led away from the car. He could feel tufts of grass and stones underfoot.

'Do what you need to do, Brother,' said a voice he now recognised as that of the one called Saul. He realised from the sounds around him that he was expected to relieve himself, and did so with some embarrassment, conscious of the other men standing close to him.

They set off again and soon the car's motion lulled him back into an uneasy sleep from which he woke intermittently, feeling cramped and uncomfortable. By now he had lost all track of time. Twice the car stopped again. The first time, another sandwich and a polystyrene cup of tea were placed in his hands. Later there was another comfort stop, which, from the nearby roar of passing traffic, was apparently in a lay-by.

Alternately sleeping and waking, Richard felt he was living in a nightmare.

Chapter 20

'We get out here, Brother.'

Richard woke with a start to find that the car had stopped yet again. He felt cold and cramped. Many hours must have passed since he had arrived at the house in Harpenden.

'What time is it?' he asked.

Unusually, he received a reply. 'It's just before one a.m.'

'One o'clock?' He was amazed. What destination had taken that long to get to? Once again he was manhandled out of the car. The air was distinctly colder now and a blast of wind struck his face like a slap, restoring him to instant alertness. They appeared to be in an exposed open space.

His two minders walked him across what felt like gravel, then onto a harder surface. A few minutes later he was half pulled, half pushed up some steep, metallic-sounding steps.

'Duck your head!' warned the man in front of him.

He lowered his head and stumbled forward. Someone pulled him to the left and he staggered and nearly fell. When he had regained his footing, he was pushed sideways and on to a hard seat.

There was a thunderous roar of an engine and he felt the seat beneath him vibrate.

'We can take that off now, Brother Richard.'

To his immense relief the blindfold was removed, but his eyes took a while to adjust. He squeezed his eyelids together and massaged his temples.

'Put your seatbelt on.'

When Richard's sight cleared, he found that he was in the cabin of a small plane. Brother Kevin was in the seat next to him and two of the other men were sitting in front of them. From the conversations he had heard in the car, he guessed they were Saul and Noah. Isaac had disappeared. Perhaps he was piloting the plane.

He was gripped with panic. Where were they taking him? Somewhere abroad? 'Where are we going?' he asked, fumbling with the seatbelt, but his voice was lost as the plane taxied off then rose steeply into the air.

He turned to Brother Kevin and shouted, 'Where are we going?'

Ignoring him, the man leaned back and closed his eyes.

Rigid with anxiety, Richard wondered if he dared take out his mobile and ring the police, but decided it would be too risky.

It was a bumpy and uncomfortable journey and several times he fought off waves of nausea. He fell into an uneasy doze but was jerked into consciousness when the plane started its steep descent and bumped alarmingly along the ground before coming to an abrupt halt.

'Follow me, Brother.'

Richard unbuckled his seatbelt and clambered after Kevin who opened the cabin door and jumped down on to the ground. There were no steps this time, and Richard's limbs were so stiff that when he jumped in his turn, he landed painfully, jarring his knees and ankles. He picked himself up, shivering in the brisk wind, and looked around for clues to their whereabouts. It wasn't entirely dark and he could make out a long landing strip fenced on either side and flanked by dark hills. A windsock flapped like an orange kite in the distance.

Noah and Saul jumped down from the passenger door and after a short, muffled conversation, walked briskly away. Brother Isaac then exited from a door in the cockpit, and stood muttering into a mobile phone.

Richard turned to Brother Kevin. 'Where the fuck are we?'

Without answering, the man seized his arm and marched him in the same direction that the others had taken. Brother Isaac walked behind.

After a while they came to a narrow path that sloped downwards. Now Richard's nostrils were picking up a salty tang and he could hear the sound of waves and the rhythmic clanking of boat rigging. Peering into the distance, he could make out a small jetty surrounded by boats bobbing and swaying in the wind. Tiny dots of light flickered in the distance.

They walked in single file to the end of the jetty where a small boat with an outboard motor was secured to a post. Brother Noah jumped in and Saul followed. Prompted by Kevin, Richard stumbled awkwardly into the vessel, feeling it rock beneath him as he tried to maintain his balance. He sat down on the narrow wooden seat on the starboard side and struggled into the lifejacket that Saul tossed across to him.

When they were all seated, the boat set off at speed, buffeted by the waves.

Richard shivered in his light clothes and his stomach churned as the vessel pitched and tossed its way through the swollen sea. The wind stung his eyes and snapped round his ears, and he was continuously splashed and sprinkled with cold water. Finally, to his relief, the boat slowed down and he could make out the dark outlines of small islands.

Brother Noah navigated expertly between some exposed rocks and headed towards a jetty that was just visible in front of some dark and craggy cliffs. As the boat bumped alongside, Isaac jumped out and caught hold of the rope that Noah tossed to him and tied it to a post.

Brother Kevin, who was sitting opposite Richard, climbed out of the boat and gestured him to follow.

Richard clambered unsteadily over the side. 'Where are we going?' he asked Isaac, not expecting an answer.

'We have come to one of our communities, Brother. Here you will be initiated as a member of the Inheritors of the New Kingdom.'

Flanked by Kevin, Richard followed the other two men along a strip of rocky shore at the base of a lofty cliff. After a few minutes they turned and started to ascend a steep path. Chilled by the fierce wind, he stumbled wearily up the slope, occasionally slipping on small stones.

When they arrived at the top of the cliff, the Inheritors quickened their pace until they reached a pair of tall gates set in a stone wall topped with barbed wire. They swung open at a shout from Brother Isaac.

Richard nervously followed the men inside. As the gates snapped shut behind them, he looked wonderingly around him. They appeared to be in some sort of compound. He could see lines of identical huts interspersed with some larger stone buildings.

Brother Isaac grasped his arm. 'Noah will show you where to go, Brother. We will meet again in a few hours.'

Noah led him down a path between two lines of Nissan huts and stopped at the door of one which he opened. He shone a torch inside. Immediately to the left of the door there was a small curtained enclosure containing a narrow bed covered by a blanket, a wooden chair and a locker, on top of which lay a Bible.

'Catch some sleep, Brother,' Noah instructed him. 'Morning prayers are at six in the Prayer Hall and breakfast at half past in the canteen. Anyone will show you where they are. The men's washrooms and latrines are behind the huts.' He pulled the door shut behind him.

Shivering in the cold, Richard sat on the bed, took off his jacket and searched the pockets for his mobile but it wasn't there. His wallet had also disappeared. The Brothers must have removed them when he was sleeping in the car. He checked his wrist. At least he still had his watch. But how could he communicate with anybody now? Would Fiona have contacted DS Johnson? If she showed him the Inheritors' message, maybe this time he would take the matter seriously. Once the police located the house near the disused railway line, they would find his father's car and realise that something had happened to him. But how would they manage to pick up the Inheritors' trail and follow them to this remote island, wherever it was?

Exhausted, he removed his shoes and trousers, relieved to discover that his keys and the rosary were still in his trouser pocket. He put them under the pillow and climbed wearily into the narrow bed. The mattress was hard and unyielding but it was a relief to lie down. He pulled the coarse blanket over him. It was scratchy and smelled unpleasant. Lying in the semi darkness, he became aware of rhythmic breathing and occasional snores. Other people were sleeping beyond his tiny curtained space.

* * *

It seemed like only a few minutes had passed before Richard was shaken awake again. For a moment he didn't know where he was and his stomach clenched with fear when he saw an unfamiliar man bending over him, holding a bundle of clothes.

'Put these on, Brother,' the man said gruffly. 'Boots are on the floor. Prayers in twenty minutes.' He dropped the garments on the bed and left.

Still weary and shivering with cold and nervousness, Richard hauled himself reluctantly out of bed. He inspected the clothes: a thick grey sweater, grey jogging trousers, long woollen socks and a yellow oilskin jacket. He pulled the jumper and trousers over his shirt and underpants. They were far too big for him. He sat on the bed to put on the socks then eased his feet into the scruffy Wellingtons that his visitor had left beside the locker. Finally, he put on the oilskin jacket and stuffed his keys and rosary into one of its pockets.

He stood up and listened. There was no sound from the rest of the hut so he assumed his sleeping companions had departed. He waited for a few moments then, drawing back the rough curtain that enclosed his sleeping quarters, he cautiously explored the area beyond his own curtained enclosure. On each side of the hut there were three identical sleeping spaces, sparsely furnished and devoid of personal possessions.

He opened the door and stumbled out into the grey morning light, shivering as a fierce blast of moisture-laden wind struck his face. The raucous cries of sea birds assailed his ears. He was standing in a narrow thoroughfare between two rows of identical Nissan huts. Behind those facing him, he could see several taller, grey stone structures. Above one of them, wisps of white smoke snaked into the air. The entire compound appeared to be enclosed within a high wall. It was a bleak, forbidding-looking place, like a prison camp.

Someone hurried past him, a gaunt bearded man wearing clothes identical to his own.

'Excuse me, where are the washrooms?' Richard asked.

The man glanced at him incuriously. 'You a new brother? I'll show you.' He led Richard to the back of the hut and pointed to some crude wooden sheds with corrugated iron roofs that had been erected on a terrace a short distance below the main compound. 'Latrines and washrooms are down there.'

Richard stumbled down the slope and examined the facilities. The latrines were primitive - mere holes in the ground from which emanated a strong smell of human waste. Outside each of them there was a spade and a bucket of sand.

In the "washrooms", there were rainwater butts with rubber hoses that could direct water into plastic washbasins or, when hooked to a wooden post, over grubby plastic shower bases.

After relieving himself, he washed his face and hands with a slimy piece of soap he found in one of the basins and dried them on a stained towel hanging on a nail. Uncertain what to do next, he returned to the door of his hut. The compound was deserted and he could hear voices chanting in the distance. He followed the sound to a crumbling, grey stone building. Standing at the open door, he saw men and women standing in rows in separate halves of the room. The women, who seemed to be more numerous than the men, were wearing grey headscarves, shapeless grey jumpers and long grey skirts.

He entered cautiously and stood at the end of the last row of men. He noticed that most of them had beards. None took any notice of him.

Brother Isaac was conducting proceedings from a raised platform at the front of the room. 'The world will pass away,' he intoned, 'and the God of Heaven will set up a kingdom that will never be brought to ruin. The wicked will be cast off. Only the upright will remain.' He raised his arm and the men and women started to chant in unison.

Richard caught some now familiar words: 'Prepare ye for the End Time, the Second Coming. The just will be saved, the unjust consumed in the fires of Hell.'

His stomach started to growl with hunger. The only food he had eaten since breakfast the previous day were the sandwiches he had been given in the car.

After about half an hour the prayers came to an end and the men started to file out of the door. Richard followed them to another grey stone building and into a draughty room, sparsely furnished with long benches and trestle tables. He sat down at one with some of the other men. Their faces were expressionless and none spoke to him.

When the men were seated, the women entered and sat at tables on the opposite side of the room. A bell rang and Brother Saul said an interminable grace, after which the men walked in single file to a table where a tired-looking woman was doling thick grey porridge into bowls and a second woman was filling chipped mugs with tea from a large kettle.

Richard followed the men and carried his tea and porridge back to the table.

The women lined up for their breakfast only after all the men had received their rations.

No-one spoke during the meal and the silence was relieved only by the chink of spoons against bowls.

Richard found the milkless tea had an unpleasant taste. The porridge was lumpy and unsweetened but at least it was filling. After eating it, the men returned their empty bowls to the counter and a woman passed round baskets of rough bread. Richard ate a piece gratefully although it was dry and there was nothing to put on it.

Eventually the bell sounded again and the men started to file out of the canteen.

Brother Isaac materialised at Richard's side. 'Come with me, Brother.'

Wondering what was about to happen, Richard followed him out of the door.

Brother Isaac strode ahead and pointed towards one of the huts. 'That's the Training Centre where you will be initiated later this morning.' He walked rapidly on, gesturing for Richard to follow.

'What is this place?' panted Richard, hurrying to keep up with him but hampered by the over-large wellington boots.

'It's a former military camp left over from the Second World War. Some of the stone buildings are abandoned crofters' cottages.'

'What island are we on?' By now he suspected it was somewhere north of Scotland, hemmed in by the unforgiving North Sea.

Isaac ignored the question. 'We locate our communities as far away as possible from the pernicious influences of the modern world. We reside here on a temporary basis.'

'Only temporary?'

Brother Isaac stopped walking and gazed at him searchingly. 'Human time is running out, Brother. Didn't you tell us you have seen a sign that the End Time is imminent?'

'Yes,' Richard said quickly, 'but the community here seems ... very well established.'

'We have been here nearly two years, ever since ...' Isaac seemed to change his mind about what he was going to say. 'As you will have noticed, we live simply and without modern innovations. We try to live in a way that does not harm the world God has placed us in. This is one of our fundamental principles. We have no electricity or mains water. We use peat for cooking and heating, and as there is plentiful rain, we have no trouble collecting water.'

'But what do you do for supplies?' Richard peered at the small area of rugged landscape that could be glimpsed over the lower perimeter wall. 'Can anything grow here? It looks virtually barren.'

'You are right. It is hard to grow food here. The winds are harsh, there is little top soil and there are only a few hours of daylight in winter. We procure essential provisions from the mainland and of course we have a plentiful supply of fresh fish. We have imported soil, compost and seeds so that we can grow some crops in the summer months when we have almost unbroken daylight. We have erected greenhouses in a more sheltered area, down there.'

Brother Isaac led him behind a hut and pointed down towards two rudimentary wooden and glass structures that had been erected on the lower level of the slope behind the main compound. He then led Richard further through the settlement, pointing out several other grey stone buildings. One functioned as a laundry, where members could go once a week to get clean clothes; a larger one, at the far end, had a combined use as a nursery and a schoolhouse.

Richard was puzzled. 'But where are the children? I haven't seen or heard any.'

'They are kept apart,' Brother Isaac replied, striding ahead. 'After they are weaned, the children are taken from their mothers and housed in the nursery with the trusted women. As soon as they are able to talk, they move into the schoolhouse where they are taught only the Bible and practical skills. This is so that their minds will not be contaminated by erroneous information from the outside world.'

Richard stared at him, horrified. 'But it's cruel to take children from their mothers.'

Brother Isaac frowned. 'The Healer has forbidden personal attachments as they dilute devotion to God and the Truth.'

'How do the women tolerate being separated from their children?'

'They are obliged to accept it. Girls are taught to be obedient, to keep house and have children. After age twelve, they are given in marriage.'

Richard was even more shocked. 'That's underage. It's against the law.'

Isaac smiled. 'It is not against *God's* law. Inheritors are allowed to have three wives.'

'Three?' Richard spluttered.

'Yes, three. Women in our community are subservient to men, as is right and proper. The women take care of all the cleaning, washing and cooking. They are not allowed to leave the compound.'

Richard looked pityingly at the women who were now scurrying around the compound in their shapeless clothes, carrying brooms and mops. All of them studiously avoided eye contact with him. 'What do the men do?' he asked, striving to keep his tone casual.

They had now reached the perimeter fence and were passing the gates through which Richard and his abductors had entered in the early morning. Next to it was a kind of wooden sentry box. A man stood inside, a pair of binoculars in his hand.

'The highest echelon,' responded Brother Isaac, 'is the Persuaders some of whom you have already met. We are responsible for religious training and spreading the Truth. The next echelon, the Trustees, is responsible for keeping accounts, procuring supplies and ensuring that the compound is managed and run according to our principles. Then we have a third group - the Anglers. Fish is an essential part of our diet here. Finally there are the Subordinates, to which you will belong.'

Richard gulped. 'What do the Subordinates do?'

'The Subordinates do the heavy work - maintaining the buildings, digging trenches for latrines, preparing the fish, that kind of thing. The Subordinates are not allowed to leave the island.'

'Why not?'

Brother Isaac was silent for a moment and when he replied his voice was hard. 'In the past, some of our members deserted the commune and returned to the path of untruth and wickedness. Now only the Persuaders, the Trustees and the Anglers are allowed off the island.' He gripped Richard's arm. 'The Inheritors of the New Kingdom do not tolerate traitors, Brother Richard.'

Richard attempted to conceal his alarm.

The grip on his arm tightened. 'Remember this, Brother,' Isaac continued, 'the gates here are permanently locked and the boats are chained up when not in use.' He released Richard's arm. 'You will have noticed on our journey here that the sea is extremely rough and there are dangerous rocks. There is only one navigable channel to the island. Only the most experienced boatmen among us can get on and off the island safely.'

Richard decided to probe. 'Where does the community's funding come from?'

'You ask many questions, Brother. In each of our settlements, there is a Trustee who keeps accounts for our leader, the Healer. All new adherents are required to give any money and worldly goods they possess to our community, as you yourself will be required to do ...'

Not bloody likely, Richard thought, although his "worldly goods" didn't amount to much; he hadn't paid off his credit card and his bank account was overdrawn. 'Why do they call him the Healer?' he asked.

'Because he heals souls by leading people on to the paths of right-eousness.'

They turned back towards the main compound and Isaac accompanied him to the door of his hut. 'The Subordinates are allocated specific daily tasks,' he announced. 'As you have not yet been allocated yours, Brother, this is a good time for silent prayer and contemplation. You still have your watch? At eight thirty, please come to the Training Centre where you will be initiated. Eight thirty,' he repeated and walked away.

Richard entered the hut and found that a small towel, a tiny square of soap and a toothbrush had been placed on his bed. He took the Bible from his locker and strolled back through the door, pretending to peer earnestly at the open pages. Several women carrying mops and brooms hurried past without giving him a glance.

He ambled behind the hut and descended the slope that led to the lower level of the compound. In case he was being watched, he continued to glance at the Bible, occasionally moving his lips as though in prayer. After a while he realised he was approaching the ramshackle greenhouses. Curiosity led him towards the door of the largest one. Through the salt-lashed glass walls, he could see the shapes of numerous plants. He ventured inside, relishing the warm humidity and peaty smell that provided a welcome contrast to the sharpness of the brine-laden wind outside.

He wandered up the narrow passageway between shelves covered with pots and trays of sprouting greenery. Towards the back of the greenhouse, a small, plump woman, dressed in the baggy jumper, shapeless skirt and headscarf all the women wore, was bending over some plants and pruning their stems. Not wishing to disturb her, he was about to tiptoe back to the door when his elbow collided noisily with some plant pots.

Startled, the woman turned round. 'Jesus, Mary and Joseph!' she exclaimed, dropping the secateurs. 'It's yourself, so it is!'

Richard stared at her, stunned. 'Sister Francis!' he exclaimed joyfully, 'you're here! You're safe!' Overcome with relief, he bounded towards her, tripped on an uneven board and nearly toppled the little nun over.

She steadied herself against a shelf. 'Ay, I'm safe, thanks be to God, so don't you go knocking me through the glass, now!'

She adjusted her spectacles, then caught hold of his hand, shook it vigorously and continued to hold on to it. 'This is a miracle, so it is, a miracle! There was I thinking I'd never see anyone I knew ever again. The Good Lord has obviously been watching over me. But how did you find me, Richard? How did you know I was here?'

Richard beamed. 'When I found out you were missing, I suspected the Inheritors had something to do with it. I hope they didn't hurt you.'

She relinquished his hand. 'Och no, thanks be to God ... but they frightened me, they did indeed.'

'What happened? How did they get you?'

'Two of those men, the ones with the teeth I told you about, they broke into the convent garden and made me get into a car. Then they drove me to this place. It was a terrible long journey in a car, so it was. They made me get in a bumpy wee plane, then a wee boat that tossed and turned-- '

'Did they tell you *why* they brought you here?'

'They said I've been specially chosen because I saw that thing in the sky that you and I saw, Richard. And because I've dedicated my life to God, they think the Messiah will reveal Himself to *me* when He comes again, poor deluded souls that they are!' She gazed at him sadly. 'Between you and me, I think they're a bit queer in the head. But if the Good Lord has seen fit to send me to this place then it means He has a job for me to do. Now tell me, Richard, how did *you* get here? Have you brought the police with you?'

'Unfortunately not, I'm on my own. I told the police I thought the Inheritors had taken you but they weren't convinced, so I thought that if I could locate them myself, I'd be able to find you. I looked them up on the internet and went to meet them, and ended up here, the same way that you did.'

She seized his hand again and squeezed it. 'God bless us and save us, then it's a miracle that you found me, it is indeed.'

'When I told the police I thought the Inheritors had kidnapped you, they thought *I* had something to do with it!'

'You?' She looked astonished. 'And why would you be wanting to kidnap an old woman like myself?'

'That's what I said! Oh, sorry, Sister, I didn't mean to say you're old.'

She smiled at him indulgently. 'I've seen many more summers than you, young man!'

'You've lost weight,' Richard said with some concern. 'How have you coped in this awful place?'

She smiled gently. 'Don't you be worrying about me, now. It's the other poor souls we should be worrying about, the women and the children. Those so-called brothers don't give me any grief. They keep me apart from the other women. I have a sleeping hut to myself and my task is working in the greenhouses. No-one else comes down here except some of the men, and that's only when there's heavy stuff to move.'

For Richard's benefit, Sister Francis outlined the commune's daily routine: a monotonous sequence of communal prayers, frugal meals and manual work.

'I suppose it's not that different from my life in the convent,' she said sadly, 'but we sisters embraced that life with joy. There's no joy in this place.' She took off her glasses and mopped her eyes with her sleeve. 'I've been at Our Lady of Lourdes nearly forty years you know. It's my home. I miss it and the other sisters.'

He smiled sympathetically. 'Of course you miss it. Do you know what island we're on?'

She shook her head. 'I've been told it's part of the Shetlands but I haven't been out of this compound since I was brought here.'

He caught her hand. 'We've got to get away from here, Sister. I could try and steal one of the boats.'

She regarded him sadly. 'Are you an experienced sailor, young man? We'd drown for sure. Did you see the rocks and how rough the sea is when they brought you here? Besides, you'd never be able to leave the compound. The gate is always locked and there's someone watching it at all times. And you must be very careful, Richard. We can't be seen speaking to each other.'

'Why not?' Richard looked warily at the salt-caked glass walls of the greenhouse. He didn't think anyone could see in from outside.

'Men and women are only supposed to communicate with each other if they're married. Did you know the men are allowed to have *three* wives?' She clucked her tongue disapprovingly. 'The poor women can't even keep their own children. It's sinful, so it is, unnatural!' She gazed sorrowfully into the distance, then brought her attention back to him.

'Tell me what's been happening, Richard. I've lost all track of the world outside since coming to this God-forsaken place.'

Richard told her that the fire attacks were still spreading round the globe.

She looked horrified. 'Lord bless us and save us. It's must be the work of the Devil himself.'

'Well *they* …' Richard gestured in the direction of the main compound '… *they* think it's the work of God; a sign that the day of reckoning is coming.'

Sister Francis lowered her voice. 'One of the women told me that a healer is coming to prepare this group of souls for the end of the world. Would you believe that? That's why the men they call Persuaders are returning to the island. The one they call Saul has gone to fetch the others. I suppose they can't get all of them in that wee plane at once.'

Richard felt a stab of excitement mingled with fear. 'You mean Abraham R is coming here?'

She looked bewildered. 'Abraham R? Who's that?'

'The leader of the Inheritors. They call him the Healer.' He glanced at his watch. 'I'd better go. I'm having some kind of initiation. I'll try to come and see you again as soon as I can. We have to think of a way of getting out of here.'

She accompanied him to the door of the greenhouse. 'You take care, Richard. These men are dangerous. Pray to the Lord to protect you.'

He fished inside one of the pockets of his oilskin jacket and drew out the rosary. 'Don't worry, Sister. I've still got this.'

She smiled. 'Then Our Lady will keep you safe from harm.'

Chapter 21

Brother Isaac, attired in a long-sleeved white robe, was waiting outside the hut that served as the Training Centre. His expression was severe. 'I said eight thirty, Brother Richard. Here, everyone is expected to keep to the prescribed times.'

'I know, I'm sorry,' Richard stammered, red-faced from the exertion of running back to the main compound. 'I lost track of time. I was contemplating some … passages in the Bible.'

'Which passages in particular, Brother?'

Richard sought desperately to remember some words or passages in the Bible. 'Erm…the Book of Revelations, Armageddon.'

'That is appropriate,' Brother Isaac murmured as they entered the hut.

Richard found himself in a narrow room that was empty of furniture except for some benches stacked against the walls. A large image of Abraham R was suspended from the ceiling at one end. Posters with quotations from the Bible were hung at intervals along the walls. In the middle of the room a number of men were standing together, talking. They too were wearing long white robes.

Richard felt a prickle of fear as they formed a circle round him.

'Brother Richard! Are you ready now to take the vows?' asked Isaac.

'Vows?'

'Those who join the Inheritors of the New Kingdom must swear allegiance to its beliefs, principles and rules. Are you ready?'

'I suppose so.' Richard felt anything *but* ready.

'Then you must kneel and hold the Bible in front of you with both hands.'

Richard lowered himself reluctantly on to his knees.

'Now, each of us will put a question to you in turn. In your answer you must repeat the words and each time you take the vow, you must bow down and kiss the Bible. Is that clear?'

'Yes,' he muttered, feeling extremely vulnerable in a kneeling position, encircled by white-robed men with beards.

'Brother Richard,' continued Brother Isaac, 'do you vow to carry out the Holy Word as written in the Good Book?'

'Er…yes,' he stammered.

'No!' snapped Isaac impatiently. 'Do as I told you. Make the declaration, then kiss the Bible!'

Richard gulped but felt he had no choice but to follow the man's instructions. 'I vow to carry out the Holy Word as written in the Good Book.' He bowed his head and kissed the Bible.

Each of the men then addressed a question to him in turn.

Do you vow to dedicate your life to God? Do you vow to live according to the principles of the Inheritors of the New Kingdom? Do you vow to obey the commands of our prophet and healer, Abraham R? Do you vow to give up the multiple evils of the outside world? Do you vow to give your worldly goods to the community?

Richard mechanically repeated the words, barely taking in what he was saying until one of the vows - *Do you vow not to fornicate with the wives of other brothers?* - nearly reduced him to hysteria. Did they think he would want to fornicate with one of those drab, harassed-looking women? He bit his lip and concentrated on his knees, which had started to hurt.

After he had repeated the vows, Brother Isaac ordered him to prostrate himself on the floor.

Uneasily he obeyed.

Isaac stood over him. 'Brother Richard,' he declared portentously, 'you have taken the vows! You are now a member of the Inheritors of the New Kingdom. Your thoughts and actions will henceforth be dedicated to the Holy Word as written in the Good Book. You shall join us in the new kingdom that has been prophesied. But …' his voice had a chilling edge '… should you break your vows or try to leave the sect, we will wreak a terrible vengeance. You must lie there for a while and meditate.'

Richard shivered as he lay face down on the cold wooden floor. These people weren't just crazy, they were psychopaths. If only he could recover his mobile and ring Fiona. He castigated himself for not having formulated a clear plan of action once he had met up with the Inheritors. His mission had been to find Sister Francis. This had been achieved, but now what? The situation she was in, that they *both* were in, was worse than he ever could have imagined.

He heard the sound of advancing footsteps and Brother Isaac's voice.

'You may rise now, Brother. The ceremony is over.'

He hauled himself stiffly to his feet and found that he and Isaac were alone in the room.

'Soon you will meet the Healer,' Isaac announced as they left the hut.

'The Healer is coming here?'

'Yes, he is coming to instruct us on the preparations we must make for the End Time. In the meantime, Brother, we have decided on the daily tasks you are to perform. Your morning task will be to prepare the fish for the day's meals. You will start tomorrow. '

'What?' exclaimed Richard who had never prepared a fish in his life, 'can't I do something else?'

Brother Isaac smiled unpleasantly. 'All new brothers must start with the humblest of tasks. As the Good Book says, "in all labour there is profit!" Your afternoon task will be to dig some new trenches for the men's latrines. Every month, we fill in the old ones.'

Richard suppressed a groan.

* * *

The rest of the day passed in a blur. He dozed through several tedious sessions of communal prayer and sat uneasily through frugal meals eaten in complete silence. He glanced round the prayer hall and canteen to see if he could spot Sister Francis, but didn't persevere in case his looking at the women was misconstrued.

The Inheritors retired to bed distressingly early, straight after evening prayers, when it was still light outside.

Richard also returned to his hut where he fretted at the lack of any form of distraction. The sole reading matter available was the Bible. No books, newspapers, radios or electronic devices were permitted to pollute the minds of the members of the Inheritors. He attempted to converse with some of the men sharing his hut but their responses to him were terse and unfriendly. Maybe they had been forbidden to speak to him. He wondered how they could bear the isolation and claustrophobia of the place. And when did they visit their "wives"? He assumed marital relations were strictly regulated.

Although still exhausted from the journey and stress, he couldn't sleep. Hours passed and all was quiet in the hut except for the heavy breathing and occasional snores of the other occupants. He tossed restlessly on his hard bed, reflecting on the day's events and the joyless nature of the sect's daily routine. He had been on the island less than twenty-four hours but felt he had been there for days. He longed to be back in his room in Coronation Close, sitting at his laptop calmly writing his thesis. *His thesis!* How long it was since he had even given it a thought. Why had he abandoned it when it was so near completion?

Eventually he got up, quietly opened the door and stepped outside. It was a cold, clear night and the sky was a revelation: a fathomless dome, sparkling with great clusters of stars, the like of which he had never seen further south. He gazed upwards for a long time, marvelling at the jewelled immensity. He wondered if it was possible to witness the Aurora Borealis from the island.

A brilliant dot of light slid suddenly, and with speed, across his line of vision - an aeroplane or another UFO going about its deadly business?

He shivered and went back inside.

Chapter 22

After breakfast the next day, Brother Isaac informed Richard that in order to perform his first task, the preparation of fish caught early that morning by the Anglers, he would have to leave the compound. Two "Trustees", Jacob and Ezra, accompanied him through the gates. They were carrying round metal containers, one of which they handed to him.

A watery sun appeared as they passed through the perimeter gates and for the first time Richard became aware of the scenic grandeur of the island. After the drabness of the compound, he found it uplifting to feast his eyes on the colours around him — the vertical tumble of cliffs dotted with multi-coloured wild flowers, the deep violet waters below, spattered with the inky reflections of rocks. In the far distance he could see a rugged, treeless landscape, its thin layer of topsoil scarred by pitiless winds, and the jagged ruins of some ancient stone habitations. Despite the screeching of seabirds wheeling and diving above the cliffs, the scene had a tranquillity that seemed at odds with the thinly masked tension he sensed among the Inheritors.

As they strode along the cliff path, Ezra remained silent but the other Trustee, Brother Jacob, a tall, wiry man with a tanned and deeply seamed face, engaged him in conversation. 'This a new place for ye, laddie?'

'Yes,' Richard replied cautiously. 'I've never been here before.'

'The weather takes some getting used to. We're lucky today. It's a clear morning. We call days like this "between weathers". When it's like this, you can see islands many miles away. But it can all change. We often get four seasons in a single day here. We could have a thick fog by lunchtime.' Jacob pointed across the sea towards the jagged protuberances of some Lilliputian islands in the distance. 'Those are the Out Skerries--'

The other man scowled and muttered something that sounded like a warning.

Richard gazed blankly ahead as though he hadn't heard, but mentally filed away this clue to his whereabouts.

'The light's unique up here,' Jacob continued. 'We have nineteen hours of daylight in the summer and it never really gets dark. Have ye heard of the "Simmer Dim"?'

'The what?'

'The Simmer Dim. In a few weeks time, and then until July, the sun will set around ten thirty in the evening and rise again at about three thirty. The five hours in between are a kind of dusk. We call it the Simmer Dim. If the sky is clear, you can even read outside during the night. In winter, though, we only have about six hours of daylight.'

'Wow!' Richard thought it must be intolerably bleak to be stranded in the compound during so many hours of darkness. 'What a lot of birds there are,' he observed.

'Ay.' Jacob scanned the sky. 'It's a birdwatcher's paradise up here. There are gannets, guillemots and fulmars round the coast, as well as terns, shags and cormorants. Birds come here from all over Europe, sometimes from Asia and America. It's quite common to see puffins, razorbills and kittiwakes. On some of the islands you get Bonxies.'

'Bonxies?'

'Great Skuas. They're quite rare. If you look over there --'

'We're not here for bird-watching, Brother!' snapped Ezra. 'Hurry or we'll be late.' He strode angrily ahead of them.

'Is this a kind of nature reserve, then?' Richard asked. After the taciturnity he had encountered among other members of the sect, he was relieved to meet one who seemed friendly and had interests beyond his religious beliefs.

'Ay, ye could say that,' Jacob replied. 'Seals are common here and sometimes you can see Harbour Porpoises and Minke whales. They're a bonny sight!' He lowered his voice. 'We mustn't let our beautiful world be destroyed, Brother! It must be prevented.'

Richard stared at him in astonishment. He had believed the Inheritors were hell-bent on seeing the planet consumed by flames. Was the man trying to convey a message to him? Before he could respond, Brother Jacob gave him a warning glance. They had caught up with Brother Ezra who was standing waiting, his expression hostile.

They continued down the cliff path in silence. When they reached the shore they turned right, passing a small jetty which Richard recognised as the one where he and the four men had disembarked early the previous morning. The boat that had brought them to the island had gone. Maybe Brother Saul had taken it on his way back to collect the other Persuaders. As they walked, he noticed a strong smell of fish.

After rounding a craggy point lapped by waves that washed over their boots, they arrived in a small rocky bay littered with nets, buckets and fishing tackle. Two fishing boats were tied up at the highest level of the shore. A bearded Angler in yellow oilskins was hauling a net over the side of a third boat at the edge of the water. Another was busily emptying wriggling fish into a container. Scores of screeching birds wheeled and swooped over his head.

A crude wooden hut had been erected at the base of the cliff. Brother Jacob took the container from the second Angler and filled a bucket with sea water before leading Richard inside. The hut contained two canvas chairs, an empty bucket and a large flat rock with red stains on its upper surface. As there was only room for two people inside, Brother Ezra stood watchfully at the door.

Brother Jacob put down the filled container and the bucket of water. He produced a sharp knife from the pocket of his oilskin. 'Have ye done this before?'

'Never,' Richard replied with a shudder.

Jacob sat down on the chair. 'Then watch me.' Taking a fish, he laid it on the rock, made a v-shaped cut at the anus, then slit it up to the gills and pulled out the entrails. 'Put the innards in the empty bucket,' he instructed Richard, 'then wash the fish in the one I've filled with sea water. We don't have ice but the water here's plenty cold enough. Then put the clean fish in one of the empty containers. When you've done them all, we'll take them back to the canteen. The birds will have the innards.'

Richard felt slightly nauseous. Some of the fish in the container were still wriggling. He preferred his fish cooked, covered in ketchup and on a plate. 'What kind of fish are they?' he asked, trying to conceal his discomfiture.

'These are mostly mackerel and herring, but the Anglers sometimes catch whitefish - haddock, whiting and cod. Now you have a go. Gut the fish with a smooth belly cut and make sure you don't leave any blood or viscera in the body cavity.' Brother Jacob stood up and Richard replaced him on the chair. He gingerly plucked a fish from the bucket, hating its wet, slithery feel and even more, its smell. He took the knife and plunged it into the fish then clumsily slit upwards between the gills.

'That's right,' Brother Jacob said approvingly. 'Now widen the gap with your hand and pull out the entrails.'

Richard reluctantly obeyed. He wanted to ask Jacob why he had mentioned saving the planet but was aware of the other man watching them intently through the door.

When he thought Richard had sufficiently mastered the skill, Brother Jacob joined Brother Ezra outside the hut.

Gutting fish on a remote, windswept island, Richard experienced a strong sense of unreality. By midday his hands were chilled and red raw and he was relieved when it was time to carry the prepared fish back to the compound. Neither of the men spoke as they ascended the steep cliff path, but he noticed that Jacob was observing him keenly.

After they arrived at the compound, he scrubbed his hands in the washroom. He was aware that his clothes smelt strongly of fish and when he entered the prayer hall, the men nearest to him recoiled.

Lunch was an unappetising mess of boiled fish and swedes then, after the obligatory twenty minutes for prayer and contemplation, he was given a spade and shown a spot where he should dig trenches for the men's new latrines. Although it was strenuous work exacerbated by the soreness of his hands, he found it more congenial than gutting fish as he was on his own and, as far as he was aware, not under constant surveillance.

He wondered when there would be another opportunity to slip down to the greenhouses to see Sister Francis. He wanted to tell her that he had found out that the island was near a place called Out Skerries.

Chapter 23

Over a week passed and Richard began to find life in the compound increasingly unbearable. He could put up with the fierce winds and occasional driving rain, but he loathed the histrionic prayer sessions, the unappetising meals eaten in silence and the overall tedium. He fretted at the absence of conveniences such as a comfortable bed, electric light and hot water. Although he had willingly put up with such privations during his field research in Kashmir and Bangladesh, here, in this remote outpost of the British Isles, he found them intolerable. The bleakness of life on the island, the inability to engage in normal social intercourse and the absence of music or laughter, weighed heavily upon him. He never heard the children in the fenced-off nursery playing. Instead, he occasionally heard them crying and chanting the prayers they were forced to learn by heart.

A major torment was the impossibility of making contact with the world outside the compound. Most nights he lay fretfully awake for lengthy periods, wondering whether Fiona had persuaded the police to track the Inheritors down and how long it would take them to find their way to the island.

The physical exertion of digging trenches provided a welcome release from tension, and he used the time trying to imagine a means of escaping from the island. He was engaged in this activity one day when the peace of the afternoon was disturbed by a faint clattering sound. The noise was continuous and rhythmic and grew steadily louder. Squinting up at the sky, he spotted a small dark shape moving diagonally towards the compound beneath some wispy clouds - a helicopter. For a moment, his heart leapt. Had the police discovered his and Sister Francis's whereabouts?

As it drew nearer, the machine went into a steep descent and swooped deafeningly over the compound, creating a blinding hurricane of dust. Richard dropped his spade and rushed away from the latrines and on to the main concourse. Male and female Inheritors appeared from every door, shouting excitedly. The helicopter disappeared over the roofs at the far end, its engine slowed then stopped, leaving a silence that was almost as dramatic as the preceding noise.

Intrigued, Richard waited to see what would happen next, but when Brother Isaac appeared and sharply ordered everyone to return to their tasks, he had no option but to return to his digging, which he did reluctantly, desperate to know who was in the helicopter.

About an hour passed then the peace of the afternoon was disturbed again, this time by the loud clanging of a bell. A few moments later Richard heard shouting in the distance and a man called down to him, 'Hurry, Brother. The Healer has come! We're summoned to the Prayer Hall.'

Richard uttered a gasp of surprise. He stuck his spade in the earth and hurried towards the hall, conscious of his muddy boots and dirt-encrusted hands. People were streaming through the door as he arrived, many, like him, still in their work-stained clothes. Everyone took their usual place in the hall and waited expectantly. Several minutes passed then the Persuaders, all of whom had apparently now returned to the island, swept up the aisle and on to the platform.

'Brothers and Sisters,' announced Brother Isaac, gazing gravely down at the assembled congregation. 'Our reverend leader is about to bring us a message of the utmost importance.'

There was an air of hushed anticipation in the hall, followed by a murmur of excitement as a tall figure with shoulder-length dark hair and a greying beard, entered the hall and advanced slowly to the platform. The Inheritors bowed their heads respectfully as he passed, then raised their arms in the air and shouted in unison, 'All praise to our holy leader, the Healer! All praise to the bringer of God's message!'

On reaching the platform, Abraham R raised his arm and the chanting abruptly stopped. He was dressed in a long purple robe and a profusion of crosses and amulets dangled from his neck. He was stockier than Richard had expected, in fact there was the distinct bulge of a paunch beneath the robe. And Richard could swear that he was wearing make-up, with rings of kohl around his deep-set eyes.

There was an expectant hush in the hall.

After a few seconds' silence, the "Poet, Philosopher and Healer" began to speak in a deep and sonorous voice.

'Inheritors of the New Kingdom, Brothers and Sisters, the signs that the End Time is approaching are unmistakable.' He gazed fiercely around the hall as though someone might have the audacity to contradict him. 'We have squandered the riches of our Garden of Eden. We have brought about the destruction of our planet by plundering and polluting the elements that foster life. God has signalled his displeasure by sending us ever more severe disasters - earthquakes, hurricanes, volcanic eruptions and floods. But Man has ignored these warnings and has not mended his evil ways. So now God has sent a more potent sign of his anger. He has sent his servants billions of miles across the universe to cleanse the Earth by fire, and to prepare us for the End Time and the Last Judgment.'

There was a pause while he waited for this information to sink in, then in rising tones, he proclaimed, 'Our planet is dying so we too must die!'

There was a moment of silence.

'In my seminal work, *Preparing for the End Time*, I prophesied that when the Earth started to die, we would have seven months in which to prepare ourselves to die at the appointed time.'

His words were greeted by an excited buzz of voices. He waited for the noise to fade before continuing. 'But when is the appointed time?' His voice dropped dramatically. '*This* is what I have come to reveal to you.'

His audience waited, transfixed.

'It will be ...' He paused for theatrical effect. 'It will be the twenty-fifth of December!'

There were gasps throughout the hall.

'The twenty-fifth of December, the date of the First Coming of our Lord Jesus Christ, will also be the date of His Second Coming! On that day, those who have been sent from another world to cleanse the Earth will bring the Messiah back to us.'

A buzz of excitement rippled through the rows of listeners.

Richard felt prickles of apprehension down his spine. Now he knew why the Inheritors were so interested in the UFOs that he and Sister Francis had witnessed. It was because they believed they confirmed their loony beliefs. He gave a start as voice near his ear whispered, 'Merry Christmas, Brother!' He spun round.

Standing behind him, Brother Jacob put a warning finger to his lips.

'On that day ...' Abraham R spread his arms for emphasis. '... On that fateful day, the Day of Judgment, we must be ready to die!' His voice dropped to a lower, more intimate tone. 'But, fellow believers, because we are the righteous ones; because we are the ones who have lived by the Holy Word in isolation from the wicked ways of the world, we will rise again!' His voice rose to a thunderous shout. 'For without are dogs and sorcerers and whoremongers and murderers and idolaters!'

There was complete silence in the hall.

Abraham R raised his eyes heavenward. 'We alone will be resurrected and transported with the Messiah to a new world, billions of miles across the universe; the world from which our visitors have come to cleanse the Earth.' He paused, then enunciated slowly and clearly, 'We are the Inheritors; the ones who will inherit God's new kingdom! We are God's *Herrenvolk*!'

A shiver ran down Richard's spine. Despite the studied theatricality of his performance, the man was completely bonkers. Could he seriously believe that those destroying swathes of lush vegetation across the planet were enacting the divine will and that they were bringing the Messiah? Could he seriously believe that the Inheritors were a divinely chosen master race?

Abraham R moved to the edge of the platform. 'Brothers and Sisters, at the time of the Last Judgment, a mediator must argue your case so that you can be saved. That person is among you.' He gestured towards the women's section of the room. 'She has been chosen for this task because she has witnessed the bringers of divine justice and has dedicated her life to God's service. Brother Isaac, bring forth the mediator.'

Isaac stepped off the platform and went to the left side of the hall. Pushing through the rows of grey-clad women, he seized the arm of a small, plump individual. Richard caught a glimpse of her frightened expression as he led her up to the platform.

Abraham R took Sister Francis by the hand and presented her to the assembled Inheritors. 'Followers of the Truth, here is your mediator! When the time comes, she will testify to your righteousness before the Messiah. Assisted by an acolyte, she will conduct the ceremony that will precede your communal leaving of this world.'

Sister Francis gaped at him then at the people in the hall. She seemed to be in a state of shock and Richard could see her lips quivering. She looked absurdly tiny by Abraham R's side.

'On the twenty-fifth of December,' continued the Healer, still holding on to Sister Francis's hand, 'you will follow this procedure. Brother Isaac, leader of this Chapter, will distribute to each of you the substance that will carry you to oblivion before the time of your resurrection. When he rings the first bell, the women will give the pills to the children. When he rings the second bell, you will all assemble in this hall where the final ceremony will take place. Immediately after the ceremony, you will each take the substance that will bring about your liberation from this sinful world and ensure your passage to the next.'

A moment of complete silence in the hall was followed by a murmur that gradually increased in volume as the Inheritors absorbed these words.

Richard was rigid with disbelief. The maniac was proposing mass suicide! After a moment, he started to tremble with shock. He and Sister Francis had to get away. They had to inform the police before it was too late. Would anybody help them? He looked at the men standing near him. A few appeared elated but most seemed profoundly disturbed. None made any protest, but surely there were some among them who wouldn't meekly accept what the so-called "Healer" was ordering them to do? He glanced behind him, but Brother Jacob was staring unblinkingly into space. What had he meant by his cryptic words? Was he a genuine sceptic or was he trying to trap Richard into revealing that he wasn't a true believer?

His thoughts were interrupted by a different sound. Abraham R. had started singing in a deep voice. After a few bars the congregation joined in. It was the chant Richard now knew by heart, *Prepare ye for The End Time* ...

The chant was followed by a lengthy period of fervent prayer, accompanied by the habitual raising and lowering of arms.

Now it was Brother Isaac's turn to address the gathering. 'Brothers and Sisters, our Reverend Leader has brought us a message of sublime importance. It is the announcement we have long been waiting for - the date of the culmination of our lives on this earth. This is not something to be absorbed in a moment. We must reflect and start to prepare ourselves. You may return to your quarters now and spend the next hour in prayer and contemplation.'

Richard was about to follow the men filing out of the door when he was startled to hear himself summoned to the platform by Brother Isaac.

He turned and walked up the aisle, exchanging a horrified glance with Sister Francis who was still standing beside Abraham R. He noticed, as he reached the platform, that the "Healer" exuded a sharp and overpowering scent that reminded him of the smell of a joss stick. His face was pock-marked and seemed to be covered in a layer of tan-coloured make-up.

'Reverend Leader, this is Brother Richard,' said Brother Isaac, 'the one I told you about who has elected to join us. He has been initiated.'

Abraham R's piercing eyes bore into Richard's. 'You have seen the Light, Brother?'

Richard assumed what he hoped was a pious expression. 'Indeed I have--'

'Reverend Leader,' prompted Brother Isaac.

'Indeed I have, Reverend Leader.'

'You have left your life in the outside world, with all its evils, completely behind?'

'I have, Reverend Leader.'

'You have sworn to live according to our beliefs and principles during the short time left to you?'

'Yes, Reverend Leader.' Richard studiously avoided Sister Francis's eye.

The Healer placed a meaty hand on his shoulder. 'As you have also witnessed the sign of the Second Coming, you will be the acolyte who will assist the mediator in the final ceremony preceding death.'

Richard stared at him, petrified with terror. He took a deep breath to control himself and stuttered, 'Oh ... right. That will be a ... great ... honour.'

* * *

His legs were shaking as he walked back through the compound but he couldn't face returning to his cramped sleeping quarters. Instead, he went to a side of the hut that was out of the wind and sat on the ground with his back against the wall, wondering frantically how he and Sister Francis could escape. As far as he could see, there were only two possible courses of action, both fraught with danger. The first was to try and steal a boat. But even if he succeeded in breaking its padlock, he lacked the navigation skills to steer one safely between the rocks, let along find his way to the largest island. The second option was to try and recover his mobile phone. But he had absolutely no idea where that was.

A spasm in his abdomen forced him jump to his feet and make a dash for the men's latrines. He saw a number of Inheritors also hurrying to the same destination. Their white faces and the stench emanating from the trenches suggested that the End Time was an appealing prospect only when assigned a date in the distant future.

Drained after the explosive emptying of his bowels, he wandered slowly back to his hut and resumed his position against the wall. He had been there a few minutes when a deafening burst of noise in the distance announced that the helicopter was taking off again, presumably conveying Abraham R and his terrifying message to another unfortunate Inheritor community.

The sound accelerated to a clattering roar and the compound was rocked by a powerful horizontal current as the aircraft passed low over the hut roofs. This time no excited spectators emerged from their huts to watch its flight.

The noise gradually receded and the helicopter became a tiny dot in the afternoon sky.

Richard closed his eyes. He wondered how Sister Francis was feeling after the announcement that she was to preside over a ceremony preceding mass suicide. Not surprisingly, her expression had been one of profound shock. Maybe she had retreated to the solitude of the greenhouses. He decided to go and find her. Hauling himself to his feet, he took a few steps, then hesitated. This was supposed to be a time of prayer and contemplation. Best not to take any chances. He returned to his sleeping quarters to fetch his Bible. As he entered the hut, he could hear whispering from the other curtained areas.

He took a roundabout route down to the greenhouses, walking slowly and occasionally glancing round to see if he was being watched. The wind, which had strengthened, lifted his hair and created little eddies of dust in front of his feet. To avoid suspicion, he opened the Bible at random and glanced down at the page.

It was an unfortunate choice: *Isaiah, 28, 15: We have made a covenant with death and with hell we are in agreement.* With a shudder, he snapped the book shut.

He peered through the salt-encrusted glass of the larger greenhouse then cautiously entered and tiptoed up the aisle between shelves laden with plant containers and densely-packed trays of greenery. He couldn't see the little nun. Disappointed, he was about to turn back when he heard a soft murmuring. He followed the sound to the far end of the greenhouse. She was on her knees, rocking backwards and forward and crossing herself. As he got closer, he could hear her muttering: 'Lord Jesus Christ save us! Holy Mother of God help us! God forgive them.'

On hearing him approach, she started and turned. Her face was wet with tears.

'I'm sorry, Sister.' He held out a supporting hand as she rose stiffly to her feet. 'I didn't mean to startle you.'

She clutched his arm and spoke in spasmodic gasps. 'Richard ... that man! That terrible man! Such a wicked thing he's suggesting. God forgive him. What can we do? All those poor souls ... We must put a stop to it. We must save them. To think they want *me* to participate in ... mass suicide ... I can't be a part of it. It's a terrible sin ... it's against the law of God. What can we do?' She took off her glasses and mopped her eyes.

Richard tried to sound reassuring. 'We won't let it happen. I promise you I'll think of something.'

She gazed at him mutely.

'I'll think of a plan,' he added without conviction. 'I'll try to find my phone and call the police.'

Her face flushed with anger. 'That fiend has the audacity to call himself a healer. He's no healer; he's a murderer!' She stopped and stared past him with a look of alarm. 'Whisht. I think there's someone coming; a man. He may have seen you. You must hide.'

Richard panicked. 'Where?'

She gestured at a shelf behind her. 'Squeeze yourself under there. I'll stand in front of you.'

He flung himself on to his knees and crawled under the shelf. She dragged a plant container in front of him.

From his cramped hiding place, Richard heard heavy footsteps advancing up the central aisle of the greenhouse

'Are ye alright, Sister?' It was a familiar voice.

'Who are you?' she replied, her voice quavering with fright.

The man spoke in an urgent whisper which Richard had to strain to hear. 'They call me Brother Jacob. Don't worry, ye can trust me. I've come because I want to help. I know you were brought here against your will. What we just heard … I can't go along with it. The man's mad. What he's suggesting is wicked; a travesty of the Christian faith. You mustn't get mixed up in this business, Sister. I can help ye get away.'

Richard peered between the leaves in the container in front of him but all he could see was Sister Francis's tiny pair of wellingtons and the much larger ones worn by Brother Jacob.

'I don't know you, Mr…Jacobs,' he heard her say. 'Why should I trust you?'

'Because what the Healer is proposing is wrong; an abomination! It has to be stopped. I'm a Trustee. I have access to the boats. I can get you out of here. I can take you to Lerwick.'

There was a brief silence and when Sister Francis responded she sounded bewildered. 'I don't understand. You're one of them aren't you?'

'You have to believe me, Sister. I could get away on my own, but I don't want to leave you here. You don't belong here.'

'No, I don't,' she replied, 'but if the Good Lord saw fit to send me here, it must be for a purpose. Now I know what that purpose is. It's to save the poor souls here from this wicked perversion of the Faith.'

'You can't do anything to help them on your own. If you come with me to Lerwick, I promise you I'll contact the police and get them to put a stop to this business. Will ye come?'

There was a brief silence before she answered. 'You have an honest face, Mr. Jacobs, and maybe I'll give you the benefit of the doubt. But I fear you may be leading me into more danger.'

'As God's my witness, you can rely on me, Sister. But one other thing; there's a new young man here. The Persuaders brought him. I heard them talking. He's been initiated, but they're not really sure of him and I have the impression he's not really committed.'

Richard was genuinely surprised. He thought he had done a pretty good job of fooling the Inheritors up to now.

'If he puts a foot wrong, the Brothers will turn on him,' Jacob continued. 'They're vicious buggers, some of them… begging your pardon, Sister. I could get him out too, before he gets into trouble. I'll try and sound him out. D'ye know the young man?'

Richard held his breath. This could be a trap.

'You men all look the same to me,' said Sister Francis with a trace of her former mischief. 'But you must try and help the poor wee fellow, whoever he is.'

'We'll have to leave at night when everyone's asleep, Jacob told her. 'The rocks around here are treacherous, but I know these waters. I must away now. When the time's right, I'll bring you word. In the meantime, Sister, don't say anything about this to anyone.'

Richard heard Jacob's footsteps retreating and was about to emerge from his hiding place when he heard them coming back again.

'Tell me, Sister, I heard the Persuaders say that huge aircraft have been destroying parts of our planet. We don't receive news from the outside world here, but they say you have seen one of them. Is it true?'

'Ay,' she said hesitantly. 'I did see one of the accursed things, a great whirling, glittering thing, so it was. The next morning we heard that part of a common near the convent had been burnt to a cinder, totally destroyed.' She snorted. 'They're instruments of the Devil, so they are. It's blasphemy to say they're bringing Our Lord and Saviour back to Earth for his Second Coming.'

'I agree with you, Sister.'

'But isn't that what all of you believe?' she challenged.

'I…' Brother Jacob stopped suddenly. 'The meditation time is nearly up. It would be dangerous if anyone sees me here. I'll be in touch with you soon. Trust me, Sister.'

Once again Richard heard his footsteps recede. He waited for a moment then eased himself out from his hiding place and stretched his cramped limbs.

Sister Francis was gazing after Brother Jacob with a bemused expression.

'Do you think he's genuine?' Richard asked.

'Och, it's hard to tell,' she said pensively. 'But it sounds as though he wants to renounce his beliefs. Maybe we should give him the benefit of the doubt.'

Richard nodded. 'You may be right. He's made some comments to me that suggest he's not really one of them. He could be our only chance.' He clasped her hand. 'Don't worry, Sister. We will get away from here, with him or without him.'

A bell clanged. The meditation was over.
He returned reluctantly to his digging.

Chapter 24

It was a miserable morning. As Richard and his two minders walked down to the shore, sheets of rain were falling horizontally. This time there was no open vista to brighten his mood. The sea heaved with angry, spume-laden waves and the horizon was obscured by thick dark clouds. When they rounded the craggy point, the fishing boats had already been pulled up on to the shore and the Anglers were returning to the compound. One of them told Ezra that the weather had become too bad to continue. They had managed only a small catch which they had left in the hut.

Unable to mend nets in the pouring rain, Brother Ezra decided to return with the Anglers to the compound. Jacob and Richard installed themselves inside the hut. Jacob sat on the floor while Richard resumed his task of preparing fish. Because of the bad weather there were only two buckets. By now he had established a rapid routine. It took him only a few seconds to pluck a fish from the bucket, gut it, and toss the cleaned article and the innards into their respective containers. Although he still loathed the feel and the smell of the fish, he found it a relief to be away from the compound where the habitual atmosphere of tension had been intensified by a palpable air of shock.

Brother Jacob was watching him thoughtfully.

Now, Richard thought. *He'll say something now.*

'So, Brother,' Jacob murmured after a short pause, 'are ye looking forward to Christmas?'

Richard didn't intend to give anything away. He gave a non-committal grunt and remained bent over his task, mechanically slitting a fish with the sharp knife.

'Ye know that wee lady they brought up to the platform yesterday?' Jacob continued.

Richard kept his head down and didn't interrupt the rhythm of his work. 'You mean the one the Healer said was a mediator?'

'Ay.'

'What about her?'

'She doesn't belong here.'

'She doesn't?'

'No. She's a nun.'

Richard feigned surprise. 'A nun?'

'Ay. From a convent.'

'I didn't know the Inheritors *had* convents.'

'They don't,' said Jacob impatiently. 'She's from a convent *outside*, an RC convent down in England.'

'Oh? What's she doing here, then?'

The man lowered his voice. 'She was taken by the Persuaders. They brought her here against her will.'

Richard pretended to be shocked. He dropped the fish he was gutting and turned to face his companion. 'You mean she was ... kidnapped?'

'Ay, you could say that. Like yourself?'

'I *chose* to get in touch with the Inheritors,' Richard said cautiously. 'I went to meet the Persuaders of my own free will, although I wasn't expecting to be brought here.'

'Why did you make contact with them, laddie?'

Richard felt a prickle of suspicion. He chose his words carefully. 'It was after I saw... something in the sky'.

'You mean you saw a flying object, like the one the wee nun saw?' Jacob's eyes lit up with interest.

Immediately Richard was on his guard. 'Did *she* see something, then?'

'Ay, she did. That's why they brought her here. What was it you saw?'

'Something huge and incredibly dazzling in the sky. It was on the same night that a large recreation ground was incinerated in my neighbourhood. Then I heard that there had been a spate of similar incidents all over the place. Everybody kept saying there must be a rational explanation but I didn't think there could be or the people responsible would have been stopped by now. I came to the conclusion that the thing I saw must have come from another world and could be a sign of the end of *our* world. I wanted to find other people who believed the same. So I looked on the internet and found the Inheritors and their beliefs seemed to coincide with mine. I left a message for them to contact me, and they did.'

Such a long silence followed his words that Richard began to feel uneasy.

Eventually Bother Jacob spoke. 'Why do I feel that's not quite the whole story?'

Richard was perplexed. 'What do you mean?'

'You don't seem ... comfortable here, Brother. You have an air of disbelief; scepticism.'

'Do I?' Richard was genuinely surprised.

Brother Jacob looked at him searchingly. 'Ay, and I have to warn you that the Brothers aren't sure of you. They had a discussion after your initiation and asked Brother Ezra and me to keep a watch on you.'

Richard's hand jerked and the point of the knife pierced his thumb. 'Ouch!' He sucked the blood oozing from the wound. His mind was racing. *Were they on to him?*

Brother Jacob spoke again, so quietly that his voice was almost drowned by the sound of the rain and the waves outside the hut. 'Let me put something to you, Brother. I don't think that you are a true believer and it shows. The Healer and the leading brothers ... they're dangerous; vicious. They take their beliefs to the extreme. You must know that by now. They procure young girls, just to breed, provide children. They believe men must "seal" many wives so that they can go to heaven. They kidnapped the nun, then they brought you. They won't let you go. Only the Persuaders, Trustees and fishermen are allowed to leave the island. But I can help you get away. I'm familiar with these waters. '

There was a silence, then, meeting Richard's incredulous gaze, he added, 'I know what you're thinking. Why am I telling you this when I'm one of them? Why haven't I tried to leave?'

'Yes,' Richard sucked his bleeding thumb. 'Why haven't you?'

Jacob gazed out of the hut door towards the sea. 'I used to live on Fetlar. I was a nature conservationist there, with my wife Kirstie. We worked together, the two of us, for many years. We had our little house and regular supplies. A while ago she fell ill ... very ill. I took her to the hospital in Lerwick. They said it was uterine cancer ... advanced ... She was airlifted to Aberdeen ...' His voice thickened with emotion. 'She died within the week. We'd been together twenty-one years. No children.' He paused, turned away from Richard and wiped his eyes with the back of his hand.

Richard waited in silence.

'After Kirstie died, I went back to the island, tried to carry on the work but I couldn't go on. I went to pieces; started to drink...whisky.

One night I drank a lot, too much. I took the boat. It was windy and the sea was rough. I lay down and just let the boat drift, wherever it wanted to. I didn't care. I had nothing else to live for. I don't know how long I was out there. It could have been several days. Then *they* found me.'

'Who?' Richard was transfixed. Either the man was genuine or he was a wonderful actor.

'Two of the Anglers. I was apparently dehydrated and delirious. They brought me back here and the women looked after me. When I got better, one of the Persuaders came to see me. He talked to me about God's will and the world being on a mission to self-destruct. It made sense to me. It's an angry religion, you will have noticed that, Brother Richard, and I was angry. I didn't care if the world was going to end. I *wanted* it to end.'

Jacob sighed and gazed out of the open door of the hut. 'To cut a long story short, I embraced their beliefs. I knew there was something unpleasant about them, but I liked the simplicity and the hardness of the life here. It was balm to my soul. I worked hard and after a while they began to trust me and made me a Trustee. But as I began to heal inside, I started to realise what they were really like.' He gave a bitter laugh. 'I heard the Brothers describing how they treat people who try to leave; how they punish "traitors". And I realised that they were forcing very young girls into marriage. But I didn't do or say anything. I decided to watch and wait. When they brought the wee nun here, I knew that was wrong. What happened yesterday has forced me to make a decision. That man isn't a healer, he's a maniac.' Jacob spat on the ground. 'Now I intend to leave and inform the police what he's planning. I have to put a stop to it.'

He paused and looked searchingly at Richard. 'I'm taking a big risk telling you this, laddie, but I've an inkling ye'll be of the same mind. I'm going to take one of the boats. It would be by night, a couple of hours before high tide. It's light enough at night at this time of year and I'm an experienced sailor. I'll take you and the nun if you're willing. Are you with me?'

Richard felt put on the spot. He prevaricated. 'How will you get past the gates at night?'

Jacob laughed. 'That's the easy bit. Trustees take it in turns to man the gates. I'd plan to leave on one of my nights. But I'll have to watch the weather ...'

Before he could say any more, there was a sound outside and Brother Ezra's tall figure appeared at the door. Rain was dripping from his oil-skins. 'Have you nearly finished?' he asked Richard curtly.

Richard pointed to the container he had filled. 'That one's ready. I need a few minutes to finish the other one.'

Jacob joined Ezra outside the hut, giving Richard time to reflect before coming to a decision. The man's tale was so dramatic it could almost be true. For why would he think up such a story? He could simply have claimed that he had become disillusioned with the sect or admitted that he didn't want to commit suicide. If he was genuine, he was taking a real risk in revealing his plan to a newcomer. But his plan was risky. What if they were caught attempting to escape? On the other hand, what could the Inheritors do to them that would be worse than forcing them to participate in mass suicide?

He flung the last few fish into the container. Sister Francis was good-hearted but shrewd. If she had decided to trust Jacob, shouldn't he also give the man the benefit of the doubt?

* * *

Several days passed and Richard had no further opportunity to speak to Brother Jacob since, either by coincidence or by design, tight-lipped Ezra always stayed close to them when they conducted their morning's work on the shore. He desperately wanted to discuss Jacob's escape plan with Sister Francis but that opportunity was also denied him. There was no possibility of sneaking down to the greenhouses in the afternoon for, without prior warning, another man had suddenly joined him in his task of digging the trenches.

The enforced inaction left him in a state of helpless frustration. How many days had he been here? He had lost all sense of time since arriving on the island. He caught sight of himself one morning in a tarnished mirror hanging in one of the washrooms, and was dismayed to see the coarse beard that had sprouted since his arrival on the island. It made him look old.

His nights were restless and disturbed by nightmares. In one of them, Abraham R. stood before him offering him a small, white pill. When he resisted, the man forced the pill into his mouth. He had woken with a scream, to the annoyance of the other occupants of his hut.

Some time after their conversation, he finally found himself alone again with Brother Jacob. It was a quiet misty morning after a stormy night and Ezra had been summoned to help repair the outboard engine of one of the fishing boats. As soon as he was out of sight, Jacob seized the opportunity to join Richard in the hut. 'Have ye given any thought to my proposition, Brother?'

'Yes, I've been thinking about it,' Richard replied cautiously, without interrupting the rhythm of his work.

'And?'

'I'm not sure.'

'The nun has agreed to come with me.'

'Has she?' Richard wondered how he had managed to visit Sister Francis again without arousing suspicion.

'Are you going to join us?'

'I'm not sure.'

Brother Jacob shrugged. 'If you want to remain here, it's your choice, laddie. But I'll thank you not to say anything to anyone as it could repercuss on the wee nun as well as on myself.'

Richard plucked another fish from the bucket and took a little time before he replied. 'Are you sure the boats are safe?' he asked eventually.

Jacob laughed. 'Ay, they're bonny wee boats, Norwegian-made, aluminium and virtually unsinkable. They take up to four people. Not fast, mind; they only do up to about five knots. But I told you I'm an experienced sailor.'

'But how would we get away without anyone seeing or hearing us?'

'Some have managed it.'

'Oh?' Richard leaned towards him eagerly. 'Did you know a man called Paddy McAllister?'

Jacob looked puzzled. 'McAllister?'

'An old guy, always quoting bits from the Bible. He escaped from the Inheritors. I think he may have come from here.'

Brother Jacob stroked his beard and reflected. 'One of the Anglers, Brother Patrick I think he was called, took a boat one night; broke the chain. That could be your man. The Brothers went looking for him.'

'I know. They found him!'

Brother Jacob looked startled. 'How d'ye know that?'

Richard told him about the attack on Paddy. 'I've been looking after his dog since he died. At least I was, till I came here'.

'D'ye mean the Brothers killed him?'

'Not directly. He apparently had a heart condition, but what they did to him obviously exacerbated it.'

Jacob frowned. 'Ay, they're a vicious bunch, and I may as well warn you now, laddie, if you come with me, they'll come looking for us too, unless we can get the police to stop them. But if you stay here, what future d'ye have?'

'None,' replied Richard. His decision was made.

'Does that mean ye'll come?'

'If the nun has agreed to come, so will I.' He didn't want to admit yet that he already knew Sister Francis. 'So what's the plan?'

'It's my turn for gate duty tomorrow night. I'll get word to the wee nun. Come to the gates at one a.m. and try not to disturb anyone. If it's stormy, we'll have to wait for another night.'

Richard hesitated. 'Are you sure no-one suspects anything?'

Jacob looked surprised. 'Why d'ye say that, laddie?'

'I may be wrong, but I have the impression that Brother Ezra has been watching us; you as well as me.'

Jacob looked thoughtful. 'Ay,' he said. 'I was becoming aware of it myself. All the more reason to go soon. Most of the Persuaders left the island yesterday, so that should make it easier.'

Richard was surprised. 'Where have they gone?'

'They don't tell me, laddie. Maybe they're following the Healer to another commune ... to prepare people for the Christmas cull.'

'Where are the other communes?'

'I'm not sure. I only know what I've heard from some of the Brothers. Since the original sect was proscribed in America, they've been trying to establish new settlements elsewhere, but they're very secretive, they don't give much away.'

Richard nodded. 'I know. They even choose derelict buildings for their meetings.'

'How d'ye know that?'

'Because I went to meet the Persuaders in one.' He decided to come clean. 'I suspected that they'd abducted Sister Francis, the nun they brought here. That's the real reason I contacted them.'

Brother Jacob looked bewildered. 'D'ye mean you already knew the nun?'

'Yes,' Richard replied apologetically.

Jacob pursed his lips. 'If I'd known that before, I wouldn't have wasted so much hot air trying to convince you to come away with us. How did you know the Persuaders had taken the nun?'

'She told me that two men had accosted her in the street a few days before she was kidnapped. They sounded like the ones who had attacked the one you knew as Brother Patrick. I told the police but they didn't believe me. I also told them I'd witnessed a bunch of Inheritors meeting in an abandoned theatre, but when they went to investigate, there was no sign of them.'

'Ay, they're a clever bunch.' Brother Jacob fingered his beard thoughtfully. 'It may be hard for us to convince the police what they're up to. They may not believe *us*, but they'll surely believe the wee sister.' He glanced warily at the open door of the hut. 'We may not get a chance to speak again. Remember, we'll meet at the gates tomorrow night if the weather holds. If not, I'll try to get word to you in the afternoon.' He left the hut.

After he had gone, Richard sat motionless. He was exhilarated at the prospect of escaping from the island, but also felt a huge sense of apprehension. Had he put his trust in the right person?

He spent the rest of the day in a state of feverish excitement. Never had time passed so slowly. Although he tried to maintain an appearance of calm, he occasionally found Brother Ezra's eyes resting thoughtfully upon him during meals and prayer sessions. It made him feel uneasy.

Luckily the man who had started to help him dig new trenches didn't join him that afternoon, so he decided to risk a visit to the greenhouses.

Sister Francis was bending over some plant trays. She straightened up when she saw him, looking relieved. 'It's good to see you, so it is.' She grasped his hand. 'I've been so anxious. The man Jacobs told me yesterday that he's planning to go when he's on gate duty tomorrow night. He wants me to go with him but I wanted to speak to you first. Are you coming, Richard? I don't want to go without you.'

He smiled at her reassuringly. 'Don't worry. I wouldn't let you go with him on your own. Are you sure we can trust him?'

'Ay, I believe we can. He has an air of honesty about him. I think he has had sadness in his life that led him to this place.'

'Then everything's set for tomorrow night, if the weather holds.'

'I'll pray that it will.' Her round face creased with anxiety. 'But there's a wee problem. The sea was terrible rough when they brought me here and I can't swim.'

He squeezed her hand. 'Brother Jacob is an experienced sailor and there'll be lifejackets on board. And he told me the boats are virtually unsinkable.'

'It's a big risk we'll be taking, Richard, that's for sure.'

'Yes, but it could be our only chance to prevent them carrying out the Healer's command.'

'Ay, you're right. It's a sin to be thinking about my own safety at such a time. If this is the best way of helping the poor souls in this place, then Jesus our Saviour will protect us.' She crossed herself.

Richard looked anxiously at the door. 'I'd better get back before anyone sees me. Brother Jacob will let us know tomorrow at meditation time if he thinks the weather looks favourable.'

She pressed his hand. 'May the good Lord and his blessed Mother watch over us, Richard!'

'Amen to that!' He hurried out of the greenhouse.

Chapter 25

There was a stiff breeze the next morning and the sea was choppy. Lines of foaming waves swelled ominously as they advanced towards the shore. Richard interrupted his labours at frequent intervals in order to check the sky for signs of a storm. Through the open door of the hut he could see Brother Jacob occasionally raise his head from the net he was mending and scan the horizon. They studiously avoided catching each other's eye and had no chance to exchange any words as stony-faced Ezra was constantly within earshot. An opportunity arose when the burly man ran to retrieve a net the wind had blown on to some distant rocks.

Jacob quickly turned and raised his thumb. He mouthed some words that Richard strained to hear over the sound of the waves and the screeching of the gulls: 'One a.m. tonight. Wear an extra jersey ... carry your oilskin.'

Richard dropped the fish he was gutting and put his head through the hut door. 'How will you break the padlock?' he mouthed back, remembering the stout chain that secured the boats to a large piece of driftwood.

'I know where they keep the key. Get back to work before he sees us talking.'

* * *

For the rest of the day, Richard remained in a state of acute nervous tension. After finishing the afternoon's digging he went to the laundry to get a clean set of clothes. The unsmiling woman on duty handed him a pile of the standard issue trousers, jumper, socks and underpants, and made a note on her ledger. He returned to the hut, changed into the clean clothes then returned with his dirty ones. As the woman stooped to put them in a large laundry basket, he grabbed another jumper from a shelf, stuffed it under his oilskin jacket and hastened out of the door.

That night he lay fully dressed on top of his bed, rigid with anxiety. The snoring and mumbling from the other occupants of the hut seemed extra loud. Every time he checked his watch, its luminous hands seemed to have barely moved. When the dial showed ten to one, he slid off the bed and pulled on the extra jumper. He put his keys and rosary in the pocket of his oilskin jacket, crept through the hut door and closed it noiselessly behind him. He waited outside for a moment but could hear no sound other than the occasional rattle of a door or window shaking in the wind. Despite wearing two jumpers, he shivered without the extra protection of the jacket which he was carrying over his arm.

He took a deep breath then set off through the compound. As he passed the line of Nissan huts, he was alarmed to see an oil lamp burning through the window of one of them. Someone must still be awake. He stopped and listened, his heart thudding so loudly he thought it must be audible. But nobody emerged and challenged him. Keeping to the opposite side of the path, he crept on, past the prayer hall and past the canteen. *Nearly there ...*

At last the high, double gates loomed before him. He halted and held his breath; someone was coming towards him. Panic-stricken, he shrank against the perimeter wall, but was relieved when he recognised the dumpy little figure cautiously approaching the gates from the opposite direction.

Before he had time to greet her, Brother Jacob stepped out of the "sentry box" next to the gates, carrying his oilskin jacket and a large flashlight. He put a warning finger to his lips. Richard and Sister Francis waited silently as he gently drew back the heavy bolt that fastened the gates. It gave a creak, which, in Richard's state of heightened anxiety, sounded deafening. Why, he wondered, was every sound so magnified at night?

Jacob opened the gates just wide enough for a single person to pass through. He paused, listened, then motioned Sister Francis and Richard to go through before him. After following them, he pushed the gates gently back into position, securing them at the bottom with a large stone in case, unbolted, they swung open in the wind.

'Don't put the jackets on till we're out of sight of the compound,' he whispered.

The three of them set off down the steep cliff path. Having already followed this route a number of times, Richard negotiated it with relative ease, but Sister Francis slithered and stumbled and would have fallen had he not helped her over the rough terrain.

When Brother Jacob was satisfied that they could no longer be seen from the compound, he halted. 'You can put the jackets on now.'

They pulled on their yellow oilskins and he strode rapidly ahead.

Richard grasped Sister Francis's arm again and they scurried after him, occasionally slipping on loose stones.

The sound of the waves increased as they neared the bottom of the slope. They passed the jetty where the Persuaders' boat was kept, and hastened towards the craggy point that divided the two bays. Then they heard it: the clanging of the compound bell!

They froze and gazed at each other in horror. A shiver ran down Richard's spine.

Sister Francis crossed herself.

Brother Jacob uttered a curse. 'Ezra! Man's been watching me like a hawk. Come on! We've a good twenty-minute start.' He broke into a run and disappeared round the point.

Richard stumbled after him, pulling Sister Francis by the hand. By the time they got to the second bay, Jacob had already pulled off the tarpaulin covering one of the fishing boats and unlocked the padlock connecting it to the security chain. 'Quick, laddie!' he called to Richard, 'give me a hand.'

The two of them dragged the boat down to the water's edge and pulled it through the narrow inlet between the rocks. When it was deep enough to launch the vessel, Brother Jacob climbed over the side and pushed it further out to sea with an oar. 'Fetch the nun,' he called urgently.

Richard waded back to the shore where Sister Francis was waiting. Taking her hand, he guided her towards the boat. By the time they reached it, the bottom of her long skirt was sodden. Jacob leant over the side, put his hands under her armpits and hauled her into the boat. With a grunt and a groan, she toppled on to the seat in the stern.

Richard hoisted himself over the side and sat down beside her. He pulled off his wellingtons which had taken in seawater and emptied them over the side.

Sister Francis started to scrabble in the recesses of the boat, making it wobble alarmingly from side to side.

'Sit down, Sister,' Jacob said sharply. 'You're making us unsteady.'

'My glasses, I can't see without them.'

Richard pulled her gently back into a seated position. 'We'll find them later.'

Jacob tossed two lifejackets over to them. 'Put these on. It'll be rough.' He picked up the oars.

Richard pulled on one of lifejackets then helped Sister Francis, who was fumbling ineffectively at the straps, into hers. He gathered up the crumpled tarpaulin that Jacob had thrown into the boat and draped it over the nun. 'This will keep the wind off you.' As he tucked the tarpaulin around her, something slid off it. He reached down to pick it up. 'Your glasses!'

'Thank God!' she said gratefully and replaced them on her nose.

'Shine the flashlight on the rocks,' Jacob called to Richard. 'It's by your feet. Once we're past the worst of them, I'll start the motor.'

Richard grabbed the flashlight and obediently directed the light over the surface of the water.

Using the short oars and grunting with effort, Jacob manoeuvred the boat around the jagged dark shapes that protruded above the water's surface. Occasionally they scraped over submerged rocks. Richard's heart was in his mouth. What if they capsized? He had a horrifying vision of Sister Francis being sucked beneath the waves.

At last they emerged into open sea. Richard and Sister Francis moved cautiously to the central seat while Jacob took their place in the stern, lowered the outboard motor into place, then pulled the starter cord and the choke. As it spluttered into life, Richard thought he could hear shouts in the distance.

'They'll guess we're heading for Mainland,' Jacob told them, his words just audible above the sound of the engine. 'The Anglers will take the ski boat. We'll go in the opposite direction.'

Richard nodded, happy to leave the decisions to the older man.

Jacob turned the boat at a sharp angle. It started to pitch and toss on the choppy waves. Richard glanced anxiously at Sister Francis. He hoped she would be able to cope with the boat's motion as well as with the cold.

After about twenty minutes, Jacob pointed to something in front of them. As they drew closer, Richard could make out a dark cliff, at the base of which a small pier or jetty was just about visible. Occasional spouts of foaming water cascaded over its surface. Jacob navigated carefully towards it. 'We'll tie up there and take cover,' he shouted above the noise of the waves. 'Hopefully they'll have gone in the opposite direction.'

When they reached the jetty, he cut the motor, steered alongside and turned the boat so that the prow was facing towards the open sea. He jumped out and secured the rope tightly to a post then clambered back in. 'We'll stay here a wee while to create some distance between us. I don't want to use up too much fuel. Take my place in the stern.'

Richard and Sister Francis huddled together in the stern and as the boat bobbed and banged against the side of the jetty, Richard abandoned himself to the rhythm of the waves.

* * *

He heard it first: the distant drone of an outboard motor. Screwing up his eyes, he was horrified to see a boat approaching. He shouted a warning to Jacob who was slumped on the central seat.

As soon as he realised what was happening, Jacob jumped up and clambered on to the jetty. But before he had managed to untie the rope, the other boat had already reached them. It was steered by Brother Ezra. Behind him were two brawny Anglers whom Richard recognised from when he had spent the mornings gutting fish. He was gripped with despair. His heart sank. Their one chance of escape had failed.

Ezra navigated alongside, neatly wedging them between his boat and the jetty. He cut the engine. 'What a touching sight!' he sneered. 'The traitor Jacob, our new initiate and the holy nun! Did you think you could get away? You two stay where you are,' he ordered Richard and Sister Francis. 'Brothers, get the traitor!'

The Anglers stood up and one of them started climbing over the sides of the two boats in an attempt to reach the jetty.

'Keep down, Sister,' roared Brother Jacob, abandoning the rope and preparing to fend off an attack.

Ignoring his command, Sister Francis rose shakily to her feet. She seized Jacob's long flashlight with both hands, swung it over her right shoulder then, with a shout of 'God forgive me!' struck the Angler who was climbing into their boat, heavily on the chest. He screamed and toppled backwards, falling against the other Angler who was standing ready to follow him. The second man staggered back then tumbled over the side of the second boat into the water.

Bellowing with rage, Ezra attempted to steady the violently rocking vessel before turning his attention to the Angler who was floundering in the sea.

During the commotion, Jacob succeeded in unfastening the rope. 'Hold tight!' he yelled to Richard and Sister Francis. He leapt back into the boat and pulled a fishing net from under a seat before starting the outboard motor. He gave the other boat a sharp push sideways then dropped the net overboard and quickly took Richard's place in the stern. Once clear of the other vessel, they chugged away.

None of them spoke until they had put a safe distance between them and the jetty. Then Richard gazed admiringly at Sister Francis. 'Wow! Where did you learn to hit like that?'

She smiled coyly. 'I used to play tennis when I was at school in Belfast. I always had a ferocious forehand.' Her expression became anxious. 'I hope I didn't hurt that man too badly.'

'Well I hope you did!' muttered Jacob. 'It was a blow for the greater good.'

'Why did you throw a net in the water?' Richard asked.

Jacob grinned. 'It'll wrap round their propeller. That should slow them up for a while.'

The wind had dropped and the sea was calm, allowing them to make rapid progress through open water studded with small islands. The sun was up now, though obscured at intervals by scudding clouds.

They travelled for a while in silence. Although Richard kept looking behind them, there was no sign of the other boat.

Eventually, Brother Jacob pointed to a land mass in front of them. 'That's Whalsay, the Bonny Isle. North Mainland's behind. We'll pull in at Symbister. It has a big harbour and there'll be plenty of other vessels. There's a marina there where small boats can tie up.'

Richard breathed a sigh of relief.

A picturesque harbour crowded with yachts, small fishing boats and trawlers came into view. Beyond it, Richard could see a flat expanse of green with a scattering of white and grey buildings. Despite the early hour, there were already signs of life: small boats were heading out to sea, a solitary person walked a dog along a path, a red car disappeared into the distance

'Symbister,' Jacob called above the growl of the engine. He turned the boat so that it was heading for the harbour. 'There's a ferry from here that goes to Mainland and from there we can get to Lerwick.'

'How far is Lerwick?' Richard shouted back. Now that his fear had subsided, he had become acutely aware of physical discomfort, he was shivering with cold in his damp and clinging clothes. He glanced down at the nun who was slumped next to him, her head nodding on her chest. Her glasses had slid comically to the end of her nose.

'About twenty miles from Laxo where the ferry terminal is.'

Richard surveyed the scene in front of him. 'Is there a police station here?'

'Ay, there is. But we'd better clean ourselves up and have something to eat before we go there.'

'How will we do that? Do you have any money?'

'No, but I used to know someone here,' replied Brother Jacob. 'If she's at home, I'm sure she will help us.'

He navigated carefully through the mouth of the harbour and around bobbing vessels. After cutting the engine, he steered into an empty berth then jumped out of the boat and secured it. 'Wake up, Sister. It's time to go ashore.'

Sister Francis opened her eyes and gave an exhausted sigh. Richard helped Jacob hoist her over the side then climbed out himself.

Jacob covered the boat with the tarpaulin then led them to the shore. 'This way. It's not far.'

They followed the harbour wall, passing a jumble of boats and marine buildings, then took a road along the side of which a few wild flowers spouted colourfully among the hardy grasses.

Richard felt dizzy with hunger and weariness and his legs wobbled as he walked. White with fatigue, Sister Francis tottered stiffly beside him, hanging on to his arm. A passing group of fishermen stared at them curiously and Richard realised what a strange trio they must appear; he and Jacob with their unkempt hair and straggly beards and Sister Francis with her broken spectacles and long, wet skirt that clung to her legs as she walked.

At the end of the road, they came to a dry-stone wall and a line of small white buildings. Jacob stopped in front of one and knocked at the door.

Richard glanced at his watch. 'Isn't it a bit early to call on someone?'

'Not if I know this lady. She'll have been up this last hour.' Jacob knocked again and they heard a female voice inside calling impatiently, 'OK, I'm coming.'

The door was flung open and a stout woman dressed in baggy slacks and a long woollen cardigan appeared. 'Well?' she asked suspiciously. 'What d'you want at this hour of the morning?'

Jacob took a step towards her. 'Agnes ... Aggie. Don't you know me?'

She peered at him then moved a little closer. After studying him for a second, she put a hand to her mouth and shrieked, 'Jacob! Jacob Cameron! Can it be? Is it really you?'

'Ay it is, Aggie.'

'But ...' White-faced, she held on to the door frame to steady herself. 'I heard you were dead... drowned ...'

'Well, as ye can see, Aggie, I'm very much alive.'

She continued to gaze at him, transfixed. 'But the coastguards found your boat; they said it was empty ... they searched for you for days. We all assumed--'

'I was rescued.'

'But it's been nearly ... two years ... Where have you been all this time, Jake? Why didn't you let us know you were alive? '

'It's a long story, Aggie. I'll tell you all about it, but for the moment me and my friends here, we're very tired and we urgently need your help.' He gestured at Sister Francis and Richard who were standing behind him. 'This good lady is a nun and this young man is Richard. They're from England.' He turned to Richard and Sister Francis. 'This is my old friend, Aggie. We worked together in Aberdeen, many years ago.'

Aggie regarded Sister Francis who was still clinging to Richard's arm, barely able to stand, and her expression changed to one of concern. 'Look at the poor wee soul. Come inside. You'll be needing breakfast and a rest. Then I'll hear all about your resurrection, Jake Cameron, turning up here like a ghost after all this time, looking so thin, and with that dreadful beard, not letting folk know you were still alive and well...'

Still scolding, she led them inside. 'Take off those wet boots now, and those oilskins. I'll not have you dripping over my carpet.' She eyed Sister Francis's wet skirt. 'Come upstairs with me, my darling, and I'll give you something dry to wear. You two wait in the sitting-room. I'll be down in a minute.'

While she led Sister Francis upstairs, Richard and Jacob left their wet things in the porch then sank gratefully into soft armchairs in the tiny living room.

'I've given the lady some of my things to wear.' Aggie told them when she returned downstairs. 'Poor wee soul was drenched and chilled to the bone. She was so exhausted, I've left her in my bed. Now I'll make some tea to warm you up.'

After gratefully drinking the hot beverage, Richard fell asleep on his chair. When he woke, he found he was alone in the room and could smell something cooking; something he hadn't smelt for a long time - bacon! His mouth watered. Checking his watch, he saw it was after nine. He could hear Jacob and Agnes talking in another room. Following the sound of their voices, he found the two of them in a small kitchen. Jacob was now wearing unfamiliar clothes - trousers that were a bit large for him and a colourful, diamond-patterned jumper.

Aggie looked up from her frying pan as Richard entered. 'Ah, you're awake. Jake's been telling me about your adventures.' She clicked her tongue disapprovingly. 'It's a wonder you weren't all drowned or murdered by those villains.' She looked him up and down. 'You'll be wanting a wee wash before breakfast. The bathroom's at the top of the stairs. I've left a clean jersey and some trousers out for you. They belong to my son. They may be a bit big for you, but at least they'll be dry.'

Richard obediently went upstairs. He felt much better after he had washed and put on the oversized garments he found in the bathroom. He took care to transfer his keys and the rosary from the pocket of his oilskin jacket to the pocket of the voluminous trousers.

A short time later, he, Jacob and Sister Francis were sitting in the kitchen, consuming with relish the hearty breakfast of eggs, bacon and sausages that Aggie had prepared for them. Richard thought it was the best meal he had ever had. He was pleased to see that some of the colour had returned to the nun's cheeks.

Aggie put a rack filled with thick pieces of toast on the table. 'When you've finished eating,' she said to Jacob, 'you'd best go and talk to the sergeant in charge at the police station.'

'Ay.' Jacob spread a thick layer of butter on his toast. 'That's exactly what I intend.'

Richard decided to broach a subject that the hair-raising escape from the island had temporarily driven from his mind. 'Aggie, what's the latest news on the Blitzgreen? 'Have there been any more attacks?'

She frowned. 'Not for a week or so, as far as I know. We haven't had any problems up here, mind.'

'Have they discovered who the perpetrators are?'

She snorted derisively. 'Some are saying it's an alien invasion. But I don't hold with any of that nonsense. I believe it's foreign terrorists. If they're not caught soon, it'll be the end of the world as we know it, you mark my words.'

Richard exchanged an uneasy glance with Sister Francis.

Chapter 26

The sergeant in charge at the police station looked at them askance when they entered, and was frankly incredulous when they related their strange and complicated story. He told them he knew nothing about missing nuns or a sect called the Inheritors of the New Kingdom and made it clear that he had far more pressing matters to attend to.

When they pressed him to take action, he disappeared into another office to ring Area Command at Lerwick for advice. After a lengthy interval he returned and informed them that they would be put on an afternoon ferry to Mainland where a police car would convey them to Lerwick police headquarters. He seemed relieved at the prospect of getting rid of them.

* * *

'Be sure to keep in touch, now,' Aggie waved an admonitory finger at Jacob as the three of them were about to embark on the ferry. 'No more disappearing acts.'

'No, I promise, Ag.' He gave her a hug. 'I'll call you when I'm settled in Aberdeen.'

'We'll send you back your clothes,' Richard promised.

'Och, don't bother,' she replied. 'They're old.'

The chief inspector at Lerwick Area Police Command was as baffled by their narrative as the officer at Symbister had been. He listened with an air of puzzlement then, with a gesture of helplessness, contacted Northern Constabulary. After some time had elapsed, a fax arrived containing a blurred photo of Sister Francis and confirmation that she was on a central list of missing persons. Convinced now of the truthfulness of at least this part of the story, the inspector made several more phone calls. One of them, to Shetland Islands Council, elicited the information that a community claimed to be conducting a long-term experiment in sustainable living had taken over a disused army camp on a formerly abandoned island off the Skerries.

He looked questioningly at Jacob. 'That would be your Kingdom folk?'

'That's them alright,' Jacob, who had recognised the name of the island, replied grimly.

The chief inspector promised that the community would be investigated and arranged for the three of them to be transferred by air to Aberdeen. There, after making separate statements at the police headquarters, they were put up in a hostel for the night.

The following morning, a car arrived to take Richard and Sister Francis to the airport where they were to board a flight to London.

Jacob's face was flushed with emotion as he wished them goodbye. 'God be with you, Sister,' he said, pumping Sister Francis's hand. 'It's been a privilege knowing you. And God be with you too, Brother.' He gave Richard a bear hug and murmured in his ear, 'I hope they get the vicious bastards and lock them up for a very long time!'

Richard was still so exhausted that the return to England passed in a blur. At Heathrow, he and Sister Francis were met by four police officers who conducted them to separate cars.

The little nun clasped Richard's hand as they parted. 'God bless you, Richard. Now that Our Lady has brought us home safe and well, we must pray for her help in the battle against that devil who calls himself a healer.'

He experienced a rush of emotion as he watched her climb into the back of the waiting car.

* * *

There were two people in the small and windowless interview room - a policewoman and a male officer with whom Richard was already familiar - DS Johnson.

'Oh dear, Mr. Jarman!' The officer looked him up and down with a faint smile, making him acutely aware of his growth of straggly beard and the baggy, rolled-up trousers belonging to Aggie's giant son. 'You look a bit … rough, if I may say so.' He indicated a chair. 'Do sit down.'

Richard sat facing him across the table. The policewoman left the room and returned with a mini cassette-recorder, a folder and some sheets of fax paper. She placed these on the table in front of the officer, then closed the door and stood in front of it. Reading upside down, Richard could see his name and several dates written on the cover of the folder.

'Well, Mr. Jarman,' DS Johnson began, 'I gather you found our missing nun.'

'Yes,' Richard couldn't keep the note of triumph from his voice. 'I told you the Inheritors of the New Kingdom had abducted her.'

'So you did, Mr Jarman, so you did. And it seems you may have been right.' DS Johnson picked up the papers in front of him and scanned them rapidly. 'This is a copy of the statement you made in Aberdeen. Perhaps now you would tell me exactly what happened before and after you went to that island.'

Richard sighed. All he wanted to do was go home, shave and have a bath. 'It's all written down.'

'Well I'd be grateful if you would describe those events for me again, so that I have a complete record.' DS Johnson switched on the cassette recorder and informed it of the date and time and the identity of the three people in the room. He turned back to Richard. 'Can we go back to a day shortly before you and I had our last little chat? I've been informed that after your visit to that disused theatre in Potters Bar, you made contact with a religious sect called the Inheritors of the New Kingdom, in the belief that they had abducted the nun, Sister Francis.'

Richard realised that Fiona must have divulged this information. 'Yes, I contacted them through a religious forum on the internet.'

'But you didn't mention this before when you and I spoke about the nun's disappearance.'

'No.'

'Why not?'

Richard felt flustered. 'Because you didn't seem convinced when I said I thought the Inheritors had taken her.'

DS Johnson ignored this. 'I understand that you posted a message on an internet forum in the name of "Witnesser of the Light". Is that correct?'

'Yes, I thought the name might catch their attention. As I told you before, the Inheritors have a particular interest in the very bright flying objects some of us saw on the nights of the arson attacks.'

'And after posting your message, you received a response.' The officer stated this as a fact rather than a question.

'Yes, I found a coded message inviting me to meet them.'

'Is this the message?' DS Johnson took a sheet of paper from the folder and read out its contents in a slightly mocking tone. 'Witnesser of the Light, those who are prepared for the End Time will be spared. Come forward into the light. Redemption will be found where end follows harp, one high place eleven of five fifteen.' He tossed the paper on to the table.

'Yes, that's the message I received.'

'Curious message, isn't it? It was given to me by a young lady who reported you missing, Mrs Fiona Harris. Apparently you gave her my card.'

Richard made no comment.

'The young lady said she managed to decipher the message. She told me she believed it was an invitation to you to meet members of the sect called Inheritors of the New Kingdom, somewhere in or near Harpenden. She thought you might be in danger. *Close* friend is she?'

Richard disliked his insinuating manner. 'She's an old friend. We were at school together.'

'So after your *old* friend interpreted the message, you went to a derelict house in Harpenden.'

'If you know that already, why are you asking me?'

'Because that is where your trail went cold.'

'My trail?'

'Given your previous connection with the missing nun, I thought your disappearance must be more than a coincidence. So we sent some officers to find the address in Harpenden that the young lady said was hidden in the message you received. They found a *Golf* car, registered in the name of a Mr. Gordon Jarman, abandoned in a disused railway yard.'

'Yes, that's my dad's car. I've been using it while he and my mother are on holiday.'

DS Johnson picked up one of the papers on his desk and glanced at it. 'My colleagues also found numerous tyre marks nearby and signs that an empty, boarded-up building had recently been broken into. But *you*, Mr. Jarman, were nowhere to be seen. And that's where we lost your trail. So now I would like you to give me a full account of all that happened at that site and on the days that followed.'

Richard launched wearily into the long story of everything that had occurred after he had met the Persuaders at the boarded-up house in Harpenden.

DS Johnson interrupted at frequent intervals, asking for clarification and further details. After Richard had completed his account of the escape from the island, he switched off the cassette recorder and sat for a moment in thoughtful silence.

Richard twitched impatiently.

The officer looked across at him and the corners of his mouth quivered slightly. 'Thank you, Mr. Jarman. You can go home now. We'll be in touch.'

Richard stared at him incredulously. 'Is that all? What are the police going to do about the Inheritors? Abraham R has to be stopped.'

'Don't worry, Mr. Jarman. We'll be working on the case with our colleagues in Scotland and, if it turns out to be an extradition situation, with the authorities in the United States. In the meantime, I suggest you go home and wait for us to contact you.'

'I can't get home. The Inheritors took my wallet as well as my clothes and my mobile. I only managed to keep my keys.'

DS Johnson rose to his feet. 'I'll ask someone to drive you.'

'Where's my dad's car?'

'It was taken to a location in Hertfordshire. The sergeant at the desk will give you a number to ring. You can collect it when you're ready.' He chuckled. 'But may I suggest you have a shave and a change of clothes first?'

* * *

When the police car drew up in Coronation Close, Richard was surprised at the surge of affection he felt for his boyhood home. For once the suburban dreariness of the place with its net-curtained windows and overly neat front gardens, failed to irritate him. His spirits sank, however, as he clambered out of the car and spotted a stout figure watching from the door of number three.

He hastened up the path, unlocked the door and trampled over the scattering of mail on the doormat. The house smelled stale and unaired. He opened some windows then went to the landline to ring Fiona only to find, to his frustration, that he couldn't remember her number. It was listed on his mobile and he didn't have a clue where that was. After fumbling through a local telephone directory, he rang her parents' number and left a message for her.

Before going upstairs, he sorted through the mail. Most of the items were for his parents, but among those addressed to him he was delighted to find a cheque; the fee for a series of articles based on his research that he had contributed to a scholarly journal. He breathed a sigh of relief. The funds should keep him going for another few months.

After scrutinising the contents of the other envelopes, he went to his room and switched on his laptop. Scrolling rapidly through his emails, he found one from his mother.

Darling, I hope you're OK. We're still having a marvellous time but we're worried about those dreadful terrorist attacks. What is the world coming to? I expect you're busy on your thesis. Drop us a line soon to let us know how you're getting on. Dad sends his love, and mine as always,

Mum xxx PS Have you remembered to water the garden and house-plants?

No, he hadn't!

A less welcome message was from Phil Banks.

Didn't you get my message? Yours truly has been plucked from the dole queue by World Weather Review. Starvation wages but could lead to glory. Celebrations on Friday 9th June. Get bladdered at Green Man, followed by dessert at HOT TOTTY!!

Another email was from Dan.

Hi, what's up? Mobile on blink or have you been kidnapped by the Happy Clappies? Give me a bell some time.

Richard rang Dan from the phone in the hall. 'You weren't wrong about me being kidnapped by the "Happy Clappies", though "happy" isn't a word I'd use to describe them!' He gave Dan a severely abbreviated account of his recent experiences.

Dan punctuated his narrative with whistles of astonishment. 'Blimey, Ric!' he exclaimed after Richard had finished describing the hazardous boat journey. 'What the fuck were you thinking of? Those Inheritors sound a right bunch of nutters. I warned you not to get mixed up with them. You were lucky to get away when you did.'

'I know, and I'm really grateful to that guy Jacob. If it hadn't been for him, Sister Francis and I would still be on that island.'

'Well at least the police are taking you seriously this time.'

'They have to, Dan. They can't dismiss the nun's evidence. I'm hoping they'll act quickly in case those thugs come after us again.'

'You think they only abducted the nun because she'd seen something on one of the nights when there was an arson attacks?'

'I don't think it, I know it. It sounds crazy but they genuinely seem to believe the UFOs are a sign of the Messiah's second coming. They apparently kidnapped Sister Francis because they thought she'd been divinely chosen to reside over some absurd end of world rite before they all committed suicide.'

'Blimey! They must be insane.'

Richard laughed. 'You can say that again. What's been happening here, Dan? The woman who helped us in Symbister said there haven't been any more arson strikes.'

'Not here, there haven't. They've moved away from the major cities. Now they're targeting forests. Last week they destroyed a chunk of the Russian Taiga Forest region and some of the Brazilian rainforest.'

A shiver ran down Richard's spine. He recalled that the Amazon rainforest and Taiga Biome provided a significant amount of the Earth's oxygen levels.

'And you'll be interested to hear,' Dan continued, 'that around the time of the most recent attacks, some people witnessed lights and objects in the sky, like the ones you saw.'

'Is anything being done?'

'The UN Security Council's holding another emergency meeting to discuss the possibility of a concerted international response, and the PM's going to make a statement when he gets back in a few days.' Dan's voice shook slightly. 'It's very worrying, Ric.' His voice sank to a whisper. 'I wish I could take Kate and Liam somewhere safe, but where the fuck's safe these days?'

'Better stay where you are,' Richard replied. 'From what you say, I reckon the safest place to be is in the middle of a built-up environment.'

He replaced the phone and went upstairs to have a long and refreshing bath.

Fiona rang him back later that afternoon. 'Thank God you're back. Where on earth have you been? Are you OK? What happened? Did the Inheritors harm you?'

'It's a long story, Fi. I'll tell you all about it when I see you. I just wanted to let you know I'm home.'

'Thank God,' she repeated. 'I was sick with worry when you didn't come back. I kept trying your mobile and when you didn't answer, I knew something awful must have happened. I rang that policeman, the one who gave you his card. I took him the message--'

'I know. I've already seen him. Thanks for doing that, Fi. How's Maggie?'

'She's fine. She and Polly are a good team. Ric, are you sure you're OK?'

'Yes, I'm fine, really.'

'I want to know everything that happened. Can we meet?'

'Yes, I can come over to your place later if you like?'

'Cool. I can't wait to hear.'

'There's a heck of a lot to tell.'

Chapter 27

Richard left the house feeling considerably better for being clean-shaven and dressed in his own clothes which were now slightly too big for him.

As he turned out of his front path, he met Doris Perkins who was just turning into hers. She stopped when she saw him. 'Ricky, I hope you don't mind, but I need to ask you about ...'

'Let me guess, Mrs. Perkins ... the police car?'

'Yes.' She lowered her voice. 'Is it true, Ricky? It will be such a shock for your Mum and Dad when they get back.'

'Is what true, Mrs. Perkins?'

'That you've been in prison?'

'In prison?' he exclaimed, flabbergasted.

'Marjorie told me this morning ...'

'What did Marjorie tell you?'

She peered anxiously at him. 'She said that you'd been arrested ... for ... for ...'

'For what?'

She moved closer and whispered, 'for watching that stuff... on the internet.'

He stared at her. '*What* stuff?'

She flushed. No sound issued from her mouth but he was able to read her lips, 'Porn...o...graphy.'

'*Pornography*?' Richard gave a gasp of outrage then a shout of bitter laughter - abducting a nun, downloading pornography, what else would he be accused of? He took a deep breath and leaned towards his neighbour.

'I can assure you, Mrs. Perkins,' he articulated loudly, hoping his voice would carry further down the Close, 'that I have *neither* been arrested *nor* have I been in prison and I have *never* watched pornography. You do realise such suggestions are slanderous?'

She took a nervous step back. 'Well, your mum did mention that you're always on the computer. And because you've been away for a while and the police brought you back this morning looking ... like you did, Marjorie thought ...' Her voice tailed off.

Richard felt himself go red with anger. 'Watching porn isn't the only thing one can do on a computer you know. Didn't my mother mention that I'm writing a doctoral thesis for the University of London?'

He turned away and strode towards the corner. His earlier feeling of affection for Coronation Close had completely evaporated. As he passed number three, he thought he could see a plump face behind the net curtain in the front window. Turning back to Mrs. Perkins who was still standing where he had left her, he shouted, 'And you can tell Marjorie Phelps to mind her own bloody business!'

His anger subsided as he walked through the quiet suburban streets to Fiona's parents' house. The scent of flowers permeated the afternoon air and the few people he met on the way nodded pleasantly to him. They seemed calm, unruffled, as though nothing was wrong with the world. His enforced stay on the bleak island already seemed unreal, a lifetime away.

When the door opened in response to his knock, Maggie shot out and jumped up at him, barking excitedly.

He staggered back. 'Hello, girl. What have you been feeding her on?' he called to Fiona who had followed the dog out of the door. 'Doughnuts? She's really filled out.'

'Well that's more than I can say for you!' She descended the front steps and eyed him critically. 'You've lost weight, Ric.'

'That's because I've been on a diet.' He gave her a hug.

She hugged him back. 'It's great to see you again. I was so scared when I didn't hear from you. Where have you been all this time? It's been weeks.'

'Is that all? It felt more like months.'

'Why didn't you ring me? Did you find Sister Francis? Did you meet Abraham R?'

He laughed. 'One question at a time! Hi, Polly.'

The girl hung back shyly and plucked at her mother's sleeve.

'What is it, Poll Doll?'

Polly whispered something in Fiona's ear.

Fiona smiled. 'She wants to know if you're going to take Maggie home with you.'

'Why?' he asked. 'Don't you want me to take her home with me, Polly?'

'No. I want her to stay here, with us.'

'But what about your gran and grandad?'

'They won't mind.'

He looked enquiringly at Fiona.

'They weren't keen on having Maggie,' she said, 'but as Polly's so fond of her, I'm sure they'll let her stay. That's if you're sure.'

A wave of relief swept over him. 'Absolutely sure. My mother doesn't like dogs and it'll be difficult for me to keep her if I get a new job.'

'Wicked!' Polly jumped up and down while Maggie scampered round them, barking furiously.

Fiona grabbed her by the collar 'Calm down, Maggie!' She looked at Richard. 'Are you free? Fancy a walk?'

'Sounds good to me.'

They strolled through an old churchyard behind which there was a winding path alongside a narrow stream. It led to a grassy clearing with a playground at one end. After the bleakness of the island compound, Richard took pleasure in the scene confronting him - people strolling in the late afternoon sun; parents pushing their toddlers on swings; children chasing each other on the grass.

Fiona turned impatiently to him after Polly had run off to throw a ball for Maggie. 'Come on. Tell me what happened.'

They sat down on a bench and he related, once again, the details of his enforced stay on the remote island.

She listened, aghast, uttering occasional gasps of shock and amazement.

'They took my phone. That's why I couldn't contact you,' Richard said finally, 'or anyone else for that matter. I probably couldn't have got a signal up there anyway.'

She clutched his arm. 'Thank God you and Sister Francis got away. That guy Abraham sounds a maniac.'

'I can't decide whether he's mad or just evil,' muttered Richard. 'Probably both.'

Her grasp on his arm tightened. 'He can't get away with it, can he? Are the police going to arrest him?'

'I bloody well hope so. Northern Constabulary were going to investigate what's really going on that island. They must have enough evidence by now. I hope they find him and those other Inheritor thugs soon, or they might come after Sister Francis and me again.'

Fiona looked anxious. 'You must be careful, Ric. If they managed to spirit Sister Francis away, they could easily get to you. You don't live in a walled convent.'

'Yeah, that's why I hope the police will act quickly.'

She frowned. 'How could those people on the island meekly accept an order to commit suicide? Do you think they're *all* mad?'

'More likely brainwashed. They think what's happening is the fulfilment of an ancient prophecy. They genuinely believe that the arson attacks are the beginning of the end of the world and that spaceships are about to bring the Messiah on his second visit, and that when he comes, he's going to carry them all off to a "New Kingdom" ... after they've died, that is!'

She shuddered. 'But that's crazy.'

'Yes, most of it is.'

She stared at him. 'What do you mean, *most* of it?'

'You must have heard that some people think that the arson attacks may have been perpetrated by ... something that's come from outer space.'

'Yes, but that's rubbish, isn't it?'

'The thing is, Fi, no-one has yet come up with a more plausible explanation. I'm even beginning to think there could be something in Mark Davenport's theory.'

'Whose theory?'

'Mark Davenport's. He's a former colleague of mine. He suggested that whoever or whatever has been destroying areas of vegetation, could be deliberately trying to reduce the planet's oxygen levels.'

'That's an awful idea.' She stared at him, her face puckered with anxiety. 'What about you, Ric? Do you think they've come from outer space?'

He hesitated before replying. 'I can't dismiss the idea out of hand. Those machines have such amazing acceleration that nothing's been able to catch them, not even the most sophisticated warplanes.'

'You're freaking me out.' She glanced uneasily up at the sky. 'Surely you don't believe in aliens?'

'I'm keeping an open mind,' Richard said cautiously. 'Ever since that night when I saw that weird thing in the sky, I've been trying to find out more about space and UFOs and stuff. There was this American guy called Drake. He calculated that there could be ten thousand planets in the Milky Way where intelligent life may have developed.'

'Ten thousand? How could he know that?'

'He used some sort of complicated mathematical equation that astronomers still refer to. But even if intelligent life has developed elsewhere in the universe, it's difficult to imagine how aliens could get here. The distances are unbelievable. The nearest stars to us, the ones called Alpha Centauri, are over four light years away from our sun.'

'How far is that?'

'Incredibly far. A light year is about six trillion miles. If we were travelling at the speed of our fastest rockets, it could take over seventy thousand years to reach the nearest of the three - Proxima Centauri!'

Her mouth dropped open. 'Wow! That's mind-blowing.'

'Even if we travelled at the fastest speed any man-made spacecraft has ever achieved, it would still take thousands of years. And if we wanted to reach a planet orbiting one of the next nearest stars, like Sirius, that would be double the distance.'

'Wow!'

'So if aliens have come from another solar system, they've either got an incredibly long lifespan or they've had to produce a series of generations in transit! The only other way they could get here would be by taking short-cuts through wormholes, like something out of *Star Trek*! What I'm saying, Fi, is if we have been visited by beings from another planet, they must have developed technology so incredibly advanced that it's completely beyond our comprehension.'

She looked baffled. 'But if it takes so long to get here, why would anyone from another planet bother?'

'Good question. It's not as though Earth would be easily detectable from a remote star system or another galaxy. Though I did read somewhere that as we've been leaking signals from radar and TV for the last sixty years, it's quite possible that extraterrestrials could have picked something up. Or they could have intercepted a specific contact signal like the *Arecibo* message.'

'The what message?'

'*Arecibo*. It's some kind of radio message that was sent to contact extraterrestrials in the 1970s, but there's been no reply yet. It's probably still travelling through space. Another possibility is that aliens could have hit upon our planet by mistake rather than by design.'

'How could that happen?'

Richard reflected then grinned. 'OK. Imagine there's this bunch of ... scaly creatures living on Planet Zong, trillions of miles away. One day their leader says, "Look, guys, our star's dying and unless we find somewhere else to settle we're not going to survive." So they set off in spaceships that can travel at the speed of light and then spend thousands of years whizzing along in complete emptiness. And just when they're getting totally fed up with each other's company and bored with their stock of DVDs, one of them shouts, "What's that over there?" They pick their way through a cloud of asteroids, zoom past some pretty in-hospitable-looking planets, then they see this shimmering blue globe, and their leader says, "That looks interesting, let's go and see.' And bo-ing! Here they are!'

She smiled. 'But if a bunch of scaly creatures are looking for a new planet to settle in, why would they set out to destroy it? It wouldn't make sense.'

Richard shrugged. 'Maybe they've been trying to find out what makes Earth so abundant, what all that green stuff is and what happens if it's eliminated. But hey! I'm only fantasising. I don't have a clue what's going on.'

The jingle of an approaching ice-cream van interrupted their conversation and Polly bounded up to them. 'Can I get an ice-cream, Mum?'

'Sure you can, Poll Doll.'

'Cool!' Polly raced off to wait for the van.

Richard looked wonderingly round the park. 'It's weird. There's this potentially huge threat to the planet, yet people are getting on with their lives as though nothing's happening. I would have expected panic.'

'There haven't been any attacks in this country for a while. Perhaps we've become complacent.'

He nodded. 'Yeah, it's easier to contemplate disasters from a comfortable distance. But this threat's of a different order isn't it? It's worldwide.'

They sat lost in thought for a moment then she smiled at him. 'It's good to have you back, Ric.'

Touched, he took her hand.

She leaned forward and kissed him on the mouth. He put his arms around her and responded eagerly.

A peal of giggles caused them to draw abruptly apart. Polly was watching them, rocking with mirth. 'Are you two in lerv? Are you going to get married?'

Fiona looked embarrassed. 'Don't be silly, Poll!' she said dismissively, but her eyes looked into his a trifle too long and alarm bells rang in his head. He *liked* Fiona, he more than liked her, he really fancied her. But he wasn't ready for another serious relationship or for taking on a ready-made family. He had a sudden nightmare vision of being trapped somewhere like Coronation Close for the rest of his days, if the end of the world didn't occur before he had completed his allotted span.

He stood up. 'The van's here. Let's get that ice cream.'

'Yes!' shouted Polly.

After buying her a cone, he pleaded exhaustion and said he needed to go home.

'When will I see you, Ric?' Fiona asked.

'Soon,' he replied cautiously, 'when I've recovered from my holiday in Scotland.'

'Perhaps we could go out to dinner one night?' she suggested. 'My treat.'

'Great,' he replied, 'as long as it's not a fish restaurant!'

Chapter 28

As he made his way home, Richard reflected on his conversation with Fiona. Were the aerial attackers really intent on wiping out the world's ecosystem? If that was the case, he needed to put his life in order. No more distractions; no more chasing after missing nuns and religious maniacs. He would concentrate on completing his thesis. Then, if the world did come to an end, at least he would have achieved something.

He slept for fifteen hours that night and in the morning resumed work on his concluding section. He was surprised to find it comparatively easy to pick up where he had left off. His experiences on the island had thrown his subject into sharper relief and he now felt even greater admiration for the survivors of natural catastrophes he had interviewed during his research. The fortitude with which they bore the calamities that had befallen them contrasted shamefully with his own pusillanimous reactions to relatively minor privations on the island.

He spent the next few days bent over his laptop, leaving the house only to buy essential provisions.

He was typing busily one morning when Fiona rang him on his parents' landline.

'Have you seen the papers?'

'What papers?'

'It's in several of them.'

'What is?'

'You'd better take a look,' she said enigmatically and rang off.

Intrigued, he opened the internet and scrolled through some of the national papers. It didn't take him long to find what she had been alluding to - a headline in one of the tabloids: *Missing Nun Found!* He gave a grunt of dismay on reading the short piece below it.

A Roman Catholic nun who was abducted from Our Lady of Lourdes Convent in May, has been found safe and well. According to a source, Sister Francis (68) was kidnapped by members of a shadowy religious sect and taken to a remote Scottish island. She managed to escape with the help of other members of the sect. The police are investigating.

Another paper contained a brief paragraph headed, *Nun's Liberation from Captivity.*

Richard groaned. Who could have leaked the story? Surely not the police while their investigations were at such an early stage. And he couldn't imagine the nuns wanting any publicity.

Later that morning, Fiona rang back, 'Have you seen it?'

'Yes. Who could have leaked the information?'

'Does it matter?'

He sighed. 'I suppose not, as long as I'm not identified. '

'There's no way anybody would know you were involved, unless Sister Francis or the police gave your name to the press. But that's unlikely isn't it?'

'I hope so.'

'When will I see you, Ric?' she asked rather plaintively. 'We were going to have that meal, remember?'

'I'll call you to arrange something soon, Fi. I've just got stuck into my thesis again.'

'OK, fine.' She sounded disappointed.

He returned to his work but was again interrupted by the phone in the hall. This time the voice that addressed him was deep and belonged to a man.

'Richard Jarman?'

'Yes?'

The caller abruptly rang off.

Richard felt a pang of unease. Could it have been one of the Inheritors? He rang 1471 but didn't recognise the number the call had been made from. He returned to his desk and resumed writing his final chapter, stopping only to make a sandwich for lunch. He was about to take it upstairs when he heard voices outside. Peering out of the hall window, he saw two men at the bottom of the garden path. They were staring up at the house. For a second he panicked, then relaxed. Unlike the Persuaders, they were casually dressed and looked slightly scruffy.

Shortly afterwards, the bell chimed.

He cautiously opened the door.

One of the men held out his hand. He had a strong scent of aftershave. 'Richard Jarman?'

'Yes?'

'I'm from *The Hertford Chronicle*.' The man waved a business card at him and before Richard knew what was happening, the other one held up a camera and took a picture of him.

He took a startled step backwards. 'Hey, what…?'

The two started firing questions at him. 'Can you give us a statement, Mr. Jarman? Were you on that island? Was it you who helped the nun escape? Give us the story, Mr. Jarman!'

'I don't know what you're talking about.' He slammed the front door and stood in front of it, breathing heavily.

Almost immediately the bell chimed again and he could see a blurred image of the first man's face through the frosted glass door pane. 'Mr. Jarman? Mr. Jarman?'

Richard ignored the voice. Soon afterwards, the telephone in the hall started to ring insistently. He removed the receiver.

For several hours he skulked indoors while the men waited outside, occasionally banging on the door and peering through the windows. Finally, in desperation, he rang DS Johnson and left a message asking him to call back.

It was a while before the officer rang and he sounded irritated when Richard told him what had happened.

'I hope you haven't been loose-tongued, Mr. Jarman. You know this is an ongoing investigation.'

'It wasn't me who spoke to the press,' Richard retorted indignantly. 'I don't know how they found out I was on that island.'

'Well don't tell them anything.'

'Of course I'm not going to tell them anything. Has the Inheritor commune been closed down?'

'I'm afraid I don't have that information. By the way, Mr. Jarman, you're presumably aware that you'll be required to identify the persons you claim abducted you and took you to that island?'

Richard sighed with relief. 'Does that mean they've been caught?'

'I believe some of the male members of the organisation have been apprehended in Scotland.'

'Won't Sister Francis's testimony be enough?'

'No, they'll need both of you, and the man who engineered your escape, to identify the ringleaders.'

'Will we have to go to Scotland to do it?'

'No. We can conduct identity procedures on a computer these days. It's called Video Identification Parade Electronic Recording, VIPER for short. You can do it at a police station or at home, if you prefer.'

Richard thought another police visit to Coronation Close would be unwise. 'I'll come to the station.'

'We'll call you when we need you. Oh and by the way, the police in Scotland are sending us some items they believe belong to you. You'll need to come and identify them as well.'

Richard heaved another sigh of relief. The police had obviously searched the commune.

It wasn't until late afternoon that he risked venturing outside. Looking cautiously around to make sure that the reporters weren't lurking in wait for him, he descended the path and had only taken a few steps towards the corner when the door of number three was flung open and Marjorie Phelps emerged.

She waddled rapidly down her steps to intercept him. 'What's going on? First the police, now the press! They've been calling at our houses, asking about you. What have you been up to now, Ricky Jarman?'

He looked at her defiantly. 'Nothing, Mrs. Phelps.'

Her billowing chins quivered with indignation. 'Nothing? This is a respectable neighbourhood, Ricky, at least it was before *you* moved back here. What's going on?'

'I'm not at liberty to say.' Richard dodged past her, scurried round the corner and hastened down the hill.

Before he had managed to go more than a hundred yards, a man leapt out of a parked car and barred his way. 'Can you spare a few minutes, Mr. Jarman?'

Richard was dismayed to recognise one of his earlier callers, the one with the sickly-smelling aftershave. 'Get out of my way!' he snapped, sidestepping the man and striking off down the hill.

Hurrying footsteps followed. 'Hang on, Mr. Jarman; I only want to ask you a few questions.'

Richard quickened his pace but the journalist rapidly caught up and trotted alongside him, panting. 'Please, Mr. Jarman, just a few minutes of your time.'

'What the hell do you want?'

'Can you confirm that you were on that island in the Shetlands at the same time as the missing nun --?'

'What island? What nun?' Richard strode on without turning his head or slackening his pace.

The man gave an incredulous laugh. 'Give me a break, Mr. Jarman. The nun who was kidnapped and taken to an island in the Shetlands.'

Richard hastened on, looking straight ahead. 'What's that got to do with me?'

'Come on, Mr. Jarman. I'm pretty sure you were also on that island.'

Richard came to an abrupt halt and swung round to face him. 'What are you talking about?'

'Your name *is* Richard Jarman?'

'It is, but I can't be the only person with that name. Why are you harassing *me*?'

The reporter took a tissue from his pocket and mopped his face. 'We found you by a process of elimination. We've been contacting all the Jarmans listed in the London directory. Fortunately there aren't very many. I rang your house this morning. You answered, remember?'

'That was you?'

'Yes. And when we came here, a lady told us that you've been away from home and only came back a few days ago ... in a police car.'

'What lady?'

'A little lady with a shopping bag. Irish accent.'

Richard sighed. *Thank you, Mrs. Brennan.* 'Just because I'm called Richard Jarman,' he snapped, 'it doesn't mean I have anything to do with the nun who escaped from an island.'

The reporter winked at him. 'I think you have *everything* to do with her, Mr. Jarman.'

Richard's curiosity overcame his better judgment. 'Where did you get the name Jarman from in the first place?'

'The nun. Someone overheard her telling the story of what had happened to her.'

'Who overheard her?'

'An electrician. He was doing some rewiring at the convent when the nun was brought back by the police. He contacted *The Chronicle* and for a ... small consideration, told us what she said. He said she told the other nuns that she'd been kidnapped by a religious cult and taken to an island in the Shetlands. She said she was kept there against her will. But you know this already, don't you, Mr. Jarman?'

'No, why should I?'

'The electrician heard her say that she escaped with some Scottish bloke and a younger guy called Richard Jarman from London. We contacted the convent but the nuns refused to talk to us. That's why we've been looking for you, so we can get the full story. So come on, Mr. Jarman. You arrived home in a police car the same day that the nun returned to the convent, didn't you?'

'Piss off!' Richard wheeled away from the reporter and sped across the road to the shopping parade. Dodging behind a delivery van, he peered round the side of it and saw the reporter running across the road in pursuit. Richard watched him hurry, panting, towards the minimarket, look up and down, then set off towards the petrol station.

Richard scuttled in the opposite direction and turned into a nearby side street. When he was sure he hadn't been followed, he slowed his pace to a stroll. It was a warm evening and groups of people were sitting at tables outside bars, chatting and laughing as though they didn't have a care in the world. He glared at them resentfully. Why weren't they as anxious and as pissed off as he was?

To kill time, he bought an evening paper and sat down outside a coffee bar to read it. The headline on the front page announced the return of the Prime Minister from the United Nations Security Council meeting. A photo showed him arriving, grim-faced, at Number Ten where he was due to prepare his address to the nation, scheduled for eight o'clock that evening.

Inside the paper, a double spread featured a map of the world with the words *Global Trail of Destruction* written in glaring red across the top. The devastated areas were marked with small white crosses. They covered a disturbingly wide area of the globe. At the bottom of the pages was a question, printed in strident upper case: *WHO IS RESPONSIBLE?*

Peering at the map, Richard recalled with a shiver how the Persuaders had rejoiced on hearing news of the latest attacks on the car radio. He folded the paper, tucked it under his arm and set off for home. As he turned into the Close, he peered anxiously around but there was no sign of any reporters, nor, thankfully, of Marjorie Phelps. He dashed past her window, unlocked his front door and went inside, locking it securely behind him.

At eight, he switched on the television.

The Prime Minister's lined face stared out from the screen. 'As you are all aware,' he started, 'persons as yet unidentified have destroyed significant areas of plant life across the globe, increasing levels of carbon dioxide in the atmosphere and reducing the supply of oxygen on which life on this planet depends.' He gazed grimly at the camera. 'Mercifully, the United Kingdom has not been targeted over the last few weeks, but we cannot be complacent as the attackers could strike again. So far, about twelve countries besides our own have suffered these incendiary attacks.'

He paused and a map of the globe appeared on the screen with the chronology and location of the strikes marked in red.

'We don't know the perpetrators' motives,' the Prime Minister continued. 'No-one has yet been able to identify any specific political or religious reason for these actions. But despite some of the more fantastical rumours in circulation, I can assure you that those responsible are *not* extraterrestrials. The Ministry of Defence has seen nothing to date that could be classed as proof that extraterrestrial life exists.' He gazed gravely into the camera and cleared his throat.

'The Secretary General of the United Nations has declared that these acts of terrorism present the greatest threat to the world since the Cuban missile crisis of 1962. In consequence, the Security Council has held a second emergency meeting to consider what measures can be taken to defend the world against further attacks. The Security Council has a responsibility to protect populations and it has the power to take whatever action it believes is necessary to restore international security. That includes military action. All member states have put their security services on full alert and have pledged to cooperate in any joint military action to combat this menace. Those in a position to do so are sending trackers to intercept any suspicious over-flying aircraft.'

He blinked at the camera then enunciated slowly and clearly, 'There is no need to panic. Everything that can be done to safeguard the planet and, of course our own country, will be done. Here, in the United Kingdom, our defence and emergency services are on high alert and Her Majesty's Government is ready to use emergency powers to deal with any threats to national security. We are also instructing local authorities to prepare contingency plans and to set off warning sirens whenever an enemy attack is detected.'

'Blimey,' muttered Richard. He had occasionally heard air-raid sirens in radio and television documentaries about the Second World War, and had been struck by the eerie quality of their high-pitched wail.

The Prime Minister's voice increased in strength and sonority. 'I repeat, everything that can be done to contain and oppose this menace will be done, and I am absolutely confident that we will defeat those responsible. These islands have a history of brave resistance to external aggression and I assure you that we will overcome this new threat. Thank you and goodnight.'

The Prime Minister's address was followed by a report on the recent attack on Brazilian rainforests. Video footage taken from a helicopter showed scores of blackened trees, some of which were still smouldering.

'The Pope,' the newsreader announced, 'has declared next Monday a day of special prayer for world peace and security.'

Richard switched off the television and sat hunched in his chair. He wondered whether he was any different from the insouciant groups he had seen sitting outside cafes and bars earlier that evening, fiddling while the world literally burned. On the other hand, what else was there to do? What could *anybody* do, except carry on as usual and wait to see what happened next?'

He went upstairs and with a shaking hand, searched his pockets for the rosary. With a grunt of relief, he found it in the pocket of the oversized trousers Aggie had lent him. He tucked it under his pillow.

* * *

The next morning he rang the number DS Johnson had given him and arranged to collect his father's car. To his relief, no neighbours or reporters accosted him as he left the Close and descended the hill. While he waited at the bus stop, a beautiful black girl glided past. He stared hungrily at her swaying hips and jutting buttocks. Sex. That was what he needed! He had been chaste for far too long. It wasn't that he had taken a vow of celibacy; it had just happened that way. He made an effort to ignore the surge of sexual desire that was assailing him, but in the warm early summer, the streets seemed full of attractive girls; girls in shorts and strappy tops; girls in skimpy dresses and ridiculously high heels; girls with swinging dark hair like Fiona's.

Fiona…He knew she was as attracted to him as he was to her, but she might get ideas about commitment, and he didn't want her to get the wrong impression. On the other hand, she had interpreted the Inheritors' message for him and had contacted the police when he didn't return from the rendezvous in Hertfordshire. She had also looked after Maggie while he was away and was willing to keep her on a permanent basis. He felt a rush of guilt at not having contacted her.

When the bus arrived, he sat on the upper deck. Soon bored with looking at the passing suburban streets, he picked up a discarded copy of *The Hertford Chronicle*. The front page focused on the Prime Minister's address and he wondered whether the speech had acted as a wake-up call to a public that had suppressed its fears remarkably quickly after the panic following the initial attacks had subsided. Was it due to complacency, as Fiona had suggested? Yet as he tuned into the buzz of conversation around him, he had the impression that the mood had changed and had become more sombre.

'What's the world coming to?' he heard the elderly man in front of him say to the woman beside him. 'We didn't win the last war for this.'

'I think it's immigrants,' the woman responded irrelevantly. 'All them foreigners. We've allowed too many people into this country.'

'Fancy using air-raid sirens,' the man continued as though she hadn't spoken. 'I remember them from when I was a nipper. Nasty sound it was. Sent shivers down your spine.'

In the seat behind Richard, another man was patiently explaining the Prime Minister's message to a woman who was obviously confused by its import.

'But what does it mean?' she asked tremulously

'It means we've got to be vigilant and prepared, Mum.'

'Why do we need gas masks?'

'Not gas masks, Mum, facemasks, like those that protect you from infections or traffic fumes, but only if there's another attack.'

'Oh.' She sounded baffled.

Not everyone seemed to be fazed by the threat hanging over the world. Richard could hear a young girl speaking loudly on her mobile phone about something of infinitely greater importance: the outfit she was going to wear that evening.

He turned his attention back to the newspaper and started idly flicking through the inner pages. Then, *Christ!* He was looking at his own face, frozen in a stupid open-mouthed expression of surprise, under the headline, *Man Denies Assisting Nun's Escape*. He uttered a silent curse. Bloody reporters! He wished he had smashed their camera. The photo was accompanied by a brief and inaccurate version of Sister Francis's abduction and escape.

He cast a furtive glance behind him but no-one was looking his way. He hoped the paper had a limited circulation and that the story hadn't been syndicated.

After retrieving his father's car, he drove home and was dismayed to see Marjorie Phelps hovering on the pavement near the foot of his path. She was holding a newspaper. Bracing himself, he got out of the car and walked nonchalantly up the Close. When he reached her, she brandished the paper at him. He could see it was a copy of *The Evening News*. With a sinking heart, he caught sight of his photo on the page facing upwards. She jabbed her finger at it and trumpeted, 'I *knew* you were up to something, Ricky Jarman!'

'What do you mean, Mrs. Phelps?'

'It says here that you had something to do with that nun who was kidnapped.'

'Does it?' He assumed an expression of extreme surprise.

'Don't try to be coy with me! How did you get involved in the kidnapping of a nun?'

'Why?' he retorted. 'Do you have a problem with nuns, Mrs. Phelps?'

'No,' she snapped, 'I don't have a problem with nuns, but I do have a problem with young men who bring our neighbourhood into disrepute.'

Richard struggled to keep his voice calm. 'Are you implying that helping an abducted nun to escape, assuming that I did, is something disreputable?'

Her face flushed with anger. 'Of course not. But your general behaviour *is*, and as president of the Residents' Committee, I am empowered to tell you that we ...' she waved her arm in a gesture to embrace the whole Close '... we are not prepared to tolerate any more disruption, so unless you -- '

'Unless I what?' He lowered his voice to a conspiratorial whisper. 'If you must know, Mrs. Phelps, I'm helping the police with a very important enquiry. It's top secret and I'm not at liberty to talk about it, not to the press, not to you, not to anyone. The police have warned me that if anyone goes shooting their mouth off to reporters, it could jeopardise the outcome of the enquiry.' He turned on his heel, walked up the path and entered the house, slamming the door behind him.

He went straight to the TV and checked for a news update. Reports of panic-buying suggested that the Prime Minister's address had increased rather than calmed the public's fears. He wasn't surprised. One of the final news items, however, did surprise him.

'Police have swooped on a small island in the Shetlands,' announced the glamorous female newsreader. 'They are investigating a commune set up by a religious sect that originated in the United States. Members of the commune are believed to have abducted a nun from a convent in Hertfordshire. She managed to escape and has given evidence about her ordeal to the police. A number of men have been taken into custody on suspicion of abduction, underage sex and child abuse. A group of women and children are being temporarily looked after at a special centre and are awaiting repatriation. An Interpol Red Notice has been issued for the sect's leader, Abraham Rosenberg, who also goes by the names of Solomon Godworthy and Harold Martyr. He is believed to be in hiding somewhere in Europe.'

'Yes!' Richard punched the air.

'Rosenberg,' the newsreader continued, 'spent some years in a psychiatric institution before founding the sect which is now proscribed in the United States. He is wanted on charges of fraud, extortion and abduction of women and minors.'

Richard stood up and danced round the room. So the great "poet, healer and philosopher" was also a fraudster, as well as a deranged religious nut. So much for his having a hotline to the Messiah! He went to the landline in the hall to share his glee with Fiona. However it was her mother who answered the phone, sounding distinctly unfriendly. She told him that Fiona had taken Polly to Cornwall as it was half-term, and wouldn't be back for another couple of days. 'Her father and I,' she added with some asperity, 'have been left with that ugly dog.'

Disappointed, he was about to go upstairs when the doorbell chimed. He peered cautiously out of the hall window. A man with a camera was standing on the step and another was waiting at the bottom of the path.

'You can piss off!' Richard muttered and hastened up the stairs.

He resumed work on his thesis and after several hours of concerted effort, emailed the final chapters to Professor Salter for his comments.

Chapter 29

Now that his thesis was finished, Richard found time hanging heavily on his hands. To avoid being waylaid by journalists, he spent most of the daylight hours listening to music and watching DVDs, in between checking the news on the television and internet.

News bulletins now contained daily statements from the UN Security Council about the global "terrorist threat". Despite the growing number of reports that brilliantly coloured, spinning objects in the sky had been seen on the nights the arson attacks took place, any suggestion that the threat might emanate from extraterrestrials continued to be rubbished. This assurance didn't allay increasing public fears, however, and in some parts of the world, groups of zealots were reported to be heading for hills and mountain tops to prepare for the end of the world.

After several days of inertia, Richard set about cleaning and tidying the house with a vigour that would have astonished his mother. He had a vague hope that imposing order on his living space might do something to mitigate his growing anxiety. He scrubbed the kitchen and bathroom and dusted the living room, before turning his attention to the back garden. For the first time since his parents had left on their cruise, he watered the flowerbeds and weeded the borders. He was amused to catch a glimpse of Mrs. Perkins watching him with an astonished expression from her bedroom window.

When a message arrived from his supervisor, approving the final section of his thesis and suggesting possible dates for the *viva*, he felt a huge sense of relief. Now he could get on with something that would take his mind off the global crisis: a search for job opportunities with overseas aid agencies.

He spent some time producing a CV that he felt was sufficiently flexible and comprehensive to win him some interviews, then sent copies, together with appropriate covering letters, to a number of prominent international aid and development agencies.

Fiona called him at the weekend. 'Mum said you rang.'

'Yes, she told me you were in Cornwall. Did you have a good time?'

'It was fine. We stayed with my cousin in Truro. Polly enjoyed herself.'

He noticed that her voice sounded flat. 'But you didn't?'

'It was OK, I suppose. Not warm enough to swim, though.'

'That's a shame.'

'I'm scared, Ric,' she blurted. 'I listened to the PM the other night. What's happening? It seemed kind of unreal before, but now they're implying the world's on a knife edge.' Her voice shook. 'It's hard to carry on as though nothing's happening.'

'That's all we can do, Fi, all anyone can do. At least there have been no more attacks in this country.'

'I suppose so.' After a brief silence that he found uncomfortable, she added, 'How have you been?'

'Me? Fine. I've finished my thesis.'

'That's great. You must be pleased.'

'I am. I've started job-hunting. I've just sent my CV to a bunch of aid agencies.'

'That's good.'

There was another silence and he searched for a new topic. 'Did you hear that the police have raided the island I was taken to and closed down the commune?'

'No, I hadn't heard.'

'I don't know if they've arrested all the Persuaders yet, but they're after Rosenberg. He's wanted on a whole bunch of charges.'

'Oh,' she replied without apparent interest.

'How's Maggie?' he asked in an attempt to keep the conversation going.

'Mum and Dad didn't enjoy having her on their own. She's very unpopular at the moment.'

'Why's that?'

'She ate the cake Mum made for our return.'

'What, all of it?'

'Every crumb.'

He was relieved to hear her laugh. A thought struck him. 'You wouldn't be free on Friday night, would you, Fi?'

She hesitated before answering cautiously, 'I could be, why?'

'A former colleague of mine, Phil, between you and me he's a bit of a prat, but he's got a new job and a group of us from my old journal, *Global Geographic*, are celebrating at a pub in Town. I'm afraid *The*

Green Man's not the greatest venue in the world, but it'll be better than sitting indoors brooding about what might happen. And afterwards you could buy me that meal you promised me?'

'OK,' she said after a third pause. 'I expect Mum and Dad will enjoy having Polly to themselves.'

'Cool. I'll pick you up about seven.'

Later that evening the phone rang again. Fearing that it could be another reporter, he picked it up warily and was relieved to find that it was his sister.

'What on earth's going on, Ricky? Mike saw your picture in the paper. Something about a missing nun?'

He groaned. 'Oh, bugger!'

'What's it all about?'

'It's complicated, Sass. The police know about it and I can't say any more, not to the press, not to anyone. '

'But--'

'Sorry, Sass, all I can tell you at the moment is that the police are investigating.'

Saskia sounded baffled. 'I don't understand. I thought you were writing your thesis.'

'I was,' he said wearily. 'And you'll be pleased to hear that I've finished it.'

'That's great. But how did you get mixed up with that missing nun?'

'I found out that she'd been kidnapped by a religious sect and helped her get away.'

'*What?*'

'That's all I can tell you for now, Sass. I promise you I'll explain soon. Please don't say anything about it to Mum and Dad when you email them. You know how Mum worries.'

Reluctantly she agreed.

* * *

Fiona seemed subdued when he called for her on Friday evening. She gave him a casual peck on the cheek and on the journey into central London, gave only brief and uninformative responses when he attempted to make conversation. He cast covert glances at her. Her hair had grown longer and now fell smoothly to the top of her shoulders. A strand was caught on one of her silver loop earrings. The close-fitting blue top she was wearing clung to her small pointed breasts. He tried not to stare at them. He thought that he would definitely like to take the relationship a stage further though not, perhaps, as far as she wished.

That was the problem.

'Did you see my picture in the paper?' he asked, fearing that she might be reading his thoughts.

She looked surprised. 'No. What paper?'

'A local Hertfordshire rag and *The Evening News*. Could have been in others. Your parents may have seen it.'

'Well if they have, they haven't mentioned it. Did the reporters find out where you live?'

'Unfortunately yes, and they've been hounding me ever since.' He noticed that her eyes looked blue this time rather than their habitual green-grey.

'That's bad luck. I suppose you can't tell them anything.'

'No, it might prejudice the case. But it doesn't matter how often I say "no comment", they keep coming back.'

'Poor you. I bet you wish you'd never heard of the Inheritors.'

'You can say that again.' He was relieved that her manner towards him seemed to have thawed. 'And I've had a letter from the police. I've got to pick some of them out in an identity parade.'

His spirits sank as soon as they entered the dingy interior of *The Green Man*. A raucous burst of laughter immediately directed his attention to the far side of the room where Phil Banks was standing drinking with some of his other former colleagues. Richard prayed that none of them had seen his picture in the paper.

Phil approached, waving his glass in greeting. 'Ric! Glad you could come.' He leered at Fiona. 'And who's *this*? You've been keeping her very quiet, haven't you, Professor?'

Richard made the introductions, then, as Phil bustled Fiona up to the counter to get drinks, went over to greet the other men. After the customary exchange of banter, he drew Mark Davenport aside.

'What did you make of the PM's address? Do you believe they're terrorists?'

'The jury's still out, Ric. My mate in Washington says the Pentagon's playing the whole thing down. They're peddling the line that what's happening is part of a plot to destabilise certain nations. But he also told me something else. One night when those airships or whatever they are, were spotted over the States, some radio and light signals were picked up on radar. They were coming from the ground.'

Richard was puzzled. 'From the ground?'

'They think someone has been signalling to them.'

'Christ! Do they know who?'

'Yes, some religious fanatics, can't remember their name. Apparently they'd set up a kind of observatory in a remote area on the Arizona-Utah border. A number of people have been taken into custody. Now they're looking for the leader, the founder. Nasty bit of work by all accounts. Abraham something or other.'

Richard's heart gave an unpleasant lurch. 'You mean Abraham Rosenberg?'

Mark looked surprised. 'Yes that's the name. Have you heard of him?'

'More than that. 'I've actually met him.'

'You've *met* him?'

'Yes, it's a long story.' Before Richard could say any more, they were joined by Fiona and Phil Banks.

Phil thrust a pint into his hand. 'I've just been telling the lovely Fiona about my onward and upward career march.' He proceeded to regale Richard with a detailed account of the masterly interview he had given to secure his new job. While he was still in full flow, the other GG colleagues drifted across from the bar. One of them, Luke, nudged Richard in the ribs.

'Hey, Ric, did I see your ugly mug in *The Evening News* the other day?'

Richard's heart sank.

'What's this?' interrupted Phil. 'Picture in the paper? What 'ave you been up to, Professor?'

'Nothing,' Richard muttered. 'A case of mistaken identity'.

Luke jabbed him playfully in the chest. 'Come on! What's the story? Spill the beans.'

'There are no beans to spill.' He adopted a jocular tone. 'They got the wrong man: the wrong *Jar* man.'

'It was something to do with that nun,' Luke insisted. 'The one who was kidnapped?'

'A nun?' spluttered Phil, nearly choking on his beer. 'You old pervert!
I never 'ad you down as a nun-fancier, Ric. We're you taken with 'er
'abits?' He laughed uproariously. 'I always said you needed a *good*
woman! Fiona, you tell us, what's our professor been up to?'

'Nothing,' Fiona said frostily. 'Ric just told you, they got the wrong
person.' She turned to Richard. 'Could we find somewhere to sit down,
Ric? It's too noisy here.'

Gratefully, he conducted her to a vacant table. 'Do you want to go?'
he asked as they sat down.

'No.' She took a sip of her wine. 'Let's stay for a while. At least finish
our drinks.'

Phil and the others trailed after them and started dragging chairs up
to the table. Within minutes they had forgotten about his picture in the
paper and were exchanging ribald anecdotes.

A blizzard of questions swept through Richard's mind as he pretended to listen: Why had the Inheritors been signalling to the mysterious aircraft? Was there a direct link between them and the attackers?
And did this mean that Rosenberg was now back in the States? Frustrat-
ingly, the group round the table had become too boisterous for him to
discuss these questions with Mark, and when Phil suggested moving on
to *Hot Totty*, he decided it was time for him and Fiona to leave.

'You can't go yet,' protested Phil.

'We're going to get something to eat,' said Richard, 'then I'm taking
this young lady home.'

Phil sniggered. 'So early? *You're* not a nun, are you, Fiona? '

'Not yet.' She forced a smile.

As the group rose to say goodbye, Richard took Mark aside and muttered, 'I'll give you a bell tomorrow,' before shepherding Fiona towards
the door.

'You were right,' she said as they made their way to an Italian
restaurant they had spotted on their way to *The Green Man*.

'What about?'

'Phil. He *is* a prat.'

Richard laughed and slipped an arm around her waist.

When they were in the restaurant, he related what Mark had told
him about the Inheritors.

'I don't understand it. Why would they be signalling to those airships or whatever they are?'

She looked thoughtful. 'Well, I suppose it makes a kind of sense.'

'What do you mean?'

'Look at it this way. They're expecting the Second Coming, right?'

'Right.'

'Well where exactly is the Messiah going to arrive? It could be any-where on the planet. If they believe they're the chosen people, they've got to guide him to where they are.'

'But I thought Rosenberg was hiding out in Europe somewhere, not in a remote part of Arizona.'

'Maybe the Inheritors' headquarters is still in the States.'

Richard was still puzzled. 'But if they believe in an all-powerful Mes-siah, wouldn't they think he'd *know* where to find them?'

She smiled. 'As you've said yourself, the Inheritors' beliefs aren't par-ticularly rational or logical.'

* * *

It was after eleven by the time they arrived at her parents' house. She smiled at him as she unfastened the gate. 'Thanks, Ric. It's been an in-teresting evening.'

Without answering, he crushed her to him and kissed her urgently. She responded with gratifying enthusiasm and they remained locked together until there was a volley of barks inside the house and a light came on in an upstairs window. Two faces peered down at them.

'Bugger!' Richard exclaimed. 'Thanks a lot, Maggie!'

Flustered, Fiona extricated herself from his arms. 'I'd better go in. See you, Ric.' She darted towards the door.

Trudging grumpily home, he gazed up at the cloudless sky. The moon, a fading glimmer in its last quarter, was surrounded by sparkling pinpricks of light. Was one of them the home of the flying objects that were now terrorising the Earth? Or had the attackers come from a planet orbiting a star so remote that its ancient light wasn't yet detectable by even the most powerful radio telescope?

Part 3
The Bobblers

Chapter 30

Richard was in the middle of a dreamless sleep when something jerked him abruptly awake. It was a noise, a very unpleasant noise: the wailing of an air raid siren. He gasped and sat up. The room was illuminated with an unnaturally brilliant light. He jumped out of bed and ran to the window, then gasped again. For the sky was ablaze with streaks of amazing colour - crimson, yellow and orange.

Thrusting his head out of the window, he craned his neck upwards, but could see nothing. He shut the window, pulled on some clothes and ran downstairs. As he opened the front door, the volume of the siren intensified, the sound mingling with furious barking from Pugwash next door. He stepped outside and saw his neighbours emerging rapidly from their houses, calling to each other in alarm, and gathering in small pyjama-clad huddles on the pavement. Some were tying on facemasks.

He joined Reg and Doris Perkins and Stan and Marjorie Phelps under the street lamp. They were staring towards the south. Looking in the same direction, he gasped on seeing saw two astonishingly bright objects suspended high in the sky.

'What are they, Reg?' Stan Phelps shouted over the sound of the siren. 'Are they military aircraft?'

Reg looked bewildered. 'I don't know. I've never seen anything like them before.'

Marjorie Phelps, majestic in a pink bed jacket over a billowing white nightgown, pumped her husband's arm. 'Do something, Stanley,' she ordered.

'What do you want me to do, woman?' he snapped irritably. 'Tell them to turn off the siren?'

'It's an air-raid warning,' she retorted. 'We've got to do *something*!'

Mrs. Brennan joined them, whimpering with fear as she fumbled with her facemask. 'Holy Mother of God! What's happening?'

Doris Perkins took her by the hand. 'We don't know yet, dear. Let me help you with that.'

'Look!' Reg shouted excitedly, gesticulating at the sky.

Following the direction of his finger, Richard saw four tiny winged shapes gliding upwards in a pincer movement leaving white trails in their wake.

'Fighter planes,' exclaimed Reg excitedly. 'Go gettem, boys!'

'Fighter planes?' gulped his wife. 'Are we at war, Reggie?'

'I think ... blimey! Look at that!' Reg pointed at the two dazzling objects in the distance.

The group gave a collective gasp, for the objects had started revolving. They spun slowly at first, then progressively faster until they became two pulsating orbs of brilliant light. Then suddenly and with unimaginable speed, they shot upwards and disappeared from view.

Dazed, Richard gaped at the empty space where they had been. The coloured streaks in the sky were already starting to fade. Almost immediately the fighter jets roared overhead then separated and wheeled away into the distance. After a few minutes the siren stopped. A heavy silence descended on the Close, only broken when a baby in a nearby house started to cry.

'Bloody' ell,' muttered Stan Phelps. 'Bloody 'ell!'

'Language, Stanley!' snapped his wife.

Reg Perkins was opening and shutting his mouth like a fish. 'I've never seen anything like that in my life,' he stuttered. 'Never.'

His wife tugged anxiously at his dressing gown sleeve. 'Are we at war, Reggie?' she repeated.

'I don't know, dear. I just don't know.'

'It's curious,' Richard mused aloud. 'I wonder why there weren't there any sparks this time?'

They stared at him.

'What do you mean, "this time"? What sparks?' Marjorie Phelps asked sharply.

'The night Fonthill Recreation Ground was hit, I saw sparks coming from one of those things.'

'You mean you've seen one of them before, Ricky?' asked Stan Phelps.

'Yes, I told you, Mr. Phelps. Don't you remember? When you were cutting your hedge the morning after Fonthill Park was destroyed, I asked you if you'd seen anything during the night.'

Stan looked confused. 'Did you, Ricky? I don't remember.'

'Yes,' Richard glanced sideways at Marjorie Phelps. 'I reported it to the police. They came round to take a statement. You remember that, don't you, Mrs. Phelps?'

'You said your bicycle had been stolen,' she retorted accusingly.

'That was because it was top secret. Maybe we should go indoors to see if there have been any announcements.'

After a few moments of anxious discussion, the group dispersed.

Once indoors, Richard switched on the TV. Programmes on all channels had been replaced by a repeated announcement. Its message was stark:

People in the London area, do not panic. Stay in your homes. Everything is under control. The unidentified aircraft above the capital have been put to flight. The armed forces are on standby to deal with any further incursions into our air space. The Government is taking every precaution to protect the public from any external threat. The Cabinet is meeting today to discuss invoking emergency powers under the Civil Contingencies Act.

Richard didn't bother to return to bed. He sat in front of the TV in a state of agitation, replaying in his mind the scene he had witnessed and trying to figure out what it signified. When news programmes caught up with events, film footage showed the mysterious flying objects rotating then accelerating away at mind-blowing speed, while the crowds that had come out onto the streets watched in stupefaction.

A grim-faced government spokesman appeared on all channels and strove unconvincingly to reassure people that everything was under control. He repeated the claim that the mysterious aircraft had been forced to retreat, adding that there had been no reported acts of destruction.

Politicians, representatives of the armed forces as well as astrophysicists and scientists were hastily summoned to television and radio newsrooms to discuss what had occurred. Most pronounced themselves baffled and several cautiously expressed the view that the objects' extraordinary powers of acceleration and manoeuvrability were way beyond the capacity of any man-made flying machines.

Subsequent reports from around the world indicated that unidentified objects had also hovered threateningly over a number of other major cities during the night. Eye witnesses described how they had streaked away with amazing velocity after fighter jets were sent to intercept them. In some countries, panic-stricken crowds had gathered outside government buildings, demanding explanations and reassurances.

As Richard watched the news, his apprehension increased. He waited until nine then rang Mark Davenport. 'Did you see them?'

'Yes!' Mark sounded excited. 'Quite extraordinary!'

'What do you think they are?'

'I'm pretty sure now that we're not dealing with a human agency.'

Richard expelled a long breath. 'I've thought so all along, but didn't want to believe it. The implications are too scary.'

'An alien invasion in our lifetime? All the evidence says it's impossible but if it is, it's history in the making, Ric!'

Richard felt it was a piece of history he would prefer not to be experiencing, although (and he was slightly ashamed at the thought) it might have the welcome effect of diverting press attention from Sister Francis and himself.

'What do you think they're up to? Are they just watching us?'

'It's possible. Maybe they're planning a new offensive.'

Richard shivered. 'But what do they want? What are they trying to achieve?'

He heard Mark sigh. 'I'm not acquainted with the thinking processes of aliens, dear boy. One thing you can count on is that their minds, if they *have* minds, won't be anything like ours. For all we know, they might be machines ... robots ... feats of technology we can't begin to imagine, which presumably is how they've managed to escape detection so long by satellites and tracking devices. That reminds me. You were telling me the other night that you actually met that guy, Rosenberg, the religious nutter the police are after.'

'Yeah, worst luck. He's the leader of a proscribed sect called Inheritors of the New Kingdom. I sort of ... got involved with them.'

'Jesus, Ric! How did you manage to get mixed up with a bunch like that?'

Richard sighed. 'I suspected some of his followers were behind that nun's disappearance, so I stupidly went to find them.'

Mark whistled. 'You mean Luke was right? You *were* involved in that nun's escape, like it said in the paper?'

' 'Fraid so. Some of Rosenberg's followers took me to an island in the Shetlands and that's where I found her. We managed to get away, but I've got to keep schtum because the police are investigating the whole business.'

'But how did you get involved with that nun in the first place?' Mark sounded bewildered.

'It's far too complicated to go into now, not with all this happening. I'll tell you all about it when I see you.'

After speaking to Mark, Richard left the house, deciding that a walk might help to steady his nerves.

It was an unusually hot morning, noisy with the clamour of church bells. The traffic beyond the Close was busier than usual and as he reached the bottom of the hill, he could see an unusual number of people milling around the shopping parade. When he crossed the road, he discovered the reason. A straggling queue extended from Mr. Patel's shop right to the end of the parade, then looped back to make a parallel line alongside. A long queue of cars had also formed at the petrol station.

Some of the people outside the minimarket were carrying facemasks and a few were even wearing them. Richard overheard snatches of conversation. Unsurprisingly there was only one topic.

I never thought I'd hear that noise again … It was just like during the Blitz … My nan was hiding under the kitchen table … I didn't know what them things were … They looked like spaceships to me … Rubbish, there aint no such thing … The Prime Minister said it's terrorists doing this … What's the army doing?

A hand-written notice outside the shop informed Richard that certain items - bread, rice, flour, tinned soup, bottled water, candles and toilet paper - had already sold out. He hovered uncertainly for a few moments, wondering whether to join the queue of panic-buyers, but as it was so long, rejected the idea. Instead, he walked on to the newsagents, picking his way past another long and impatient queue that had formed in front of the cash dispensing machine. With a pang he recalled poor Paddy McAllister squatting on the pavement there with Maggie sprawled beside him.

At the newsagents, he joined another line of people queuing to buy the Sunday papers. Most had been printed too early to include coverage of the morning's dramatic events, but one of the tabloids had been quick off the mark and had produced a front page that screamed *The Terror Returns* above a photograph of the UFOs that someone had managed to take with a powerful camera.

The text beneath the image seemed intent on increasing panic. It declared that emergency measures were being prepared in hospitals in all major towns and cities, and that, should the unknown aircraft return, the police, assisted by the army, would be given special powers to maintain public order. Readers were offered several helpful pieces of advice: *Take your masks with you every time you go out. Stock up on essentials. Stay indoors when the siren goes. Make sure you know where children are at all times. Watch out for elderly relatives and neighbours, especially those living on their own.*

The page concluded with a list of emergency telephone numbers.

'Hot innit?' muttered the shopkeeper as Richard paid for the paper. He gestured at the front page. 'Terrible business, this. Dunno what to make of it, do you?'

Richard shook his head. Wiping the perspiration from his forehead, he retraced his steps along the parade and started back up the hill.

By the time he got home, a clammy and oppressive heat had settled over the Close. Then with startling suddenness, the sky darkened and purple-black clouds massed ominously across the sky. Seconds after he had shut the door, a clap of thunder exploded like a sonic boom, causing the house to shake alarmingly. Blinding streaks of lightning illuminated the living room like neon lights, followed, a few moments later, by some of the loudest bangs he had ever heard.

Awestruck, he watched the storm through the patio windows. A howling wind tore round the house, rattling doors and forcing the branches of trees and shrubs into a frenzied dance. Rain pounded aggressively on the roof and battered at the windows. Within minutes the back garden resembled a lake. Although Richard had experienced massive storms in Asia, he knew enough about weather systems to recognise that this one was out of the ordinary.

The storm had been raging for about half an hour when the doorbell rang. The wind pushed him violently backwards as he opened the door. As he steadied himself, someone leapt inside and stood dripping on the mat.

'Jesus, Fi,' he exclaimed, using all his strength to push the door shut. 'You're soaked. What are you doing out in this weather?'

She pushed her dripping hair away from her face. 'Sorry to barge in on you like this. I went to get stuff from the shops but there were incredible queues. I waited for ages then got caught in the storm. It was quicker to come here than go home. You don't mind?'

'Of course not.' He led her to the cloakroom in the hall. 'Take off your wet things and I'll put them in the tumble dryer. I'll find you some dry ones.'

She joined him later in the living room, looking incongruously young in his mother's voluminous pink bathrobe and fluffy slippers. She flopped down in an armchair, dabbing ineffectively at her wet hair with a hand towel.

'Here, let me do that.' He took the towel from her and rubbed her hair vigorously, causing it to stick out in points round her face.

'You'll make someone a good mum one day, Richard Jarman,' she commented, raising her voice to make herself heard against the howling wind.

He grinned. 'Maybe that's my new vocation.' He put down the towel and returned to the window. 'I've never seen a storm like this before, not in England.'

'Neither have I. It came on so suddenly. People were running in all directions looking for shelter. And after the siren this morning...' She rose from the chair and joined him at the window. 'What do you think is happening, Ric?'

'I've no idea, Fi.'

'Mum's really freaked out. She thinks it's the start of World War Three.'

'What about Polly?'

'She seems OK, thank goodness. She doesn't understand what's going on.'

'Nobody does. Whoever was up there seemed to be making some kind of statement.'

'Mum wants us to go and stay with my aunt in Suffolk. She thinks we'll be safer there. But I said they should go without me. I don't want to be separated from Polly, but I'm needed here at the hospital. They've set up a special emergency unit and we're all on call.'

Richard felt selfishly relieved.

She put a hand on his arm. 'Do you mind if I call home? They'll be worried about me.'

'Go ahead. I'll put the kettle on and see if I can find my mother's hair dryer.'

He went into the kitchen and filled the kettle. But when he switched it on nothing happened. He tried the light switch. Nothing. He boiled the water in a saucepan on the gas stove and made two cups of tea.

'No point in looking for the hair dryer,' he told her as he carried the cups into the living room. 'There's a power cut. Your clothes will have to stay wet I'm afraid.'

'I have to put them back on anyway. Dad's coming to collect me.'

'Well, have some tea first.' He handed her a cup.

After she had drunk the tea, she returned to the cloakroom and changed back into her wet clothes.

He took her hand when she entered the sitting-room. 'Fi ...'

'Yes?'

'If your parents go away and you don't want to be on your own, you can always stay here.'

She smiled at him. 'Thanks, Ric.'

He caught her in an embrace. Seconds later the doorbell chimed. 'That'll be Dad.' She broke away from him.

He bit back his disappointment as she disappeared through the front door.

* * *

By the early evening the storm had burnt itself out, leaving not the freshness Richard would have expected, but oppressive heat and humidity. As soon as power was restored, he switched the television back on to see if there was any further news. The previous night's happenings were now superseded by images of the tempest that had burst so aggressively over the country. They presented an alarming picture. Rivers had burst their banks and bridges had collapsed, leaving residents in flooded, low-lying areas marooned in their homes. In some exposed areas, roofs and chimneys had been hurled into the air and trees had toppled dangerously across roads and gardens, causing some buildings to capsize. Transport was severely disrupted in all regions. Motorways had been reduced to chaos by multiple pile-ups. Airports had been forced to close while storm-tossed ships and ferries had limped to the safety of the near-est ports. Damaged power cables had forced trains to stop miles away from railway stations and tube lines had ground to a halt, trapping hun-dreds of people underground. Emergency services were working flat out to try to reopen roads and help marooned or injured people to safety.

As the evening wore on, the global scale of the tempest became clear. During the previous twelve hours, much of the planet had been sub-jected to an unprecedented battering. There were reports from across the world of hurricane winds, tidal waves and flash floods. A meteorol-ogist interviewed for a television news programme admitted that the ferocity of the weather events had taken him and his colleagues by sur-prise, but suggested that it was part of the inexorable process of climate change.

Richard, however, couldn't help wondering whether the perpetrators of the attacks on the world's vegetation were responsible for what was happening.

Later that evening, the phone rang in the hall.

'Ricky, darling?' His mother's voice was faint and distorted by crackle.

'Mum? Is everything alright?'

'Oporto … terrible storm … incredibly seasick …'

Straining to hear, he managed to piece together her story. On its re-turn from a few days in the Azores, the cruise liner had found itself battling against mountainous waves and winds of near hurricane force. Badly damaged, it had managed to get to Oporto where it was now waiting for repairs.

The line suddenly cleared and he jumped as his mother's voice in-creased sharply in volume. 'Are you still there, Ricky?'

'Yes, Mum.'

'Do you know what's happening? People are picking up all sorts of rumours from the internet and phone calls. They're saying it's not ter-rorists who've been destroying so many places, it's aliens! That's non-sense isn't it, darling? Have you heard anything?'

Richard attempted to sound reassuring. 'There are lots of rumours going round, Mum, but no-one really knows who's behind the attacks. You know how the media sensationalise things when there's a crisis. You shouldn't worry.'

His mother sounded relieved. 'We thought it had to be poppycock, but it's hard to find out exactly what's going on. Are you alright, darling? We heard there's been really bad storm damage in the UK.'

'I'm fine, Mum. It was pretty rough here yesterday but it's over now.' He decided not to mention the ruined back garden and the fact that the shed roof was embedded in the hedge.

'I don't know how long we're going to be stuck here. We're still on board though they say we should be flown back in a day or two. Your dad's still feeling poorly ...' Her voice grew faint again.

'Sorry Mum, the signal's breaking up.'

Checking the computer for a news update, he found the internet buzzing with rumours and counter-rumours about the causes of the devastation. Many, like him, suspected that the UFOs were in some way responsible. The official line was that there had been a storm of unprecedented force.

Chapter 31

The next morning was stiflingly hot. The temperature had soared to over ninety degrees Fahrenheit and a flurry of special radio and TV broadcasts warned people to drink lots of water, to use high factor sun block and to wear protective clothing when venturing outside.

It was the day Richard was due to go to the police station to identify the Inheritors. Checking the news before he set off, he heard that unprecedented high temperatures were being experienced not only in the UK but in many parts of the world, even those accustomed to long periods of ice and snow. Death rates in Europe had risen especially among the more elderly members of the population. In some countries where, following prolonged drought, the blistering heat had ruined crops, bans had been placed on grain exports and food prices were rising. In other areas, however, massive storms and heavy rainfall had resulted in flooding and catastrophic landslides.

On leaving the house, Richard found a letter addressed to him on the mat. As he didn't have time to read it, he stuffed it in his pocket and set off towards the corner, nearly colliding with Mrs. Perkins who was surveying her broken garden fence and shaking her head in disbelief.

'I've never seem a storm like it, Ricky, have you? Reg said it's due to global warming. Do you think he's right?'

Richard kicked a broken roof tile into the gutter. 'It's possible, Mrs. Perkins. We've been having unusual weather patterns for some time now.'

'Well I hope we don't have more storms like that one. It's ruined our back garden. And it's so hot.'

The roads beyond the Close displayed further evidence of the devastation wrought by the storm. As Richard descended the hill, he was obliged to pick his way past severed branches, upturned recycling boxes, fragments of glass and occasional lumps of masonry. A wooden chair with splintered legs lay on its side in the gutter. Several vehicles had been abandoned at hazardous angles in the road. He noticed that the sounds of passing traffic and people clearing up after the storm were muffled, as if everything was blanketed in an invisible coating of snow. The sky wasn't the clear blue of a few days before; it was pale, bleached almost white.

At the police station he was met not by dour DS Johnson but a younger and more affable officer, DC Pike. He led Richard into a room with a computer and showed him video clips of groups of men. Richard picked out a number of Persuaders – Isaac, Saul, Ezra, Kevin and several others he recognised although he had forgotten their names. Seeing their scowling faces reawakened unpleasant memories of his sojourn on the island. He wondered how Sister Francis was. They hadn't spoken since their return from Scotland and he decided he would call the convent when he got home.

Before he left the police station, he was reunited with his mobile phone and wallet which been sent from Aberdeen. He wasn't surprised to find that money and his credit card had been removed from the wallet and that the battery of his mobile was dead.

He remembered only now that he had a letter in his pocket. Opening the envelope, he discovered it was from *Immediate Response*, one of the overseas aid organisations he had contacted, offering him an interview. At any other time he would have been overjoyed. Now he merely thrust it back into his pocket.

Visiting shops on his way home, he found many of the shelves stripped bare and it was only after a long search that he managed to stock up on pasta, biscuits and tinned soup. The Government's exhortation to the public to desist from panic-buying had obviously fallen on deaf ears.

The heat and humidity became increasingly oppressive during the morning, and as soon as he got home he had a cold shower and put on clean clothes. Then, after recharging his mobile, he rang the convent's number and asked to speak to Sister Francis.

Mother Ignatius's response was curt. 'You will appreciate that Sister Francis is not a young woman and she needs time to recover from her ordeal. Since she has been restored to us, we have been protecting her from contact with people outside the convent.'

'I do understand,' Richard said placatingly. 'I just wanted to know how she is.'

The Reverend Mother's voice softened slightly. 'She is well and I will tell her that you called.'

Having abandoned hope of speaking to Sister Francis, he was

delighted when, later that afternoon, his mobile rang and he heard her slightly teasing tone. 'Mother Ignatius told me I'd had a call from a young gentleman.'

'She wouldn't let me speak to you.'

'Och, she's only trying to protect me. Since I came back, I've been advised to have no contact with anyone outside except Father Doyle and the police. But I persuaded her to let me ring you back.'

'I'm glad you did,' he said. 'It seems ages since we were on the island. How have you been?'

'I'm grand, thanks be to God. The sisters insist that I rest for much of the time, though I keep telling them there's no need. Why bother with the likes of me when the world's in danger and there's poor souls out there in need of protection from the evil threatening our beautiful world?'

'I'm sure the sisters are right,' Richard demurred. 'You had a terrible time on that island, and the journey back wasn't a picnic either.'

'Ay!' She chuckled. 'I can't believe how we got away in that wee boat. It seems like a dream now, so it does. '

'More like a nightmare!'

'And yourself, Richard? How are you?'

'I'm fine. Did you know that some huge machines, like the ones you and I saw, came again? Did you hear the siren?'

'Ay, and the sound nearly froze the blood in my veins. Mother Ignatius told us what had happened. Do you have any notion what they are?'

He took a deep breath. 'I know it seems impossible and there's no proof, but people are beginning to believe they could have come from another planet.'

'Lord bless us and save us!' she exclaimed faintly and there was a short silence before she spoke again, this time in a stronger voice. 'Well, if there is life elsewhere in the universe, then God must have created it, just as he created life in our own world. We're holding special prayer vigils in the chapel to ask for His protection.'

'We need more than prayer,' Richard exclaimed rather more sharply than he intended. 'Something has to be done.'

Her voice was gentle. 'Have you still got it, Richard? The rosary?'

'Yes.'

'Whenever you feel afraid, take it out and ask our Holy Mother to protect you, and she will. You will do that now, won't you?'

'Yes,' he muttered. 'Have you heard anything about the Inheritors since you got back? Have you been called to take part in an identity parade?'

'I have indeed. I did it this morning, here at the convent. The police brought a computer, one of those like a wee attaché case. They showed me some men and asked me to pick out any I recognised. I saw some of those rough fellows from the island.'

'I did it too, this morning, at the local police station.' Richard assumed the identity process had been organised at roughly the same time to avoid collusion. Jacob had probably also been asked to do it that morning in Aberdeen. 'Did you hear that the commune has been closed down?' he asked her.

'No. That's good news, so it is!'

'Some of the men have been taken into custody and the women and children have been taken off the island. They're being looked after by Social Services.'

'Praise be to God.'

'And I heard something about Abraham R.'

'That fiend! What about him?'

'His real name's Rosenberg and he's wanted in the States for extortion, abducting young girls and forcing them to marry much older men.'

He heard her give an angry snort. 'He's the devil incarnate! I could see how unhappy the young women on the island were, and the poor wee children.'

'And wait till you hear this,' Richard continued. 'The Inheritors have been caught trying to send signals from a remote desert observatory in America. My theory is they thought they were contacting the Messiah on his second coming.'

He heard her gasp. 'Sad deluded souls! If that man's involved, then it won't be Our Lord Jesus Christ who's coming back to Earth, more's the pity. It'll be Old Nick himself.'

Richard chuckled. 'You could be right.'

'I have to go now, Richard. I promised Mother Ignatius that I'd only be a few minutes. We must pray for the world's deliverance. And I'll pray for you too. Goodbye and God bless you.'

* * *

That evening the doorbell chimed and Richard heard a faint bark outside. Opening the door, he was surprised to find Fiona standing on the step, with Maggie panting beside her on a lead.

'Are you at home?'

'As you see. Come in.'

He bent to kiss her as she walked through the door but she was abruptly jerked out of his reach by Maggie who made a purposeful dash for the kitchen.

'I see you brought your chaperone,' he said, following them.

Fiona crouched down to unfasten the lead. 'I did and she's thirsty.'

'I'm not surprised, it's bloody hot.' He filled a bowl with water which Maggie slurped noisily. 'To what do I owe the pleasure?'

'Mum and Dad have gone to Suffolk. They've taken Polly. The house felt really empty when I got home, and I didn't want to be on my own. So I thought I'd come over. You don't mind?'

'Of course not.' He feasted his eyes on her. She was wearing a short summer dress that revealed her long, slim legs. 'You weren't tempted to go with them?'

'I can't. Not while the hospital's on emergency alert.'

He opened the fridge door and extracted two bottles of beer. 'I expect you could do with one of these.'

'Now you're talking!'

'Let's go and sit on the patio, it'll be cooler there. But I warn you, the garden's not a pretty sight and the shed's lost its roof.'

While they sat facing the devastated lawn and flower beds, Maggie nosed busily along the side fence, sniffing the air for Pugwash.

'I wasn't exaggerating, was I?' Richard said ruefully. 'My mother will be heartbroken when she gets back. The garden's her pride and joy.'

Fiona laughed. 'I thought *you* were her pride and joy! Our garden's nearly as bad, but we don't have a shed roof in the hedge.' She pushed a lock of dark hair back from her forehead and took a sip of the cold beer. 'Just what I needed. We have fans going at the hospital but they don't make much difference when it's this hot. By the way, I passed a very large woman a few doors up from you. She gave me a really dirty look.'

'That'll be Marjorie Phelps, our resident battleaxe. She's convinced I've joined the criminal fraternity.' He mimicked Mrs. Phelps' high-pitched voice. ' "You're bringing the Close into disrepute, Ricky Jarman!" She thinks Maggie's the Hound from Hell.'

Fiona looked incredulous. 'Maggie? She's as gentle as a lamb! Hang on, that's my phone.' She took her mobile out of her bag. 'That'll be Polly. I'll take it inside.'

She stepped back into the sitting-room and Richard heard her trying to persuade her daughter, and then her mother, that she would be perfectly fine staying in the house on her own. Her eyes were moist when she returned to the patio and he tried to distract her by relating details of his eventful morning - the identity parade, the conversation with Sister Francis and finally, the letter he had received from *Immediate Response*.

'An interview already?' she exclaimed. 'You must be pleased.'

'A short time ago I would have been. But the way things are now, it's impossible to think ahead. Everything's so ... uncertain.'

'I know. It's like we're all waiting for something even more dreadful to happen.' She regarded him gravely. 'Do you think things are more serious than they're letting on, Ric?'

'I'm afraid so. Some people think those flying machines have affected the climate and that's why there have been so many natural disasters happening at once.'

'Strewth!'

'But there's no evidence,' he added hurriedly. He tried to think of something more reassuring to say but failing, changed the subject, 'Are you hungry, Fi?'

'Yes, a bit,'

'Then why don't I rustle us up something? I'm afraid the larder's a bit bare at the moment, like the shops. Is pasta OK?'

'Fine, if you're sure.'

'Of course I'm sure. I may even have a tin of dog food ... for Maggie, that is!'

After feeding Maggie, he cooked some pasta and concocted a simple sauce with an onion, his remaining two tomatoes and grated cheese. They carried their plates and another two bottles of beer out on to the patio. 'At any other time, this would be fun,' he muttered as they sat down.

'Well why don't we try and make it fun,' she replied. 'Let's not talk about what's happening. Let's talk about something else.'

'OK.'

As they ate, they reminisced about their schooldays before events, marriage in her case, university entrance in his, moved their lives in totally different directions.

It was getting dark by the time they finished eating.

Richard sighed as he picked up the empty plates. 'I suppose we'd better go and check the news.'

'No,' Fiona said firmly. 'I've had enough of doom and gloom. Why don't we try and live for the moment?' She looked shyly across the table at him, her eyes glowing. 'I could stay the night, if you like.'

Chapter 32

Richard couldn't stop smiling when he got up the next morning. It had been a long time since he had slept with a woman. Fiona had already left for the hospital. She had been right. *Carpe diem*: it was far better to live for the moment than agonise over future catastrophes that might never happen.

Maggie greeted him enthusiastically when he entered the kitchen, then pointedly sniffed the empty bowl on the floor.

'OK, I can take a hint.' He gave her the last of the dog food which she gobbled down noisily. He washed up the dishes from the night before, ate a perfunctory breakfast, then put her on the lead and left the house to go to the shop.

It was another sweltering day and he wondered, as they left the house, whether he should take her back to the dog grooming parlour to have her thick fur clipped. He was thinking about this when he heard loud banging on a window. He turned to see Marjorie Phelps' plump face framed by a frilly lace curtain. What did the wretched woman want now?

She gestured for him to wait. A few seconds later the front door opened and she appeared at the top of the steps. He steeled himself for a complaint about Maggie but was surprised to see that her expression was more anxious than angry or accusing.

'Ricky,' she called in a tremulous voice. 'Have you heard?'

'Heard what, Mrs. Phelps?'

'Those things ... on the telly.'

'What things?'

'Those flying things ... the ones we saw the other night. Some have come down.'

His heart gave a painful thud. 'Do you mean they've landed?'

'No ...but some have come down really low.'

'Where? Here?'

'No, America and some other foreign places yesterday. Come and see for yourself. It's on the news.' To Richard's surprise, she descended the steps and tugged him urgently by the arm, apparently forgetting that he was her *bête noire*.

Intrigued, he allowed himself to be led through her front door, taking care to keep Maggie close by his side.

'Look,' she whispered, pointing at the enormous flat-screened television that took up most of one side of her sitting-room. She collapsed on to a sofa which gave a protesting groan as her bulk depressed the springs.

Richard gazed at the picture on the screen. It was showing a wide and darkened street on which lines of police, some on horseback, were struggling to hold back an excited crowd. Blue and white police cars with flashing lights were ranged next to the kerb and he could see the angular shapes of skyscrapers in the distance. In the background there was a deep humming sound and the throbbing of helicopters. Above the noise, a loud voice, speaking in American-accented English, was sharply ordering the crowd to disperse and clear the area.

Stunned, he sank on to the nearest chair. Maggie sprawled untidily at his feet.

The picture disappeared from the screen and was replaced by a British television news desk where two grave-faced news presenters, a middle-aged man and a younger woman, were sitting side by side.

'American military forces have been put on full alert,' declared the man. 'This was the scene captured by television cameras in New York yesterday afternoon.'

The camera panned over the scene to show a queue of armoured vehicles carrying missiles. Positioned in front of them were lines of troops wearing visors and full protective gear. They were pointing automatic weapons at the sky. Richard gasped as the camera swung upwards to reveal a gigantic spaceship suspended high above the street, casting a massive shadow over everything on the ground beneath. It was identical to the one he had witnessed in April. To his astonishment, it seemed to be made not of metal but of some kind of translucent material that was constantly changing colour from within, shifting from deepest crimson to orange, from orange to bright yellow, then back to red again. The machine was emitting a low throbbing hum and a cloud of white vapour was issuing from its middle section.

An American reporter was stumbling nervously over his commentary of which Richard was able to catch only fragments:

Invasion of air space ... federal state of emergency ... imperative to defeat threats and aggression aimed at the United States ... Northcom operations

... Consequence Management Response Force ... Air-to-Air and Surface-to-Air missiles on standby ...'

In the pauses between the reporter's words, Richard could hear another male voice loudly repeating something over some kind of loudspeaker system. It took him a few moments to understand the message which was evidently directed at the occupants of the spacecraft.

You have entered an American Air Defense Identification Zone. This is a hostile act. Surrender immediately or face punitive military action.

There was an ear-splitting roar that reached a crescendo as a line of fighter planes zoomed menacingly past the spacecraft then retreated into the distance. Compared with the colossal flying machine, they looked minuscule, like toy models.

There was a renewed cacophony of shouts from the crowd.

'What the...? Oh boy, just look at that!' shouted the reporter, his voice reduced to a hysterical squeak.

The camera refocused on the flying object. From the bottom of its middle section, some large spherical objects were emerging, one after the other, like gigantic eggs, prompting hysterical screams and shouts from the crowd below.

'Christ!' Richard leapt to his feet.

'Oh my God!' Marjorie Phelps was almost sobbing with fear and clutching at her blouse convulsively. 'What are they?'

'Lord knows.' He sank shakily back on to the chair.

There were four of them. They floated a few feet below the host machine for several seconds. Then Richard heard someone bark an inaudible order and the TV camera zoomed downwards to show the soldiers training their guns up at the objects.

The warning voice over the loudspeaker increased in volume. 'Surrender immediately. You have precisely thirty seconds before we fire.'

Why don't they fire *now?'* whispered Mrs. Phelps.

The fighter planes zoomed back into view and Richard heard a series of deafening reports as each fired at the objects. But instead of penetrating them, the missiles fizzled harmlessly off the surface of the eggs and spun downwards to an accompaniment of shouts and screams. The camera showed people on the ground running in all directions. 'Move away! Move away,' an authoritative male voice was shouting. 'Everybody leave the area immediately!'

The camera focused again on the four round objects which Richard now decided looked more like bubbles than eggs. He watched, awestruck, as they separated and moved away from each other sideways, then they regrouped, floated upwards and were literally sucked back into the middle section of the machine. The vivid colours started to fade and the machine became a dazzling white, so bright that he found it painful to look at. The hum increased in volume and the airship accelerated sharply upwards, creating a massive down blast that knocked some of the watching troops off their feet.

As the noise receded, the picture on the screen revealed the spectators on the ground looking paralysed with terror. Some remained staring open-mouthed at the sky, others were shouting hysterically. The servicemen, their firearms now lowered, looked dazed.

Richard could hear a loudspeaker making a series of inaudible announcements.

The TV news reporter was gabbling hoarsely, presumably attempting to analyse events that had rendered him literally lost for words.

The two newsreaders reappeared on the screen. Both looked shocked. They quickly regained their composure when they realised they were on camera.

'We will bring you more news from the United States shortly,' said the young woman, 'and keep you informed of developments as they occur.' Her voice shook. 'During the last fifteen hours, similar scenes have been reported in other parts the world ...'

Mrs. Phelps burst into loud sobs. 'I wish Stanley was here,' she wailed.

It was the first time Richard had ever seen his formidable neighbour appear out of control.

He rose shakily to his feet. 'Try to keep calm, Mrs. Phelps. Why don't you ring Mr. Phelps and ask him to come home?'

She didn't answer, and continued to gaze at the television screen.

He looked uncertainly down at her. 'I'm going home now, but call me if you need anything.' As she remained silent, he let himself and Maggie out the front door. It was only when he reached his own door that he remembered that he had forgotten to go to the shop.

The streets were eerily quiet as he made his way down to the shopping parade. The shop was empty and there were very few items left on the shelves. Mr. Patel was watching a small television behind the counter and barely took his eyes off the screen when Richard went to pay for his meagre basket of provisions. 'Did you see them?' he cried excitedly. 'What do you think they are?'

'I've no idea.'

As Richard hurried home along the empty streets, he noticed the glaring rectangles of television screens in many of the windows he passed. A number of police cars overtook him at speed, their sirens blaring.

As soon as he arrived home, he tried Mark Davenport's extension at *Global Geographic*. The phone was picked up almost immediately. Mark sounded breathless with excitement and Richard could hear shouted exchanges in the background.

'Ric! We've been monitoring what's happening. Incredible! Have you seen them?'

Richard endeavoured to keep his own voice calm. 'Yes, I just saw it on TV.'

'They've appeared all over the place - Istanbul, Mumbai, Moscow, Mexico City, and ... Where else was it, John?' Mark's voice receded and Richard heard a muttered response.

Mark repeated the information. 'Sao Paolo.'

'Christ!' Richard gulped. 'I didn't realise there were so many.'

'Didn't you know? It was reported yesterday afternoon and on last night's news.'

Richard coughed. 'I was ... otherwise engaged last night. How many of them were there?'

'Difficult to say because of the different time zones. But it doesn't matter how many there were, they're so bloody huge, wherever they've appeared, everyone's freaked out. Martial law's been declared in some places.'

Richard shivered. 'What do you think it means?'

'I suppose there's a strategy behind it. What do the cities they've appeared in have in common?'

'Well, I suppose they're all pretty big ...'

'Exactly. They're among the most densely populated cities in the world. That could be significant, don't you think? And we're picking up reports that Shanghai and Beijing and several other Chinese cities may have had visitations too, though there's been no official confirmation.'

Richard gulped. 'London's a very densely populated city too. Do you think they'll come here?'

'Just a minute, Ric ...,' Mark broke off to answer a shouted question in the office.

'What do you think those round things they ejected were?' Richard asked when he resumed the conversation. 'They must have been jettisoned for a reason.'

'We thought it was an attack at first,' Mark replied, 'but there haven't been any reports to that effect. Did you know American fighter jets fired at one of them using rocket motors.'

'Yes, I saw that, but it seemed to be protected by an invisible shield. The missiles exploded harmlessly in the air.'

'Awesome!' Mark sounded even more excited. 'We don't know whether any other armies tried firing at them. But those aircraft are impossible to track once they've accelerated away. It sounds incredible, but apparently at a certain height they manage to make themselves invisible! And by the way, the attacks on forests and savannahs seem to have stopped. There haven't been any recent reports. What?' His voice receded.

Richard heard a muttered conversation in the background before Mark returned to the phone.

'Sorry, Ric, gotta go. It's bedlam here, as you can imagine.'

Richard pocketed his mobile. Things seemed to be moving towards some kind of denouement. Wasn't the next logical step for the airships to land? The idea filled him with both fear and excitement. Maggie put her head on his lap and he gently rubbed her ears. 'Are the nasty aliens coming to get us, Maggie?'

The dog gave a low whine.

He went to his room and searched the internet for news. Everything Mark had said was confirmed in the images and reports he found. The world seemed to be in uproar, caught up in a collective state of panic. Nobody was any longer claiming that the aircraft belonged to "terrorists". Social medial sites were awash with rumours that extraterrestrials were about to invade.

The Home Secretary made a statement, announcing that the government was putting emergency powers into immediate operation.

Fiona returned later in the afternoon. When he opened the door, she rushed inside looking pale and frightened. 'Everybody's talking about what's happening. I'm scared stiff, Ric. Mum rang again asking me to join them in Suffolk. I don't know what to do. I know it's my duty to stay at the hospital, but it's also my duty to be with my daughter, isn't it?'

Richard felt at a loss. 'I don't know what to say, Fi. It has to be your decision. But try not to be panicked into doing anything too quickly. You need to think it over calmly.'

He made tea and they took it on to the patio. Before they sat down, he moved the chairs into the shade as the sun's heat was still intolerable.

Fiona sat in silence for a while, staring listlessly at the ruined garden. When she spoke her voice was tremulous. 'I've never been so frightened, Ric. Every day the situation gets worse. Do you think one of those machines will come down over London, like in those other places?'

He squeezed her hand. 'It's possible I suppose. '

'There's a special service tomorrow night at Shepherd Street Spiritualist Church. Morgana Delph's coming. She'll be holding a special séance. We should go, Ric.'

He shuddered. 'No way! She freaked me out last time. That woman's spooky. She gives me the creeps.'

'It'll be a different format this time.'

'I don't care what format it is. She's a crank.'

'No she's not,' Fiona protested. 'She's got amazing psychic powers. Have you forgotten that she told you to look for the "poet, philosopher and healer"? You would never have heard of Abraham R otherwise.'

'I wish to God I had never heard of him,' Richard retorted.

She gazed at him pleadingly. 'Please, Ric, I'd like to go, but not on my own.'

He sighed. 'OK, I'll come with you, but I won't stay if she starts spouting crap at me in that awful voice again.'

'I'm sure she won't, not this time.'

'Does that mean you're not going to Suffolk?'

She sighed. 'I don't know. I'd better wait and see what happens. What about you? Have you arranged a date for your interview?'

'No, I haven't done anything about it yet.' He had forgotten all about the interview. 'Too much has been happening.'

'Well I think you should,' she said. 'I think it's better to carry on as though everything's still normal, don't you?'

He sighed. 'You're probably right.'

Fiona touched his hand. 'I could stay the night again,' she suggested timidly, 'if you like.'

He did like.

Chapter 33

The spiritualist church was full to capacity and there were few empty seats left when they arrived. Richard was pleased to find that they were in the back row. Latecomers were obliged to stand in the porch.

The interior of the church was plain. There were no pictures or statues, although a few vases of flowers brightened up the side aisles. At the front end of the room there was a platform on which stood a small upright piano, three chairs and a table furnished only with a bottle of water and some drinking glasses.

It was exceedingly hot inside the church and people were fanning themselves with the sheets of paper that had been placed on the chairs. These listed the order of service: prayers and hymns led by George, "a healing moment" with Betty, and a demonstration of mediumship by Morgana Delph.

Promptly at half past seven, an elderly woman and a tall bespectacled man entered through the door behind the platform. The woman stepped forward and motioned for silence. She was wearing a plain white blouse and a black skirt. 'This special service has been convened,' she announced gravely, 'to help us at this time of great fear and insecurity. We must pray and meditate together for the courage to face whatever trials await us in the days ahead.'

There were murmurs of assent from the congregation.

'We are very lucky,' the woman continued, 'to have a special appearance tonight by the celebrated medium, Morgana Delph. She has kindly agreed to use her psychic powers to ask our loved ones in the spirit world to bring us advice and comfort in the nation's hour of need. But first, George will begin the service with prayer and hymns.'

The tall man stepped forward and intoned a lengthy prayer for the world's salvation. It was followed by a chorus of fervent *amens* from the congregation. After the sound had died down, he sat at the piano and struck a few chords. With much shuffling and scraping of chairs, the congregation stood and sang several hymns Richard had never heard before.

When the last notes faded away, George invited the congregation to sit down and meditate in silence for a few minutes. 'Liberate your minds from fear and disturbing thoughts,' he urged. 'Imagine that you are in a beautiful place where everything is calm and serene and where no evil can reach you.'

Richard found it impossible to "liberate" his mind. He stole a sideways look at Fiona who appeared to have no such difficulty. She was gazing into space, her expression tranquil. He thought she looked beautiful and realised with a pang how bereft he would feel if she did decide to join her parents and Polly in Suffolk.

The period of meditation seemed to drag on forever. He fidgeted and his mind wandered. It had been another extremely stressful day. The descent of the mysterious airships had provoked universal hysteria and panic and there were reports that residents were fleeing many of the world's largest cities. In the UK, food and other essentials were being stripped from shops and petrol pumps were running dry, prompting warnings about food and fuel rationing. People were flocking to churches and other places of worship in unprecedented numbers.

His thoughts were interrupted by Betty who was inviting members of the congregation to come forward for healing.

A number of individuals formed an orderly queue in the aisle. One by one, they mounted the platform and sat for several minutes with closed eyes, while Betty placed her open palms on their heads and shoulders, her face rapt with concentration.

Richard glanced at his watch. They had already been there forty minutes. 'When's that woman coming?' he muttered to Fiona.

'Soon,' she whispered.

After the healing session, George reappeared on the platform.

'It is now my privilege and pleasure to welcome Madame Morgana Delph,' he announced.

The congregation stirred with anticipation as a small, dumpy woman appeared at the door behind the platform.

Richard was struck anew by the medium's cosy granny appearance which he found difficult to reconcile with the guttural male voice she had channelled the first time he had seen her.

After some preliminary words of greeting, Madame Delph addressed the congregation in soothing tones. 'At a time when unknown forces have invaded our world, bringing fear and panic, I am going to ask the spirit world to bring us insights and solace.'

The congregation murmured gratefully.

She began to pace slowly up and down the platform, her head cocked slightly to one side as though she was listening to something.

Apart from an occasional cough, there was now complete silence in the hall.

She came to a sudden standstill. 'Wait!' she cried. 'There are too many of you clamouring for attention.' She gave the congregation a conspiratorial smile and explained, 'Sometimes members of the spirit world are impatient to be heard and I can't isolate a voice because they're all shouting over each other.'

She listened again for a moment, then nodded. 'Yes, I hear you.' She gazed at the rows of people in front of her. 'Does anyone here know an Iris who has passed into the spirit world? A lady with connections to ... What's that? Where?' She listened intently. 'Southend, is that right? Yes. Southend.'

There was a moment's silence, then an elderly woman to the left of Richard and Fiona, stood up. 'My mother was born in Southend. Her name was Iris.'

'Thank you, my love.' Madame Delph listened again. 'What ... yes ... I understand.' She addressed the woman. 'Your mother wants you to know that she and your father ... What's his name?' She listened. 'Bernard?'

'Bert,' whispered the woman.

'That's right, Bert. Iris says she and Bert are happily reunited in the spirit world and they are watching over you ... What's that? Iris says don't be afraid and all will be well. You are not to panic. Remember that she and your father survived the Blitz. She says you must demonstrate the same courage in these difficult times. She sends you her love.'

The woman dissolved in tears and sat down.

To Richard's growing irritation, the medium relayed several equally anodyne messages from the other world to grateful members of the congregation. Then suddenly a change came over her. Her face seemed to broaden and become puffy. Her eyes grew wide then rolled upwards so that Richard could see only the whites. There was a collective intake of breath from the watching congregation.

Fiona grasped Richard's hand.

With Betty hovering protectively behind her, Morgana staggered a few steps across the platform, then opened her mouth and uttered the strangest sounds Richard had ever heard: a mixture of squeaks, squawks, grunts and whistles, all at different pitches, loud then soft, shrill then deep, rasping then melodic.

There were cries of alarm from the congregation.

The medium continued to make the bizarre noises for some time before subsiding with a loud expiration of breath on to one of the chairs. Her head lolled backwards and Betty rushed up to her with a glass of water. She waited for a few seconds then gently moved the medium's head forward and held the glass to her lips.

Morgana opened her eyes, took a few sips of water, then her head fell back again.

There was a stunned silence in the church.

After a few minutes, she rose unsteadily to her feet, looking white and exhausted. 'Eeeh, that were heavy,' she told the congregation in a weak voice. 'I don't know what message I received, but I hope it has given you all some comfort.' With Betty supporting her, she stumbled back through the door behind the platform.

There was a brief silence in the church then a loud buzz of excited conversation.

'We will now sing *Blessed is the Universe*,' declared George. He returned to the piano, played some notes and the congregation started to sing in wavery voices.

Richard stood up. 'I'm getting out of here,' he hissed to Fiona. He stumbled over the feet of the people sitting next to him, and pushed his way through the group standing in the porch.

After a few seconds Fiona joined him outside the door. 'What was the hurry?' she asked angrily. 'The service was nearly over. You did this last time.'

'I couldn't stand that nonsense any longer.'

'It wasn't nonsense,' she protested.

'Wasn't it? She sounded like a demented cockerel!' He uttered a few squawks then imitated Madame Delph's voice. ' "Eeeh, I hope this message has given you some comfort." '

Fiona looked so affronted that he giggled. 'I'm sorry, Fi, but I can't take any of that stuff seriously. I … I …' He started to laugh helplessly, all the tension that had been building up in him suddenly liberated.

Fiona stared at him, clearly not amused. 'For God's sake, Ric, get a grip.'

'I'm sorry, Fi, I'm, I'm ...' But he couldn't complete the sentence. He leant against the church wall and laughed until his sides ached and tears sprang from his eyes. 'I've never heard anything so ridiculous in my life,' he gasped when he finally managed to control himself. 'Look, there's a pub over there. Let's get a drink. I need one.'

She followed him across the road without a word.

The pub was deserted except for three people sitting at a table, silently watching a large television screen in the corner. It was replaying the scenes he had already witnessed in Marjorie Phelps' front room.

Fiona was tight-lipped when they sat down with glasses of cold lager. 'I don't understand what you found so funny,' she muttered. 'That was genuine channelling.'

'What of?' he chortled, 'bird and animal noises?'

'Come off it, Ric. What bird or animal makes noises like that? They were the weirdest sounds I've ever heard.'

'I grant you they were weird, but that doesn't mean she was receiving a message from the "other side".'

'Well, those noises must have come from somewhere.' Fiona pondered for a moment. 'Isn't it possible that she could have been contacted by ... someone in one of those spaceships?'

He gave a derisive snort.

'Well why not?' she asked defensively. 'Didn't you once tell me you'd heard a theory that extraterrestrials might try to communicate with us through mathematics?'

'What's that got to do with anything?'

She interrupted him impatiently. 'There was a rhythm to the noises she made. They were repeated, almost like Morse code. What if they were a code for some kind of mathematical equation?'

He gazed at her speechlessly.

'Perhaps,' she continued eagerly, 'she was giving us coordinates for the planet they've come from.'

He decided to humour her. 'Yes, maybe.'

Her face fell. 'But how would we know? I don't suppose the séance was recorded.'

'Even if it was,' Richard observed, 'how would anyone be able to decipher those noises? I don't suppose anyone has had a chance to study Alienish yet!' He wiped his brow. 'Phew! It's time pubs installed aircon. Let's go home. Are you coming back with me?'

She gave a wan smile. 'I suppose so.'

By unspoken mutual consent they dropped the subject of the séance.

* * *

That night they stayed up late, watching appalled as television news programmes showed people fleeing capital cities in cars and by public transport. In some parts of the world, protesting crowds had gathered outside administrative buildings, demanding more decisive action against the invading spacecraft. Government representatives in the affected areas were appealing for calm and some had already introduced draconian measures to protect citizens from the perceived threat.

It was now widely assumed that the huge flying machines had come from another planet, but despite the generally held belief that the aliens had been responsible for the Blitzgreen, no country had reported any further destruction of areas of vegetation. The devastation of forests and grasslands had abruptly ceased.

Richard wondered whether the descent of the spaceships was the second phase of a coordinated plan. Bearing in mind Mark's observation that cities with the highest density populations were being targeted, he had little doubt that London would eventually receive a visit from one of the huge craft and its curious clutch of eggs

The Prime Minister made another public appearance on television. He reiterated his now familiar assurances that the armed forces had everything under control, and advised the population that, in the event of any further invasion of British airspace, they should stay off the streets for their own safety.

Fiona was tearful that night and Richard held her tight, trying to calm her. He knew it was Polly she really feared for. They were too tense to make love and didn't have any further conversation about what was happening before she left for work in the morning.

Later that day he found several envelopes on the doormat. It was reassuring, he thought as he picked them up, that despite the panic gripping the world, the mail was still being delivered, the lights still came on when you pressed the switch, and most people seemed to be going about their daily business as usual.

One of the envelopes contained a letter informing him that the *viva* for his thesis would be held on the twenty-seventh of September. He put it down with a sigh. It was difficult to think that far ahead; much easier to take things day by day. He opened the patio doors to let Maggie out and the heat struck him like a blow.

The telephone rang in the hall.

When he picked up the receiver, he heard Saskia's breathless voice. 'Ric, are you OK?'

'Yes, I'm fine, how about all of you?'

'We're OK, but we're going to stay in our cottage in the Dales for a while. Mike thinks it will be safer up there. You shouldn't stay in London, Ric. Come with us.'

'I can't, Sass.'

'Why not? You said you've finished your thesis.'

'I have, but I've got a friend here.'

'A friend?'

'A girlfriend. She's on her own at the moment. Her family are in Suffolk.'

'Oh.' Saskia paused for a moment. 'Well, bring her with you.'

'I can't, Sass. She works at the hospital. Then there's Maggie--'

'Maggie? Is that *another* girlfriend?' asked his sister sharply,

'No, she's a dog.'

'A dog? You've got a dog? Since when?'

'Since ... I don't know, a while ago. She's not mine. I'm just looking after her.'

'Do Mum and Dad know you've got a dog?'

'No, and please don't mention it if you speak to them.'

'Why would I? They're worried enough already, stuck in Portugal and scared stiff about what's happening. Come with us. You could bring the dog as well.'

'No,' Richard said firmly. 'But thanks for the offer.'

He heard her sigh. 'It's up to you, but I hope you change your mind. Take care, Ric. God knows what's going to happen.'

'Don't worry about me, Sass. I'll be fine.'

'I hope so. Keep in touch. Families should stick together at times like this.'

After replacing the phone, Richard switched on the TV and found a Home Office official outlining a scheme for the rationing of essential food and supplies. This prompted him to think about augmenting his own stock of provisions. He knew that Mr. Patel's deliveries usually arrived around nine, by which time a long queue would have formed outside the shop door. He left Maggie in the garden and hurried down to the shopping parade. It was blisteringly hot and perspiration trickled uncomfortably down his back

He bought a newspaper before joining the straggling line of people outside the minimarket and scanned the front page as he waited. The main article referred to secret contingency plans for an alien invasion that had been drawn up in the 1970s and which would now be implemented. It quoted an MP's suggestion that members of the public might protect themselves from an extraterrestrial invasion by taking refuge in nuclear bunkers or in underground stations as had happened during the Second World War.

Richard snorted derisively. The nearest tube station was several miles away and he wasn't sure whether nuclear bunkers actually existed.

By the time he entered the shop, no fresh food remained on the shelves, but he managed to pick up some packets of pasta, breakfast cereal and biscuits, as well as a few tins of soup and dog food.

The rest of the day seemed unbearably long. Apart from taking Maggie for occasional walks through the quiet streets, his time was spent watching the news and listening to an endless procession of politicians, army and police chiefs grimly discussing the implications of what had happened.

The whole country seemed to be in a state of suspense, waiting.

Chapter 34

They didn't have to wait for long. Richard was jerked brutally awake the next morning by the siren, a harsh wail greeted by outbursts of hysterical barking from Maggie and Pugwash next door.

He stumbled out of bed and ran to the window in his parents' room.

Fiona, who had again stayed the night, quickly joined him, rubbing her eyes. 'What's going on?'

He slammed the window shut. 'I can't see anything. Better take a look outside.' After hastily throwing on some clothes, he ran downstairs and out of the front door.

A few feet away, on his own doorstep, Reg Perkins was trying to calm his wife who was clinging to his arm, whimpering with fear, her face almost as pink as her ankle-length dressing gown. 'Have the buggers arrived, Ricky?' he bellowed above the scream of the siren.

'Sounds like it,' Richard shouted back. 'It was only a matter of time.'

Reg muttered something to his wife who relinquished his arm and shuffled back into the house. He walked up to the low fence dividing the two front gardens, casting a lascivious look at Fiona who had followed Richard out of the front door, wearing only one of his large t-shirts.

Richard stepped rapidly in front of her. 'Can you see anything, Mr. Perkins?'

'No, but we must be prepared!' Reg adopted an upright military pose and shook his fist at the sky. 'We Brits don't tolerate invaders!' he bellowed at the invisible enemy. 'My grandfather's generation saw off Gerry. We can do it again!'

Richard suppressed a smile and peered upwards but there was nothing to see.

Reg craned his neck in an undisguised attempt to ogle Fiona. 'This your young lady, Ricky?'

Richard ignored the question.

'Bloody hot again.' Reg wiped his brow with the back of his hand. 'The missus is in a bit of a state. I told to her to go and make a cup of tea.'

'Good idea. Maybe I'll do the same. Come on, Fi. Let's go back inside.' Richard propelled Fiona through the door in front of him.

After putting the kettle on and letting Maggie into the back garden, he switched on the TV and flicked through channels, stopping at a news programme on which a minister from the Home Office was gravely warning people living or working in or near central London to stay indoors and not to venture into the city for their own safety.

The scene changed and Fiona squealed and clutched Richard's arm in terror. The screen was now showing an enormous spaceship suspended high above Trafalgar Square. It was changing from one dazzling hue to another and emitting a low, hypnotic rumble.

The events that subsequently unfolded on the screen resembled closely those Richard had watched in Marjorie Phelps' front room. Armed police were herding small groups of terrified people into neighbouring streets and up the steps to the National Gallery. At the southern end of the square, armoured vehicles were disgorging a stream of soldiers carrying rifles. An amplified voice could be heard warning the spaceship to leave the area immediately or face retaliatory action. The camera panned upwards to show fighter jets streaking across the sky and circling round it at a safe distance.

A news reporter on the ground was making a stammering attempt to give a coherent commentary. 'We don't yet know whether …What in heaven's name is *that?*'

'Bloody hell,' breathed Richard, as he watched four spherical objects being ejected, one by one, from the aircraft's middle section. They were met by a hail of fire from the jets and the soldiers below. The ammunition flared as it hit them but didn't appear to inflict any damage. Undeterred, each of the four objects began to move away from each other in a sideways arc. After a few seconds, they regrouped, floated upwards and were sucked back into the spaceship. The dazzling colours faded to a blinding white then, with startling abruptness, the huge machine shot vertically upwards and disappeared from view. With a combined roar, the jets zoomed up in pursuit.

The screen now showed police and troops gaping at the sky, and the people clustered in front of the art gallery wearing stunned and frightened expressions.

Back in the television newsroom, a female newsreader announced that the Government had convened an immediate emergency meeting and that safe places were being prepared across the country where people could take refuge in the event of an attack. She paused then continued with some breaking news. 'We have just heard that similar incidents have occurred, within a few hours of each other, in Berlin, Madrid and ...' she rattled off the names of several other capital cities.

Fiona's eyes were wide with fear. 'What do they want with us?' she whispered.

Richard put an arm around her and spoke with far more confidence than he actually felt. 'We mustn't panic.'

'But what if--?'

'There's nothing happening here, and you've got to get to work. I'll get you some breakfast.'

'I couldn't eat anything,' she said tremulously. 'Not after that.'

'You must keep your strength up.' He persuaded her to go upstairs and get dressed.

When she came down again she was still visibly upset. 'Mum just called. She wants me to drop everything and join them. But the hospital's overwhelmed. I still don't know what to do for the best, Ric. I said I'd let her know.'

'It must be very difficult for you.' He put a mug of tea and some slices of toast in front of her on the kitchen table.

She sat down and picked at a piece of toast. 'Mum said as my mobile wasn't on last night she tried to call me on the house phone. She asked where I was.'

'What did you tell her?'

'I said I didn't like being in the house on my own so I went to stay with friends.'

He smiled. 'Friends plural?'

'Well, it was only a white lie.'

He accompanied her to the hospital after breakfast. It was searingly hot and he noticed that most of the plants in the gardens they passed were shrivelled. Helicopters were clattering overhead.

On returning to the house, he checked the news which was reporting that many people were leaving London and heading for areas where they thought they might be safe.

Several questions nagged at him. Why had the attacks on the world's green areas ceased so abruptly? Could the appearance of so many space-ships be the second phase of a well thought-out invasion strategy? The idea filled him with terror. What would happen next? The only thing he was sure of was that they were not bringing the Messiah. Despite the Inheritors' attempt to signal to one of the spacecraft, he was certain there was no direct link between them and what was happening. It was far more likely, he decided, that the destruction of vegetation and arrival of the spaceships constituted such a literal confirmation of their beliefs, that they believed a divine power had dispatched the machines to Earth.

The house phone rang.

It was Saskia again. 'I know you said you wouldn't come with us, Ric, but after what's happened, you can't stay there any longer. You must come to Yorkshire with us.'

Richard refused. He felt he couldn't abandon Fiona while she was still working at the hospital. However he was more scared than he cared to admit. After speaking to Saskia, he tried Mark Davenport's mobile number.

Mark answered almost immediately, his voice competing with the shrieking of car horns. He sounded irritated. 'They've closed some of the bloody roads. Been at a standstill for over an hour.'

'You know that one's appeared over Trafalgar Square?'

'Yeah. I wish it had arrived a little earlier. I could have stayed at home.'

'What do you think's happening, Mark? Do you think they're actually going to land?'

'Of course! But I wish they'd get on with it. They've been tantalising us long enough.'

* * *

Mark's wish was soon fulfilled.

The next morning, Richard was woken from an uneasy dream by Fiona. 'Ric!' she hissed. 'Something awful's happened.'

'What?' He sat up, blinking.

'I think they've come …'

'Who's come?'

'Aliens. They've invaded.' She began to sob. 'I heard it on the radio in the bathroom.'

'Bloody hell!' He leapt out of bed and ran downstairs to switch on the television. Fiona followed him.

All of the regular programmes had been suspended in order to relay the terrible news: creatures of a kind never seen before had suddenly appeared in some central parts of London. They seemed to have materialised out of nowhere. And not just in London. According to reports, they had also appeared in other major cities across the world.

The extraterrestrial invasion had begun.

Fiona shrieked as grainy pictures appeared on the screen, revealing the strangest beings Richard had ever seen. Elongated cylindrical shapes with no visible protuberances, they were hovering, with a curious rocking motion, about eight feet above the ground. A stream of pedestrians entering and leaving Charing Cross railway station were caught on camera. They stopped, gaped at the creatures, then fled in panic. Some held up their phones and took photos of the newcomers before they ran. Police officers could be seen in the distance, stopping cars and buses and moving pedestrians to the safety of doorways and side streets.

'My God!' Fiona clutched Richard's arm so tightly that it hurt. 'What are they?' She gave a horrified gasp as the image changed to show another group of the creatures hovering in the air a bit further along the Strand. A loud voice could be heard ordering them to surrender. It was drowned by the roar of aircraft. The noise grew louder then receded. A line of police cars, their sirens blaring, was pulling up at the side of the road.

'Central London is closed until further notice,' declared the newsreader. 'Only emergency vehicles are being allowed into the area. Residents and workers are advised to remain indoors and armed forced have been deployed to repel the invaders.'

The image changed to show military vehicles moving rapidly along the Strand. They drew up alongside the police cars and soldiers in body armour jumped out, carrying automatic weapons. When someone barked an order they raised their firearms and cautiously approached a group of about dozen of the creatures floating above the station forecourt. As they moved closer, a shaft of brilliant light issued from the base of each creature and beamed down at them.

The soldiers backed away. Several of them took aim and fired at the aliens, but, to Richard's amazement, the bullets ricocheted harmlessly off them. 'Christ!' he exclaimed. 'They've got some sort of force field around them.'

The soldiers regrouped and fired a second time. Once again the bullets hit an unseen barrier, rebounded and fell harmlessly to the ground.

A camera, positioned on a balcony or inside a window, zoomed in on one of the creatures, affording viewers a close-up view.

Richard gasped. He thought he could see what looked like dark spirals or coils through the alien's outer membrane.

Fiona gave a wail of terror. 'Oh God, I can't bear to look.' She buried her head in his shoulder.

Richard watched in horrified silence as the creatures continued to direct laser-like shafts of light at the line of soldiers below and yet more trucks full of armed troops rumbled along the road. After a short while it became clear to him that the scenes he was witnessing weren't live but had been filmed earlier. They were interrupted by the news that the Prime Minister was about to address the nation and his worried face now appeared on the screen.

'As many of you will know,' he announced in a hoarse voice, 'unidentified beings have appeared overnight in central London, as they have in a number of other major world cities. We do not know what they are, where they come from, or what they intend.' He paused and gazed at the unseen audience.

'This is an unprecedented event in the history of the world, one that is bound to fill us all with the deepest fear and apprehension. But it is essential not to panic. The creatures do not appear to be very numerous, they are concentrated in a very small area and they have not so far engaged in any hostile activity. Estimates suggest that there are fewer than a hundred of them, spread out across central and west London.'

He coughed and cleared his throat before continuing. 'All the affected areas have been cleared of traffic and pedestrians and I can assure you that public safety is my Government's greatest priority. Our security forces have surrounded the invaders and we are containing them. Should you be in the vicinity of any of these creatures, take refuge indoors and do *not* approach them for any reason. I cannot stress this too strongly. Should you spot any of them in an area not yet protected by our security forces, inform the police immediately then go indoors and stay there. For your own safety, a curfew will be in place after nine o'clock in the evening.'

Fiona had started to sob loudly and Richard held her tight while he listened to the remainder of the PM's address.

'I have given orders for our troops to return from operations overseas so they can protect our country. I have also been in contact with a number of other governments and we are discussing joint strategies to deal with the situation. You will be updated on developments as and when they occur. In the meantime, I would encourage those of you outside central London to try to lead your lives as normally as possible. May God bless and protect you all.'

Fiona clutched Richard's arm. 'What do you think those creatures mean to do to us?'

He took a deep breath to steady his voice. 'I don't know but they've only been reported in central London so far. I wonder how they got here without being seen.'

'I don't care how they got here,' Fiona wailed. 'I just wish they'd go away.'

'Are you going to work?'

She shrank back against the sofa cushions. 'No, I can't go, not now.'

'The hospital may need you there.' He turned off the TV and pulled her gently to her feet. 'I'll drive you. You heard the PM. We've got to continue as normal for as long as possible.'

He drove her to the hospital and promised to pick her up when her shift was over. He had only just arrived home when he received a call from Dan.

His friend's voice was shrill with panic. 'Did you see them, Ric? Terrifying. I'm taking Kate and Liam away from here.'

'Where will you go?'

'To Kate's parents in Totnes. The further we are from London or any big city, the safer we'll be. I suggest you get away too.'

Dan's call was followed by one from Mark. He was in a lather of excitement.

'This is a once-in-a-lifetime event, Ric! If the roads weren't closed, I'd be there like a shot with my camera.'

'The police won't let you anywhere near them, Mark. And you can't get into central London at the moment. The roads are closed.'

'I know, but I want to see them for myself. I could try the side roads tonight.'

'There's a curfew. I'd wait a while if I were you. What do you think those beams of lights are, Mark? Do you think it's their way of trying to communicate with us?'

'Could be. What extraordinary times, Ric!'

Richard couldn't share his excitement. After speaking to Mark, he rang Our Lady of Lourdes Convent and, as no-one replied, left a hesitant message, saying he would call back later. He had no idea what he was going to say to Sister Francis. He just wanted to hear her voice again. Her blend of humour, common sense and religious certainty usually had the effect of calming his spirits.

Chapter 35

He remained glued to the TV screen for the rest of the morning. Every channel was dedicated to reports and speculation about the invaders. Central London remained closed to all but essential and emergency services. Vast numbers of armed personnel had been deployed in the area which was now beginning to resemble a war zone. Residents and workers were repeatedly instructed to stay indoors and warned not to approach the aliens.

As reporters and news teams had been ordered to leave the area, the media were obliged to disseminate eyewitness reports and videos taken by people trapped in their homes or workplaces in the areas where aliens had gathered.

A man who had been observing the newcomers from the safety of a first-floor window, sent his impressions to BBC News. 'They seem to want to be near people. If the soldiers move back, they follow, keeping exactly the same distance between them.'

Another man claimed to have heard the aliens make strange and unintelligible sounds, 'like animal or bird noises.'

Richard was startled. Had the extraordinary noises uttered by Morgana Delph come from an alien after all?

When he ventured outside with Maggie, he passed his female neighbours clustered in a frightened huddle on the pavement. Marjorie Phelps was clinging to Doris Perkins' arm. 'What are we going to do?' he heard her wail. She recoiled as Maggie bounded up to give her a friendly sniff.

'You should get away from here as soon as possible,' suggested Mrs. Perkins. 'We're going to join our son on the Isle of Wight. Reggie thinks it'll be safer down there.'

'Why don't you both come to St Mary's with me?' Mrs. Brennan urged the other two women. 'There's going to be a special mass this evening. We can pray together.'

Richard turned the corner before hearing the answer. As he descended the hill he could see huge queues at the petrol station at the end of the shopping parade. Mr. Patel's shop was also besieged by a jostling throng that spilled out on to the road.

There was no point in waiting to see if he could get any more supplies so he made his way home again.

His mobile rang soon after he entered the house and he was pleased to hear Sister Francis's voice. He hadn't expected her to call him back so soon.

'I got your message,' she told him.

'How are you, Sister?'

'I'm grand,' she said, 'but my vegetables aren't, not in this heat. The greenhouses are like furnaces, so they are.'

'I'm sorry to hear that,' he responded, surprised that this seemed to be her principal concern. 'But what do you think about the invasion? You must have heard the news.'

'I have indeed and it's a great challenge God has set us, to be sure. We've been holding a prayer vigil this morning.'

'Maybe they intend to attack us.'

'We don't know that, Richard. Maybe we should view those beings with open minds.'

'Open minds when they've been destroying parts of the planet?'

'We don't know that for sure either. It's possible that they've come with good in their hearts.'

'Good?' Richard expostulated. 'After all the damage they've done? And they may not have hearts!'

'They're still God's creatures, Richard, even if they don't resemble human beings. We shouldn't be repelled by difference. Perhaps it would help you to see them in a more positive light if you could consider their arrival as ... exciting.'

'Exciting?' He exclaimed, incredulous that she seemed so unfazed by such a terrifying event. 'How can it be exciting?'

'Because it informs us that God has created other worlds besides our own. We aren't alone in the universe.'

Richard was speechless.

She continued to speak to him in a gentle voice. 'We know that God made man in his image and gave him dominion over all the creatures on Earth. But there must be millions, trillions, of other planets in the universe which may have their own unique species of life. Think of it, Richard. Couldn't God in his infinite power and wisdom, have more than *one* image? Couldn't He have created a multitude of intelligent beings beside ourselves and given them dominion over the creatures in their worlds, worlds very different from our own?'

'I'm not sure,' Richard muttered doubtfully, wondering how this unorthodox perspective might accord with Catholic dogma. He found it hard to imagine a deity that looked like an elongated egg. 'I think this is more serious than you think, Sister.'

'What will happen is in Our Lord's hands,' she said soothingly. 'But tell me now, have you heard any more from the police?'

'No. I don't think they've caught Abraham Rosenberg yet even though Interpol has put out a red alert for him.'

'That fiend,' she snorted angrily. 'Well I hope they catch him soon and lock him up for a very long time.'

Richard was amused that her goodwill extended more to the invading aliens than to the leader of the Inheritors of the New Kingdom. 'Isn't Rosenberg also one of God's creatures?' he asked.

'Him?' she snapped. 'No, he's the Devil incarnate!'

* * *

At five o'clock he went to meet Fiona at the end of her afternoon shift. She was looking pale and tired. The hospital was under tremendous pressure, she told him. It had already been experiencing a huge surge of patients with heat exhaustion and respiratory problems. Now it was deluged with people suffering from panic and heart attacks.

As she looked so wan, he persuaded her with difficulty that it was safe enough to go for a short walk. He left the car in a side street and they followed the same route they had taken with Polly not long before. They walked hand in hand through the churchyard and past the stream until they reached the small recreation ground. On this occasion it was deserted. There were no smiling parents pushing their toddlers on the swings, no couples entwined on the grass, no elderly people relaxing on benches, holding their faces up to the sun.

Helicopters rumbled continuously overhead as they crossed the rectangle of sparse brown grass.

Richard told Fiona what he had heard on the news and the gist of his conversation with Sister Francis.

'How could she say it's exciting?' she exclaimed angrily. 'It's absolutely terrifying.'

Richard felt obliged to defend the nun. 'She only meant it's exciting because now we know we're not alone in the universe.'

'I'd rather we *were* alone,' she retorted, 'Anything's better than having hideous creatures like those as our cosmic neighbours.' She pulled her hand out of his and marched rapidly ahead.

He hastened to catch her up. 'Sister Francis has a point, Fi. They may look weird but they're only another form of life, a very different one, I grant you. But there are thousands of pretty weird creatures here on our own planet, aren't there? There always have been. Think of the dinosaurs. If they hadn't been wiped out, what would the dominant life form on Earth look like now? Probably not at all like us.'

'What about all the destruction those creatures have caused?' she asked angrily. 'And that may only be the start of it.'

'The attacks on vegetation have stopped.'

'How can you be so complacent, Ric?' Tears started to trickle down her face. 'It feels like the end of the world to me.'

He stopped walking and took her in his arms. 'Then let's make the best of whatever time we have left.'

He led her to a secluded spot behind a hedge and they made urgent love on a patch of cracked earth, its surface thinly covered with tufts of scorched grass.

If the world was about to end, he thought afterwards, as they lay panting and exhausted, gazing up at the cloudless sky, there was probably no better way of seeing it out.

They spent the evening watching endless replays of earlier footage showing the aliens hovering over the Strand and the unsuccessful attempts by security forces to shoot them down. All news reports were accompanied by pictures of panic-stricken reactions to the invasion. Huge traffic jams on routes out of London suggested that people were fleeing the capital in droves.

Government ministers and army chiefs were attempting to calm panic by declaring at regular intervals that the number of invaders remained relatively small and were still confined to a limited area. They assured the public that at the first sign of aggression, the military would put retaliatory measures into immediate operation.

Reports from other countries demonstrated the emptiness of this message, for it was clear that all attempts to repel or destroy the invaders were foundering in face of the invisible and impenetrable shield surrounding them.

Fiona left the room several times during the evening, and Richard heard snatches of her tearful phone conversations with Polly and her parents.

Exhausted by tension and anxiety, they retired early to bed.

Chapter 36

Richard woke with a start. Fiona was leaning over him. She was fully dressed and her face was tear-stained.

Alarmed, he sat up. 'What's the matter? Has something happened?'

'It's no use, Ric,' she whispered, 'I can't stay here any longer. I'm going to Suffolk.'

His heart sank.

'I've got to be with Polly. She has to come first, Ric. You do understand?'

'Of course,' he said with an effort.

'I need to leave this morning, while the trains are still running, otherwise I might not be able to get there.'

'So soon?'

'Yes. But I'll have to go home first to get my stuff.'

He started to lever himself up from the bed. 'I'll come with you.'

'No, I'd rather you didn't. I'll ring you when I get there.' She kissed him on the cheek, then picked up her bag and left the room.

A few seconds later he heard the front door bang and Maggie start to bark.

He went downstairs and let her out into the garden. He could hear none of the usual morning sounds from the Close. Had all his neighbours fled, like Reg and Doris Perkins, to areas where they thought they would be safe from the aliens?

Feeling very alone, he took his bowl of breakfast cereal into the living room and turned on the TV.

Every news channel was reporting the global impact of the alien invasion. People were still streaming away from cities in a desperate search for a place of safety. Airports and railway stations were besieged by desperate crowds, and the main highways were jammed with vehicles. Riots had broken out in some places where panic buying had reduced the availability of supplies, and there were widespread reports of looting. Some countries had experienced a spate of suicides.

Richard listened to the Secretary General of the United Nations pleading for calm and promising that all possible security measures would be taken to defend the world's population from the invaders.

Grave-faced officials were shown arriving at a Security Council meeting hastily convened to decide on collective action.

The international news was followed by a recorded address by a senior British police officer who warned that anyone found looting temporarily empty properties would be arrested immediately, as would those who took advantage of the situation to stockpile then resell scarce supplies. In response to reports that residents in some areas were forming vigilante groups to defend themselves, he warned people that it would be dangerous to take matters in their own hands.

Many of the news channels featured interviews with eminent cosmologists and astrophysicists who puzzled over the provenance of the aliens, marvelling at how they had managed to cover immense distances and arrive on Earth without being detected. Richard was intrigued by a theory propounded by one of these experts, that invisible "seeds" had been dropped by the spherical objects ejected by the spacecraft, and these had subsequently developed into the strange beings that were now terrifying the planet's inhabitants.

A Nobel Prize-winning biologist interviewed on one channel speculated on the physiology of the\aliens: 'Are they machines or sentient beings? If the latter, of what elements are they composed and in what proportion? How have they managed to adapt to gravity and the Earth's atmosphere? How do they reproduce? What kind of nourishment do they require? Do they need to sleep? How do they communicate with each other? Without taking one or more of the creatures into captivity,' she declared, 'it is impossible to answer such questions.'

While scientists expounded theories and sought explanations, the theologians and religious leaders called upon for their opinion, agonised over the implications for centuries-old assumptions about the nature of mankind and the universe.

Media correspondents reported that churches, mosques and temples were crowded with panic-stricken worshippers. Members of some religious persuasions had started to hold prayer vigils while others, believing that the invasion fulfilled certain ancient prophesies, had congregated in locations considered of sacred significance - caves, mountains and prehistoric monuments - to perform rituals designed to placate or communicate with the newcomers. Some occult groups were casting spells and making offerings to the aliens.

Richard wasn't greatly surprised by these reactions. He remembered reading how thousands of Americans had fled or armed themselves after hearing Orson Welles announce a Martian invasion during the notorious broadcast version of *The War of the Worlds* in 1938.

When he checked the internet, he found social media awash with apocalyptic predictions. Book-selling sites were reporting hugely increased sales of Doomsday publications about the imminent end of the world. He reflected on the irony that the works of "the Poet, Philosopher and Healer" were probably now best-sellers.

* * *

As the days passed, Richard's activities remained restricted to following news bulletins, now almost exclusively concerned with the invasion, and taking occasional short walks with Maggie. His interview with *Immediate Response* had been postponed and he wondered if it would ever take place. Since Fiona's departure his only contacts with other people were occasional phone conversations with his sister and Mark Davenport. He received a single faint and crackly call from his parents who had been moved temporarily into a hotel in Portugal. The cruise ship had been repaired, his father told him, but the return journey had been postponed as strict controls had been imposed on sea and air transport systems. Only military and commercial ships were being allowed into British ports.

Alternating between the TV and the internet, Richard followed events with increasing unease. Nations remained on full alert, waiting for the deadly attack they believed to be imminent. Drones equipped with radar sensors, TV cameras, image intensifiers and laser-guided missiles, were dispatched to the areas where spacecraft and aliens had been sighted, but every effort to destroy them failed. Firing at them proved futile and use of explosives was out of the question because of the damage it might cause to buildings and civilians. Politicians, scientists and defence experts remained mystified. The United Nations and NATO were holding almost daily emergency meetings to discuss ways of repelling or eliminating the enemy.

One evening Richard listened to a British war correspondent describing the latest attempts to capture some of the aliens on a TV news programme.

'Huge nets have been lowered from military aircraft,' the correspondent related, his voice trembling with excitement, 'but they only succeeded in subsiding limply against the barrier that surrounds the creatures. However, I have been told that an elite military unit in the United
States has now succeeded in isolating one of the creatures inside a sealed-
off hangar where infrared sensors are being deployed to try and build
up a more accurate picture of its anatomy. My source told me that they
have been bouncing radio signals off the invisible shield protecting the
alien, and conducting tests to check it for electro-magnetic frequencies.
They have applied various methods of nuclear radiation to the shield,
firing Alpha and Beta particles at it but apparently they just ricocheted
off. They then tried using more powerful radiation and directed
gamma-emitting radionuclides at the shield. These sailed through without deflection but as there was no interaction with the material, they
apparently yielded no information on the shield's composition.'

Finding these details incomprehensible, Richard switched to another
channel and heard a police chief describing how one of the aliens had
glided into a house when the door had been left open, traumatising the
residents who rushed panic-stricken into the street. After a short period
inside, the alien floated serenely out again without leaving a trace of its
presence.

Richard shuddered at the thought of how his mother would react if
an alien ever entered their house.

Public frustration at the failure to expel or repel the invaders had led
to demonstrations in Whitehall. TV cameras showed protestors waving
banners and chanting slogans calling on the Government to take more
decisive action against the interlopers. Police officers, some of them on
horseback, were standing by to prevent things getting out of hand.

Richard was intrigued to hear that groups of aliens had been seen
congregating near hospitals as well as fire and police stations. Some had
been observed following emergency vehicles - ambulances, fire engines
and police cars, to the considerable alarm of drivers and other occupants.

Others had been spotted in parts of the countryside where, according
to a newsreader, 'They have displayed an apparent fascination for
domestic animals such as cows, sheep and horses. The police are
receiving calls about sightings every few minutes. On each occasion,

surveillance helicopters and members of the armed forces are being sent to the reported locations.'

According to a high ranking army officer, it was impossible to estimate the overall number of aliens since, when pursued, they split into small groups and moved away with bursts of incredible speed.

Richard's own feelings towards the newcomers were confused. Were, they, as Sister Francis had suggested, intelligent beings created in another image of God, or killer machines dispatched from a distant planet to terrorise and destroy the Earth?

Chapter 37

Weeks passed and to Richard's amazement, nothing terrible happened. The newcomers displayed no signs of aggression and, apart from the disturbing but apparently harmless shafts of brilliant light they directed at people, they hadn't yet acted in a way that could be construed as menacing. Nevertheless, the impact of their arrival on day-to-day life was considerable. There had been an unprecedented run on the Stock Exchange and many people had started to withdraw their savings as a precautionary measure. Many banks, factories and companies had closed.

In response, the Government was making valiant attempts to keep the country going. Hospitals and emergency services were still functioning, albeit with considerably reduced staffing levels, and a skeleton public transport system remained in operation to enable key workers to reach their places of employment. To deter looting of temporarily empty properties, the night-time curfew remained in force. Anxious to avoid the kind of mayhem the invasion was causing in some other parts of the world, the Government also introduced a scheme whereby social and medical services would work together to provide a system of trauma counselling for people unable to cope with the reality of what had occurred.

As the upheaval had interrupted supplies of essentials such as food, power and other commodities, there was now rationing of fuel and essential foodstuffs. Together with scores of other local residents, Richard was obliged to queue at the nearest open post office for a book of coupons entitling him to a specific amount of essential items a week. Since he didn't qualify as a priority driver, he couldn't receive petrol vouchers.

* * *

A month after the first appearance of the aliens, the Prime Minister broadcast an appeal to those who had fled to the countryside, urging them to return to towns and cities.

'Although we are still in a state of emergency,' he declared, 'we must not allow what has happened to completely destroy our economy. So far there have been no reports of aggression from the alien visitors but I can assure the British people that our armed forces are continuing to keep a close watch on the situation. They will be deployed in all locations where aliens are spotted. Surveillance teams will remain in constant operation.'

His appeal had some effect and after some weeks, Richard was relieved to see signs that daily life was beginning to resume a semblance of normality. Businesses were reopening, the night-time curfew was lifted and people started to drift back to their homes in urban areas. He noticed too that the panic and hysteria aroused by the aliens seemed to be subsiding. Although the invaders were still loathed and feared, the prevailing mood seemed to have evolved into one of resignation. To some, they had become as much a curiosity as a threat. Because of their curious shape and bobbing motion, they had acquired a nickname - "Bobblers" - and were now often watched, at a safe distance, by gawping spectators with cameras.

Richard wasn't surprised at the speed of the transition. His research had demonstrated how time and familiarity could blunt the edge of new and difficult situations, and even prompt a kind of *modus vivendi* with them. His own mood, however, was bleak. He felt purposeless and frustrated and without employment, found time hanging heavily on his hands.

His mood changed, however, when he received a phone message one morning, informing him that the postponed interview for a post of overseas project manager with the international aid agency *Immediate Response*, had been rescheduled and would take place in a week's time. The job would involve managing and developing overseas development projects "in line with agency standards, frameworks and procedures". To demonstrate his suitability for such a responsibility, he was invited to make a short presentation to the appointment panel.

Richard felt excited but nervous at the prospect.

On the appointed day, he set off wearing a short-sleeved, open-necked white shirt and carrying his jacket over his arm. He wondered how men who were obliged to wear suits and ties at work managed in such sweltering conditions. Although it was now the beginning of September, there had been no drop in the furnace-like temperatures that had made the summer intolerable. The continuing heat wave had become almost as great a concern as the aliens. The hosepipe ban had been extended and some local councils were planning to install standpipes to limit usage.

It was the first time Richard had ventured so far out of his local area since the aliens had arrived, and he felt apprehensive. As it was too hot to travel on the tube, he took a bus. Alighting at a stop in central London, his heart missed a beat on seeing two Bobblers gliding towards him and the other passengers leaving the bus. They came to a stop a few yards away and remained suspended in the air, rocking slightly from side to side. He gaped up at them. They were smaller and more luminous than they looked on TV. Inside their outer membrane, he thought he could see the outlines of dark coils. What were they? Wires? Intestines?

As he watched, each of the aliens began to beam a shaft of brilliant white light down on him and the people around him. Hearing shouts of raucous laughter, he turned and saw some youths picking up cardboard food wrappers and polystyrene cups which they screwed up and hurled at the Bobblers, guffawing when the missiles bounced off the invisible barrier surrounding them.

A man remonstrated with the boys. 'Be careful. They could be dangerous.'

'Nah,' sneered one of the youths. 'They're just lumps of shite.' He lobbed another missile at one of the Bobblers which, seemingly unperturbed, aimed a narrow beam of light directly at him.

To Richard's astonishment, he heard faint noises coming from the two aliens: a series of shrill, rapid whistles. They were identical to some of the sounds made by Morgana Delph when she fell into a trance during the service at the Spiritualist Church. He shivered. How had she managed to tune into the sounds the aliens made so accurately? She must be a witch.

After a few moments, the creatures floated away.

* * *

The appointment process at *Immediate Response* was more daunting than Richard had anticipated. First he was taken to a tiny but mercifully air-conditioned room and given a written test that was clearly designed to detect whether he had the right qualities to work in an emergency-related context. Afterwards, he was conducted to a spacious meeting hall at one end of which four people - a middle-aged white man, a younger black man and two women of Asiatic appearance - sat at behind a large table. He was invited to sit on the single chair facing them.

The older of the two men introduced himself as Brendan Morrison, Director of Overseas Operations. He presented the other members of the panel, each of whom nodded at him courteously. Richard then delivered the short presentation he had prepared, about himself, his work to date and why he was interested in working for the organisation. During the interview that followed, the panel asked a series of searching questions about his research and his views on aid strategies. They made alarmingly copious notes and seemed especially keen to hear about his reactions to the privations he had witnessed during his field work.

After about an hour, Brendan Morrison brought the questions to a close. 'We are living in extremely unsettling times, Mr. Jarman,' he said, putting his elbows on the table and linking his fingers together. 'None of us knows what is going to happen ... or what our ... ahem ... visitors intend. But we can't sit around waiting for something to happen; we can't give up our important work because of an unknowable threat. This year many parts of the world have experienced unprecedented freak weather conditions and disasters, hurricanes, earthquakes, floods and volcanic activity. In such circumstances, we at *Immediate Response* must respond to the needs of those affected, despite the uncertainties of the present situation. We cannot let what has happened force us to abandon our mission.'

'No, of course not.' Richard shifted into a more relaxed sitting position.

'Our remit,' Morrison continued as though reading from a familiar script, 'is to deploy people with the appropriate skills and competences to meet the needs arising from such situations. The research you have conducted is very relevant to our kind of work. With so many natural catastrophes occurring at the same time, our resources are currently stretched very thin. Because of this we are obliged to recruit people on a fast-track basis and send them to the affected areas for varying periods, depending on the prevailing conditions.' He picked up some papers from the table in front of him and glanced at them. 'I see that you are single, Mr. Jarman. No wife or partner?'

'No.'

'Good. We find it preferable to send single people to remote and difficult situations. Would you be prepared to travel at short notice to wherever our services are required?' Morrison listed parts of the world, predominantly in Asia, where some of the worst disasters had occurred.

Richard took a deep breath, knowing that he must come to a quick decision. 'In principle, yes, but I can't go anywhere just yet. I have to attend the *viva* for my doctoral thesis on the twenty-seventh of this month.'

The members of the panel conferred with each other in low voices. Then Morrison addressed him again. 'That doesn't present a difficulty, Mr. Jarman. If we were to appoint you, you would be required to remain in this country for several weeks. All new recruits must undergo our standard induction process to familiarise themselves with the organisation and how it works. Afterwards there is a short period of intensive training, including a programme to acquaint recruits with the countries where they are to be sent and the conditions obtaining there.' He paused. 'Do you have any questions for us?'

After a brief discussion about employment terms and conditions, the interview came to a close and Richard was told that he would be informed of the panel's decision as soon as they finished their discussions.

As he left the building, the heat jolted him like an electric shock. He pulled off his jacket, slung it over his shoulder and walked back to the bus stop, musing on the afternoon's experience. The encouraging comments he had received from the interview panel suggested that he would be offered the job. He had long aspired to work in emergency situations overseas and working for the agency would be a great opportunity. So why did he suddenly feel so uncertain? As he waited for the bus, he explored the reasons for his unease. Was it guilt about going abroad when his own country was suffering from an alien invasion? Or was it because of Fiona. An image of her flitted through his mind and he felt a pang of longing. If he accepted a post with the organisation, it would mean being away for a period of months, perhaps longer. Would their developing relationship survive such a long separation?

After leaving the bus, he visited a supermarket to purchase his weekly rations. The shop was crowded and there were snaking queues at the checkouts where harassed cashiers were attempting to make sure that customers had chosen only the amount of goods they were entitled to under the rationing scheme.

Richard put his own shopping in a wire basket and joined one of the queues. Within a few minutes, scuffles broke out down the line as some people accused others of queue-jumping. Two men engaged in fisticuffs before they were separated by security staff. He had heard that such altercations had been happening increasingly frequently in shops and on petrol station forecourts.

As he waited in the queue, he suddenly spotted a Bobbler. It was floating above the checkout tills, aiming a shaft of light at the impatient lines of people below. Intent on paying for their purchases, few of the shoppers appeared to be paying it much attention. The woman in front of Richard, however, brandished a baguette at the interloper, and yelled, 'Bloody monsters! If it wasn't for you, we wouldn't 'ave food and water rationing. '

'It's not *just* because of them,' Richard felt constrained to point out. 'Water rationing is a result of what's happening with the weather: climate change, global warming, the shift in the Jet Stream.'

She gave him a hostile look. 'No it aint. It's because of them creatures. As if we didn't 'ave enough problems with all them foreigners comin' in. Now it's bleedin' aliens.' She glared belligerently at Richard as though daring him to contradict.

He thought it wise to remain silent.

Chapter 38

The Close was quiet when he arrived home as his nearest neighbours still hadn't returned from their safe havens. He was assailed by a bleak sense of loneliness. If it hadn't been for Maggie, he would have found the solitude unbearable.

He opened a can of beer and to counteract the silence, switched on the TV. His attention was immediately caught by an interview with a well-known linguist, Barnaby Wainwright, an expert in translating the languages of remote tribes in the Amazonian rainforest, who had been commissioned to try and decipher the strange noises the aliens made.

Wainwright, a bespectacled man in his sixties, was recounting how he and his assistants had been given permission to follow any Bobblers they could find, with a minidv camcorder. 'It's too early to come to any definite conclusions,' he informed the interviewer, 'but I think I have detected some mathematical patterns and frequencies to their language and I'm hoping to be able to make a breakthrough soon.'

To Richard's frustration, the linguist's interview was curtailed at this point and there was a rapid switch to an item on the heat wave. As he switched off the TV, his mobile rang.

'Dad thinks it's safe enough for us to come home now,' Fiona informed him.

His spirits soared. 'That's great. When are you coming?'

'The day after tomorrow, although Mum's dead against it. Dad had a really hard job persuading her. But he wants to go back to work and Polly will be starting high school soon, assuming schools will be opening. I don't want her to miss the beginning of the academic year. I've rung the hospital. They said it's OK for me to return to work when I'm ready. It'll be great to see you again, Ric.'

'And me, you.'

'Do you have any news?'

He told her about his interview.

'If you get the job, does it mean you'll be sent overseas?' she asked.

'Yes, but they haven't offered me anything yet. And I can't leave until after I've defended my thesis at the *viva*.'

'When's that?'

'On the twenty-seventh.'

'That's only a few weeks away.'

He decided to change the subject. 'When I went for the interview, I saw some Bobblers.'

'Did you? We haven't seen any here, thank goodness.'

'I saw two when I got off the bus, then I saw one in a supermarket.'

'Are they as hideous as they look on the telly? They give me the creeps.'

'More weird than hideous, I'd say. They're like ... transparent sausages. They've got this kind of spirally stuff inside them that looks like wires.'

'What were they doing?'

'Nothing much. Just bobbling about as usual, aiming those shafts of light at people. But they don't appear to be hostile, they seem non-threatening, almost ...innocuous.'

'They can't be innocuous,' Fiona said sharply. 'Think of the damage they've caused, the mayhem, and the effect on people. Mum's terrified. She's afraid one of them will kidnap Polly!'

Richard laughed. 'I haven't heard that they've kidnapped anyone yet, unlike the Inheritors. Sister Francis has a point. People like Rosenberg are probably more evil than the aliens.'

'Wouldn't you describe destruction of the green environment as evil?'

'Yes, I would,' he conceded. 'But I heard the Inheritors rejoice when they heard about some of the arson attacks. That makes them almost as culpable in my book.'

She gave an incredulous laugh. 'I don't get it, Ric. We've been invaded by aliens, about the most threatening situation the world could possibly experience and you think they're innocuous?'

'I only said they *seem* innocuous, Fi. Sister Francis says --'

He heard her give a derisive snort. 'Sister Francis! You seem to take her word as Gospel. Maybe she believes the same as the Inheritors, that the aliens are bringing the Messiah for his Second Coming!'

'I'm sure she doesn't believe that. Anyway, if the Messiah *is* about to make a return visit, I don't think he'll look like a sausage or a blown-up condom, do you?'

She giggled. 'Probably not! I'll call you when I'm back.'

* * *

He was getting ready for bed that night when Maggie started barking downstairs. In between the barks he thought he could hear thuds and muffled voices. They appeared to be coming from the front of the house. Alarmed, he went to his parents' room and peered through the window. His heart gave a painful thump. There was someone on the front doorstep! Rushing back on to the landing, he heard the front door open. Panic-stricken, he looked over the banister and was startled to see a tall figure, visible in the dim light from the streetlamp outside, enter the hallway.

'What the --?' exclaimed a male voice as Maggie, barking hysterically, hurled herself against the kitchen door.

Richard darted to the nearest light switch but before he could reach it, the downstairs light came on, illuminating the hall. 'What's that barking?' exclaimed a female voice - his mother's!

With a gasp of relief, he ran downstairs 'Mum? Dad? When did you get back? Why didn't you ring?'

His mother enveloped him in an embrace. 'Darling, it's lovely to see you. Didn't you get my message? Why is there a dog in the kitchen?'

'What message?' He thumped on the kitchen door. 'Quiet, Maggie! Hi, Dad!' He turned to his father who was hauling suitcases through the front door.

'Hello, Ricky.' His father gave him a hug. 'Who's Maggie? What an infernal racket! What's a dog doing here?'

Richard gave another thump on the kitchen door. 'Shut up, Maggie! It's long story, Dad. Why didn't you let me know you were coming?'

'We didn't know till yesterday,' his father replied, pulling the bags across the floor. 'It was very short notice. The owners of the cruise liner chartered a plane because they couldn't keep us all in hotels indefinitely. I tried to call you but couldn't get through, so your mother sent an email.'

'I never got it.'

'Obviously,' said his mother who had entered the living room and was gazing around it with a shocked expression.

Richard gulped. He hadn't tidied the room for several weeks and he knew there was an even worse mess in the kitchen. 'You must be worn out,' he said quickly. 'Why don't you sit down and I'll make you some tea.'

'Thank you, darling.' Although she was tanned, he noticed his mother looked thinner than she had been.

'How was the cruise?' he asked. 'It sounded wonderful.'

'Fabulous. At least it was before that frightful storm. I thought the ship was going to sink and we were both incredibly seasick. When we got to Portugal, it was unbearably hot, wasn't it, Gordon? And we heard that aliens had landed everywhere. We didn't believe it of course. We didn't have a clue what was happening.' Her eyes filled with tears.

His father put his arm round her. 'Calm down, Eileen. We're home now, safe. Sit down and rest. I'll take the luggage upstairs and Ricky will make you a cup of tea.' He turned to Richard. 'Your mother's very tired. It's been a long day. Can't you stop that dog barking? What's it doing here anyway?'

'I'll tell you in a minute, Dad.' He went to the door and bellowed, 'Quiet, Maggie!'

'Infernal racket!' His father returned to the hall and started bumping the luggage up the stairs. The noise prompted another volley of barks.

His mother looked exasperated. 'For goodness sake, Ricky, can't you stop that ghastly noise? It's giving me a headache and it'll disturb the neighbours.' She started to tidy the cushions on the sofa and with a cluck of annoyance, plucked an empty beer can from the floor and threw it in the wastepaper basket.

'Most of the neighbours are still away, Mum. I'll make the tea.'

Richard hurried to the kitchen, shutting the door before Maggie could escape to investigate the intruders. After switching on the kettle, he hastily cleared food wrappings and dirty dishes from the worktops.

'I'm sorry there aren't any biscuits or anything,' he said as he carried the tray into the sitting room. 'You know we've got food rationing here?'

'Yes, we heard,' his mother sighed. 'What terrible times, Ricky.'

The sound of suitcases being pulled along the landing started Maggie barking again.

'For heaven's sake,' she exclaimed. 'Can't you stop that dog barking? Whose is it anyway?'

'A friend's. I'll bring her in so you can meet her.' Richard returned to the kitchen, put on Maggie's lead and, with some trepidation, led her into the living room where he had to forcibly restrain her from leaping on to his mother.

'Good God!' she cried, collapsing on to an armchair. 'What kind of a dog is that?'

'A bit of everything.'

'Don't let it touch me! I expect it's got fleas.'

'She won't hurt you, Mum. She's very gentle, just a bit over-friendly.'

'But what's it doing here, in our house?'

'She belonged to a poor old man I knew. He died and she had no-where else to go.'

'Ricky, I don't *want* a dog in the house,' his mother wailed.

'No, we don't!' declared his father who had reappeared in the sitting room. He recoiled at the sight of Maggie who gave a joyful bark and would have leapt at him had Richard not continued to keep a tight grip on her lead.

'Good God, what an ugly mongrel! You must get rid of it.'

'I will, Dad. I'm only looking after her for a while. She's been keeping me company.' Richard gazed appealingly at his mother. 'I thought a dog would keep me safe, you know, just in case the aliens ever fetch up here, in the Close. She's a really good guard dog, you've just had evidence of that.'

His mother's expression softened. 'Of course, darling, it must have been terrible for you, all alone, with those ghastly creatures around.' She shuddered. 'What if one of them tries to get in the house?'

'Maggie would see it off!' Richard declared confidently. 'She usually sleeps in the kitchen, but I'll leave her on the patio tonight if you like.'

'No,' his mother said hurriedly. 'Leave her in the kitchen. She'll be nearer the front door there.'

Richard breathed a sigh of relief and took Maggie back to the kitchen where he gave her some dog biscuits, one of the few commodities not limited by rationing.

Now that she had seen and sniffed the interlopers, the dog settled calmly back on her blanket, uttered a deep contented rumble and was quiet at last.

Returning to the living room, Richard poured the tea and listened to a detailed account of his parents' recent experiences: how their enjoyment of the final stages of the cruise had been ruined by the terrible storm and news of the alien invasion. The enforced stay in Portugal had added to their growing anxiety and frustration.

'The main problem,' his father explained, 'was that we didn't know how or when we were going to get home. And we never knew what was going on. We had to rely on what people told us. Everybody had heard something different. You can imagine all the rumours going round, some of them quite contradictory. We didn't know what to believe. We were put up in a nice hotel but because of the storm, there was no internet signal and the only TV channels we could get were in Portuguese, Spanish or Arabic. We couldn't get CNN or find BBC World Service on the radio. We found some English papers but they were weeks out of date. And it was difficult to make phone calls from the hotel because the storm had brought down the lines.'

'And it was so hot there,' chipped in his mother, 'an inferno. You could hardly breathe.'

'It's been mega hot here too,' said Richard. 'Did you see any aliens in Portugal?'

'Not in Oporto, thank God,' replied his father, 'but there were some in Lisbon. We saw them on a Portuguese TV channel. Never seen anything like it in my life. Ghastly creatures, no legs--'

'Why have they come here?' interjected Richard's mother. 'What do they want?' She started to tremble.

'Calm down, Eileen. Why don't you go upstairs and have a nice warm bath?'

'She's very upset, you know,' his father told Richard after she had left the room. 'The taxi-driver told us there are lots of those dreadful creatures over here. Have you seen any?'

Richard began to tell him about the Bobblers he had seen earlier that day, but was interrupted when his mother suddenly re-entered the room.

'Ricky, I forgot! We haven't congratulated you. You must be *Dr* Jarman now!' Her face glowed with pride.

'Not quite, Mum. I've got to have the *viva* first.'

She looked baffled. 'What's that?'

'I have to defend my thesis in front of some academics. They'll ask me questions about it. But I did have a job interview today, at *Immediate Response*, for an overseas project management post.'

She looked alarmed. 'Oh no, darling, you can't go away again. Not now. Not the way things are. We don't know what's going to happen.'

'Your mother's right, Ricky,' interjected his father. 'Now's not the time to be going overseas again. You should stay in your own country.'

'They haven't offered me anything yet, Dad. The interview was only this morning.' He glanced at his watch and saw to his surprise that it was after midnight. 'I mean yesterday morning.'

His father frowned. 'You should be at home at a time like this, with your family.'

'Speaking of family, have you been in touch with Saskia?' his mother asked.

'Yes, they've gone to their cottage in Yorkshire.'

'I'll ring her tomorrow and let her know we're back.' His mother left the room and shortly afterwards, he heard the sound of water running in the bathroom.

His father yawned. 'I'm ready to hit the sack. We can unpack tomorrow.'

Remembering that he hadn't changed the sheets on his parents' bed since the last time he and Fiona had lain in it, Richard jumped to his feet. 'I'll make the bed up for you, Dad. You'll need clean sheets after being away so long.'

His father looked surprised. 'Thank you, Ricky, that's very thoughtful. I'll wait down here till you've finished.'

Richard dashed upstairs and took some clean sheets from the airing cupboard. By the time his mother had emerged from the bathroom, he had changed the double bed and stuffed the dirty sheets, together with some of his clothes, into the washing machine.

Chapter 39

Richard was getting dressed the next morning when he heard a piercing shriek that sent Maggie into a renewed frenzy of barking. He dashed downstairs and found his mother, dressed in her nightgown, standing at the open patio doors in the living room.

'What's happened to my garden?' she wailed. 'The roses are ruined. So is the lawn and,' she shrieked again, 'The shed roof's stuck in the hedge!'

'What? What's happened?' His father stumbled into the room, pulling a dressing gown over his pyjamas.

Richard started to explain 'It was the storm, Mum. It did incredible damage --'

She interrupted him, looking even more horrified. 'What's *that*?' She pointed at the shrivelled brown grass. 'It's … it's … *dog mess!*'

'Oh…yes,' Richard mumbled. 'I meant to clear it up. I'll do it as soon as I'm dressed.' He bolted back upstairs.

'You'd better get rid of that dog and bloody soon!' his father shouted at his retreating back.

Richard hurriedly got dressed. Glad as he was that his parents were safely home, he realised it wasn't going to be easy with the three of them living under the same roof. And it was unlikely that they would ever warm to Maggie. Perhaps he could persuade Fiona to take her back.

Fiona … His pleasurable anticipation of her return was punctured by the realisation that once both sets of parents had returned, it was going to be difficult to pick up where they had left off. Overcome with gloom, he made his way back downstairs.

His mother was fidgeting impatiently outside the kitchen door. 'Will you please remove that dog, Ricky. Every time I try to get in there, she leaps up at me.'

'She's just being friendly, Mum. I'll put her in the garden and I promise I'll clear up after her.'

His mother backed away as he opened the door and led Maggie by the collar through the hall and into the living room. He opened the patio doors and she bounded into the garden.

When he joined his mother in the kitchen, she was clucking

disapprovingly. 'All those empty beer cans. Look at that!' She gestured at the rubbish bin which was overflowing with empty tins and food wrappers. 'Is this the kind of rubbish you've been living on while we've been away?'

He flushed. 'Well, it's been hard getting stuff lately, and there are always long queues in the shops.'

'Is there anything we can have for breakfast?'

'There's cornflakes or toast,' He pulled the remains of a stale loaf from the cupboard. 'There's a bit of butter left, but no marmalade I'm afraid.'

With a loud sigh, she filled the kettle.

After breakfast, his mother set about cleaning the house with a vigour he felt was clearly intended as a reproach to him. While she noisily vacuumed the hall and stairs, he and his father repaired to the sitting room where his father questioned him closely on all that had happened during his absence to see whether it tallied with what they had heard during the cruise.

Richard told him about the UFO he had seen in April, the destruction of Fonthill Park and other green spaces around London, and the arrival of the spaceship that had expelled its strange cargo over the capital. He decided not to mention Sister Francis, the Inheritors of the New Kingdom and his enforced sojourn on the Scottish island, feeling that such details would unduly lengthen and complicate his narrative.

His father became agitated as he listened. 'Why are we tolerating extraterrestrial invaders? What have we got armed forces for? Even if we haven't got the balls to drive them out, other countries have got strong armies and high tech weapons. I can't understand why we haven't seen them all off by now.'

'There are too many of them, Dad, and they're too dispersed. Anyway, they have a sort of force field around them. There's no point in using weapons against them if nothing can touch them. Don't you think the Americans have tried? They've pulled out all the stops.' Richard described international attempts to repel or capture the aliens.

His father looked sceptical. 'Surely there must be a way of destroying them.'

Somewhat to his own surprise, Richard found himself defending the aliens. 'We shouldn't destroy other beings just because they're different from us, Dad. Difference doesn't automatically equate with evil. Some human beings are far more dangerous than the Bobblers.'

His father stared at him, puzzled. 'The what?'

'Bobblers. That's what we call the aliens here.'

'Ridiculous name!' his father snorted. 'But don't go all holy-moly on me, Ricky. We can't just stand back and let aliens take over the Earth.'

'They haven't taken over the Earth, Dad. The ones I've seen just seem …' he sought for the right word '… *interested* in what's going on. They haven't done anything since--'

'Since they were destroying the environment, the greenbelt, forests?'

'They seem to have stopped doing that now.'

Maggie tapped one of the patio doors with a paw and gazed entreatingly at Richard through the glass.

'Sorry, Dad, I'd better give Maggie her breakfast.' He fetched bowls of water and dog food from the kitchen and put them on the patio.

Maggie pounced hungrily on the food.

'You'll have to get rid of that dog,' his father repeated for the umpteenth time. 'Your mother doesn't want it in the house, and neither do I.' He wiped his brow with his sleeve. 'It's infernally hot in here. Leave the patio doors open, will you, but don't let that dog back in.'

Richard opened the glass doors a fraction.

'Has anyone managed to communicate with the aliens?' his father asked.

'Not so far as I know. They seem to communicate with each other, though. I heard two of them the other day making really weird noises. A linguist called Wainwright is trying to interpret their language, but I don't know how far he's got.'

The roar of the vacuum cleaner had ceased and now clanking sounds reached them from the kitchen.

His father frowned. 'Your mother's been extremely agitated, you know. I'm hoping she'll feel better now that we're at home.' He paused. 'Tell me about the new rationing system? How does it work?'

Richard explained how to register for and use the ration cards. 'You use them like a credit or debit card. Here, have a look at mine.' He got out his wallet and extracted his card.

His father scrutinised it. 'Impressive. How did the Government get the system in place so quickly?'

'The theory is that they were expecting an alien invasion to happen, although nothing was ever said in case there was panic. So they had emergency measures planned and ready to put into immediate operation. You must be eligible for petrol vouchers, Dad, as you need the car for work.'

'I certainly do. I couldn't do loss assessments otherwise? I rang the office this morning. Apparently they've been absolutely snowed under with claims after that big storm.'

Richard nodded. 'I'm not surprised. The storm did a vast amount of damage before everything ground to a halt after the invasion. Things are only just starting to return to normal.'

'I'm going back to work on Monday. What's the matter, Eileen?'

His mother was standing in the doorway with a strange expression on her face. 'Ricky, I just removed your dirty clothes from the washing machine and I found *this* in the pocket of your jeans. ' She held something up to show them. It was the rosary.

'Have you converted to Roman Catholicism?'

'No.' Richard tried to think of an explanation that would satisfy his mother. 'I just thought it might help in the circumstances.'

'I wouldn't have expected you to get help from one of these,' she snorted. 'Was it Mary Brennan who gave it to you?'

'No, it was a friend.'

'I'm surprised you accepted it.' She dropped the rosary on the coffee table and stalked out of the room.

'I'd keep that out of sight if I were you,' muttered his father. 'You know how strongly your mother feels about the RCs.'

Richard shrugged and placed the beads in his trouser pocket. His mother had tried unsuccessfully to instil the Baptist faith into him during his childhood.

He was still filling his father in on the events of previous weeks when the phone rang in the hall.

His mother rushed to answer it. 'That'll be Saskia. I left her a message asking her to ring me back … .Sass? … No? Who is this? *Who*? Yes he's here.' She put her head round the living room door and gave Richard another odd look. 'There's a woman on the phone for you. Sister something or other. I think it's a … *nun!*'

'A nun?' His father looked astonished.

Richard felt his face go hot. He jumped out of his chair and went to the phone. Why had she rung? It must be something important.

Sister Francis's voice was jovial. 'Was that a wee lady friend who answered the phone?'

'No, it was my mother. And Sister, please use my mobile number another time.'

'Your mother? That means your parents have returned home safely. You must be happy to see them, Richard.'

'Yes. Is something the matter, Sister? Are you alright?'

'Och yes, I'm grand, so I am. I've had an idea.'

'An idea?'

'Yes, it came to me just now so I thought I'd sneak into the office and put a wee proposition to you.'

'A proposition?' he echoed.

'Ay. Those aliens ... what do they call them?'

'Bobblers,' he prompted

'Ay, the Bobbles. Have you seen any of them, Richard?'

'Yes, I saw three yesterday.'

'And what was your impression of them?'

He was puzzled. 'It's hard to say. They look very odd, of course, but they don't seem to be malevolent. They just seem to be watching ... or waiting. Why do you ask?'

'Because I intend to go and see them for meself.'

'But I thought you couldn't leave the convent. The police thought it was unsafe.'

'I can now that those wicked men are in custody. I'm going to the bank tomorrow.'

Richard laughed. I don't think you'll see many aliens there!' He had an absurd vision of a group of Bobblers hovering over the inevitable queue at the bank counter.

'Of course I don't expect to see them *there*,' she retorted impatiently. 'The man who came for the vegetables told me there's a group of them outside the county hospital. He said they've been there for the last few days.'

'You're going to the hospital as well as the bank?'

'Yes, I thought I'd go and say a few words to them.'

'You're going to *speak* to the aliens?'

'Ay, I'm going to show them a crucifix and an image of the Sacred Heart.'

For the first time Richard began to wonder whether the little nun wasn't slightly bonkers. 'Why would you do that?'

Her voice became grave. 'Isn't it obvious? To see what effect it has on them when they see images of the Son of God. I want to demonstrate that these creatures aren't necessarily evil. They're just another manifestation of the great variety of God's creation.'

'But--'

'As long as the aliens do us no further harm, Richard, they should be protected from harm themselves.'

He was silent for a moment. It was as though she likened the aliens to cuddly small creatures that had a nasty bite but were otherwise innocuous. 'Does Mother Ignatius know what you're intending to do?'

'No, I haven't told her, may God have mercy on my soul. If she knew, she'd surely forbid it. But I owe it to Saint Francis. He loved all creatures, you know, whatever they looked like and wherever they came from. That's why I took his name. Did you know that Saint Francis found shelter in a Benedictine Monastery at the beginning of his calling?'

'No, I didn't. But if you go looking for Bobblers, it'll mean you'll be late getting back to the convent and the sisters will worry about you, especially after what happened before--'

'Not at all,' she interrupted. 'I often do wee errands for the convent when I go to the bank, and I sometimes have a wee cup of coffee with Father Doyle. So, will you come with me, Richard?'

'What? You want *me* to go with you?'

'Ay, that's my proposition. We're a good combination, you and I!' She chuckled. 'You're my partner in adversity, so you are; my young protector.'

'Oh, I'm not sure,' he faltered. 'My parents have only just come home --'

'I'll see you at eleven at the main entrance,' she said decisively. 'It's in Larks' Grove.'

He made a last attempt to dissuade her. 'I really don't think it's a good idea, Sister. No-one's supposed to approach the Bobblers. Anyway, they may have moved on by now.'

'Then we'll have to go and find them. We'll go Bobble-hunting, Richard, you and I!'

'It's not a good idea,' he repeated.

'I'll see you tomorrow, Richard. God bless you.'

Richard felt distinctly uneasy as he put the phone down. Fond as he was of Sister Francis, he didn't relish the idea of accompanying her while she brandished religious artifacts at the Bobblers. They were aliens after all, not malevolent spirits that would slink back into the shadows at the sight of a crucifix. A number of religious groups had already performed rituals to placate or communicate with them, to no apparent effect. He wished he had refused outright. On the other hand, he didn't like to think of the little nun carrying out her absurd plan on her own in case something happened to her.

He found his mother hovering beside him. 'First a rosary, then a nun?' she commented tartly. 'Are you sure you're not becoming one of *them*, Ricky, an RC?'

'No, Mum, Sister Francis is a friend.'

'A friend? Young men don't usually have nuns as friends.'

'Well I have,' he retorted. 'And I choose the friends *I* want, not the ones you approve of.'

His father's plaintive voice came from the sitting room. 'What's going on?'

Before Richard could supply an explanation, he heard his mobile ringing in his bedroom and gratefully ran upstairs to answer it. Maybe it was Fiona. He hadn't mentioned her to his parents yet. He was disappointed to hear a male voice.

'Mr. Jarman?'

'Yes?'

'Brendan Morrison, from *Immediate Response*.'

'Oh, yes hello.'

'We've come to a decision and would like to offer you a position as overseas project manager.'

Richard was speechless.

'Well? Do you accept?'

'Yes, of course I do. Thank you, Mr. Morrison.'

'Good. I'll email you the necessary details. There are some forms for you to read and sign.'

'Where would I be sent?'

'This is something we'll have to discuss with you. There are several possibilities.'

'How long would I be away?'

'Three or four months in the first instance. Could be extended to six, depending on the situation. But as I already mentioned to you, first you will have to attend the induction and training programmes. I suggest you start these as soon as possible, maybe next Monday?'

Richard agreed. He felt dazed. Too much was happening at once. He slowly descended the stairs. As he entered the sitting room, he caught fragments of a news report issuing from the television: *Security services remain on permanent alert ... No end to fierce heat wave ...*

His mother was distraught when he announced his own news. 'So soon? Where will they send you? Everywhere's so dangerous at the moment. What if terrible things happen here? What if the aliens attack us?'

'I've got to take the job, Mum. I don't want to be unemployed. And I don't know where they're going to send me yet.'

Her eyes filled with tears. 'What about *us*? We need you here.'

His father put his arm around her. 'Ricky has to accept a job when it's offered, Eileen, even if it means going away. It's not easy to find good employment these days.'

She dabbed at her eyes with a tissue. 'Well if you must go, what are you going to do about that dog? You're not leaving it here.'

'Don't worry about Maggie,' Richard said quickly. 'I'll sort something out. And I may have to go out early tomorrow.' He didn't mention his destination, hoping they would assume it was related to the job.

He escaped to his room and searched the internet to see what buses he could catch that would drop him near the hospital Sister Francis had mentioned. A few minutes later, he heard the phone in the hall ring again. Snatches of conversation reached him and he realised that his mother was speaking to Saskia. About ten minutes later, she appeared at his bedroom door, looking agitated.

'Ricky, isn't it about time you told us what's been going on?'

'What do you mean, Mum?'

'Your sister just told me there was something about you in the papers, something about a nun you helped to escape from an island in Scotland. What on earth were you doing on an island in Scotland? Was that the nun who was on the phone? Did *she* give you the rosary? What's this all about?'

He sighed. 'OK, I'll come down and tell you and Dad what's been happening. I didn't mention it before because I didn't want to alarm you.'

He accompanied his mother back to the living room.

'Turn the TV off, Gordon,' she instructed his father. 'Ricky has something to tell us.'

Richard gave them an abbreviated account of his meeting with Sister Francis, his search for the Inheritors, his sojourn on the island and subsequent flight with Sister Francis and Brother Jacob. He prudently omitted any reference to Morgana Delph and Abraham R's instruction to his followers to commit mass suicide.

His parents listened in amazement as his narrative unfolded.

'Good lord, Ricky,' his father exclaimed when he had finished. 'How did you get mixed up with those lunatics? What were you thinking of?'

'I had to find Sister Francis.'

'Why didn't you leave it to the police? It's their job to find missing persons.'

'I told them I thought the Inheritors had taken her but they didn't believe me. So I felt I had to find her myself.'

His mother looked appalled. 'You mean you deliberately put yourself in danger? I would have been beside myself with worry if I'd known what you were up to.'

'That's exactly why I didn't tell you.'

'All that time we were away we thought you were safe at home, working on your thesis.'

'Believe me, I wish I had been.' Richard said fervently.

Chapter 40

The hospital was extremely busy. A line of cars had drawn up in the road outside, each awaiting its turn to enter the drop-off parking bay. Ambulances were arriving in quick succession and disgorging their cargoes of stretchered patients. A constant stream of exhausted-looking pedestrians, some on crutches, some in wheelchairs, was passing through the main entrance. Uniformed staff were scurrying in and out of numerous side doors.

Helicopters thrummed overhead, performing their mission of surveillance of reported aliens. The noise had become so familiar that Richard barely noticed it. He did, however, spot a lone policeman patrolling round the building.

His heart sank when he spotted the three Bobblers. He had been hoping they would have moved to a different location. They were hovering by an upper window a few yards to the left of the main doors and swaying slowly from side to side. Most of the people swarming below them seemed oblivious to their presence, although one or two glanced nervously upwards before disappearing though the main entrance.

It wasn't long before he spotted a small, blue-clad figure walking up and down on the forecourt in front of the vehicle drop-off bay. She was carrying a cloth bag.

'There you are at last,' she called impatiently when she caught sight of him. 'You're late!'

'It wasn't easy getting here,' Richard muttered grumpily. 'I had to take three buses.'

'Never mind, you're here now, so let's get going.'

He looked warily at the bag she was carrying. 'Are you sure you want to do this, Sister? I mean, will it achieve anything? Won't it make you late getting back to the convent?'

'Och I've plenty of time. They'll think I dropped in on Father Doyle. Come along now, we've God's work to do.' She grasped his arm.

'Why don't we just go and have a cup of coffee?'

She stared at him, aghast. 'Coffee? Whatever are you thinking of, Richard? This is far more important.'

Reluctantly he accompanied her across the forecourt. The people they passed were too intent on their business at the hospital to pay them any attention.

Sister Francis halted below the window the Bobblers had chosen for their vantage point and extracted a small crucifix and a framed picture of the Sacred Heart from her cloth bag. 'Hold this for me, now.' She thrust the empty bag at Richard, then raising her arms, brandished the two articles at the Bobblers.

In response, they began to aim their shafts of light directly at her.

Richard shrank back in dismay and embarrassment as she began to declaim something in Latin, in a resonant voice he had never heard her use before.

'*Credemus in unum Deum, Patrem omnipotentem, factorem caeli et terrae, visibilium omnium, et invisibilium. Et in unum Dominum Jesum Christum, Filium Dei unigenitum. Et ex Patre natum ante omnia saecula. Deum de Deo, Lumen de lumine, Deum verum de Deo vero. Genitum, non factum, consubstantialem Patri: per quem omnia* (she put strong emphasis on the word) *omnia facta sunt!*

(*We believe in one God, the Father almighty, maker of heaven and earth, of all that is seen and unseen. And in one Lord, Jesus Christ, the only Son of God, eternally begotten of the Father, God from God, Light from Light, true God from true God, begotten, not made, one in being with the Father. Through Him **all** things were made.*)

During the brief silence that followed Sister Francis's declamation, Richard became uncomfortably aware that most of the people in the vicinity of the hospital entrance had stopped to stare at them. The perspiration soaking through his thin t-shirt was as much due to embarrassment as to the heat.

'Shall we go now?' he suggested. 'I don't suppose the Bobblers understand Latin.'

She gave him a withering look. 'How do you know what they'll understand? These words from the Creed have been used for over two thousand years! It's a tragedy the Latin mass was dropped, so it is. Now Richard, it's your turn.'

'My turn? What do you mean?'

'Repeat the Creed. It would be good if they could hear it twice.'

He gazed at her incredulously. 'Me? No, I can't. I don't know the words.'

'Och, I was forgetting you're not a Catholic. Well, do you still have the rosary I gave you?'

'Yes.' He extracted the beads from his trouser pocket.

'Hold it up, now, and show it to them. Our Lady will reinforce the message.'

'Is that really necessary?'

'Go on,' she urged.

Red-faced with embarrassment, Richard waved the rosary without conviction at the Bobblers.

'Now,' she instructed, 'after I say *omnia facta sunt*, I want you to say *amen* then show them the rosary again.'

Ignoring his feeble protests, she proceeded to repeat the Creed, not once, but twice, in an even louder voice than the first time. At the end of each recitation, Richard uttered a squeaky *amen* and flourished the rosary.

There was a short pause and he fervently hoped that the excruciating ordeal was over, but then, with another flourish of the crucifix, she shouted up to the aliens, 'Praise to the Lord, the Almighty, the King of Creation, praise him, for he is thy health and salvation!'

The Bobblers had stopped swaying from side to side and were perfectly still. It was almost, he thought, as though they were listening (if they had any ears). Perhaps they were just amazed by the little nun's audacity.

Sister Francis had now attracted an even larger group of curious on-lookers, some of whom were tittering. Several were holding up mobile phones to take photos of them.

Richard noticed the policeman approaching them.

'Madam, Sir! Don't you know it's forbidden to approach the aliens? I must ask you to leave the premises. We don't want any trouble at the hospital.'

Sister Francis bestowed upon him a beam of supreme innocence. 'We're just praying, Officer, so we are. We'll soon be on our way.'

Before the man could reply, there was a loud murmur from the people who had been watching the scene. The Bobblers had begun to make shrill whistling sounds, like the ones Richard had heard a few days before, but this time the sounds were more rapid, more furious, more intense. If the idea wasn't impossible, he could have sworn they were *laughing!*

Sister Francis turned to him, her round face flushed with triumph. 'You see, Richard! I've reached them! They recognised Our Lord as the son of God, Creator of all creatures on earth and in the universe. They'll be off to tell their friends. They won't hurt us now.'

'Do you think so?' Richard had serious doubts about this assertion but was unwilling to puncture her jubilation.

'I'm sure of it.' She took the cloth bag from him and thrust the crucifix and picture back inside. 'How about that cup of coffee?' She smiled again at the policeman who was standing uncertainly beside them. 'Good day to you, Officer.'

Heartily relieved to be leaving the hospital, Richard accompanied her to the nearest coffee shop.

Once she had finished enthusing over the apparent success of her attempt to communicate with the aliens, Sister Francis asked what he had been doing since their return from the island.

He told her about his job applications and confided the ambivalence he felt over the offer from *Immediate Response*.

'It's exactly the kind of job I want but it's come at the wrong time. My mother thinks that I should stay in this country when the world is in crisis.'

She listened sympathetically. 'What do your instincts tell you, Richard?'

He reflected. 'That I've got to accept the job; I need to earn a living and move on in my life.'

'Then that is what you must do. And it will be good work that you'll be doing, to be sure, God's work, helping poor souls who are suffering terrible disasters.'

'The other problem is, I have a girlfriend,' Richard blurted, surprising himself for he hadn't intended to mention Fiona.

'You have?'

'Her name's Fiona. We were at school together. She's got a daughter, but she isn't married. She was once, but not any more.'

'You mean she's divorced?'

'Yes. You'll probably disapprove of that but she's... special,' he stuttered, seeking the right word to characterise Fiona.

She gave him a shrewd look. 'And you don't want to leave her behind?'

'There's no way I can take her and a child to a disaster zone. And it's too early to think of anything ... permanent. I don't feel I can promise her anything, you see.'

She nodded. 'If the two of you are meant to be together, you will be, whether you take the job or not. You're in God's hands, Richard.'

He sighed. 'In other words, *que sera sera?*'

'I'm afraid so. You're still young. Don't try and second guess what could happen. You have your whole life ahead of you.'

'If the world doesn't come to an end,' he muttered.

'Och, now you're talking like one of those devils on the island! As I told you, those Bobbies are our fellow creatures. I don't believe they intend to destroy our world.'

'How can you be so sure?'

'Have faith in Our Lord Jesus Christ, Richard. Now I'd better be getting back or they'll think I've been abducted again, by the Bobbles this time!'

Richard was pensive as he walked back to the bus-stop. Although the conversation had removed some of his uncertainty about the job, he remained troubled.

Chapter 41

Fiona rang him the following afternoon and they arranged to meet in the tiny park where they had made love the day before she left to join her family in Suffolk. He told his parents that he was taking Maggie for a walk. He wasn't ready to mention Fiona to them just yet.

He arrived first. Unlike on the previous occasion when the park had been deserted, a few people were again using its sparse facilities. An elderly woman was sitting on a bench fanning her face with a piece of cardboard; a young woman was pushing a toddler on a swing, and four small boys were desultorily kicking a football on the short rectangle of dusty ground. The relentless heat had destroyed the remaining grass.

While Maggie trotted off to investigate the roots of a spindly hedge, Richard made for the nearest trees, seeking shelter from the glaring sun. His legs felt sticky in jeans and he wished he had worn shorts.

After a few minutes he heard voices hailing him. Looking round, he saw Fiona and Polly walking along the narrow path. Fiona was wearing a short blue dress that revealed her slender brown limbs. Her hair was tied in a ponytail, making her look almost as young as her daughter.

'Maggie!' Polly shouted joyfully.

Barking with excitement, Maggie galloped towards her and Fiona. She leapt up at Polly and placed her paws on the girl's shoulders. The two of them raced off together through the park.

Richard took Fiona in his arms and kissed her. 'It's so good to see you again,' he murmured, inhaling the fresh scent of her hair. 'I've missed you.'

She smiled at him. 'I've missed you too.'

'How was Suffolk?'

'Quiet, deadly quiet. If it hadn't been for the queues at the shop and garage, you wouldn't have known that there had been an invasion. To be honest I was bored. The village is pretty but the cottage was far too small for all of us and there was nothing to do except go for walks. At least it was a bit cooler there. Now tell me about you.'

As they strolled hand in hand under the trees, he told her about his parents' return.

'Of course I'm glad they've come home, but it's difficult. Mum's found out about Sister Francis and the island, and she keeps interrogating me. And she absolutely hates Maggie. She and Dad keep telling me to get rid of her.' He looked sheepishly at her. 'I don't suppose…?'

Fiona laughed. 'Don't worry. Polly wants her back. She talked about little else during the drive home. My parents aren't keen on Maggie either, but they'll put up with her for Poll's sake.'

He sighed with relief. 'That's great. But won't Polly be going to school soon?'

A helicopter clattered overhead.

'In about a week,' she replied when the noise had receded. 'Schools have been given the go-ahead to open, for shorter hours in the first instance. We've had a letter about security arrangements. Mum's frantic. She thinks we should keep Polly at home until the Bobblers are chased away.'

'Well, I suppose you can't suspend everything just because they're here. The country would grind to a halt.'

A football rolled near his feet. He kicked it back to the boys.

She looked enquiringly at him, her expression troubled. 'Why do you think the Bobblers haven't done anything yet, Ric?'

'I haven't got a clue, Fi. Everybody's still waiting for them to make a move.'

'Thank God there weren't any in the village. Mum would have had a heart attack. Polly's desperate to see one. She's seen them on the telly and she thinks they're cute!'

'I actually saw three of them yesterday.' Richard related what had happened when he met Sister Francis at the hospital.

She gave an incredulous laugh. 'Why did you let that silly old woman involve you in something so stupid?'

'She's not a silly old woman! What she did may have been silly, but it was out of genuine belief. She was so enthusiastic, it was hard to refuse.'

'Well I'm amazed that you joined in that mumbo jumbo.'

'That's not fair, Fi,' he responded indignantly. 'What about Morgana Delph and her messages from the dead? That's mumbo jumbo in my book, more so than waving a crucifix at a couple of Bobblers.'

She squeezed his arm. 'Don't let's argue. I just think waving crucifixes at them isn't very helpful'

'I agree with you, but I'm fond of Sister Francis. I only went with her to make sure she didn't come to any harm.' He wiped his brow with the back of his hand. 'Christ, it's hot! Let's sit on that bench in the shade.'

As they sat down, another helicopter rumbled overhead. While they waited for the noise to diminish, they watched Polly playing with the dog.

'Watch this,' the girl called across to them. She threw a stick high in the air and Maggie leapt up on her back legs to catch it.

'That's great, Poll.' Fiona called back.

He smiled. 'Maggie seems like a pup when she's with Polly.'

'Tell me about your new job,' she said abruptly. 'When do you start?'

'Next week. I've got a period of induction and training.'

'Then you'll be sent abroad?'

'Yes.'

'Do you know where?'

'Not yet.'

She chewed on her lower lip and stared moodily into the distance.

He took her hand. 'I have to take this opportunity, Fi. I can't stay in my parents' home indefinitely with nothing to do.'

'I suppose not,' she muttered, 'but why can't they give you a job you can do here, in this country?'

He smiled. 'The whole point of *Immediate Response* is to send assistance to areas where there's been a disaster or catastrophe.'

'Isn't the invasion a catastrophe? Don't people need assistance here, in this country? Anyway, what about the court case? You said you were going to be called as a witness for the prosecution? Don't you have to be here for that?'

He frowned. 'I'm not sure. I had a letter saying I have to wait for a document called a Witness Citation but it hasn't arrived yet. Everything's been held up for obvious reasons and it could be months before the case gets to court. There are legal complications because of the charges the Inheritors are facing in the States.'

'What will happen if you're away when the trial starts?'

'I don't know. I'll check the bumpf when I get home.'

'And what about *us*, Ric?' she asked in a low voice.

He squirmed uncomfortably and wiped his perspiring forehead.

'I mean, if you go away, will that be the end of us?'

He put his arm round her. 'Of course not. I won't be away for long. My initial posting may only be for three or four months, six at the most. I'll be back before you know it. And I'll keep in touch while I'm away.'

'You won't forget about me?'

'How could I? It's more likely to be the other way round. You never know, you might meet a good-looking doctor and—'

'Don't joke, Ric.' Her eyes glistened with tears.

He bent towards her and kissed her on the mouth.

'Yuck! *Gross!*'

They pulled abruptly apart to find Polly in front of them. She sniggered. 'Are you two in lerv?'

Fiona flushed pink. 'Don't be silly, Poll. Why don't you have a go on the swings?'

'Swings are boring. Anyway, it's too hot.' The girl mooched off and stood a few yards away, watching them sulkily. Maggie lay down beside her, her tongue lolling out of the side of her mouth.

Fiona rose to her feet. 'We'd better go. I told Mum we'd be back for tea.'

Richard also stood up. 'I've still got a few weeks left, Fi. Let's try and see as much as possible of each other before I'm sent away. Polly,' he called to the girl, 'you can take Maggie home with you if you want.'

Polly's face split into a wide grin. 'Wicked!'

* * *

Richard was thoughtful as he made his way home. He definitely didn't want the relationship with Fiona to end, but it was too soon to plan a future with her. Anything might happen during the time he was away.

As he opened the front door he could hear the television and sighed. After so long having the house to himself, he was finding cohabitation with his parents increasingly difficult. Being slightly deaf, his father always raised the volume of the TV to a level he found intolerably high. His mother was so afraid of the Bobblers that she wouldn't venture outside the house and expended her energies in a perpetual round of dusting, cleaning and tidying.

He put his head round the living room door. 'You'll be pleased to hear Maggie's not coming back.'

Instead of the delighted reaction he had expected, his parents turned to him with grim expressions.

His father lowered the volume on the remote. 'Marj Phelps called round this afternoon, Ricky.'

Richard braced himself for a litany of complaints. 'They're back then?'

'Obviously. She told us you've been causing mayhem in the Close.'

'Disturbing the peace is how she described it,' interjected his mother. 'She said that wretched dog kept barking and fouling the pavement, and you've been playing loud music, and the police have been coming to the house every five minutes.'

'That's rubbish. They only came a couple of times.'

His father frowned. 'Why was that?'

'I've already told you why. The first time it was to ask about the UFO I saw. The second time was when they were investigating the nun's abduction. They wanted to know why I'd spoken to her on the phone a few days before.'

His father's expression remained severe. 'Marj said there have also been journalists hanging round looking for you. What was all that about?'

'That was after Sister Francis and I escaped from the island. The press got hold of the story. It wasn't my fault.'

'And another thing,' his mother said accusingly, her face a picture of disapproval, 'Marj said you've had *women* here ... overnight!'

This was too much. 'Not *women*,' Richard retorted, '*One* woman. My girlfriend.'

'Girlfriend?' His mother couldn't have sounded more outraged if he had admitted sleeping with an alien. 'Are you back with Emma, then?'

'No, it was Fiona.'

'Who's Fiona.'

'I just told you. My girlfriend.'

'And she's been staying *here* overnight?'

'Why shouldn't she? She's my girlfriend, for God's sake, and in case you've forgotten, I'm twenty eight. Anyone would think I'd turned the house into a brothel.'

'Don't exaggerate, Ricky,' snapped his mother. 'We need to know what's been going on in the house while we were away.'

'Nothing's been "going on". Can't I have a girlfriend to stay occasionally?'

His mother ignored the question. 'Marj says it's been one thing after the other. She says you've lowered the tone of the neighbourhood.'

Richard felt himself go hot with annoyance. 'She didn't seem to mind me lowering the tone when she invited me into her house when Stan was away.'

His mother looked shocked. 'What are you implying?'

'She was so freaked out by the spacecraft, she wanted someone to hold her hand. So who did she ask? *Moi!* The local neighbourhood yob!'

'Well Marj said--'

'I don't care what Marj said,' he exploded. 'She's got a very vivid imagination. When I came home in a police car after I escaped from the island, she told Mrs. Perkins I'd been in prison for watching pornography.'

'Prison?' His mother exclaimed, outraged. 'Why did she think that?'

'Because she's a miserable old bat!'

His father bristled. 'That's enough of that language, Ricky. Mrs. Phelps may have been over-reacting but we like to get on with our neighbours. We've known them for a long time and we have to go on living here.'

'Well I'm bloody glad I don't.' Richard shut the door with a bang and retreated angrily upstairs.

After he had calmed down, he remembered the documents on witness guidance that he had received from the Scottish legal authorities. After ransacking his room he found them mixed up with discarded pages of his thesis. He scanned them rapidly until he came to the relevant details: *You will receive a witness citation with the date and time of the trial. If you fail to appear in court, a warrant may be taken out for your arrest. If you know beforehand that you cannot appear on the trial date, please let the Procurator Fiscal's Office know as soon as possible. They will decide if you can be excused from giving evidence. It is not possible to predict beforehand which trials will proceed and which witnesses will be required to give evidence.*

This left the situation unresolved. As he hadn't yet received the witness citation, all he could do was inform the Procurator Fiscal's Office as soon as he knew when and where he was going to be sent by

Immediate Response.

'Ricky!' His father suddenly called up the stairs. 'Come and listen to this. It's about the aliens.'

He returned to the sitting room in time to catch Bartholomew Wainwright being interviewed on the results of his attempts to interpret the aliens' system of communication.

The linguist was describing how he and his assistants had been studying groups of Bobblers whenever an opportunity presented itself, making notes, videoing them and recording the strange medley of sounds they made before feeding the results through computer programmes.

'I believe we have made some important headway,' Wainwright announced, looking, Richard thought, rather like a large bird with his nodding head, hooked nose and small round glasses. 'I have analysed the frequency and pitch of the noises the aliens make and, by relating them to the location they were in at the time, and what was happening around them, it has been possible to make an informed guess at what some of them may signify. To give you some examples, I have isolated some of the most common sounds they make. Listen to this.'

He pressed the start-button on a digital recorder and it emitted a strange, high-pitched squeak.

He stopped the machine. 'The aliens make this noise whenever they have positioned themselves above a group of people. I have concluded that this sound refers to us - human beings. This, on the other hand ...'

He again pressed the start-button and a series of loud clicking sounds could be heard. 'This possibly refers to animals as we only heard them utter this sound when they were observing dogs, sheep and cows.'

'Good lord!' murmured Richard's father.

Wainwright pushed back a wayward strand of grey hair before continuing.

'We believe the aliens are capable of expressing different emotions because they make this sound ...' a shrill whistling noise came from the machine '... whenever somebody tries to interact directly with them or threatens them, for example, by shouting or firing missiles at them. It appears to be an immediate reaction to what is happening. It could represent a warning. On the other hand, it could express surprise, anger, or even, and I can't rule this out, amusement.'

Richard remembered that the Bobblers had made this noise when

Sister Francis had recited Latin at them and, earlier, when the youths outside the tube station had hurled litter at them.

'Now this ...' Wainwright fiddled again with his recording machine which now emitted a series of staccato noises that sounded like hens cackling. 'This is the sound they use most. It generally lasts longer than the others and I suspect it represents an exchange or interaction between the aliens when something has happened that they consider significant or are particularly interested in. The fact that these sounds often alternate with the short squeaks you heard earlier, suggests they could be commenting on *us* - on human beings, as in this extract from one of our video recordings ...'

The picture on the screen changed briefly to show blurred footage of a group of Bobblers cackling above a circle of armed soldiers.

Richard's mother shuddered. 'Ghastly creatures!'

The linguist reappeared on the screen and continued in similar vein for several minutes before switching off the recorder and turning to the interviewer who had been listening intently. 'We are still at a very early stage of analysis and haven't yet advanced beyond phonology or sound systems. We now need to discover the language's structure - its morphology and syntax. But from what we have already deduced, I would say this is a sophisticated communication system which may have dimensions we can't even guess at. We can't, for example, rule out the possibility that they have an additional and more sophisticated means of communication such as light signals or thought transference.'

'Has your research given you any clues about the aliens' intentions?' the interviewer asked, 'and why they have come here?'

Wainwright shook his head. 'No. To decipher a language no human being has ever heard, and on which there are no known linguistic influences, is a very difficult task. When we have discovered more of their vocabulary, it may be possible to ask them questions by reproducing the sounds we have isolated. What we have discovered so far tells us only that the aliens can express reactions and possibly emotions. It is also clear that they have a keen interest in us human beings. So far as I can tell, this interest does not appear to have a malevolent purpose. None of the verbal reactions we have recorded seem to have been violent, even when the creatures themselves have been threatened with violence. What I find particularly intriguing is their apparent fascination with our emergency services.'

'What about their interest in animals?' the interviewer asked.

Wainwright looked thoughtful. 'Their interest in animals could merely imply a fascination for species that must be as alien to them as they are to us. But of course, this is only supposition. My analysis is at a very early stage. The research is ongoing and I hope in due course to compare notes with linguists in other countries who have also been trying to interpret the aliens' language.'

After the interview ended, Richard's father expelled a deep breath. 'Amazing! Hard to believe that creatures like that have a sophisticated language system.'

'It's not hard at all,' Richard declared. 'If they have the intelligence and technical skills necessary to find their way across the cosmos, it's hardly surprising that they have advanced communication skills.' But he couldn't help feeling disappointed that the linguist hadn't managed to discover more about the aliens and the reason for their unwanted arrival on Earth.

Chapter 42

He awoke with a start to find his room flooded with bright light. Glancing at his watch he saw it was just after one a.m. He jumped out of bed and hastened to the window. Leaning out, he gasped on seeing two huge and dazzling objects suspended in the sky to the west. By now he was familiar with their shape. He gazed at them in wonderment. What was happening? The spaceships had disappeared immediately after dropping their cargoes of Bobblers. Why had they now returned? And why hadn't the sirens sounded?

After he had watched them for a few seconds, the machines started revolving faster and faster until they resembled two brilliant spinning orbs. Then they shot upwards at an acute angle and disappeared. The sky darkened again and there was nothing to see except faint stars.

Richard waited for a few moments then closed the window and stumbled back to bed.

He got up late in the morning and was shaving in the bathroom, when he heard his father calling excitedly from the foot of the stairs.

'Eileen! Ricky!'

Richard leaned over the banister. 'What's the matter, Dad?'

'They've gone!'

'Who's gone?'

'The aliens, Bobblers or whatever you call them,' his father shouted impatiently.

'Gone? Where?'

'How should I know? I just heard that they've disappeared; vamoosed.'

'Are you sure?'

'Seems they took off overnight. I'll see if I can find out any more details.' His father hastened back to the living room.

Richard's mother came out of her bedroom carrying a pile of laundry. 'What's going on? What did your father want?'

'He said the Bobblers have gone, disappeared.'

'Gone?' She dropped the sheets on the floor. 'I don't believe it.'

'Let's go and find out.' Richard grabbed a towel from the bathroom and wiped the shaving foam from his face before following his mother down to the living room.

His father looked up excitedly as they entered. 'They've disappeared from other countries as well. Maybe they've gone for good!'

'Thank God!' Richard's mother sank on to the sofa, her face bright with relief. 'What wonderful news. Now we can lead a normal life again.'

Richard couldn't quite believe what he had heard. 'Did anyone actually see them go?'

His father shook his head. 'All I know is that none of them have been seen anywhere this morning. They must have gone during the night.'

'Oh!' Richard suddenly remembered. 'I saw a couple of the spaceships last night.'

His father stared at him. 'You saw some?'

'Yes. I woke up and the room was incredibly bright. I looked out of the window and saw them towards the west. They were spinning incredibly fast then they shot away. It happened in a few seconds. But the siren didn't go this time. I wonder why.'

His father looked thoughtful. 'I heard that the Government has decided not to use the sirens again because they create so much panic. You'd better call the police, Ricky, and tell them what you saw.'

Richard shook his head. 'I don't think there's any point now that they've gone.'

'Ricky's right, dear,' said his mother. 'And we don't want the police coming to the Close again, do we? It only creates gossip. Let's just be thankful that those frightful creatures have left.'

'Just a minute.' Richard's father turned up the volume of the TV. 'What's she saying?'

The three of them fell silent.

'Oh,' he exclaimed, his voice heavy with disappointment. 'They haven't disappeared completely, they've only moved on. Good God! Apparently they've relocated to disaster areas.'

Richard was stunned. 'Disaster areas? Which disaster areas?'

His father held up a hand. 'Listen.'

'It is being reported,' announced the glamorous newsreader, her eyes fixed on the autocue, 'that the aliens have moved into areas where recent catastrophes have occurred. Relief agencies have witnessed them in Pakistan, China, Chile and Africa. These pictures were taken a few hours ago in an earthquake zone in Pakistan.'

Amateur video footage showed an overcrowded, tented refugee camp. Several groups of Bobblers could be seen hovering above a food distribution point and a medical centre, both surrounded by dense, jostling throngs. People were pointing at the aliens in terror, and shoving and knocking each other over in a desperate scramble to get away from them.

Richard's father gasped. 'What the blazes are they doing there?'

'I don't know and I don't care,' declared Richard's mother, 'as long as they're not *here.*'

Richard was speechless. Once again the aliens had wrong-footed the world.

The newsreader announced that groups of Bobblers had also gathered near communities eking out a wretched living in a drought-stricken area of East Africa. A video sent by a relief worker showed a group of them floating above a dust-blown enclosure in a small village. They were beaming their shafts of light on to a circle of emaciated women sitting on the ground in the shade of their huts, holding skeletal babies. The women were watching the strange visitors fearfully but appeared too listless and exhausted to flee.

Richard had witnessed hunger in Kashmir and Bangladesh, but this looked even worse. What were the Bobblers doing in such a place? Why had they left the wealthiest nations on Earth and travelled to some of the poorest? What had motivated them to seek out the extremes of human wretchedness?

A series of government officials and foreign representatives appeared on the screen, expressing their bafflement at the latest turn of events and speculating on its significance.

After watching for a while, Richard rose to his feet.

'What about your new job, Ricky?' His mother asked as he was leaving the room. 'What if they want to send you to one of those places those creatures have gone to? Surely you won't go.'

'I'll go wherever I'm asked to go, Mum. But you needn't worry. I don't think the Bobblers will have any interest in me.'

Puzzled by the dramatic new development, he went to his room and switched on his laptop. The internet was humming with comments and speculation about the aliens' abrupt change of location. News of it had apparently first arrived via *Twitter* and when he entered the site, he found cryptic and facetious tweets on the subject appearing by the second. Among the Tweeters, he was intrigued to discover a group of dedicated "Bobbler Watchers". Defying the injunction on approaching the aliens, they had been following them for some time and exchanging information on their habits and whereabouts. Some of them had, like himself, witnessed spaceships during the night. According to one tweet, *I saw two of them disappear into thin air at speed of light.* (Apt clichés, Richard thought).

His mobile rang.

'Isn't it wonderful news?' Fiona cried jubilantly.

'They haven't gone for good, Fi. They've only moved on.'

'I know, but at least they're not here.'

'Can I see you this evening?' he asked hopefully.

'Yes, I know Mum and Dad will be at home.'

They arranged to go to a local wine bar.

'When are we going to meet her?' asked his mother when he told her. Although she had been pumping him for information about his mysterious girlfriend, he had divulged only that she was someone he had known at school. He wasn't going to mention the existence of an eleven-year-old daughter. Not just yet.

'One of these days,' he answered evasively.

* * *

'They're good people, my parents. I just can't live with them,' he told Fiona as they sat opposite each other sipping cold white wine. A ceiling fan whirred overhead. A television in the corner of the bar showed a group of talking heads having an earnest discussion about the departed aliens. Every now and then the conversation was interrupted by a scene showing the Bobblers in one of the disaster-struck areas they were now frequenting.

'Mum has very fixed ideas about some things,' he continued, 'like extra-marital sex and drinking. She went ape when she found empty lager cans in the kitchen. There were only about a dozen of them and they'd been there for ages. You'd have thought I was a closet alcoholic from the way she reacted.'

Fiona blinked at him. 'Does she know about me?'

'Yes. Ma Phelps told her I'd been having women in overnight while they were away. Shock, horror!'

'*Women?*' she exclaimed.

'Don't worry, I put her right on that score. But it's a tricky subject, Fi. Mum couldn't accept me "living in sin" with Emma, even though we were together for nearly three years.'

She gave a twisted smile. 'So the fact that you're seeing a divorced woman with a kid hasn't gone down a bundle.'

He hesitated. 'I ... haven't actually mentioned those details yet. I need to broach the subject gently.' He leaned across the table and stroked her cheek. 'There's only so much information my parents can absorb at one time. They're still reeling from finding out about the Inheritors, Sister Francis and my stay on the island. And now Ma Phelps has been round with a bunch of complaints about Maggie and the police coming to the house. I almost wish the Bobblers hadn't decamped. At least they were keeping Mum preoccupied.'

'Surely you don't mean that.'

'No, not really. But I wish she'd get off my back.' He stared moodily into his wine glass. 'I can't do a thing right at the moment. She practically follows me around with a dustpan and brush.'

Fiona smiled sympathetically. 'Well you won't have to live with your parents much longer, will you, now that you're being sent overseas?'

'I'll still need a base in this country when I get back, until I can afford a place of my own. How do you get on with your parents?'

'They're cool. They were upset when I got pregnant and they disapproved of the divorce, but they've been terrific ever since. They never really liked Paul, and they're wonderful with Polly.'

'How much do they know about me?'

She grinned. 'Only that you're single, you've just finished your doctorate and we knew each other at school. I haven't mentioned the Inheritors or kidnapped nuns or anything like that. But I'm afraid you're not flavour of the month at the moment. They weren't exactly thrilled when we came back with Maggie again.'

'Well she is an acquired taste.' Richard gazed at her hungrily. She was wearing tight-fitting jeans and a white t-shirt that revealed her boyish figure. 'You know it's going to be difficult for us to get together now that Mum and Dad are back.'

She gave him a quizzical look. 'Sleep together, you mean?'

He grinned. 'Yes.'

'I know, and we can't at home either, not with Mum, Dad and Polly there.'

She picked up her glass and started tracing circles with her finger on the wet imprint it had left on the table. When she spoke, her expression was troubled. 'Ric, what if you're sent to one of those disaster areas where the Bobblers are now?'

'It won't matter. I don't feel threatened by them.' This was true, Richard realised. He felt more intrigued than scared by the aliens.

He glanced at the groups sitting at the tables nearest to them. It seemed to him that the general mood had lightened since the news of the Bobblers' departure had exploded that morning. Despite gradually adjusting to the aliens' presence, most people had understandably remained fearful about their intentions. Although the invaders hadn't left the planet altogether, he assumed their relocation elsewhere had caused some of that fear to subside.

Chapter 43

At the beginning of his induction week at *Immediate Response*, Richard was informed that he was going to be sent to Pakistan where catastrophic monsoon rains had left about a fifth of the country's land mass underwater. The aliens' presence in this and other disaster zones hadn't been allowed to disrupt the agency's work. Since they hadn't committed any hostile acts, they were viewed as an extra, albeit unwelcome, dimension to the range of problems relief workers had to deal with.

After such a long period stuck in the house, Richard found learning about the agency's work stimulating. He enjoyed the training and found the information he was given absorbing. He continued to see Fiona whenever they were both free in the evenings, but things were no longer the same between them. She had become noticeably cooler towards him and quickly extricated herself from his embrace when he kissed her. He interpreted this as her way of protecting herself against his eventual departure.

His relationship with his parents, on the other hand, had improved now that he was out on weekdays. This situation continued, until, succumbing to his mother's pressure, he invited Fiona for tea on a Sunday afternoon. He didn't mention Polly, deciding that it would be better for his mother to discover her existence for herself.

The visit got off to a bad start. When Richard opened the door, he was disconcerted to see that Fiona was accompanied by Maggie as well as Polly. Overjoyed at being back in her former home, the dog jerked away from Polly and, with her lead flying behind her, galloped into the house, nearly tripping up Richard's mother as she emerged from the kitchen carrying the tea tray which she promptly dropped.

'What's that dog doing here again?' she snapped.

'I'm really sorry,' stuttered Fiona, 'Mum and Dad are out and I couldn't leave her at home.' She helped his mother pick up the cups, one of which had broken.

'Mum, this is Fiona, Fiona, my mother,' Richard muttered.

The two women shook hands.

His mother stared at Polly 'And this is?'

'Polly, my daughter.'

Richard's mother's eyebrows rose. 'Your *daughter*? You must have been very young when you--'

'Yes, I was,' said Fiona cheerfully, 'sixteen.'

His mother stared at her in shocked silence.

'And I'm divorced from her father,' Fiona added, anticipating the unspoken question.

Angry shouts came from the living room. 'What the...? Get off!'

Rushing into the room, Richard pulled Maggie off his father who was sitting in his usual chair in front of the TV. He hauled her by her lead through the patio doors and shut her in the back garden.

Fifteen minutes later, they were all sitting stiffly on the patio, drinking tea and eating Victoria Sponge cake.

Richard's mother kept a sharp eye on Maggie who was snuffling round the hedge, trying to pick up Pugwash's scent. Apart from asking a few conventional questions about Fiona's parents and Polly's school, she maintained a tight-lipped silence.

His father seemed more at ease and engaged Fiona in conversation about the hospital and how it had coped with the two emergencies, the invasion and the heat wave.

Polly was on her best behaviour, sitting quietly eating her cake and speaking only when spoken to.

It wasn't long before Richard began to find his mother's undisguised hostility towards Fiona and her daughter, intolerable.

'Can we take Maggie for a walk, Mum?' Polly burst out eventually, looking imploringly at Fiona.

'Great idea,' Richard exclaimed with exaggerated enthusiasm.

His parents didn't attempt to detain them and they gratefully took their leave.

As they walked along the Close, they passed Marjorie Phelps sweeping her front path, her face dripping with perspiration.

In his relief at escaping from his mother's disapproving presence, Richard greeted her with unaccustomed heartiness. 'Afternoon, Mrs. Phelps. Feeling the heat?'

She gave him a withering glance.

'Who's that fat lady?' asked Polly a little too loudly when they arrived at the corner.

'Shh, Poll,' Fiona remonstrated.

Polly giggled and trotted ahead with Maggie.

'Your mother didn't like me, did she?' Fiona commented when she was out of earshot.

Richard squeezed her arm. 'It takes her a while to get to know people. But *I* like you and that's what matters. And I think Dad really liked you too.'

'She looked shocked when she found out Poll's my daughter.'

'She'll get used to the idea. You know what some mothers are like with their sons; over-protective.'

Fiona grinned. 'Yes. Paul's mother virtually accused me of trapping him into marriage by getting pregnant, as if he had nothing to do with it!'

'I don't think Mum's as bad as that. She's just a bit old-fashioned. Dad's OK though. They're both OK really, when you get to know them.'

She looked at him quizzically. 'Will I get the chance?'

'You mean you want to repeat the experience?'

'Not just yet,' she admitted.

They spent half an hour in the park behind the church, then Fiona took Polly and Maggie home.

Richard's mother pounced as soon as he entered the house. 'You didn't tell us she had a daughter!'

'No, why should I have done?'

'Because we're your parents! Why can't you find a girlfriend who's … unencumbered?'

'I choose the friends *I* want, Mum. Not the ones you'll approve of.'

'Well she must have been really flighty if she had a child at sixteen.'

'Fiona's not "flighty", he retorted angrily. 'She's one of the best people I know. And Polly's a great kid.'

'That may be so, but I don't want you to jeopardise your future, Ricky.'

Richard could barely contain his exasperation. 'How could I jeopardise my future? Fiona and I are not getting married or anything, so why are you so bothered?'

'Because I worry about you--'

'Well don't. There's no need.'

'I think she's a very nice young woman,' said his father who until now had kept out of the conversation. 'Attractive too. And the little girl seems very well behaved.'

His mother sniffed and after a short silence, changed the subject. 'Marj Phelps called round just after you went out. She thinks a prowler's been hanging around the Close.'

Richard laughed. 'Are you sure she didn't think it was me?'

'It's not a laughing matter. Ricky. It could be a burglar.'

'In that case, shall I ask Fiona if we can have Maggie back?'

'No!' his parents exclaimed in unison.

* * *

The following evening he stayed late at the office in order to liaise with a project worker who had returned from Pakistan. The man gave him a folder of information and showed him some recent videos he had made. One of them showed small boys hurling stones at a group of aliens hovering above a makeshift camp for victims of the flood in Sukkur. Inevitably the missiles bounced off the invisible barrier surrounding the Bobblers. This didn't deter the boys who continued throwing stones until they were dragged away by concerned adults.

'They haven't attacked anyone,' grumbled the project worker. 'But they're upsetting people who have enough to put up with. Nobody has a clue what they're doing there.'

'Nobody knows what they're doing anywhere,' Richard observed.

After watching the videos, he joined the project worker for a meal at a nearby pub.

It was after ten by the time he returned home, and as he turned into the Close he thought he saw someone standing between the parked cars. He peered into the darkness but could only make out Mrs. Brennan's two cats moving stealthily along the kerb.

He had just reached the gate at the bottom of the front path, when a hand landed heavily on his shoulder.

'Bloody hell!' He jumped with fright, dropping his folder.

'I've been waiting for you, traitor!' hissed a voice.

Spinning round, Richard froze. The tall figure looming behind him, his face illuminated by the light of the nearby street lamp, was instantly recognisable despite the differences in his appearance: Abraham Rosenberg! Without his long hair, patriarchal beard and ceremonial robes, the "Poet, Philosopher and Healer" resembled an ordinary middle-aged man, albeit one who was visibly deranged. His face was contorted in fury, his eyes blazed and his grasp on Richard's shoulder tightened.

'You have thwarted God's will,' he snarled, 'and His wrath will be visited upon you.' He pushed Richard roughly back against the brick gatepost. 'Saul and Ezra were right. They suspected you were an unbeliever.'

Frantic thoughts raced through Richard's mind as he strove to shake off his assailant. Rosenberg was over a head taller than him and judging by the strength of his grip, a sight more powerful. Pinioned against the gatepost, he couldn't reach into his pocket to get his mobile.

Rosenberg thrust his savage face near to Richard's. 'You and the nun have destroyed our commune.'

'What?' Richard's fear gave way to anger. 'We didn't destroy anything. You were the one who was going to destroy the commune by ordering everyone to commit suicide.'

'That would have been resurrection, not destruction. Their souls would have been transported to the New Kingdom.'

'By the aliens? You're having a laugh!' There was no doubt about it: the man was seriously mad.

Rosenberg raised his fist menacingly. 'The aliens are God's emissaries, the vanguard of the Second Coming.'

'That's absolute rubbish.' Richard struggled violently to free himself. 'And you won't achieve anything by attacking me. The police are looking for you. You're on an Interpol wanted list.'

Rosenberg grinned wolfishly, revealing teeth so improbably even that, given half a chance, Richard would have taken great pleasure in knocking them out. 'Maybe you have forgotten, Traitor Richard, I am under God's protection.'

Richard thought it must be *he* who was under God's protection, for a light suddenly came on in the house next door and he heard a door open. Twisting his head sideways, he glimpsed Reg Perkins descending his front path with Pugwash on a lead. The dog growled as they approached.

'Is that you, Ricky?' called Reg. 'What's going on?'

'Yes, it's me, Reg,' Richard shouted then gasped and doubled up in pain as Rosenberg punched him viciously in the stomach. 'I haven't finished with you yet!' he hissed, before hurrying away.

A few moments later Richard heard a car door slam, an engine start and the sound of a vehicle accelerating away.

'Blimey!' Reg arrived at his side with Pugwash straining on his lead. 'What's going on? Are you OK, Ricky? Who was that?'

Coughing and spluttering, Richard attempted to straighten up. His eyes were streaming and it was a moment before he could summon enough breath to speak. 'Some crazy ... guy...I think he was drunk.' He found it difficult to keep his voice from shaking and his hands trembled as he adjusted his shirt.

'Are you hurt?' Reg asked with concern.

'No,' Richard panted, 'just winded.'

'Marj told us someone's been hanging around the Close. An intruder. Did he try to mug you?'

'He punched me.' Richard was still struggling to get his breath. 'He ran off when he heard you coming.'

'Well it's a good job I came out when I did. We can't have muggers round here. I'd call the police if I were you.'

Richard tried to steady his breathing. 'Too late. He had a car. He'll be well away by now. Please don't mention this to Mum and Dad, Mr. Perkins. They'll only worry.'

'If you say so, Ricky.' Reg regarded him curiously. 'Are you sure you're OK? You look pretty shaken up.'

'I'm fine, really ... Just need to get my breath back.'

'Well I'll keep an eye open. If he comes back, Pugwash will see him off. Marj is right, we ought to start a Neighbourhood Watch. You take care now, Ricky.'

After giving him another anxious glance, Reg strode off with his dog.

Richard stooped and painfully retrieved the folder he had dropped. Slowly and shakily he ascended the path, opened the front door and locked it behind him.

'Is that you, Ricky?' his mother called from the living room.

'Yes, Mum,' he replied without putting his head round the door. 'Going to bed. Early start tomorrow. Good night.' He hurried upstairs before they could answer.

In the safety of his room, he sank trembling on to the bed. The adrenalin was still coursing through his body, his heart was racing and his stomach hurt. What would have happened if Reg Perkins hadn't appeared? He imagined he would have been beaten to a pulp. He considered calling the police but hesitated. If they came to the house, it would mean telling his parents what had happened. His mother would become hysterical if she knew he had been attacked, and the arrival of yet another police car in the Close would undoubtedly provoke the unwelcome attention of Marjorie Phelps.

Another thought struck him. If Abraham R was bent on vengeance he might go after Sister Francis as well. She must be warned. But if he rang the convent and told Mother Ignatius what had happened, she was bound to contact the police, and then of course they would want to come round and talk to *him*. It was too late anyway to ring the convent. After fretting endlessly over the best course of action, he texted Fiona: *Rosenberg came here looking for me.*

She called him almost immediately and he described what had happened, keeping his voice low in case his parents came upstairs.

She sounded shocked. 'That's terrible, Ric. How did he find you? Are you hurt?'

'Not really, just winded.'

'You sound traumatised.'

'I am. The guy was violent and he might try to get at Sister Francis next.'

'You've got to call the police.'

'I intend to, but I don't want them coming round tonight. Mum would have a fit. Anyway he had a car so he's probably a long way away by now.'

'You can't risk him going after Sister Francis again,' Fiona declared. 'Why don't you call that police sergeant, the one I contacted when you disappeared?'

'He may not be on duty this late.'

'Well promise me you'll contact him first thing tomorrow.'

Richard agreed. He went to bed after speaking to Fiona, but lay nervously awake for much of the night. Early the next morning he found DS Johnson's card and rang the number written on it. Somewhat to his surprise, his call was answered immediately.

The officer sounded weary. 'What is it now, Mr. Jarman?'

Richard described what had happened.

'You'd better come down to the station,' DS Johnson said curtly. 'As soon as possible. I've got a busy day.'

After ringing *Immediate Response* to say he would be late, Richard arrived at the police station a little after nine. Was it his imagination or was the temperature slightly cooler?

DS Johnson's face appeared even more lined and mournful than he remembered.

'I seem to be seeing rather a lot of you these days, Mr. Jarman,' he observed by way of greeting. Taking a folder from a filing cabinet, he ushered Richard into the same small and windowless room he had been interviewed in before.

Richard waited while the officer extracted some papers from the folder and scanned them.

Eventually Johnson looked up. 'Yes, there's still an international search warrant out for Rosenberg. Very nasty piece of work by all accounts. You say he was waiting for you when you got home last night?'

'Yes.'

'You're sure it was him?'

'Absolutely no doubt.'

'So why didn't you get in touch with us straight away?'

Richard felt himself flush. 'I was pretty shaken up, and I didn't want my mother to hear about it. She's been in a terrible state since she got home. I didn't want to worry her.'

Johnson frowned. 'Well you've left it rather late to notify us. You say he had a car?'

'Yes I heard him leave in one.'

'What kind of car?'

'I don't know, I didn't see it. He'd punched me in the stomach and left me winded.'

The officer regarded him moodily. 'It's an extradition matter, but we could get him on a charge of criminal assault, though he doesn't seem to have done you any real harm.'

'Not this time, but he threatened to come back. There's no telling what he might do to me another time.'

DS Johnson looked thoughtful. 'After what happened before, I'm more concerned about the nun. I'll alert the convent and make sure it's put it under surveillance.'

Richard was relieved on Sister Francis's account but annoyed on his own. 'What about me? Don't I need protection too?'

The officer sighed. 'It's a question of manpower, Mr. Jarman. We already have our hands full. Are you aware how much crime has risen in this area since the invasion - theft, empty properties looted?'

'I know, but Rosenberg's really dangerous. Paddy McAllister was so badly beaten up by the Inheritors, he never recovered.'

'Well...' DS Johnson's frown reduced his brow to a mesh of deep lines and furrows. 'I'll see what I can do, but I can't promise anything. In the meantime, Mr. Jarman, it might be better if you didn't go out after dark.'

Chapter 44

Richard felt extremely nervous after he left the police station. He found himself looking anxiously over his shoulder, half expecting Rosenberg to jump out at him from every doorway. Waiting for the tube, he peered worriedly up the platform and experienced a frisson of panic whenever he spotted a tall male figure among the waiting passengers. Once inside the stifling carriage, he looked cautiously around, suspecting that every man hidden behind a newspaper could be his assailant. He realised that he feared the "Poet, Philosopher and Healer" and his followers far more than he had ever feared the Bobblers. Maybe Sister Francis was right: the Devil was more likely to be found among human beings than among the aliens. He shivered as he remembered Rosenberg's parting words: *I haven't finished with you yet...*

Even within the safety of the workplace, he remained in a state of heightened anxiety, finding it hard to concentrate on the volume of information directed at him.

As soon as he had a free moment, he rang the convent hoping to speak to Sister Francis. However, Mother Ignatius curtly informed him that the little nun was unavailable and could only receive outside calls "in exceptional circumstances". He asked her to tell Sister Francis that he had rung.

'Come and have a look at this!' The invitation came from a noisy group of fellow workers who had collected around a computer screen in the open-plan office. One of them had clicked on a scene showing a large group of aliens hovering over a cluster of circular, thorn-fenced *bomas* of the kind erected by nomadic African tribes. Inside the enclosures, colourfully dressed women were jumping up and down in front of low mud huts, gesticulating at the newcomers and shrieking with fear. Slender young men, wearing red-checked blankets and with huge earrings dangling from their elongated ear-lobes, were brandishing spears at the aliens and shouting what Richard imagined were warlike threats. Outside the enclosures, small naked boys waving sticks were rapidly herding groups of pale, bony cattle away from the unwelcome visitors.

'Bloody hell,' breathed one of Richard's co-workers. 'What the fuck are those weirdos doing there?'

Before Richard could comment, he heard his mobile ring and returned to his desk to answer it.

'Did you contact that inspector?' asked Fiona.

'Yep. He said he'd ask for the convent to be put under surveillance.'

'That's good. Have you spoken to Sister Francis?'

'I tried to but couldn't get past the Mother Fuhrer. She said Sister Francis can't receive any outside calls.'

'Are the police sending someone to protect *you*?'

'No. Apparently they don't have enough manpower to put me under surveillance.'

He heard her suck in her breath. 'That's rotten. Do you want to have Maggie back? She's a good guard dog.'

'Thanks for the offer, but my parents won't have her in the house.'

'Have you told them what happened last night?'

'Not yet. I couldn't stand the aggro.'

'Well do take care, Ric. That maniac may come back.'

They arranged to meet in the little park after work.

When Richard arrived, he found the area unusually full of people, a further indication of the more relaxed mood that had taken hold since the aliens had travelled to other parts of the globe. And the temperature was noticeably cooler; more comfortable than it had been for weeks.

It took him only a few seconds to spot Fiona. She was sitting on a bench reading a newspaper. Polly was over by the swings, throwing a tennis ball for Maggie.

'Listen to this,' Fiona said as he sat down beside her. She read from the paper: *Satellite tracking devices show large groups of aliens arriving in areas of recent desertification.* What do you make of it, Ric?'

'Not much,' he replied, scuffing the dusty earth with his foot. He was more preoccupied with the potential return of Abraham Rosenberg than with the current whereabouts of the aliens. He had another three weeks of training before going to Pakistan; ample time for the man to come looking for him again, perhaps with some of his vicious followers.

'Ric?'

He was jolted back into the present.

Fiona was looking at him enquiringly, her eyes a deep green in the early evening sunlight. 'I have an idea.'

'Yes? What?' he asked distractedly.

She put a hand on his arm. 'Don't go off the deep end.'

He stared at her, surprised. 'Why would I do that?'

'Because you're not going to like what I'm going to suggest.'

He was intrigued. 'Aren't I?'

'Nope, but I think it's the only way.'

'The only way to do what?'

She smiled at him. 'To find out what the aliens are up to.'

How can we possibly do that?'

'Promise you won't be angry.'

'OK, I won't be angry. What's your idea?'

She took a deep breath. 'I think we should go and see Morgana Delph!'

He laughed incredulously. 'Morgana Delph! You are joking?'

'No, I'm not joking. She reproduced those weird sounds the Bobblers make, didn't she? That means she can get through to them. We could ask her if she could channel one of the aliens, ask it questions about where they come from and what they want.'

'Absolutely not!' he exclaimed, horrified. 'I never want to see that old witch again. She gives me the creeps.'

'She's not an old witch, Ric. She's a *bona fide* medium. And you promised you wouldn't fly off the handle.'

'You know I hate that kind of thing, Fi. It's spooky.'

'Mum, can we go and get an ice-cream?' Polly arrived in front of them with Maggie. The dog dropped the saliva-sodden ball hopefully at Richard's feet and jumped back, poised in readiness for him to throw it.

'Not now, Doll, it's too near suppertime.'

'Oh, knickers!' The girl picked up the ball and stumped grumpily away, followed by Maggie.

Fiona turned back to Richard. 'Well? Do you have any better ideas?'

'No, why should I? It's not our responsibility to find out what the Bobblers are up to. Plenty of other people are trying to do that.'

'Well none of them have succeeded yet, have they?'

'That's true, but Bartholomew Wainwright's still working on their language. He could still make a breakthrough.'

She laughed scornfully. 'He hasn't made much progress either, apart from discovering that the aliens are interested in human beings. I could have told him that without following the Bobblers around with cameras and stuff! If so-called experts can't find out what they're doing here, why don't we have a go?'

'What's the point? I don't see how that spooky woman could help. She might just make those dreadful noises again.'

Fiona's face assumed a stubborn expression. 'Well I think it's worth a try. And if you won't come with me, I'll just go to see her on my own.'

'That's up to you,' Richard said dismissively. 'Anyway, how would you see her? You don't know where she lives.'

'I picked up one of her cards when we were at the Spiritualist church. It's got a telephone number on it, a London one and it says she does private sittings.'

He frowned. 'I don't think it's a good idea to go and see her, Fi. She claims to speak to the dead, for God's sake. That's loony.'

She scowled. 'Oh yeah? Well, talking of loony, what about waving crucifixes and spouting Latin at the Bobblers?'

'That's different.'

'How is it different?'

'Sister Francis belongs to a long-established religion which has traditional rituals.'

'You mean it's OK to have rituals involving the body and blood of a man who was crucified over two thousand years ago and allegedly rose from the dead, but to try and contact the spirits of *other* dead people is "loony"?'

'Well ...' It was a reasonable point but out of loyalty to Sister Francis, Richard was unwilling to concede it. 'I'm not a Catholic myself, but I think what happens in the mass is ... purely symbolic.'

'If you're not a Catholic, why do you carry a rosary?' she retorted.

'Because Sister Francis gave it to me,' he replied defensively. 'It's like, a talisman, a safety thing; like having a Saint Christopher medal in the car.'

She gave a derisive laugh. 'Huh! People use rosaries to pray to a mother who's supposed to be a virgin. How absurd is that? And what's all that stuff about a "Holy Ghost"?'

Richard was stumped. 'I don't think it's meant to be what we think of as a ghost, the spooky kind. It's probably more to do with the spirit.

Anyway, I'm talking about long accepted beliefs --'

She snorted. 'Beliefs change all the time. If you'd told anyone that aliens were going to invade the Earth this time last year, you would have been considered a nutcase, wouldn't you?'

'Well, yes I suppose so.'

'So why are some beliefs more acceptable than others?'

'Come off it, Fi,' he said impatiently. 'You know as well as I do that some beliefs are unacceptable: what about suicide bombers who believe that if they kill lots of innocent people they'll be rewarded with a harem of virgins in Paradise? What about the Inheritors' belief that the invasion is a warm-up act for the Second Coming? What about Abraham R's belief that after his followers commit suicide, their souls will be transported to a celestial New Kingdom?'

Fiona's face had turned pink with anger. Her eyes flashed. 'I'm not talking about madmen or extremists. Of course beliefs can be harmful if they're used as an excuse for brainwashing or abuse or violence. That's not the issue.'

'Well what is the issue?'

'You were suggesting that Spiritualism is suspect but that we shouldn't question Christianity. But what's the difference? My point is that lots of people believe mediums can communicate with the dead, so how is that any different from the belief that some guy wearing a dress is communicating with a dead man in front of an altar?'

Richard hesitated, not having an answer and unwilling to prolong an argument he felt he couldn't win. 'I only meant that getting mixed up in the ...occult can be dangerous--'

She interrupted him impatiently. 'Well I'm going to contact Madame Delph and make an appointment whether you want to come or not.' She stood up. 'Come on, Poll. It's time to go home.'

They left the park in silence.

Richard made his way home in an agitated state. He was annoyed with Fiona for her ability to outsmart him in an argument and angry with himself for not making a more forceful case against Spiritualism. He hadn't realised Fiona felt so strongly about Catholicism. He had no particular affiliation to any religion himself. Any beliefs he might have held had been destroyed during his field work with the survivors of terrible catastrophes. It was hard to believe in a merciful god when whole communities had been wiped out in the space of a few seconds.

By the time he reached the bottom of Bridlington Hill, however, he had begun to change his mind. Maybe he should accompany Fiona. It might smooth things over. Moreover he had to admit that Morgana Delph couldn't be a complete fraud. The first time he had seen her, she had alerted him to the existence of Abraham R, and the second time, she had uttered exactly the same extraordinary noises that the Bobblers used to communicate with each other. She clearly had a mysterious power that he didn't understand and which made him feel deeply uneasy.

Perhaps Fiona was right, he decided. Was channelling any more bizarre than some of the rites and rituals involved in Christianity and other established religions; stuff like exorcism, speaking in tongues or faith-healing? He had always viewed such activities with extreme scepticism. But, as recent history showed, circumstances change beliefs. Not that long ago, he wouldn't have believed in the existence of aliens. Maybe he should approach Spiritualism with a more open mind. Maybe he should accompany Fiona after all.

Preoccupied with these thoughts, he had completely forgotten about Rosenberg until, on reaching Coronation Close, he recalled the man snarling with rage in the light of the streetlamp. With a frisson of fear he hastened up the path to his parents' front door.

His mother called out a greeting as he entered the house. Savoury smells from the kitchen informed him that she was preparing the evening meal. This was one aspect of his parents' return that he did enjoy - home-cooked meals. Since the Bobblers had departed, life in the Jarman household had resumed a semblance of normality. His father had returned to work and his mother had begun to pick up the pieces of her social life, reconnecting with groups attached to the Baptist church she attended. She hadn't mentioned Fiona since the day she and Polly had come to tea, and neither had he.

He went upstairs and sent Fiona a text: *I will go with you to see MD*.

His mobile rang almost immediately. When he answered, expecting it to be her, he heard a different female voice, one that was soft and accented.

'Mother Ignatius told me you called.'

'Yes. She gave me a rather dusty reception.'

'She was only trying to protect me. The police told her I mustn't leave the convent for a while and to be very careful. That devil is back among us, Richard. He's here, in England.'

'Yes, I know.'

'Did the police warn you too?'

'No, I rang them.' He told her about his encounter with Rosenberg but didn't mention the physical assault to which he had been subjected. 'He claims you and I destroyed the commune. And now that he's tracked me down, the police think he may come to find you.'

'Did he do you any violence, Richard? That fiend is capable of anything, so he is.'

'No, a neighbour came out with his dog and frightened him off.'

'Thanks be to God! But he might come back. You must take care, Richard'

'Don't worry about me, Sister, I'll be fine. But what about you? Are the police keeping watch on the convent?'

'They're sending a car round at regular intervals. They said I shouldn't even go into the kitchen garden without one of the other nuns accompanying me.' Her voice sounded small and scared. 'You don't think he'll try to kidnap me again, do you?'

'It's very unlikely,' Richard said reassuringly. 'The commune on the island's been closed down.'

'Well we must pray that he'll be caught soon. God be with you, Richard and do be vigilant.'

Fiona's texted response, which he found when the call ended, was brief: *Ok will arrange with MD.*

Chapter 45

The day of the *viva* arrived and Richard was given a day's leave from *Immediate Response*. He borrowed one of his father's suits and made his way into central London. On his arrival at the university, he was met by his supervisor who led him to a small lecture room and introduced him to the internal and external examiners. A small group of interested staff and students had assembled in the seats in front of the platform.

For several hours, Richard parried the examiners' searching questions, overcome with nervousness at first. He grew more confident, however, when he realised that they weren't trying to catch him out but were genuinely interested in his experiences with communities affected by catastrophic natural disasters.

As he had expected, the questions eventually turned towards the overall significance of his thesis; what new thinking it contributed to the field of Social Anthropology and what it revealed about the efficacy of overseas aid.

He had already rehearsed his answers to these questions and was able to hold forth on them for some time. 'I believe,' he said in conclusion, 'that my work demonstrates the effectiveness of self-reliance at individual and small group level. It shows that helping survivors to self-organise and use their own ingenuity and resourcefulness, encourages them to regain a sense of purpose and rebuild their communities. This is preferable to over-dependence on outside agencies. Local people, not governments, not aid agencies, know best what is needed.'

The examiners clucked approvingly and it was finally all over. He was now officially Dr Jarman. He rang his parents to tell them the news then accompanied his supervisor to a restaurant for a celebratory lunch.

It was in unusually high spirits, somewhat assisted by the wine that had accompanied the lunch, that he set off for home that afternoon. The knowledge that he had acquitted himself well in the *viva* put a spring in his step as he ascended Bridlington Hill. He was still replaying in his mind the answers he had given, when he became aware of the purring of a car engine close to him. Some sixth sense sent a warning signal to his brain. Without slackening his pace or fully turning his head, he gave a cautious sideways glance. His stomach knotted with panic. A shiny black saloon car was being driven slowly alongside the kerb only a few feet behind him. He had seen that kind of car before: when he had gone to meet the Inheritors at the disused railway yard near Harpenden. In such a car he had been forcibly conveyed to the island in the Shetlands.

Two men were sitting in the front seats, one of whom had a familiar hawk-like profile. He caught a quick glimpse of the number plate and tried to commit it to memory.

His mind went into overdrive. There were other pedestrians walking behind him and he thought it unlikely that the men would strike in front of witnesses. Trying not to betray his nervousness, he strolled casually on. When he came to the next side road, he walked straight across as though continuing up the hill, but on reaching the opposite corner, turned left and sprinted along the road. As he expected, he heard the car brake and go into reverse.

On the upper side of the road, there was a narrow alley between two houses, leading to the almost identical road above it. He ran up the alley then turned right and turned back into Bridlington Hill. He stopped briefly on the corner to catch his breath. The black car wasn't in sight but he knew it wouldn't be long before its occupants realised the manoeuvre he had made. He fingered his mobile in his pocket but before he could take it out, he saw the black car nosing out of the lower road. Fortunately, there were two other vehicles ascending the hill which forced it to wait.

He took off again at speed. The two cars passed him, then he heard a third. Glancing over his right shoulder, he saw it coming rapidly up the hill behind him. He darted into another side road and into a narrow lane that ran alongside the detached garage belonging to the house on the corner. The top of the lane joined another which bisected the back gardens on the lower side of Coronation Close and those on the upper side of the road below it. When Richard was a boy, it had been the access route to a scout hut in a small rectangle of open land, but the hut was now derelict and the lane had become a repository for rubbish and fly-tipped furniture. It wasn't visible from the road and there was a slim chance his pursuers wouldn't realise it was there.

He stumbled past overflowing plastic bags and a torn and filthy mattress, then stopped and listened. To his dismay, he heard a car stop and two car doors slam. He was seized with renewed panic. The back gardens of Coronation Close were enclosed by brick walls in front of which residents had planted a bulwark of hedges and prickly shrubs to deter intruders. Over the years, these had expanded into dense and impenetrable thickets. He ran a few yards along the lane, desperately searching for a way through. Spotting a slight but unpromising gap in one of the hedges, he hauled himself up on to the wall, pushed his father's jacket through the gap, then pulled the branches violently apart and attempted to squeeze through them. The jacket provided only flimsy protection from twigs and thorns. They scratched his arms and hands and clutched and tore at his clothes, and it was only after a desperate struggle that he managed to squeeze himself head first through the hedge. As the branches closed behind him, he fell clumsily on to a flowering border and lay there for a moment, panting from his exertions.

He stumbled to his feet, grabbed the sleeve of his jacket and pulled it out of the hedge, noticing as he did so that blood was seeping from the cuts in his arms and hands. His heart was beating painfully fast and his legs were trembling from the unaccustomed exercise.

Hearing footsteps on the other side of the hedge, he froze. They came nearer, then receded. A few moments later, they approached again and stopped alarmingly close to where he had broken through the hedge. He held his breath as he heard Abraham R. shout to his companion, 'He must have got through there.'

Panic-stricken, Richard picked up his jacket, scrambled across a parched lawn and made for a garden shed he had spotted near the house. He was about to conceal himself behind it when to his alarm, a woman's voice bellowed his name: 'Ricky Jarman!'

The owner of the voice came waddling towards him, waving her arms in fury. 'What in heaven's name are you doing in my garden?'

Richard groaned. Of all the gardens in the Close, he had chosen the one belonging to number three! For a moment he wasn't sure who he would rather face, Abraham Rosenberg or Marjorie Phelps. He plumped for the lesser of two evils. 'Please keep your voice down, Mrs. Phelps,' he hissed.

'Keep my voice down?' she bellowed. 'You break into my garden and have the nerve to ask me to keep my voice down?' Crimson-faced with rage, she marched up to the flowerbed and uttered a shriek of outrage.

'You've trampled my chrysanthemums!'

'I'm sorry,' he stuttered. 'I didn't mean to--'

'You didn't mean to?' She gazed at him, aghast. 'And just look at the state of you!'

Mortified, Richard tucked his loosened shirt into his waistband. He realised he had ruined his father's suit. There was a tear in one of the jacket sleeves and a jagged hole in one of the trouser legs. He decided that honesty, or *near* honesty, was the best policy. 'I'm really sorry, Mrs. Phelps, but it was the only place I could get through the hedge. I've been helping the police find a wanted criminal --'

'A wanted criminal?' she exclaimed incredulously. 'The only criminal around here is you! You're trespassing on private property.'

'He's behind the hedge,' Richard whispered, 'with one of his accomplices. He's violent.'

'Poppycock!' She picked her way carefully round the trampled plants and stood listening in front of the hedge, then marched back to him.

'No-one there! I knew this was another of your lies. You've been nothing but trouble since you came back here, Ricky Jarman, and I'm not putting up with it any longer. I'm going to call the police and tell them you've vandalised my garden.'

Richard took a deep breath. 'Please do, Mrs. Phelps. And while you're about it, ask to speak to Detective Sergeant Johnson. In fact I'll ring him now myself.' He fumbled in a jacket pocket, extracted his mobile and, under her outraged gaze, rang DS Johnson's number. This time he got the officer's message service.

'Detective Sergeant Johnson, it's Richard Jarman,' he said in a loud voice that he hoped would be heard in the lane behind the hedge. 'Abraham Rosenberg has returned to this area. Please call me as soon as possible.'

Marjorie Phelps was momentarily speechless.

Richard adopted a placatory tone. 'I'll pay for the damage to your garden, Mrs. Phelps. Now please may I go through your house? I need to get home.'

Muttering a litany of furious complaints, she reluctantly allowed him inside and accompanied him to the front door.

He stood for a moment on the step, looking anxiously around, but there was no sign of Rosenberg or his companion. With a sigh of relief, he hurried to his parents' house. As he entered he noticed that the door had a red balloon bearing the word *Congratulations!* bobbing above it.

He wondered what he was going to tell them. His arms and hands were bleeding and his father's suit was badly torn. He would have to give them some explanation but decided to play down the danger he had been in. His mother had bought a bottle of Champagne and was preparing a special meal to celebrate the achievement of his doctorate. He didn't want to upset her more than necessary.

He tiptoed inside as quietly as he could, intending to sneak upstairs before his mother heard him, but he was too late.

'Is that you, darling?' She emerged from the kitchen with a wide smile on her face that froze as soon as she saw him. 'Ricky, whatever's happened? Have you been in an accident? You're bleeding.'

'I'm OK, Mum. It's nothing. Just a few scratches.'

'It doesn't look like nothing.' She stepped closer. 'What on earth have you done to yourself?'

He started to edge up the stairs. 'Just let me wash these cuts, then I'll tell you--'

'No,' she said firmly. 'Tell me now. You can't leave me guessing when you come home looking like this. And I don't know what your father will say when he sees the state of his suit.'

He gave a resigned sigh. 'OK, OK. It's no big deal. You remember I told you about that island Sister Francis and I were taken to? Well, the leader of the sect, Abraham Rosenberg is pissed off because the commune was closed down after we reported what was happening to the police. So he came looking for me and chased me up the hill. The only way I could escape was through Mrs. Phelps' garden.'

She looked shocked. 'He chased you? What was he going to do?'

'I dunno. Thump me, I suppose.'

'That's terrible, Ricky. He sounds dangerous. You should never have got mixed up with that nun.'

'It's not her fault the man's a nutcase, Mum.'

'What if he's still out there?'

'I think he's gone now. Hearing Ma Phelps shouting would have frightened him off.' He tried to laugh. 'It would have frightened anyone off.'

'But what if he comes back? Ricky, you must call the police at once.'

'I've already rung them. They know all about Rosenberg. They're already looking for him.' He started to mount the stairs.

She made as if to follow him. 'I'll clean those scratches for you. There's some Iodine in the bathroom cupboard.'

'There's no need, Mum, I'll do it myself.' He hastened up to the bathroom, washed the blood from his cuts and covered the largest ones with strips of sticking plaster. Afterwards he went to his desk and wrote down what he could recall of the car's number plate - *SW ...57 ... H.* He was trying to remember the rest of it when his mobile rang.

'You called, Mr. Jarman?' DS Johnson sounded, as usual, slightly sarcastic.

Richard told him what had happened and gave as many details as he could of the car Rosenberg had been driving.

'Scottish registration,' the officer murmured thoughtfully. 'We'll have an alert put out. Our Super has been in contact with the American authorities. They're keen for us to catch Rosenberg. In the meantime, we'd better keep an eye on your area for the next day or two as he seems to have a special interest in you. You're obviously an easier target than the nun.' He paused. 'You seem to make a habit of getting into these scrapes, Mr. Jarman.'

'Not by choice,' Richard replied huffily.

* * *

When his father returned from work, he told his story a third time without mentioning his earlier encounter with Rosenberg.

His father shook his head in dismay. 'You must look out for yourself, Ricky. The chap's obviously dangerous. Maybe you should stay at home for a few days.'

'I can't do that, Dad. I'm half way through my training.'

'Are the police going to provide you with protection?'

'DS Johnson said they'll keep an eye on this area in case he comes back.'

'Well make sure you always have your mobile handy when you're out.'

'I will. Sorry about your suit, Dad. I'm afraid it's a bit the worse for wear.'

His father waved a dismissive hand. 'Your safety is far more important than a suit.'

The doorbell rang. A policewoman had arrived to take some details.

Richard told his story yet again and took her round the corner to show her the lane where he had climbed through the hedge. She examined some footprints and made notes before driving away. As the police car left the Close, Richard noticed Mrs. Phelps watching it from her front window.

It took a while for him to reassure his parents that the police had the situation under control. By the evening, however, they had calmed down sufficiently for his father to open the bottle of Champagne before the celebratory dinner his mother had prepared. He chuckled when Richard again described the scene in Marjorie Phelps' garden.

His mother, however, was not amused. 'It's not a laughing matter, Gordon. Marj said she spent the whole summer watering her flower beds during that terrible heat. No wonder she was annoyed.'

'Battered flowers are preferable to a battered son!' Richard's father raised his glass. 'Congratulations, Dr. Jarman!'

After one small glass of Champagne, his mother relaxed and had it not been for the fright he had experienced, Richard himself would have felt extremely content.

When they had finished eating, he and his father took the remains of a bottle of wine to the living room and switched on the television to catch up on the latest developments.

They learned nothing new. The aliens were continuing to frequent disaster-stricken parts of the developing world and surveillance drones were keeping a round-the-clock watch on their whereabouts. A relief worker interviewed by video-link in the Philippines, commented that although the creatures hadn't displayed any overt aggression, the terror they provoked was exacerbating the misery of traumatised communities.

Richard's father shook his head. 'What's their agenda, Ricky? Why are they harassing those poor devils?'

Richard drained his glass. 'It's a complete mystery, Dad. Nobody knows.'

His mobile buzzed and his spirits sank on finding a text from Fiona: *Private sitting with MD arranged for 10am Sat in Finchley.* The last thing he needed was another session with the crazy medium.

'She's had a cancellation,' Fiona told him when he rang her back in the privacy of his room.

'How much will it cost?'

'Fifty pounds.'

'Fifty quid?' he exclaimed in dismay. He was coming to the end of his remaining funds and had yet to receive any payment from *Immediate Response*.

'That's not much between the two of us. Now, tell me about this morning. How did you get on?'

He gave her a brief account of his *viva* which already seemed a long time ago. He decided not to tell her about his latest encounter with Abraham R just yet. It would only worry her and having already related the story four times, he was bored with repeating the details.

Chapter 46

He waited until they were travelling to Finchley before giving Fiona an account of his second escape from Abraham Rosenberg.

She looked troubled. 'Do you think he'll try again, Ric? Remember what happened to Paddy McAllister. I know you're a lot younger than he was, but --'

'Don't worry. I'm being ultra careful.'

He had, in fact, been extremely vigilant during his journeys to and from *Immediate Response*, but there had been no sign of Rosenberg since that memorable afternoon. And DS Johnson had been as good as his word. He had arranged for an unmarked police car to park in the Close several times a day.

When Morgana Delph opened her front door, Richard thought once again that she looked more like his granny than "The World's Greatest Medium". Her grey hair had been set in tight curls and her dumpy frame was squeezed into a frilly white blouse and an ankle-length black skirt.

She led them into a room crammed with over-sized furniture. Richard winced as he looked around. Virtually every surface was covered with china ornaments, predominantly pirouetting ballerinas and winsome kittens. Different sized crystals dangled in front of the net curtains covering the bay window. Framed photographs of the medium, posing with minor show-business celebrities, lined the walls. Amongst them, Richard spotted a charcoal sketch of a Native American wearing a feathered headdress and smoking a long clay pipe.

Morgana invited them to sit at a small table on which she had placed a pack of Tarot cards, a box of tissues, a bottle of mineral water and a glass.

Richard's chair was squashed against a large bookcase filled with volumes with titles such as *Voices from Beyond the Grave* and *Rediscover your Seventh Sense*.

The medium sat down at the table opposite them and looked at them enquiringly. 'How can I help you? Is there someone you need to get in touch with in the spirit world?'

'Not exactly.' Fiona glanced at Richard. 'We were at the Spiritualist

Church in Shepherd Street when you made a special appearance after the invasion. You went into a trance and channelled one of the aliens.'

Morgana looked astonished. 'One of the aliens? Eeeh, I don't think so.'

'But you did,' Fiona stammered. 'You made very strange sounds just like--'

Richard took over. 'We didn't recognise them at the time, but later, when I heard some aliens communicating with each other, I realised that you had made exactly the same kind of noises that they do. So we concluded that you must have channelled one of them.'

'Well now, fancy that!' Morgana stared at them, her pale blue eyes magnified by the thick lenses of her spectacles. 'All I can remember is that it were one of what I call my "heavy" sessions. When I'm in an altered state, I'm not aware what voices are coming through me. The only memory I have afterwards is of an atmosphere; a state of mind. I don't recall the words I speak. They're not *my* words.'

'On that occasion, they weren't *words* at all,' Richard pointed out. 'They were just noises. But we believe it was Alien Language and we wondered whether you might be able to channel an alien for us again.'

The medium looked at him severely. 'Eeeh, I can't channel to order, young man. *I* don't choose who speaks through me; they choose *me*. I'm just a communication vessel, like a telephone. I never know who's going to call up. It could be someone that you've completely forgotten, or it could be your old granny.'

'It won't be my old granny,' Richard chortled. 'She's in a nursing home in Torquay.'

Morgana glared at him. 'There's no need to be flippant, young man. What you must understand is that I have no control over who decides to make contact through me or the words that come out of my mouth. And as far as I know, the alien invaders haven't passed over to the other side, into spirit, more's the pity. So I'm not sure that I can help you.'

Fiona gave her one of her winning smiles. 'We'd be really grateful if you would try.'

'Well ...' The medium stared at them dubiously. 'I suppose I can see if anyone else wants to contact you. That's all I can do, but there's no guarantee it'll be who you want. Have you brought a tape with you?'

'No.' Fiona looked crestfallen. 'We never thought of that.'

'Then it's just as well I've got a spare one.' Morgana went to a sideboard and took an old fashioned-looking cassette recorder from a drawer. Returning to the table she switched it on. 'You can take the recording home with you.' She picked up the pack of Tarot cards and handed them to Fiona. 'Shuffle these for me, my love. And while you're doing it, think about what you want to know.'

'Hey!' Richard protested. 'We haven't come to have our fortunes told.'

Morgana drummed her fingers crossly on the table. 'I'm not a fortune-teller, young man, I'm a clairvoyant. When people come to me asking for a reading, I do the cards first to get an insight into their psyche. I like to give people their money's worth.'

'Of course,' said Fiona soothingly. 'And we're very grateful.' She gave Richard a warning glance before shuffling the cards and handing them back to the medium who fanned them out, face downwards, on the table.

'Now pick any ten cards, my love, at random.'

Fiona picked ten cards and gave them to her. Morgana turned them over so that they were face upwards. She laid them out in a pattern, some overlapping others. 'Now let me see …' she began to stab at the cards with her index finger. 'The Empress! That means motherhood, birth.' She gazed meditatively up at the ceiling. 'I sense there's a young lass who's very close to you.'

'Yes,' Fiona gazed at her, wide-eyed. 'There is.'

The medium tapped another card. 'And now the Knight of Swords: there's also a young man around you. He's a bit unreliable. There've been arguments?'

Fiona was silent.

'The card's opposed by Four of Cups. Eeeh! Discontent, tears! You need to reassess the situation, love. Look at it in a new way…Now, what's this?' She paused for a moment. 'This is a healing card. Are you a nurse, my love?'

'No, but--'

'Is your work related to healing?'

'Yes,' breathed Fiona. 'I work in a hospital. That's amazing!'

'Now, let's look at your past influences.'

Richard mentally switched off. He shifted impatiently, irritated with

Fiona who was gazing raptly at Morgana and drinking in every word. Bored, he gazed around the room and tried to occupy himself by counting the number of porcelain ballerinas. By the time he reached forty, Morgana's voice reinstated itself in his ears.

'Nine of Cups: a wish card. You'll have to wait, my love, before you get what you desire.'

Fiona sighed.

'Now your turn, young man. Pick ten cards.'

Resignedly Richard obeyed.

Madame Delph repeated the same procedure, turning them up and laying them out in a pattern on the table. 'Queen of Cups,' she muttered, peering at one of them. 'There's a young woman close to you.'

Richard guffawed and Fiona kicked him under the table.

'Ah, the Wheel of Fortune! Lots of things have been happening in your life, but the card is opposed by the Two of Swords. You've been stuck in a situation. Vacillation! You're not ready to come to a decision, young man.'

Richard felt uncomfortable.

'Seven of Swords: adventure and misfortune have followed you around. You've needed to use your wits.'

'That's true enough,' he muttered, impressed in spite of himself.

'And here's the Hierophant: someone you like and respect; a wise person. I think it's an older woman, a spiritual person ...'

Richard's interest was now fully aroused.

'But,' she frowned, 'here's someone else connected with you ... the Devil, the shadow side. Someone's giving me the letter R ...' She uttered a shriek, 'Oooh! A right bad one, is this! Evil incarnate!'

Richard froze.

Morgana gazed at him with a concerned expression. 'You must take care, young man, keep out of this one's way.'

He gulped.

She studied another card. 'Five of Pentacles. You've been exposed to risks but you haven't liked to confront them, have you?'

He felt discomfited under her gaze. 'Well, I --'

'You must settle something once and for all.' She peered closely at the next card. 'Here's the Fool in the Major Arcana. You're about to escape; embark on a new journey, foreign lands; a new chapter in your life is starting …' Her voice started to fade, she started to breathe heavily and her eyes rolled upwards. Slumping back in her chair, she uttered a long drawn-out sigh then a groan, 'Ahhh.'

Richard and Fiona exchanged an anxious glance.

'Do you think she's alright?' he whispered.

'I don't know,' Fiona murmured back. 'Maybe someone's trying to get through.'

After a few seconds, Morgana sat up with an abruptness that made them both jump. Her eyes snapped open and gazed unseeingly past them. Then, to their astonishment, she started to utter a series of squeaks, cackles and whistles.

'Bloody hell!' exclaimed Richard. 'It's Alien Speak!'

'Who are you?' Fiona asked in a loud voice. 'Where do you come from?'

Morgana continued to make the strange sounds.

'You say something,' Fiona hissed to Richard.

Self-consciously he addressed the medium. 'What do you want? Why have you come to Earth?'

Morgana uttered a succession of short staccato grunts as though she was having difficulty breathing. She gave a snort then, to their even greater astonishment, started to speak in a preternaturally high woman's voice: 'Sphère … espèce … élément.'

Richard was baffled. 'What's that she's speaking?'

Fiona looked astounded. 'It's French!'

'Why's she speaking French for God's sake?'

The strange high voice continued to utter a series of seemingly un-connected words. 'Besoin … survivre … nourrir … chaleur … perte …végétation … adaptation … l'eau … bientôt … fin … rentrer.'

Richard and Fiona gazed at each other in bewilderment.

Morgana fell silent. After a second, she toppled forward, banging her head on the table and scattering the Tarot cards, some of which fell on to the floor.

Fiona leapt to her feet, poured a glass of water and hovered uncertainly beside the medium's chair.

After a few moments, Morgana recovered consciousness and sat up, looking exhausted. 'By 'eck, that were 'eavy, were that,' she murmured weakly, her native Yorkshire accent sounding much stronger than it had done before. She took some deep breaths, grasped the glass Fiona was proffering and gulped down some water.

'Well? Did you get what you were expecting?' she asked, replacing the glass on the table.

'Not exactly,' Fiona said hesitantly. 'You were speaking French.'

'French?' She stared at them. 'Fancy that. Do either of you have French ancestors in spirit?'

'Not that I know of,' Fiona replied. 'Have you, Ric?'

'No. But maybe you spoke in French because you call yourself *Madame* Delph.'

'Don't be flippant, young man.' Morgana rose wearily from her chair. 'That's me done for this morning. I'll have to go and rest now.' She took the tape out of the recorder and handed it to Fiona. 'I hope it were useful, my love.'

Fiona's eyes shone with gratitude. 'Yes, thank you. It was amazing.'

They paid her and left.

'Wasn't that incredible?' Fiona breathed as soon as the door closed behind them.

Richard muttered something non-committal.

'Come on Ric, you must admit it was impressive.'

'I could have done without all that Tarot malarkey, but I admit the last bit was fascinating. How much did you understand, Fi?'

'Most of it. It wasn't sentences, just unconnected words. I'd have to listen to it again.'

'Before speaking in French, she made Alien noises. Why would an alien speak in French?' Richard wondered aloud.

'It must have got its linguistic wires crossed.'

'Well she did say to think of her as a telephone.'

Fiona giggled. 'Don't be flippant, young man! But how are we going to listen to the tape? Have you got anything to play it on? I haven't.'

'I think my parents have got an old cassette recorder somewhere. Why don't you come home with me and we can listen to it there?'

She hesitated. 'What about your mother? I'm not exactly flavour of the month.'

'Don't worry about her. This is important.'

When they arrived at the house, Richard saw the unmarked police car doing a slow circuit of the Close. He hadn't given a thought to

Abraham Rosenberg for several hours and the memory of their last encounters made his stomach give a sudden lurch.

'Ricky?' called his mother as he opened the front door. 'Lunch will be ready in about half an hour.' She came out of the kitchen and her face fell when she saw Fiona. 'Oh, hello...Felicity.'

Fiona gave a wan smile.

'Hi, Mum,' Richard said cheerfully. 'There's a tape *Fiona* and I want to listen to. Do you still have an old cassette tape-recorder?'

She looked puzzled. 'We used to have one. Ask your father. He's in the garden.' She gave Fiona a cold glance and retreated into the kitchen.

His father was standing with his back to them, cutting down the branches of a heat-blasted shrub.

'Hi, Dad,' called Richard.

His father wheeled round. 'You startled me. Hello, Fiona. Nice to see you again.' He sucked at his thumb. 'Bloody thorns. Just cut myself.'

'Mum said you had an old cassette recorder. Do you know where it is?'

'Cassette recorder?' His father wiped his forehead with the back of his hand. 'We used to have one. It may be in the cupboard under the stairs. Why?'

'There's a tape we want to listen to.'

'Well I think it's in there. Have a look. I'll see you later.' He resumed his work.

They went back inside and Richard rummaged in the hall cupboard. After a few minutes he gave a shout of triumph and emerged brandishing a dusty tape recorder. 'Hope it still works. Let's take it up to my room.'

As they climbed the stairs, he looked back and glimpsed his mother standing at the kitchen door, watching them with pursed lips.

He put the recorder on his desk and plugged it in. Fiona perched on the side of his bed while he inserted the tape and pressed *play*. He fast-forwarded through the Tarot readings until he got to the point where Morgana Delph fell forward on her chair.

They listened in awed silence to the strange alien sounds she uttered and Fiona began to write as the strange high voice then uttered the words, 'Sphère ... espèce ... élément ... besoin ... survivre ... nourrir ... chaleur ... perte ... végétation ... adaptation ... l'eau ... bientôt ...

fin ... rentrer.'

Richard switched off the tape. 'Can you write the words in English?'

'Well *sphère* is--'

'Sphere, obviously, which could mean the Earth or the sun or another planet, don't you think?'

'I suppose so.' She wrote the words down. '*Espèce* means species.'

'That could mean us?' he suggested. 'The human species.'

'Or them,' she countered, 'extraterrestrial species?'

'Maybe. What's the next word?'

'Well *élément* is the same as in English but it could be plural because the "s" doesn't sound in French. *Besoin* means need, but again it could be plural - needs. *Survivre* is to survive, like in English. *Nourrir* means to feed or nourish.'

She wrote down the words. 'Next, *chaleur* is heat and *perte* means loss. *Végétation* and *adaptation* are the same as in English. And *l'eau* is-'

'Water!' Richard leaned towards her eagerly. A picture was beginning to emerge. 'Go on.'

'*Bientôt* means soon. *Fin* is end or finish and *rentrer* means to return or go back. Could that mean they're soon going to return to wherever they came from?'

He bent to read her notes. 'It's possible. We've got a sphere, which we can take to be a planet, and a species' needs for survival. Survive what? The elements, heat and loss of vegetation.' His heart began to pound with excitement. 'Maybe it's referring to the effect of the Blitzgreen, and something about water.'

She frowned in concentration. 'Well, the word before that is "adaptation". I suppose that could mean that we, the human species, need to adapt to what's happening as a result of global warming.'

'Or it could apply to them and the planet they come from? Maybe the aliens are the ones who have to adapt because their star is dying.'

She gazed at him. 'In that case, it could mean they're looking for--'

'A more congenial environment to move to?' He felt another surge of excitement. 'That could be it.'

Fiona looked troubled. 'But if they think ours is a more congenial environment, why would they have destroyed some of it? Should we tell someone about this, Ric?'

'Who would we tell?'

'I don't know. The police?'

'No, not a good idea. If we tell them we consulted a medium and she channelled an alien who spoke to us in French, they'll just think we're taking the piss! There have already been too many crazy ideas about the aliens' intentions.'

'I know. One guy has been putting out tweets saying they're going to carry the entire human race off to another planet.'

'Exactly. The thing is, Fi, we have no evidence that it *was* an alien speaking through Ma Delph.'

'But you said the noises she made sounded like their language.'

'They did, but if it was one of them, why on earth would it then start speaking in French? Anyway, there's no point in telling the police about it, or anyone else for that matter.'

'Not even your mum and dad?'

'Least of all them.' Richard shuddered at the thought. His mother hadn't yet recovered from the series of shocks he had inflicted on her: his friendship with a nun, imprisonment on an island, relationship with a divorced single mother and pursuit by a psychopath. Informing her that he had consulted a medium who channelled a French-speaking alien might just send her over the edge!

'No,' he repeated firmly. 'Let's keep it to ourselves for the time being.'

At that moment, his mother shouted up the stairs. 'Ricky, lunch is ready.' There was a pause before she added, 'Would ... Fiona like to stay?'

Richard looked questioningly at Fiona and whispered, 'Could you bear it?'

'I can if you can.'

He went to the top of the stairs and called down to his mother. 'Yes, she'd like to stay. Thanks, Mum.'

Fiona gave one of her gap-toothed grins. 'I wonder what she thinks we've been doing up here.'

He pulled her into his arms. 'What a pity we don't have time to realise her worst fears!'

Chapter 47

'I'm sorry it's only soup and bread and cheese,' Richard's mother said stiffly. 'I wasn't expecting a guest.'

'Soup and bread and cheese is fine,' Fiona replied quickly. 'Thank you for inviting me, Mrs. Jarman.'

She produced a frigid smile. 'How is your daughter?'

'Great, thanks. My parents took her to the Science Museum this morning.'

'Oh. How interesting.'

An uncomfortable silence was broken by Richard's father. 'So where did you two get to this morning?' he asked cheerfully.

Richard gave Fiona a warning glance. 'We went to visit a friend who lives in Finchley.'

'Ah, and what was that tape you wanted to play? The cassette recorder still works, I take it?'

'It worked fine, thanks,' Richard replied. 'It was something our friend gave us --'

'A language tuition course,' Fiona interjected.

Richard's father looked surprised. 'Oh? What language?'

'French,' she replied quickly. 'I'm brushing up on my French.'

'I thought language courses were all online or on CDs these days.'

Fiona went slightly pink. 'Yes they are, but this is an old method, one you can't get hold of any more. I was pleased Morg ... our friend, still had a copy. Lovely soup!' She swallowed a spoonful. 'What is it? Leek and potato?'

'No,' Richard's mother said coldly. 'Chicken.'

There was an awkward silence.

'What's the method called?' asked his father, busily cutting a loaf of bread into thick slices.

'It's the ... Delph Method,' Richard replied. He heard Fiona give a kind of choke and felt a giggle rising in his throat. He didn't dare catch her eye. To suppress his mirth, he tried to think of something unpleasant. Abraham Rosenberg came immediately to mind. This provided him with an opportunity to change the subject. 'I saw the police car in the Close when we got here.'

'Yes,' said his father, 'I suppose it means they haven't caught that psychopath yet.'

His mother put down her soup spoon. 'I still don't understand how you got mixed up with such dreadful people, Ricky. What if that man tries to break into the house?'

'Don't worry, Mum. I've got a police hotline number to call if he turns up again.'

'But what if the police don't come quickly enough? I've been on tenterhooks ever since you came home that afternoon, all scratched and bleeding. I don't think you realise how worried I've been.' Agitatedly she crumbled a piece of bread onto her plate.

'Eat your lunch, Eileen,' Richard's father murmured soothingly. 'The police have been coming round at regular intervals and I'm sure they have the situation under control.'

After another awkward silence, he turned to Richard. 'I heard on the news that the aliens have fetched up somewhere in Chile, in an earthquake zone. I wonder how those poor people cope with seeing those grotesque creatures on top of all they've been through. How long will this go on, for God's sake?'

'Who knows?' Richard cut himself a large slice of Cheddar.

'And now you're about to go to one of those disaster areas yourself, Ricky,' cried his mother. 'Why must you keep putting yourself in danger? Couldn't you ask *Immediate Response* to give you an office job here, in this country?'

He shook his head. 'There's no point, Mum. I've been appointed as an overseas development officer.'

'But it could be dangerous where you're going.' She turned to Fiona, clearly hoping to find an ally. 'I don't think he should go, do you, Fiona?'

Fiona hesitated. 'I think it's up to Ric, Mrs. Jarman. It's his career after all.'

Richard glanced at her gratefully.

His mother scowled.

* * *

'Sorry about that,' he muttered to Fiona after they had made their escape. 'Mum's been a bag of nerves ever since she got home.'

She slipped her hand into his. 'It's understandable, Ric. No mother likes to think of their children going somewhere potentially dangerous, however old they are.'

'She nearly went berserk when I told her about Rosenberg chasing me the other day.'

'That's understandable too, isn't it? He's obviously a psychopath.'

'True,' Richard muttered gloomily. 'If he believes the aliens are the advance guard for the Second Coming, why doesn't he go in search of *them* instead of me?'

She thought for a second. 'I suppose it's too early.'

'Too early for what?'

'The Second Coming. You told me Rosenberg believes it will happen on Christmas Day, the date of Christ's first "Coming". That means he thinks he still has plenty of time to come and terrorise you.'

'I suppose so.' Richard's heart suddenly missed a beat. 'Quick. Get out of sight.' He crouched behind a parked van and pulled her down beside him.

'Hey,' she squawked. 'What's going on?'

'There's a black car coming up the hill ...'

'Is it Rosenberg's?'

'I don't know, but I'm not taking any chances.' He peered cautiously round the back of the van. The car was now in full view and there were two men in the front seats. He ducked quickly out of sight as it passed the van on its way up the hill. 'It *is* him and the gorilla he was with before.'

She clutched his arm. 'Do you think they saw you?'

'I don't think so or they would have stopped.' He straightened up. 'I'd better go back in case he's heading for Mum and Dad's house. The police car wasn't there when we came out.'

She rose to her feet and gazed at the car disappearing up the hill. 'If you go back they'll see you.'

'I'll keep out of sight. I'll ring DS Johnson. He said they'd come immediately if Rosenberg showed up again. You go on home, Fi.'

'No,' she protested. 'I'll come with you.'

'I'd rather you didn't. I don't want to worry about your safety as well as my own.'

She hovered uncertainly beside him. 'Are you sure you'll be alright?'

'Yes, I'll be fine. Go!' He gave her a gentle push. 'Didn't you tell me you were going to take Polly out on her rollerblades this afternoon?'

'You will call me? Let me know what happens?'

'Of course I will.'

'Please be careful, Ric.' Reluctantly she left him and continued down the hill with occasional worried backward glances.

After leaving an urgent phone message for DS Johnson, Richard crossed the road and proceeded cautiously up the hill on the right side, staying close to parked cars. When he arrived opposite the turning into Coronation Close, he positioned himself between a grimy campervan and a red hatchback spattered with bird excrement, and peered across the road. He couldn't see the BMW in the Close and wondered whether Rosenberg had driven it into one of the residential parking bays beyond his line of vision. If not, he could have parked the car further up the hill.

He looked cautiously round the back of the campervan then ducked back again. He had spotted it. The car was parked about a hundred yards further up the hill, facing downwards, affording the occupants a clear view of anybody who entered or left Coronation Close. From this vantage point, they would also be able to see all the vehicles ascending the hill. As this was the route Richard expected a police car to take, he again rang the hotline DS Johnson had given him.

This time Johnson answered. 'Stay where you are, Mr. Jarman,' he warned, after Richard had given him details of the BMW's position. 'Let us deal with this. We don't want any gung-ho heroics.'

Richard spluttered incredulously. Taking on Rosenberg and his beefy companion was the last thing he intended. He would rather confront a bunch of aliens any day.

Leaning uncomfortably against the back of the campervan, he waited nervously for something to happen.

An interminable period followed. As it was a Saturday afternoon, there was little traffic on the hill. He watched an aeroplane moving deceptively slowly overhead, leaving feathery trails in its wake. A young woman walked by pushing a toddler in a buggy with a yellow balloon attached to its handle. She stared suspiciously at Richard as she passed, and the balloon brushed lightly against his face in the breeze.

Suddenly Richard heard a car door slam. Peering round the back of the campervan, he saw Rosenberg's thickset companion walking casually down the hill. His heart missed a beat as the man turned into the Close. What was he intending to do? Knock on his parents' door? Threaten them? His instinct was to rush down and warn them, but he realised that would be dangerous. Glancing back at the BMW, he breathed a huge sigh of relief on spotting a police car moving swiftly down the hill behind it.

At first Rosenberg didn't seem to notice it and it was only when the police car drew near that he started the engine. By then it was too late. Another police car sped up the hill, braked, made a ninety degree turn and parked sideways, cutting off his escape. At almost the same time, the first car came to a halt immediately behind the BMW. Two police officers alighted from each vehicle. One of them was DS Johnson. He opened the BMW driver's door and ordered Rosenberg to get out.

As Rosenberg emerged, he was seized by Johnson and a second officer. He struggled violently and Richard could hear him bellowing curses and threats: 'The Messiah will punish you for your abominations! You will burn in Hell!'

Two more police cars, their sirens blaring, raced up the hill. They stopped in front of the three stationary vehicles and four uniformed officers jumped out. Two of them stationed themselves in the middle of the road to stop other traffic passing up and down the hill.

Rosenberg's accomplice suddenly reappeared on the corner of the Close. He glanced up at the row of cars then started to walk rapidly down the hill.

Richard leapt into the road. 'One of them's getting away,' he yelled, pointing at the retreating figure. 'He was in the car with Rosenberg.'

The man broke into a run and two of the officers set off in pursuit. One of them caught up with the fleeing figure and brought him down in a rugby tackle. The two of them then dragged him, struggling, back up the hill where Rosenberg, spread-eagled against the side of his car with his palms pressed against the roof, was being searched.

Richard watched with satisfaction as Johnson handcuffed his wrists behind his back and two officers marched him to one of the police cars. Before he was bundled inside, Rosenberg turned his head and bellowed, 'You'll burn in Hell, traitor!'

Richard gave him a cheery wave.

Rosenberg's accomplice was searched and handcuffed in his turn, before being unceremoniously pushed into the back of the horizontally-parked police car. Two officers then climbed into the BMW, and with gloved hands, removed various articles which they placed in plastic bags. The other police officers stood in a huddle, conferring, while DS Johnson spoke animatedly into a phone. Richard saw him take a notebook out of a pocket and write something down.

After finishing the call, he beckoned Richard over. For once he seemed genuinely friendly. 'Nice work, Mr. Jarman. Now that we've picked Rosenberg up, you won't need to keep looking over your shoulder. The wheels ...' he nodded in the direction of the BMW '... are registered in the name of ...' he glanced at what he had written '... Solomon Godworthy. Curious name, that.'

Richard grinned. 'It's one of Rosenberg's aliases. I've been told he has several. Will you ring the convent and tell them he's been caught? Sister Francis was really nervous after you told her he was still on the loose.'

The officer nodded. 'The convent will be informed. I'll be in touch if we need any more information from you. Do you want to bring a case against him for assault?'

Richard shook his head. 'No, as far as I'm concerned, the sooner he's extradited the better. I'm just grateful you've got him.'

Johnson gave one of his sardonic smiles. 'Well, try and keep out of danger in the future, Mr. Jarman, and perhaps we'll see a little less of each other.'

The officers climbed into the cars and after much slamming of doors and firing of engines, the vehicles were driven away.

In the silence that followed, Richard noticed that groups of curious onlookers had gathered to watch what was going on. Among them he spotted Reg and Dorothy Perkins, Stanley and Marjorie Phelps and his parents.

His father rushed across the road. 'Was that him, Ricky? Rosenberg? Have they got him?'

'Yes and his mate.'

'We saw you come out from behind that van but the police told us not to move. Did he try to harm you?'

Before Richard could answer, his mother arrived breathlessly at his side and threw her arms around him. 'Thank God you're safe. When we heard those police cars, we didn't know what was going on. Your father said he thought that awful man might have come back. Did he hurt you?'

Richard gently extricated himself from her embrace. 'No, he didn't know I was here until after the police arrived.'

He accompanied his parents across the road to the corner where their neighbours were still standing, talking in hushed tones.

'Ricky Jarman,' Marjorie Phelps commented sourly as they passed, 'whenever there's trouble, you tend to be mixed up in it.'

Before Richard could utter a rejoinder, his mother turned indignantly on her neighbour. 'My son should be congratulated, Marj,' she snapped. 'He's just helped the police catch a wanted felon.'

Mrs. Phelps looked deflated. She gave Richard a look of undisguised hostility then turned on her heel and waddled back into the Close. 'Come, Stanley!' she called over her shoulder. 'It's nearly tea time.'

With an apologetic grimace, her husband followed.

'Now the excitement's over I think we could all do with a cup of tea,' declared Richard's father.'

It was only when Richard was safely indoors that he realised his legs were shaking. After a day like this, he mused, six months in a disaster zone in Pakistan would be a doddle.

Before joining his parents in the living room, he rang Fiona. 'It's over, Fi. The police have got Rosenberg and his accomplice.'

He heard her expel a breath. 'Thank goodness you've called. I've been so worried.'

He described what had taken place after she had left him earlier that afternoon.

'Thank God they've caught him at last. You must be terribly relieved.'

'You can say that again!'

'Ric, something occurred to me after I got home this afternoon,' she said, after they had exhausted the subject of Rosenberg's capture.

'Oh? What was that?'

'It's about the French message.'

'Oh.' The dramatic events of the afternoon had completely obliterated his interest in what had happened when they visited the medium.

'Do you remember the first time we went to see Morgana Delph, at the theatre?'

He groaned. 'How could I ever forget it?'

'And do you remember her introductory spiel, when she talked about mediumship and what the process involves?'

'I can't say I do.' His principal memory of the event was the humiliation he had felt at being singled out in front of so many people. 'Why?'

'Well, she mentioned the spirit guides who help her.'

'Did she?'

'Yes,' Fiona said impatiently, 'don't you remember?'

'No.'

'She said she had two principal spirit guides: a Chinese healer and an Indian, a Native American, chief.'

Richard snorted derisively. 'An Indian chief? That's such a cliché!'

Fiona ignored this. 'She also said that she has a third guide…someone who steps in to help when a spirit has difficulty getting through.'

'So?'

'She said the third guide was a *French* woman.' Fiona sounded triumphant. 'Someone who lived a very long time ago. Her name began with an S. Madame D. referred to her as *Tante* which means Aunt. *Tante* … What was the name? Sa … Sa … Sabine! That's what it was. She called her *Tante Sabine.*'

'What about it?' The last thing Richard wanted to think about was Morgana Delph's spirit guides.

'Don't you see? Madame D was having difficulty receiving the alien's communication so Tante Sabine must have stepped in. And because she's French, or rather, *was* French, she translated what the alien said into French. Either that or the alien communicated with her in French.'

He snorted dismissively. 'Come off it, Fi. You can't possibly believe that.'

'Well, do you have any better ideas?' she asked huffily.

'No. I've had more important things to think about this afternoon. But if it's so obvious, why didn't La Delph mention Auntie Whatsaname herself? She seemed just as puzzled as we were that the message was in French.'

'She was probably so exhausted after the séance, it didn't occur to her.'

'Huh,' he muttered, unconvinced.

'Well if you have any better ideas, let me know.' Fiona abruptly ended the call.

Richard sighed. He seemed to have acquired an unfortunate knack of rubbing her up the wrong way. But when he joined his parents in the living room, he reflected on what she had suggested. Perhaps Fiona was right. She usually was. He didn't remember the medium mentioning a French spirit guide but if she *did* have one, improbable though that seemed, perhaps it could explain why someone, or some *thing*, had spoken through her in that language.

Chapter 48

Richard was enjoying a leisurely shower when his father banged on the bathroom door. 'Ricky! Come downstairs. Something's happened.'

Alarmed, he wrapped himself hurriedly in a towel and rushed downstairs.

His father, still in his dressing gown as it was a Sunday morning, was in his usual armchair opposite the television. He looked up excitedly as Richard entered the sitting room. 'They've gone, Ricky!'

'Who?'

'The aliens of course!'

'What, again?' Richard had a strong sense of *déjà vu*. 'You mean they've left the disaster zones? Where have they gone to this time?'

His father pointed upwards. 'Up there! Who knows where? They've apparently disappeared.'

'Are you sure?'

'Well that's what they're saying on the news.'

'Crikey!' Richard secured the towel around his waist and sank on to the sofa. 'Does Mum know?'

'She hasn't come back from church yet.'

Every television channel was buzzing with the news: the aliens had abandoned all their recent locations and there were reports from around the world that spaceships had been seen hurtling upwards at unimaginable speeds.

Experts hastily summoned to media newsrooms, were invited to speculate on the significance of this latest twist in the story of the invasion. As usual, their deliberations were inconclusive. The general assumption was that the aliens had left because they had accomplished their task. But what had been their task? And where had they gone? Would they return? As usual, no-one could supply answers to such questions.

The front door banged and Richard's mother appeared in the living room. She gazed aghast at Richard. 'Ricky, for heaven's sake! Is that towel wet? The sofa will be soaking--'

'Forget about the sofa, Eileen!' his father said impatiently. 'The aliens have gone!'

'What do you mean, gone? Gone where?'

'They've disappeared. Left the planet altogether.'

Her mouth dropped open. 'They haven't just moved on somewhere, like last time?'

'No, it seems they've really gone this time.'

'Thank God!' She said faintly, clutching the back of a chair. 'Are you sure it's true, Gordon?'

'It seems to be. All the reports say they've gone.'

She collapsed on to an armchair. 'That's wonderful, fantastic.'

'Shh!' hissed Richard. 'Listen!' He leaned forward eagerly as the face of the linguist, Bartholomew Wainwright, appeared on the screen at the start of an interview with a news presenter.

'Dr. Wainwright,' the presenter began. 'Can your recent analysis of the aliens' communication patterns shed any light on their sudden departure?'

The linguist pushed a rebellious lock of hair back from his forehead. 'Not exactly--'

'Or on the original reason for their invasion?'

'Well ...' Wainwright noisily cleared his throat. 'We haven't yet found the key to why the aliens came here in the first place, but after re-examining our recordings and the video footage, we have made an additional discovery.'

'Oh? What is that?'

'We have discovered that the aliens made a particular sound that we missed before. It was so low-pitched that we didn't hear it when we first listened to the recordings. We only heard it when someone mistakenly turned the volume up to full.'

'What kind of a sound?' the presenter asked eagerly.

'It was ... a deep rumble, a bit like this ...' Wainwright inhaled deeply then uttered a low growling sound.

The presenter was momentarily speechless. Rapidly collecting himself, he asked, 'And what do you think that ... sound means?'

'If we consider it in the context in which it was uttered, I would say it represents a kind of observation or commentary.'

'A commentary? On what?'

'On us; on human beings.' the linguist declared triumphantly. 'You may remember that in our previous analysis, we found that the aliens made a specific sound when they appeared to be observing people. Like this...' He raised his head and uttered a loud cackle.

The presenter looked startled.

'We interpreted that sound,' Wainwright continued blithely, 'as a communication between the aliens in relation to the people they had been observing. They tended to make the new sound when the people they were watching were in specific situations.'

'What kind of situations?'

'Emergency situations. We have detected a pattern in their behaviour. Initially, the aliens tended to frequent areas where there were a large number of people, city centres, railway stations, for example. After that, they started following emergency vehicles to locations where an accident or serious incident had occurred. Then they moved into areas where there had been some kind of disaster such as a flood, earthquake or catastrophic drought. As you know, the most recent sightings of them were in refugee camps, places where desperate people were queuing for food, water or medicines. In short, they seemed to be fascinated by situations in which human beings were experiencing anxiety and stress.'

The presenter nodded thoughtfully. 'Yes, there does seem to be a pattern. What do you think it means?'

Wainwright frowned. 'We don't know for sure, but, I would interpret the new sounds we have discovered as the aliens' take on what was going on at the time.'

'You're suggesting that they merely represent the aliens' reaction to witnessing human beings in difficult or stressful circumstances?'

'In a word, yes. Interestingly, while the aliens were making those sounds, they were simultaneously directing a kind of laser beam on to the individuals or groups they were observing. We haven't worked out what that actually was, but as far as we know, it didn't actually harm anyone --'

'Maybe not,' interjected the presenter, 'but the damage they inflicted on the Earth's environment could have consequences far into the future. They have also caused an incredible amount of fear and panic.'

'That, unfortunately, is true,' Wainwright replied. 'They showed us that they are capable of destruction on a large scale, which is why their subsequent lack of aggression is such a mystery.'

'And you still have no idea from your research what their intentions were?'

Wainwright shook his head. 'Alas, no. We will continue to interrogate the data we have collected, but unless the aliens return, it is possible, indeed likely, that we will never know what their intentions were.'

The interview concluded.

Richard's father turned to him, baffled. 'Well, I'm none the wiser, are you?'

'No.' Richard was equally puzzled. 'Why were the aliens so interested in crisis situations? It doesn't make sense.'

'Well as long as they've gone, I don't give a fig what their intentions were,' declared his mother. 'I'll go and ring Saskia and ask if she's heard the good news.' She rose from her chair and disappeared into the hall.

'Good news for now, maybe,' muttered Richard's father. 'But how do we know they won't come back? '

'We don't.' For a moment Richard was tempted to tell his father about the visit to Morgana Delph, but he thought better of it. Feeling uncomfortable in the damp bath-towel, he stood up. 'I'd better get dressed.'

While he was upstairs, Fiona rang. She sounded excited. 'If they've really gone this time, it could mean some of the stuff Morgana Delph came out with was true. Two of the words were "soon" and "return", remember?'

'Yes, the message could have been authentic.'

'And it could have come from her French spirit guide!'

'I suppose so,' he muttered grudgingly.

* * *

As the day went on, there was only one topic in the news: the aliens' departure. Political leaders and heads of state round the world made statements in the media, cautiously expressing relief that the planet had been let off so lightly, but warning that it might be only a temporary reprieve as the unwelcome visitors could return at any time.

It occurred belatedly to Richard that in one respect, the aliens had done his own country a favour. The restrictions introduced at the beginning of the invasion had forced him and his compatriots to live leaner and probably healthier lives. Rationing had encouraged the purchase of essential rather than superfluous foods and there was less conspicuous waste. Greater care was being taken with water consumption and the fuel shortage had ensured that the streets were no longer permanently clogged with traffic.

That afternoon he received a call from Mark.

'Exciting news!' exclaimed his friend. 'They've certainly been keeping us on tenterhooks all this time.'

'Did you hear Barnaby Wainwright?'

'Yes, he seemed to put another piece of the puzzle in place.'

Richard was intrigued. 'Another piece? Do you have an idea what the Bobblers were up to, then?'

'I have a suspicion, don't you?'

'Yes. Actually I do.'

'Then maybe we should put our ideas together. See if they coincide.'

'OK,' Richard responded eagerly. 'You go first.'

'Not now, Ric. How about lunch tomorrow?'

They arranged to meet at a brasserie that was equidistant from their respective offices.

Richard lay awake that night in a state of fevered excitement. Had the aliens really departed for good?

Chapter 49

The morning's headlines screamed the news: *The Aliens have Gone. The World is Spared.* Cartoons on the inside pages featured comic-book spaceships streaking away from Earth. One depicted a flock of winged Bobblers soaring upwards into outer space. The caption read, *We came, We saw, We didn't conquer.*

According to all commentaries, the most curious episode in the history of mankind had come to an end. The aliens' departure was greeted with relief and joy across the globe; the planet was off the hook.

Or was it? This question was preoccupying Richard when he arrived at the brasserie to meet Mark Davenport.

'You seem to have landed on your feet with *Immediate Response*,' Mark observed after they had given their order.

'Yes, it's exactly the kind of job I was looking for.'

'Are you ready to go to Pakistan?'

'As much as I can be. Jabs up-to-date, travel arrangements made.'

'What about that nice girlfriend of yours? Janice?'

'Fiona.'

'Of course, Fiona. Very attractive I thought.'

'What about her?'

'She can't be delighted that you're going to be away for so long. Six months did you say?'

Richard shifted uneasily. 'Yes, six initially, and no, she's not delighted. But what can I do? This is something I've been working towards for a long time.'

'Hm.' Mark took off his glasses and raised them to the light to inspect for smears. 'In my admittedly limited experience, most women want commitment.'

Richard picked up the wine list and studied it with exaggerated interest. 'Fiona's great,' he muttered eventually. 'We get on terrifically well, but I can't commit myself to a permanent relationship at the moment. I don't know how my role in *Immediate Response* is going to pan out. And she's got a kid, so she's stuck with schools and stuff.'

Mark smiled. 'Sensitive subject?'

'How are things at *GG*?' Richard asked quickly.

'Hotting up again now that we're all back at work. I saw Phil Banks the other day.'

'Oh? How's he getting on with the new job?'

Mark started to polish the lenses of his glasses with a paper napkin. 'You know Phil! Already grumbling about the workload. He wants to arrange another piss-up now that things are quietening down.'

'They haven't been quietening down in my neck of the woods,' Richard muttered morosely.

'Why? What's been happening?'

Richard described his recent encounters with Rosenberg.

Mark stared at him. 'Fuck! You had a lucky escape there, Ric. The guy sounds crazy.'

'He is; a total fruitcake.'

Mark carefully replaced his glasses on his nose. 'Do you think he really believed the Bobblers were going to bring the Messiah on his Second Coming?'

Richard gazed at him reflectively. 'I honestly don't know. But when I did an internet search for the Inheritors, I found a number of cults who believe that alien visitors will transport their souls to another world. And it wasn't that long ago that members of the Heaven's Gate sect committed mass suicide, believing their souls would be beamed up to a spaceship following the Hale-Bopp comet.'

He paused. 'On the other hand, Rosenberg may have just opportunistically latched on to what was happening to confirm the Inheritors' beliefs. Though he might have been intending to force them all to commit suicide then take all the money and stuff they were obliged to donate to the cult, for himself.'

'What do you think will happen to him now?'

'He's going to be extradited so I should be safe from now on.'

Mark gave a bark of laughter. 'Safe? In Pakistan? Stomping ground of the Taliban and El Qaeda?'

'You're beginning to sound like my mother!'

'Well you certainly have a talent for getting into dangerous situations.'

They fell silent as a waitress appeared and served them with their order.

Mark scrutinised his pizza and picked up his knife and fork. 'You go first. What do you think the Bobblers were up to?'

Richard poured a blob of Ketchup on to his plate. 'Only if you promise you won't laugh.' He described what had transpired during the visit to Morgana Delph.

Mark gazed at him incredulously. 'You don't believe in that stuff, do you?'

'Well I didn't at first. I thought it was a load of hogwash. But now I think there could be something in it, Mark.' He speared a chip with his fork. 'I know this kind of stuff is hard to take seriously, but it sort of made sense when Fiona remembered the medium said she had a French spirit guide. We thought the words she came out with could have suggested a credible motive for the invasion: they might have been searching for a new planet to settle on.'

Mark looked sceptical. 'You don't think the medium's a fake?'

'I did at first but now I believe she's genuine.'

Mark looked thoughtful as he chewed a mouthful of pizza. 'So you think the aliens may have earmarked Earth as a possible new planetary home because their sun is about to die and their natural resources are running out?'

'Something like that, and what she said also implied that they would soon be going back to wherever they came from.'

Mark made no comment.

'Well, what do you think?' Richard asked impatiently.

'Hasn't it occurred to you that there might be another reason for the invasion?'

'No. Why? What's your theory?'

'It may not be entirely unrelated to yours. Bartholomew Wainwright sort of hit the nail on the head.'

'Did he? I didn't think he'd come up with very much.'

Mark waved his fork at him. 'You of all people should recognise what the Bobblers might have been up to!'

Richard stopped eating and stared at him. 'Me? Why?'

'What is it you've been doing for the last year or so?'

'Writing my thesis.'

'No, before that.'

'Doing research, field research.'

'On?'

'On people's behaviour during and after a crisis; how they react to a catastrophe or a natural disaster--'

'Exactly!' Mark rapped the table with his fork. 'And what have the aliens been doing according to Wainwright?'

'Observing human beings in stressful situations. But that's not the same as --'

'Isn't it? Think about it, Ric. The Bobblers liked to congregate near people in difficult circumstances, didn't they? People suffering from fear, panic or sickness; people suffering the consequences of extreme weather conditions and natural disasters. They could have been observing how the Earth's dominant form of life, human beings, reacts in the face of crises. In other words, they could have been doing exactly what you were doing in Kashmir and Bangladesh.'

Richard was stunned. 'You're suggesting they might have been conducting field research on us?'

'Yes. That searchlight they kept shining at people could have been some kind of recording device, their equivalent of a camera or camcorder, though infinitely more high tech.'

'Strewth!' Richard remembered uneasily how three Bobblers had directed a laser-like beam at him when he had joined Sister Francis in that absurd ritual at the hospital. For a moment he felt a sense of fellow feeling. Were the aliens now on their way to some distant planet's equivalent of a university to submit their findings?

Gales of raucous laughter from a neighbouring table prevented him from pursuing the conversation. He sipped his lager and reflected on Mark's idea while waiting for the noise to subside.

'But how would that fit in with what Fiona and I think?' he asked as soon as he could make the question heard. 'You said your theory wasn't entirely unrelated to ours.'

'Well, assuming the old girl, your medium, *is* genuine and what she said wasn't a hoax, there does seem to be a connection. Your French message could mean we humans will have to adapt to natural forces and climate change in order to survive.'

'You mean it could have been referring to *our* ability to withstand extreme conditions rather than theirs?'

'Exactly.'

Richard took a moment to absorb this. 'We thought it was possible that the Bobblers' star was dying and they were looking for another planet to settle on. But I suppose your idea makes more sense.' He paused. 'Though your theory doesn't explain why they destroyed so much vegetation.'

'True.' Mark pondered for a moment. 'Maybe it was part of their overall agenda, a research experiment if you like. They may have wanted to observe how we humans cope when our ecosystem is damaged and the supply of oxygen reduced. If it was an experiment, it didn't work very well as the targets were too dispersed. They may also have realised that they didn't need to create emergency situations themselves. They arrived during a period of extremely volatile weather conditions when there were an unprecedented number of natural disasters around the world. So they had ample opportunity to observe how we humans behave in situations beyond our control, including how we reacted to their arrival of course.'

Richard gazed at him pensively. 'This has been the worst year in living memory for natural disasters. Do you think they did something to affect weather systems?'

'No. We've run a bunch of articles on this year's crop of catastrophes and according to the data, they can all be attributed to natural geological or climatic causes, though they could have been exacerbated by the Bitzgreen.'

Richard was relieved. He didn't want to believe that the Bobblers had deliberately set out to destroy the human race. But he still wasn't entirely convinced. 'If you're right about this, I don't understand why the aliens would *want* to study us? What would be the point?'

Mark waved an arm in the air. 'You name it, Ric: thirst for knowledge, the need to understand the universe, to discover what forms of life have developed elsewhere and the conditions that enable their survival. Why did *we* put men on the moon, build massive telescopes, send space probes to Mars and the other solar planets? We can't assume that curiosity is restricted to us humans. I imagine the need to enquire, explore, discover and understand is a characteristic of all intelligent forms of life. But hey, I'm only thinking aloud! We'll never know for sure what they were doing here.'

Richard swallowed his last mouthful of burger and wiped his mouth with a paper napkin. 'Well, even if intellectual curiosity was the motive, it doesn't rule out the possibility that they could also have been searching for a new home.' He shuddered at the thought of sharing the planet with millions of oversized chipolata sausages.

Mark put down his knife and fork and pushed away his empty plate. 'That's still a possibility, I grant you. It was evidently an exploratory visit, albeit an extremely scary one from our point of view. We don't even know if the Bobblers are representative of dominant life in the world they came from. They could be pre-programmed machines, exploratory probes or a lower-order species working on behalf of a far more sophisticated form of life. I think the Americans still have one in captivity, so they're probably trying to find out exactly what it is.'

'Well whatever they are, why would they have come *here* and not somewhere else?'

'Why not here? And we don't know that they haven't visited other planets, do we? If they had the technological expertise to get here, they might equally well have visited other worlds where intelligent life has developed. There are far more planets capable of harbouring life than we previously thought. They could be checking out any number of them as possible candidates for a future house move.'

'So how can we find out where they came from?'

Mark laughed. 'We can't, unless they choose to tell us ... in French or in Bobblerish! We're not sufficiently advanced to trace their whereabouts. We'll just have to wait and see what happens next, but what happens next may not be in our lifetime.' His expression became pensive. 'Perhaps this has acted as a wake-up call, Ric.'

'In what way?'

'By warning us that we haven't been taking sufficient care of the world's natural resources. And ironically, despite everything, the aliens' visit has had some positive results.'

Richard stared at him. 'Has it?'

'Did you hear that Russian scientists have succeeded in developing a formula that acts as an antidote to the substance that's destroyed vegetation?'

Richard nodded. 'I knew they were working on it.'

'Well it's been distributed to all the areas destroyed in the Blitzgreen and work has already started on restoring and replanting forests and grasslands. All the countries that have been affected are collaborating;

helping each other out, and there's a far greater awareness now of the importance of protecting the natural environment.'

'You're right.' Richard had been dimly aware of these developments but had been too preoccupied with other events to register them.

'The other positive thing,' Mark continued, 'is that virtually every nation has now agreed to work on a plan to combat global warming. The invasion has actually brought countries together like nothing else has ever done. It's cooperation on a global scale.'

He glanced at his watch. 'Must get back. Lunch is on me, by the way. See you, Ric.'

Fat rain drops began to fall as Richard left the brasserie. The devastating heat wave was finally over.

Chapter 50

He had two final farewells to make.

It was raining hard when he pressed the buzzer at the wrought-iron gates.

After a muffled exchange on the intercom, the elderly nun who had opened the gates to him once before, shuffled down the drive carrying a huge black umbrella. 'What do you want with Sister Francis?' she asked, peering suspiciously at him through the wrought iron scrollwork.

'I've only come to say…' Before he could complete the sentence, he saw Sister Francis herself bustling round the corner of the convent. She was holding an identical black umbrella and carrying a large covered basket.

Her face lit up with pleasure when she spotted him. 'Richard! What a lovely surprise. It's my young friend, Sister Benedict. The one who helped me escape from that island.'

The gates swung noisily open and Richard entered, brushing the rain from his face.

Sister Francis lowered her umbrella and handed the basket to the other nun. 'The apples are for the shelter. Mr. Carter will be picking them up shortly.'

Beaming, she turned to Richard and pumped his hand. 'This is an unexpected pleasure, so it is. Come along inside now, out of the rain. We'll go and have some tea.'

She raised her umbrella to cover them both, but as it barely reached his eyebrows, he took it from her and held it over their heads as she led him round the building and through a side door. After she had deposited her muddy overshoes and the dripping umbrella inside the porch, she led him along the corridor, past the chapel where she had once taken him to pray and into a formal parlour. It was furnished only with a large mahogany table and four upright wooden chairs. Pictures of the Sacred Heart, the Virgin Mary and various haloed figures Richard didn't recognise, covered the walls.

Sister Francis indicated one of the chairs. 'Take off your raincoat and sit yourself down while I make the tea.'

Obediently he draped his wet raincoat across the back of the chair and sat down.

She bustled away and returned a few minutes later carrying a tray with tea things and a plate of biscuits. She put them on the table, poured the tea into two cups and handed him one before settling into a chair opposite him with a contented sigh.

'Well, this is grand, so it is. To what do I owe the honour of a visit?'

'I've come to say goodbye.' Richard sipped his tea, declining her offer of a biscuit. 'I told you I'm being sent to Pakistan? I'm leaving next week.'

'So soon?'

'Yes. I've spent the last few weeks preparing.' He described his induction programme and the project management role he would be performing for *Immediate Response*.

She beamed at him. 'It's good work you'll be doing, Richard; God's work.'

'It will certainly be a challenge. But I'm looking forward to it.'

She stirred her tea thoughtfully. 'I envy you, Richard, I do indeed.'

He gazed at her, surprised. 'You do? Why?'

'Going to another country, helping poor souls in distress.'

'But you help people in distress here, don't you? What about all your work for the homeless shelter and the food banks?'

'Ay, we do good work here, but it lacks ...' She paused as if seeking the right words. 'It lacks urgency ... excitement ... You know, Richard, that time we spent on the island, hard though it was, I felt ... invigorated.'

He pretended to be shocked. 'Sister Francis! You're not telling me you *enjoyed* it there?'

'Och no, indeed I did not. It was a dreadful time, so it was. But I've spent over four decades in this convent, Richard. Don't get me wrong, now. This is my home and I've never regretted dedicating my life to God. But what happened on that island made me feel that the good Lord had a special job for me there. You and I were sent there to achieve a purpose. With the help of our friend Jacobs, we managed to liberate those poor people. We saved them from the terrible thing that devil Rosenberg wanted them to do, thanks be to God.'

'Well with any luck he'll be locked up for a very long time.'

'The world will be a safer place without him, it will indeed.'

Richard put his empty cup on the table and she refilled it. 'And will the world be a safer place now that the aliens have gone?' he asked mischievously.

'Well, they didn't attack us and now they've left us in peace.'

'But they did attack us,' he protested. 'They attacked us by harming the planet and causing so much chaos and panic. Some people were so frightened they had heart attacks. Some even committed suicide.'

'Ay, that's true,' she said, crestfallen. 'There was a lot of panic, I grant you. It's terrible what fear of the unknown can lead to, so it is. But they were still God's creatures, just as you and I are. We should have stayed calm when they arrived, given them the benefit of the doubt, and all that could have been avoided.'

'You think so?' he muttered dubiously. 'I'm not so sure. And what if they come back again?'

'Then we must greet them in the spirit of love and friendship,' she said firmly. 'Not try to destroy them.'

'I'm afraid not many will think the same as you.'

'Ay,' she sighed. 'That's the pity of it. It's hard for us to accept that we're not the sovereign race and that there are other intelligent beings in the universe.' She smiled at him fondly. 'Now tell me. What about your wee lady friend?'

He blinked at the sudden change of subject. 'What about her?'

'You told me you were troubled about leaving her.'

He gave a nervous laugh. 'I was...I am...but I can't give up the job.'

She gave him a shrewd look. 'And does she accept that?'

'She's not happy about it.'

'Well, if you're the one she wants and she's the right one for you, then you must both wait for the right time.'

'Maybe. Of course I'll miss her, but I'm not in a position to make a commitment, not yet.'

She nodded. 'Then you're doing the right thing by making her no promises.'

'Yes, that's what I think,' he said gratefully.

After conducting him back to the gates, she took his hands in hers. 'God bless you, Richard.' Her eyes misted over behind her glasses. 'You will keep yourself safe now, won't you?'

'I will.' He took the rosary from his jacket pocket and showed it to her. 'I've still got this. It's served me pretty well so far.'

* * *

On his final evening he took Fiona to her favourite Italian restaurant and while they were waiting for their meal to be served, told her about his conversation with Mark.

'Do you believe the Bobblers *were* on a research mission, like he suggested?' she asked.

'It's possible. But that doesn't mean we weren't right too. They could also have been looking for a new planet to settle on.'

She smiled. 'It would be an extraordinary coincidence if they were doing the same kind of research as you were.'

'If there's one thing I've learnt in the last six months,' Richard commented ruefully, 'it's that extraordinary things do happen. Pakistan will seem like a vicarage tea party by comparison. Though there's one thing I'm grateful for.'

'What's that?'

He gazed at her, thinking how attractive she was with her green eyes and glossy dark hair. He realised that she meant more to him than he had allowed himself to admit. 'If it hadn't been for that UFO I saw in April, I probably wouldn't have met you again. Though maybe you wish we hadn't … met again, I mean.'

She managed a wan smile. 'No, I don't wish that. It's the best thing that's happened to me this year.'

He leant over to take her hand but at that moment, a waitress arrived with their meals. They ate in silence for a while, then, in an attempt to lighten the mood, he launched into an account of his mother's incessant fussing. 'She keeps putting things in my bag and when she's not looking, I take them out again. Yesterday it was a thermal vest. She's afraid I'll catch cold over there, would you believe it?'

Fiona pulled a wry face. 'Mothers are like that. Even me, I'm afraid.'

'You mean you'll still be doing things like that when Polly's nearly thirty?'

'I expect so, but if you're anything to go by, I won't get any thanks for it!'

'Well, by the time she's my age, Polly should be able to stand on her own two feet.' He refilled her glass. 'I can't wait to get away from home and from that old Battleaxe Ma Phelps.'

She laughed. 'Pakistan is a long way to go to escape your mother and a nosy neighbour, Ric.' She toyed with the food on her plate and he noticed that her eyes had filled with tears. 'You will keep in touch while you're away?'

'Of course. I hope I'll have access to email and Skype.' Seeing her devastated expression, he added hastily, 'Six months will pass in no time, Fi, and the chances are I'll have some home leave during the tour.'

'But what will happen when you've finished the six months? Will they send you somewhere else?'

'I don't know,' he said helplessly. 'It depends on how I get on and how *IR* rates my work.' He put down his knife and fork, reached across the table and took her hand. 'I'm sorry, Fi, but this is what I've been working towards for three years. You know I care for you, but I can't–'

'Promise anything?' She brushed away her tears. 'I know that, and I do understand how much the job means to you.' She smiled at him bravely and lifted her wine glass. 'Here's to you, Witnesser of the Light. I wish you luck. We'll have to let the future take care of itself.'

Richard raised his own glass. 'And here's to you, Fiona.'

* * *

There was an autumnal chill in the air when they left the restaurant. It had stopped raining and the clouds had cleared, revealing a cluster of bright stars.

On the path outside her parents' house they clung to each other in a long embrace.

'Take care of yourself and Polly while I'm away,' he said when they finally broke apart, then, on hearing a faint bark, 'and Maggie, of course.'

'Don't worry, Polly will take care of Maggie. Goodbye, Ric, I'll miss you.' Fiona's voice broke and she turned and ran up the steps. Without looking back, she unlocked the front door and went quickly inside.

He lingered for a while in the absurd hope that she might come out again, then walked sadly away.

As he reached the corner of Coronation Close, he glanced upwards and came to a halt on glimpsing a shooting star. He gazed wonderingly up at it. Was it a star or something else? Were the Bobblers still on their unimaginably long journey through space? Would they return? And if they did, would the world greet them in a spirit of love and friendship as Sister Francis had suggested? He thought it was extremely unlikely.

Yet, as Mark had pointed out, the aliens' visit had resulted in one extremely positive outcome. It had brought about an unprecedented spirit of global cooperation. Mutual suspicion and traditional enmities had been put aside as nations worked together to restore devastated parts of the environment and combat global warming. Cooperation and mutual help seemed to have replaced xenophobia and conflict. In this respect at least, the aliens had brought about a new and better world order.

Richard smiled to himself. Rosenberg and his deluded band of followers had been wrong. The new kingdom they had hoped to inherit wasn't somewhere in outer space; it was here on Earth.

If you want to read more by V K McGivney, her debut novel, *Aftermath of a Murder*, (a Chill4Books award winner) is available in e-book format and paperback.

A great plot that leads the reader deeper and deeper into the secrets and lies on which the main character's life has been unknowingly based. A gripping read that was very hard to put down.

Page-turning murder mystery with a gripping plot and a heart moving family story to go with it - highly recommend and an excellent first novel.